THE HARDY BOYS CASEFILES™

Books in The Hardy Boys Casefiles™ series

FRANKLYN W DIXON

SINISTER PLOTS

THE HARDY BOYS CASEFILES™
3 STORIES IN 1

BLOOD MONEY
COLLISION COURSE
FINAL CUT

AN ARCHWAY PAPERBACK
Published by SIMON & SCHUSTER
New York   London   Toronto   Sydney   Tokyo   Singapore

BLOOD MONEY, COLLISION COURSE and FINAL CUT first published in Great
Britain by Simon & Schuster, 1992
First published together in this combined edition by Archway, 1997
An imprint of Simon & Schuster Ltd
A Viacom Company

Simon & Schuster Ltd
West Garden Place
Kendal Street
London
W2 2AQ

THE HARDY BOYS CASEFILES is a trademark of Simon & Schuster Inc.

Simon & Schuster of Australia Pty Ltd
Sydney

A CIP catalogue record for this book is available from the British Library.

ISBN 0-671 00540 5

Printed and bound in Great Britain by Caledonian International Book Manufacturing,
Glasgow

BLOOD MONEY

Chapter

1

"WHO SAID CRIME doesn't pay?" Joe Hardy asked.

Frank Hardy turned and shot his younger brother, sitting directly behind him in the backseat, a disapproving look.

"Oh, it's not that it doesn't pay." Their father, the famous private detective Fenton Hardy, spoke up from the driver's seat. "If money is all you count, then crime certainly does pay."

"But ninety-nine percent of the time, it doesn't pay for very long," Frank added.

"I give up," Joe said, throwing his hands up in mock surrender. "All I meant was, this is a pretty elegant neighborhood for a crook to live in."

"Well, Moran didn't spend all his time

here," Fenton Hardy said, backing his car into a parking spot. "In fact, he spent the last ten years of his life in a cell about the size of your van." Looking out the back window, he glanced at Joe, who nodded sheepishly.

"I get the message, Dad."

"I knew you would," Fenton said, nosing the car up to the curb. He turned the key and slid it out. "Better lock the doors, boys. We're not in Bayport anymore."

As he stepped onto the sidewalk, Frank had to admit his brother was right about one thing. It was an expensive-looking, elegant neighborhood. Immaculate three-story townhouses, with bay windows and elaborate ironwork fences, lined both sides of the block they had parked on. The street itself was clean and quiet, with large trees (bare now that it was the middle of winter) planted at regular intervals along the sidewalk. Past the last of those trees, at the end of the block, the Manhattan skyline was clearly visible.

Since the building of these Jefferson Heights townhouses twenty years earlier, this area had become one of the most exclusive residential districts in Brooklyn. Apartment space was at a premium because the area was just over the river from Manhattan, convenient to the subways, and the neighborhood was safe.

All in all, it looked like a model for the perfectly planned urban development. But

2

from what Fenton Hardy had been telling them on their drive from Bayport, this model of urban development had a major flaw. The beautiful townhouses had been bought by one of the country's largest criminal organizations.

"I remember when some of this block was a park," Fenton Hardy reminisced. "In the summer there were a half-dozen ball games going at one time." He was silent for a moment, then shook his head, clearing out the memories. "I don't understand this invitation. I helped to get Moran sentenced to jail twenty years ago. He delayed going for ten years, of course. But the last thing I ever expected was an invitation to Josh Moran's house."

"He can't hurt you now, Dad," Frank pointed out. "He's dead."

Which was the reason they were there. Fenton Hardy, much to his surprise, had been notified that he had been named a beneficiary in Josh Moran's will. Along with the notification had come a request to attend the reading of the will that afternoon. Frank and Joe, on break from school, had been only too eager to accompany him.

"I wonder what Moran could have left me," Fenton Hardy said.

"Probably a time bomb," Joe replied.

Frank laughed. He and Joe followed their dad across the street and up the steps of one of the few townhouses that had not been split up into apartments.

"This whole building was all Moran's," Fenton Hardy said, stepping forward and ringing the bell.

Joe whistled in admiration, just as the front door swung open and a tall, dark-haired man, dressed in a fashionable, expensive-looking suit, was revealed. He appeared to be about thirty and had the solid, trim build of an athlete.

The man smiled expectantly at Fenton. It was obvious the two didn't know each other.

Joe, on the other hand, recognized the dark-haired stranger instantly.

"I'm Fenton Hardy—these are my sons, Frank and Joe."

The man shook hands with Mr. Hardy. "Glad to meet you, sir. I'm Tommy Poletti."

Joe managed to shut his mouth, which had dropped open when the man answered the door, and mumble a quick hello.

"I'm glad you could make it today," Poletti continued, opening the door wide for them and motioning them inside. As he took their coats, Joe nudged Frank excitedly.

"Do you know who that guy is?"

Frank shook his head. "One of Moran's goons, right?"

"One of Moran's goons?" Joe shook his head excitedly, his eyes wide. "That's Tommy

Poletti. He was a quarterback for the University of Southern California—and won the Heisman trophy about ten years ago."

Joe was something of a fanatic about football—not surprising, considering that he played for the Bayport High football team.

"I never heard of him," Frank whispered to his brother.

"Never heard of him? He used to hold all the single-season collegiate passing records!" Joe exclaimed, a little louder than he'd intended.

"Except touchdowns in a season." Poletti turned and smiled. "But that was a long time ago."

"Joe's a running back for his high school team," Fenton Hardy put in. "A pretty good one, if I say so myself."

"Dad—" Joe protested, flushing slightly.

"Fullback, right?" Poletti asked, looking Joe up and down.

Joe nodded. "Yeah."

"We never had a good fullback at USC when I was playing," Poletti said. "Might've won a few of those Bowl games if we had." He leaned forward and spoke directly to Joe. "You want my advice, bulk up a little. They're growing linebackers bigger every year."

"I'll try," Joe said, smiling. As Poletti turned away, a sudden and obvious question occurred to Joe.

5

What was Tommy Poletti, a former Heisman trophy winner, doing mixed up with a gangster like Moran?

The question echoed in his head as Poletti led them down the hall and through a set of double doors into a large living room. About twenty people were standing there, talking to one another.

Joe recognized none of them.

This time, his father did.

"Hugh!" he called out.

A thin, dark-haired man standing by himself near the fireplace turned. When he saw Fenton Hardy, his eyes lit up.

"Fenton!"

The two men met in the middle of the room and embraced.

"Looks like your dad found an old friend," Poletti said. Just then the doorbell rang again.

"Excuse me." Poletti disappeared through the double doors.

The man their father had recognized looked somewhat older than Fenton Hardy. There were huge bags under his eyes, and as he'd crossed the room to greet Fenton Hardy, Joe noticed that he walked with a slight limp. He wore a wrinkled, ill-fitting green sport coat and baggy gray pants that hung loosely from his skeletal frame. In one hand he was carrying a drink.

Joe, with Frank a step behind, crossed the room to stand beside their father.

"It's good to see you again, Fenton," the man said, his eyes glistening a little. "These are your sons?"

Fenton Hardy nodded. "Boys, this is Hugh Nolan. He worked with me on the force."

"A long time ago. I retired more than fifteen years ago."

"Pleased to meet you, Mr. Nolan," Frank and Joe said almost simultaneously.

"You look a little like my son Ned," Nolan said to Frank, shaking hands with each of the boys. "I tried to get him to come with me today, but he just got out of the army, and . . ." He shrugged. "What's this all about, Fenton?"

"Your guess is as good as mine, Hugh."

"I don't have one," Nolan said. "To tell you the truth, I don't understand why I'm here at all—"

Nolan stopped talking abruptly, and stared over Joe's shoulder at the double doors. His face tensed.

"What's wrong, Hugh?" Fenton asked.

Joe followed the thin man's gaze.

A tall, powerfully built black man, dressed in a navy blue suit and white shirt, had just entered the room and was scanning the crowd.

"Chief Peterson!" Frank called out.

The man turned at the sound of Frank's voice and began heading toward them.

Police Chief Samuel Peterson's appearance there was no surprise to any of the Hardys. Immediately after he'd been named a beneficiary in Moran's will, Fenton Hardy had called the chief and discovered that his old partner (the two had been detectives together) had been named a beneficiary as well.

"Whatever Moran wants to leave me I guess applies to Sam as well," Fenton had said. "After all, we're the ones who put him away." The two men had talked, and both had agreed to show up for the reading.

Peterson crossed the room quickly, nodded hellos to both Frank and Joe, and shook hands warmly with their father. Fenton Hardy was clearly glad to see the chief.

Nolan, just as clearly, was not.

When the chief turned to shake hands with him, Joe felt the temperature in the room drop.

Nolan ignored Peterson's extended hand, and the chief finally lowered it and spoke.

"Hugh," he said, nodding. "It's good to see you."

"Good to see me, is it?" Nolan asked, biting off each word. "That must be it. You didn't return any of my calls fifteen years ago when I needed your help—because you were waiting to see me in person."

"I told you I had nothing to do with that decision, Hugh," Peterson said calmly.

"You could've helped me!" Nolan spat out, with such bitterness that Joe took a step aside.

What did Hugh Nolan have against Chief Peterson, anyway?

Joe glanced at his father and received a look that told him to save his questions for later.

"You've got to try to understand that was a long time ago, Hugh," Peterson was saying.

"Oh, I understand," Nolan said bitterly. "I understand, all right." He stepped closer to Peterson, till the two were only inches apart. The top of Nolan's head barely reached the collar of Peterson's jacket.

"Now you try and understand this," Hugh Nolan said.

He drew his arm back and before anyone could stop him, threw the entire contents of his drink in Chief Peterson's face!

Chapter

2

FRANK AND JOE were shocked as Nolan turned and stalked away angrily.

"Hugh—" Fenton Hardy began, then sensed it was useless to start after the man. He turned to Peterson. "Sam, are you all right?"

"Fine," Peterson said, pulling out a handkerchief and dabbing at his face. "Just fine."

"He has no right to blame you," Fenton Hardy said.

The expression in his father's eyes told Frank he'd have to save his questions for later.

He and Joe hadn't seen the chief since the events that had resulted in Fenton Hardy's kidnapping several months before, in the case *Edge of Destruction*. At that time Peterson had just entered the mayoral race in New York

City. Since then, he had withdrawn from the campaign after suffering a mild heart attack.

The chief was supposed to be taking it easy now, Frank knew, and this situation with Hugh Nolan, whatever it was, couldn't be helping matters any.

"I hate to break up the party," Fenton Hardy said. "But look who just walked in."

He nodded over his shoulder.

In the doorway at the far end of the room stood a group of five men, all in dark suits. One, clearly the leader of the group, looked as thin as Hugh Nolan, and somewhat older. But where Nolan's clothes and demeanor had indicated a man who was having trouble making ends meet, this man's bearing spoke of someone who was used to money—and knew how to enjoy it.

With him was a younger man, as powerfully built as Tommy Poletti, but with a crueler, meaner face. The other three—Frank guessed they were bodyguards—formed a rough circle around them.

"The old guy is Johnny Carew. The one talking to him is his son Daniel," Peterson was saying. "They're—"

"You don't have to tell us who they are," Frank said. The Carew crime family was the most powerful on the East Coast, and Johnny was its head—a man who had supposedly controlled judges, congressmen, and even a vice-president.

At one time, Frank knew, Josh Moran had been Carew's most trusted crime lieutenant. That was before he broke away to start his own crime "family." The two groups had been feuding since then—for about twenty years. About the time that Dad got Moran convicted, Frank realized.

"Say," Joe said, nudging Frank. "Who's that?"

A pretty dark-haired woman had just entered the room from another door and was scanning the crowd.

"That's Moran's daughter, Emily." Peterson smiled. "She's a little old for you, Joe." A big heavyset man came over and spoke briefly to Emily. "Billy Delaney," the chief continued. "Moran's second-in-command. He's been running the gang the last few years, and the word is, he's not unhappy that the old man died. The big question is, now that Moran's dead, can he prevent Carew from taking back the territory Moran stole from him?"

Daniel Carew, who had been talking softly to his father, suddenly caught sight of Emily Moran. He called her name and quickly crossed the room to her side.

Carew had barely begun to talk when Emily started to move away. He grabbed her arm. An expression of anger crossed Emily Moran's face, and she coldly removed Carew's hand.

It looked as if, at least as far as she was concerned, the feud between their two families was to continue.

"If I could have your attention, ladies and gentlemen." A tall thin man, wearing wire-rimmed glasses and a bow tie, stood behind a large, antique mahogany desk at the far end of the room.

"My name is Vance Johnson, and I was Mr. Moran's lawyer. I'm here in that capacity to execute his estate—beginning with the reading of the will. If you will all take seats—"

Tommy Poletti crossed the room to sit with Emily Moran. Johnny and Daniel Carew took seats next to each other. Frank and Joe remained standing with their father and Chief Peterson. Across the room, Hugh Nolan also stood.

"Thank you for coming today." Johnson picked up a stack of papers from the desk and began reading.

" 'I, Joshua Sean Moran, being of sound mind and sound body, do hereby bequeath the entire body of my estate, its assets and capital, to my only daughter, Emily—' "

"No surprises there," Daniel Carew interjected. Tommy Poletti shot him a dirty look.

" 'With this exception. I have set aside in a safe-deposit box ten million dollars in cash.

This money is to be divided equally among the following individuals: Hugh Nolan, Johnny Carew, Daniel Carew, Samuel Peterson, Fenton Hardy, Thomas Poletti, and William Delaney.' "

There was a moment of stunned silence. Frank and his father exchanged a puzzled glance. Johnson continued reading.

" 'These shares will be payable three months from the date of the reading of this will. They may not be transferred or assigned, nor may they be renounced, except in the single following instance.' "

Johnson looked up over his glasses. " 'The only way one of the named beneficiaries shall not receive his due share of this money is if he meets his demise before the aforementioned date. In that event, the shares of the remaining beneficiaries will increase proportionately.' "

Fenton Hardy didn't look pleased—nor did any of the other people named as beneficiaries.

"Say it again—in English, Van," Daniel Carew said.

"It's simple enough," Tommy Poletti interjected. "Everyone whose name was called is due a share of ten million dollars—if he can stay alive for the next three months."

"This is why Moran wanted you all here," Frank said, his eyes wide. "Revenge.."

Fenton Hardy nodded grimly. "He's made it open season on every one of us."

Chapter

3

JOE STUDIED THE COLLECTION of gangsters assembled in the room. It wasn't hard to figure what the next three months would be like.

With ten million dollars at stake, murder would be in the air.

Chief Peterson rose, his face twisted in anger. "I don't know about anyone else, but I don't want any part of this will—or that ten million dollars."

"I don't intend to become involved either," Fenton Hardy said.

"We should all refuse to take part in Moran's sick little exercise," the chief added.

At that precise moment, Joe turned and saw Hugh Nolan's face. Clearly, he wanted his slice of Moran's fortune.

"If you're so uncomfortable with your

share, you could give it to me, Chief," Daniel Carew offered. "In three months, of course."

"I'd rather burn it," Peterson said.

"That's against the law," Daniel said, smiling wickedly. "I'd have to report you. Besides—if some screwball wants to leave me a share of ten million dollars, who am I to argue?" He smiled at Emily. "No offense."

"Watch your language, Carew," Poletti said. "How about a little respect for the dead?"

"You're a fine one to talk about respect for the dead," Carew replied. His eyes went to Emily. "Why don't you give the lady a decent amount of time to mourn her father before you marry her—"

"You need to learn some manners, pal," Poletti said, springing to his feet.

"From you?" Carew asked. "Don't make me laugh."

Emily put a hand on Poletti's arm. He shrugged it off, and stood waiting, his eyes blazing.

Joe wondered if the former Heisman winner knew how dangerous it was for him to be threatening the son of one of organized crime's biggest kingpins.

"Tommy, Mr. Carew, please—" Johnson began.

"Daniel!" Johnny Carew, who had remained virtually silent during the reading of the will and the exchanges that followed, now spoke up for the first time. "Apologize to Mr. Poletti—and to Miss Moran."

The elder Carew's voice was clipped and couldn't hide the fact that Carew was furious with his son. Daniel mumbled a reluctant apology, first to Poletti, who accepted reluctantly, and then Emily.

The two men sat down again.

"I, for one, intend to honor Joshua's wishes regarding the disposition of his estate," Johnny Carew continued. "If he wanted all of us"—he raised a hand and held it out palm up—"to share equally in his wealth, that is how we will share it."

"You can't be serious," Peterson said. "You know Moran wants us to kill each other for that money—"

"I am perfectly willing to accept my share of Josh's estate," Carew continued, ignoring the chief. "I hope everyone else here will do the same."

"None of us wants any trouble, Chief," Delaney added. "But I'm not giving up my share, either."

Peterson shook his head in disgust.

"I'm afraid the whole question is beside the point. It's quite impossible for any of you to renounce your shares." Johnson placed the papers he'd been reading from into a manila folder on the desk. "Mr. Moran has written his will so that it will be impossible for any of you to step aside as a beneficiary. The shares of the other beneficiaries only increase if—"

"If we die," Daniel Carew said.

"Yes, that's essentially correct." Johnson cleared his throat. "If there are no other questions . . ."

Joe shock his head. Why had Moran made Poletti a target? For that matter, why was Delaney, Moran's right-hand man, a beneficiary as well? He doubted that Johnson had the answers to those questions.

The lawyer cleared his throat again and looked around the room. "I thank you all for coming. We'll meet back here in three months—at which time we'll discuss the formal distribution of Mr. Moran's estate."

The gathering broke up quickly after that. The Hardys, after seeing Chief Peterson off, found themselves outside on the street just as Hugh Nolan emerged from the brownstone.

"Don't say it, Fenton," Nolan said as he reached the bottom of the steps. His limp was much more pronounced now, and he was clearly straining with each step.

"You know I've got to, Hugh," Fenton Hardy said. He stepped forward to give Nolan a hand, but the older man waved him off. "Sam did everything he legally could to see that you got your money. He got outvoted—"

"I don't want to hear it!" Nolan snarled. He bit his lip then and was silent a moment. When he spoke again, he was much calmer. "Sorry, Fenton. I shouldn't have snapped at you—or thrown the drink at Sam. Just lost my temper again." He checked his watch. "Anyway, I've got to go."

"It was good to see you, Hugh." Fenton took Nolan's hand and shook it vigorously.

"And you, too, Fenton. But I'm afraid I've made a bad impression on your sons," he said, turning to Frank and Joe. "Maybe I can make it up to you next time by telling you some stories of when your father was a rookie cop."

"Next time?" Joe asked.

"Why—three months from now."

And with that, Nolan turned and walked off down the street.

"Looks like he's anxious to get his share of Moran's cash, Dad," Joe said as they climbed into the backseat of their gray four-door sedan.

"I'm afraid things haven't gone well for Hugh for the past twenty years since he was charged with taking bribes," Fenton replied. "His wife left him, there were problems over his pension, and he had to retire early without getting it."

"So I gathered," Frank said. "And he blames Chief Peterson for those problems."

"That's right." His father checked the rearview mirror and pulled out into traffic. "I wouldn't doubt Hugh Nolan could put his share of that money to good use."

"Who couldn't?" Joe asked. "Seven people, ten million dollars, that's—"

"Almost a million and a half each," Frank said.

"I for one don't intend to share in any of that money," Fenton Hardy said firmly. "As soon as we get home, I'm going to put in a call to my lawyer and see what we can do."

"Johnson said you couldn't change the terms," Frank pointed out.

"Then I'll give the money to charity," Fenton Hardy said. "And that will be the end of it."

Joe, in the backseat, watched out the rear window as the skyline of Manhattan disappeared. He thought about the group of people they'd seen that day and the amount of money at stake.

Somehow, he knew his father was wrong. That wouldn't be an end to it.

A month and a half passed.

It was a blustery morning, two days into winter break, and Frank and Joe had come to New York City to do some research at the public library. They were browsing through a subway newsstand, waiting for a subway train: Frank bought a computer magazine; Joe, one of the New York City papers. They had just sat down in the subway when Joe tossed the paper he was reading onto Frank's lap, right on top of his magazine.

"Take a look at this," Joe said.

"Crime Kingpin Murdered," the headline screamed. Beneath it, in bold print, the article continued.

Daniel Carew, reputed heir to the crime family run by his father, Johnny Carew, was gunned down late yesterday evening in front of his Brooklyn home.

Frank looked up.

"Read on," his brother said. "There's a lot more."

Frank picked up the paper.

The police discovered Carew's body on the stoop of his Brooklyn brownstone. He had been shot once in the chest. The police are holding Tommy Poletti, former Heisman trophy winner, who, according to police reports, had argued violently with Daniel Carew earlier that day.

Frank shook his head. "Tommy Poletti—a killer?"

"I don't believe it either," Joe said.

Frank continued reading and learned that the police had found no gun. However, Carew's own revolver, which "he always carried with him," according to sources, was missing.

The paper suggested that the shooting might be the start of a gang war over Joshua Moran's territory, now that he was dead.

But Frank knew there was another, better motive for Carew's murder.

It seemed that the game of killer-take-all that his father had predicted was beginning.

"I bet Chief Peterson has involved himself in this case," Frank said.

"And I bet you're right." Joe nodded. "Which makes me think we ought to take a little detour."

Frank nodded. "They're holding Poletti at the eighty-fourth precinct house in Brooklyn," he said. "And I bet that's where we find Peterson."

They got off at the next stop to change trains and an hour later were standing in front of the precinct house on Gold Street.

"This is the place," Joe said. "Now, how do we get in to see Chief Peterson?"

"I'll think of something," Frank said, just as a limousine was pulling up next to them. Emily Moran emerged.

"Miss Moran," Frank called out.

She turned and stared at Frank and Joe, a puzzled expression on her face.

"I'm Frank Hardy, and this is my brother

Joe—we were at the reading of your father's will. . . ."

"Of course," Emily said distractedly. She looked exhausted: dark circles formed half-moons below her eyes, and her skin was sallow, as if she hadn't slept all night. "You'll have to forgive me— This whole business with Tommy—that the police think he's involved in murder . . ." She shook her head.

Frank smiled understandingly. "It seems a little unlikely to us, as well."

Someone cleared his throat behind the threesome. "And who are the two of you?"

A thin man with a close-cropped black beard, who must have just emerged from the precinct house, was standing on the steps, eyeing the Hardys suspiciously.

Frank approached him, leaving Emily standing next to the car with Joe.

"I'm Frank Hardy," he said, extending his hand.

"Detective Mike Lewis," the man said, shaking Frank's hand firmly. He looked at Frank closely, then snapped his fingers. "You're Fenton Hardy's kid, aren't you?"

Frank nodded, somewhat surprised. "How did you—"

"You look just like him," Lewis said. The detective nodded in Emily Moran's direction and lowered his voice. "I can guess what brings you here."

"You'd probably guess right," Frank said. "We want to know if this shooting ties in to Josh Moran's will."

Lewis hesitated. "You know, I really can't talk about the case with you. . . ." His voice trailed off.

"I understand," Frank said. "But if Chief Peterson okays it?"

Lewis smiled. "Anything's okay then. He's just inside. If he doesn't have a problem talking about the case with you there, then I—"

"Good," Frank said. "Lead the way."

The four of them entered the precinct house together.

"First I've got to pick up Poletti," Lewis said. He pointed to his right. "The holding cells are this way. Miss Moran?" She nodded that she wanted to accompany the detective.

"Actually, I'd like to talk to the chief first," Frank said. He wanted to find out just how strong the case was against Tommy Poletti— information he didn't think he'd get with both Poletti and Emily Moran present. Joe indicated he'd go with Lewis and Emily.

"The chief's in the office at the top of the stairs—follow this corridor—you can't miss it."

To Joe, the precinct house looked like his high school. The cinder-block halls were painted the same dull beige and decorated (more accurately, not decorated) in the same dull style.

Off to the right was a sign that said Holding Cells, with an arrow pointing down the stairs. Lewis, who had obviously been to the station many times before, led them down a flight of stairs and then into a long, narrow basement corridor. They were about halfway down it when Joe stopped short.

"Did you hear something?" he asked.

Lewis and Emily Moran looked at each other and shook their heads. "I didn't," Lewis said.

"Wait." Joe held up his hand. "There it is again." He listened closely for a second, then turned back the way they'd come and stopped in front of a door marked Utility Closet.

Faint thumping noises could be heard coming from inside.

Joe tried the knob. It wouldn't budge.

"Hey!" He banged loudly on the door, then threw his weight against it.

In response, there came a renewed series of thumps, louder and more insistent than before.

"In here!" Joe said excitedly. "There's somebody trapped inside!"

Chapter

4

"I DON'T BELIEVE IT," Chief Peterson said. He was sitting behind a large gray metal desk, a lot of papers fanned out in front of him that he had obviously been studying until Frank interrupted him. Now he was staring up at the source of the interruption with a half-shocked, half-pleased expression on his face.

Frank Hardy stood in the doorway of the chief's borrowed office, looking slightly ill at ease.

"This case isn't twelve hours old, and the boy genius is here to help already." Chief Peterson gathered up some of the papers he'd been studying and slipped them into a manila folder. "Where's your brother? Working with the detectives?" the chief asked, smiling to let Frank know he was kidding.

Frank smiled back and nodded. "He is. He's downstairs with Lewis and Emily Moran."

"I give up!" Peterson threw up his hands. "What took you so long?"

"We just got into town."

"Well, you might as well have a seat," the chief said. He indicated a chair in front of the desk.

"Do you mind if I ask you a few questions about the shooting?"

Peterson laughed out loud and shook his head. "Matter of fact, I was just going to call your dad and tell him about this."

"So you also think this has something to do with Moran's will?" Frank leaned forward, catching a glimpse of the police report on the shooting, which lay open on the desk. Poletti's record was the top sheet of the file.

"No, I think this has nothing to do with the will," Peterson replied.

"But I thought you said—"

"I was going to tell your dad not to worry when he read about this. As far as we can tell, this is a case of jealousy. Two men fighting over the same girl."

"The papers thought that it might be the start of a gang war," Frank said.

Peterson pursed his lips. "I don't think so. Poletti's only involvement with the Moran crime family seems to be with Emily."

Frank nodded. "The papers also said you hadn't charged him with anything yet."

"That's true," the chief said. "But Lewis and I are hoping he'll confess—the evidence is pretty convincing."

"I don't know," Frank said slowly. "I just can't see Poletti killing Carew—"

"Why? Because he's a former Heisman winner? A lot of things could have happened to him since then. We don't really know anything about him," Peterson said.

Frank nodded a little sheepishly.

Just then, a bell began ringing outside in the hall. Frank raised his eyebrows. "What's that?" he asked.

"That," Peterson said, standing up, "is the coffee cart—more popularly known around here as the 'roach coach.' " He smiled at Frank. "Come on—I'll buy you a soda."

Frank rose and followed him, but he wasn't sure he wanted to eat anything from a "roach coach."

"How could anyone get locked inside a closet—inside a police station?" Emily asked.

"I don't know if it is a 'someone,' " Lewis said, shaking his head. He rapped the door sharply with his knuckles, then stood for a moment with his ear pressed to the door, listening. "But something's in there, all right. I'll see if I can find some keys." He disappeared down the hall.

"Hang on!" Joe yelled at the door. "We'll have you out of there in a second!"

In fact, it took more than five minutes for Lewis to return. All the time Joe and Emily Moran stood, listening to the muffled thumping on the other side of the locked door.

Finally Lewis arrived with a ring of keys about the size of a softball; the fifth key opened the door.

A man, hands and feet bound behind his back and a gag stuffed into his mouth, lay on his stomach next to the door.

Lewis rolled him over.

"It's Ed!" Lewis said, bending down and undoing the man's gag. Joe helped Lewis untie the man's bonds and get him into a sitting position. The man began taking in huge gulps of air.

"Take it easy," Lewis said, kneeling down by him. "Are you all right?"

"What happened?" Joe asked.

"Beats me," Ed said, his words punctuated by faint gasps. "I was coming out of the service elevator when I hear this noise behind me. Next thing I know, I'm lying in this closet all tied up—with a whopper of a headache. Somebody thumped me over the head but good!"

Lewis looked puzzled. "What would anyone

want to knock you out for?'' he asked, shaking his head.

"What do you do around here?'' Joe asked, kneeling down next to Ed.

"Him?'' Lewis spoke first, before Ed could answer. "He's from the food service company. Runs the coffee cart.''

"What can I get you today?''

The coffee cart, Frank saw, was similar to the pushcarts that were rolled up and down the aisles of airplanes. This one had sandwiches and an assortment of beverages and snacks.

"Where's Ed?'' Chief Peterson asked.

"Oh—he called in sick today,'' the man pushing the cart said. He was a couple of inches shorter and a few years older than Chief Peterson, with graying hair that hung almost to his shoulders. He had on a white button-down shirt and black pants.

"Anything serious?'' Peterson asked, rummaging through the contents of the cart. He picked up a sugared doughnut and looked at it longingly.

"Might be—I wouldn't count on seeing him for a while,'' the man said, shrugging. "That's fresh,'' he said, pointing at the doughnut the chief had picked up.

"Looks it,'' Peterson said. "But I'm on a diet.'' He patted his stomach and put down the doughnut. "Give me a decaffeinated coffee—

black. And I'll take one of these." He picked up a small bran muffin and shook his head ruefully. "Good for the old ticker, they tell me," he said.

The man behind the cart nodded and handed Peterson his coffee. "That's what I hear, too. You got heart problems?"

Peterson shrugged. "Nothing serious."

"Good. Just make sure you take it easy," the man behind the cart said.

"I plan to," Peterson said. He raised the cup to his lips and took a sip. "That's good coffee. Almost tastes like the real thing."

"I'm glad you like it," the man behind the cart said. "It's a fresh pot." His eyes were the most piercing shade of blue—almost a purple, really—that Frank had ever seen. They were also remarkably unlined for a man who otherwise looked to be in his late forties.

"You want something?" the chief asked Frank.

"A cup of coffee, maybe?" the man asked.

Frank shook his head. "Joe and I had a big lunch."

"Okay, then." The chief nodded to the man behind the cart. "See you later."

"Take it easy," the man said, and disappeared down the hall.

Frank and Peterson returned to the office the chief was using and sat down again.

Peterson took a bite of the muffin, and then

another sip of his coffee. "Anyway, no, I don't think this has anything to do with the will. We have about fifteen witnesses who saw Carew and Poletti get into a shoving match on the Brooklyn Heights promenade early yesterday evening. Poletti threatened Carew in front of all of them."

Frank nodded. "One of the other beneficiaries could be setting Poletti up—"

"In order for somebody to get a lot more money, he'd have to knock off Johnny Carew and Billy Delaney—the heads of two of the largest East Coast crime families. Nobody's that dumb." Peterson wiped a hand across his forehead and grimaced. "It feels hot in here all of a sudden. Did they turn up the heat?"

Frank shook his head. "Feels the same to me."

The chief loosened his tie and unbuttoned the collar of his shirt. "Anyway, not only would they have to kill Carew and Delaney, they'd have to get at yours truly, the chief of police. And how are they going to do that?"

"I see your point, but—"

Frank looked at Peterson. The chief was really sweating now, and he also looked very gray. "Are you all right?"

Peterson shook his head. "I'm not sure. I feel dizzy, I—" He stood suddenly and gasped, swaying on his feet.

Frank was at his side in an instant to help

ease him back down in his chair. The back of Peterson's shirt was drenched in sweat.

"Frank," the chief said slowly, a look of horror spreading across his face. "I'm having a heart attack!"

Chapter
5

"I JUST HOPE whoever's got the cart hasn't wrecked it," Ed said, leading Lewis down a long, narrow hallway. Joe trailed a few paces behind; they had left Emily with one of the officers in charge of the holding cells. "I'm responsible for whatever happens to it, you know."

"Let's just find the guy," Lewis said. "Then we'll worry about what he's done."

And why, Joe added silently.

The basement of the police station was a maze of identical cinder-block corridors. Again, Joe was reminded of high school: any second, he expected to hear bells ring and to see students pour out of classes into the halls. There were even lockers along one wall, he saw.

As they crossed another corridor, Joe heard a noise off to his left. He turned and looked in that direction.

About fifty feet away a man in a white shirt had his back to them. He had long gray hair and was stooped over, and he was pushing a food cart with a coffee pot on top. A police officer was walking next to him, and the two were talking animatedly.

"Hey," Ed said, stopping so suddenly Joe almost crashed into him. "That's my cart!"

"Hey!" Joe yelled. The man in the white shirt and the police officer both turned.

"Stop that man!" Lewis called out.

The officer recognized Lewis. With a puzzled look on his face, he reached for the man walking beside him, putting a hand on his shoulder to detain him.

The man in the white shirt straightened up, and it was as if he'd shed twenty years. He moved like lightning, spinning to free himself from the policeman's grasp. He continued his spin into a side-kick. His foot slammed into the officer's chest, sending him crashing against the wall.

The officer slumped to the ground and lay still.

The man in the white shirt shoved the cart out of his path and raced off down the hallway. The cart smashed into the wall, spilling plastic-wrapped pastries and coffee all over.

"Hey!" Ed yelled. "Look what that guy did!"

"Forget it—go get help," Lewis told Ed, physically turning him around and pointing him in the direction they'd come from.

The second the officer hit the wall, Joe was racing full tilt after his assailant.

As he sped through corridors, Joe quickly realized two things. The man he was chasing was fast—and he couldn't be as old as his stooped-over posture had suggested. Or if he was old, he was in fantastic shape, because Joe, who was anything but slow, was losing ground.

He bore down harder. The corridors were deserted. As Joe ran, the only sounds he was aware of were his own labored breathing and the squeaking of his sneakers on the linoleum floor.

He was still losing ground, though he told himself that all he had to do was keep the man in sight—after all, he was trapped in a police station. How could he possibly escape? Up ahead, Joe saw his quarry disappear to the left, as the corridor they were running down ended.

Joe slowed. Lewis jogged up beside him, breathing heavily.

"He turned down here," Joe said as they came to the end of the corridor.

Off to their left, about twenty feet away, was a bank of elevators—and the mysterious man in the white shirt, who stood there, waiting silently.

"You can't get away," Lewis called out. "Why don't you make it easy on yourself?"

The man said nothing. He seemed completely unconcerned by their presence—as if they couldn't do a thing to stop him, whatever he decided to do.

"Give it up," Joe added, continuing to move toward him. Behind them, he could hear running footsteps—more police, no doubt, coming to help them. "You're outnumbered."

The ghost of a smile crossed the man's lips—and at that second the elevator doors opened.

The man stepped inside quickly.

Joe, who was about five feet away, sprang toward him, just as the door was starting to slide shut.

The man spun into another side-kick. But Joe was ready for it. He sidled out of the way, so the kick only caught him a glancing blow.

It still felt as if he'd been struck with a lead weight. He bounced off the closing elevator door and landed on the floor just outside the car.

Joe struggled to his feet and launched himself into the elevator. Something hard slammed into his stomach, knocking the wind from him. He reached up, trying to grab the man to stop him from getting away. He did manage to clasp something—just as another kick sent him spinning backward through the open elevator door.

Whatever he'd grabbed came with him.

Joe landed on the ground, flat on his back. He looked at what he was holding in his hand, then up at Lewis.

"It's a wig," Joe said, holding up a clump of gray hair. "The guy was wearing a wig."

"Stay calm, Chief," Frank said.

"My pills, Frank," Peterson gasped. He was having trouble catching his breath now. "Nitroglycerin—my coat pocket." He reached up with his right arm and shakily pointed to the back of the door.

Frank unhooked the coat and reached into the pocket to pull out a small bottle.

"That's it," the chief said. "Give them to me—quick." He took the bottle from Frank and tried to pop the cap off. But his arm was shaking so badly now that he dropped it on the floor.

"Hurry!"

Frank picked up the bottle and got a pill out. He placed it beneath the chief's tongue.

"It's not working," Peterson said, and now there was panic in his voice.

From his CPR course, Frank knew that whatever panic the chief was feeling was only making his condition worse.

"Try to stay calm," Frank said. "I'll get

help." A group of three officers was standing just outside the door. "Call an ambulance!" he yelled. "The chief's having a heart attack!"

They stared at him for a second, trying to place him.

But before Frank knew it, they were inside the office, snapping out orders. Two pulled the chief to his feet; the third spoke to Frank.

"We'll take a squad car."

The two officers carrying Chief Peterson held him as easily as if he were a baby and practically ran through the station and outside with him.

Would they get to the hospital in time to save him? Frank wondered as he climbed into a squad car. They were following the one carrying the chief. His mind ran on that treadmill until they arrived at the hospital emergency room. He and the police officers he'd ridden with spent half an hour in the waiting room, not knowing anything.

Finally one of the emergency room technicians emerged.

"He's over the worst of it," the man told them. "We seem to have stabilized his heartbeat. Took a long time to do it, though," he said, shaking his head. "Anyway, if you hadn't gotten him here so quickly—"

Someone tapped Frank on the shoulder just then.

Joe was standing there, looking concerned.

"Heard all about it at the station," he said. "How's the chief?"

"He's going to make it." Frank studied his brother, who looked somewhat disheveled. "What happened? Did you run all the way?"

"We had a little excitement of our own," Joe said. He told him about the intruder at the police station. "Anyway, by the time we got out to the street, the guy was gone. And nobody had seen him or anything." Joe shook his head. "Lewis is still trying to figure out why this guy was so anxious to impersonate a coffee vendor. . . ." His voice trailed off suddenly as he caught the look in his brother's eye.

In Frank's mind, things were starting to click into place. "The chief started having his attack a few minutes after drinking his coffee," he said.

"You think he might have been poisoned?" Joe asked.

"All we can do is find out."

They waited until Peterson's own doctor had arrived and finished briefing the police. Then they pulled her aside and told her about their suspicions.

"Chief Peterson's been very good about taking care of himself," she said thoughtfully. "I'm surprised that this attack came on so suddenly. Let me run a blood test, check for poison. It'll take a couple of hours," she added. "So make yourselves comfortable."

By this time a large crowd of police officers and relatives had assembled outside the emergency room. Among them, Frank caught sight of Detective Lewis and Chief Peterson's wife, Anne. He and Joe crossed to her side and sat down with her, to wait for the test results. Almost two hours to the minute, they had their answer.

"The chief was definitely poisoned," his doctor said. "We found traces of an amphetamine in his system. The drug would have simulated all the symptoms of a heart attack—palpitations, shortness of breath, chest pain, and would probably have been fatal to him, without his nitroglycerin pills and prompt treatment. If you hadn't gotten him here so quickly . . ." Her voice trailed off.

Frank thought of the unexpected circumstances that had led him to Brooklyn and to his talk with the chief and what might have happened if he hadn't been there to reach those nitro pills when the chief started having his attack.

"You think this might have something to do with the will?" Joe asked, pulling his brother aside.

Frank pursed his lips. "I do. Granted, there are probably a lot of people who'd like to see the chief dead, but this, right on the heels of Carew getting shot—"

Joe broke in. "I think we'd better call Dad to make sure he's okay."

Frank nodded grimly. "And then we'd better find out a lot more about that man in the white shirt—before he strikes again."

Chapter
6

FRANK SPENT the next forty-five minutes on the phone to Bayport.

The first fifteen minutes he spent reassuring his aunt Gertrude that he and Joe were fine. Then he spent fifteen minutes reassuring his mother that their schoolwork wasn't suffering. Finally he was able to speak to his father and reassure himself that Fenton Hardy was all right. Frank briefed his father on the mysterious goings-on at the police station that afternoon. When Fenton heard Chief Peterson was in the hospital, he decided to drive down to see him. By nine o'clock all three Hardys were assembled in Peterson's hospital room.

"I got here as quickly as I could," Fenton Hardy said. He laid a hand on Samuel Peterson's shoulder. "And I'll have you know I had to miss one of Laura's foreign film festivals to get here."

Peterson laughed. "It's good to see you." The chief still looked a little weak, but he was in good spirits. "And I'm flattered you came just to make sure I was all right."

"I didn't," Fenton said. "I came to see Anne, too." Peterson's wife was sitting in a chair on the other side of the bed, holding her husband's hand. Frank thought she looked a little worse than the chief at that point. "And my boys, of course."

"If it wasn't for that one boy of yours," Peterson said, nodding toward Frank, "I might not be here now."

Frank flushed beet red.

"And if it wasn't for the other"—Peterson nodded at Joe now—"we wouldn't have found out that I was poisoned."

Now it was Joe's turn to blush.

"They'll make good detectives someday," Fenton said. His expression turned serious then. "There's actually another reason I rushed in," he said. "After hearing about Daniel Carew, and now this—"

"I know," Peterson said, looking at Frank. "I may have been wrong. The Carew killing might have something to do with Moran's will."

"So Poletti has to be innocent," Joe said,

thinking fast. "He couldn't have drugged you."

"Maybe. He could have hired someone to poison me," the chief pointed out.

"Or there could be more than one killer among the beneficiaries. More than one person willing to commit murder to increase his share," Fenton put in.

"That's a scary idea," Peterson said. His brow creased as he thought. "First thing tomorrow, I'll see about getting some kind of report together on where all those beneficiaries are—"

"You'll do nothing of the sort!" Anne Peterson said. She looked angry. "Sam Peterson, you're supposed to be taking it easy!"

"You're right, dear. I'll have someone else take care of it." He and Fenton exchanged a hurried glance, and Fenton nodded, indicating he'd pick up the slack.

"You be careful, Fenton. It couldn't hurt to take precautions—"

"I will," Mr. Hardy said. "And I'll call Hugh Nolan, if you like," he offered.

"Good," Peterson said. "Any warning from me and he'd be likely to disregard on principle."

"All right," Fenton said. "We'll get started right away. Good night, Sam. Good night, Anne."

When they got out into the hall, Fenton

spoke privately to his sons. He'd rushed right in to see the chief as soon as he'd gotten to the hospital and hadn't had a chance to talk to them yet.

"I'm very proud of both of you" was the first thing he said. "Now, what can you tell me about this man who poisoned the chief?"

"Not much, I'm afraid," Frank said. "He was pretty well disguised."

"Yeah," Joe said. "First time I saw the guy, I thought he was about fifty. But he moved like a young guy. Whoever he was, he was really well trained in karate—or something."

"Something?" Frank asked.

"You know—kung fu, tae kwon do—one of those martial arts. I knew what he was going to do, but I couldn't stop him. It was like I was moving in slow motion the whole time."

Fenton turned to his eldest son. "Frank? Anything else?"

"Not really. Just like Joe, I thought he was a lot older at first, but then—" He shook his head. "I don't know. He could have been twenty-five or fifty-five, I really couldn't tell."

"You said he had blue eyes," Joe offered.

"That's right—I noticed them right away," Frank said. "They were so—" He looked up at his dad. "They were too blue," he said suddenly. "I think we were supposed to notice them."

Fenton nodded. "Probably tinted contact lenses. Sounds like a pro."

"What do we do now?" Frank asked.

"*We* don't do anything," Fenton said. "I'm going to make sure Hugh Nolan's all right—and then do a little detecting on the case. And you two are getting on the last train back to Bayport."

"We did come into the city to use the library," Frank pointed out. "And it's a little late to do that now."

Joe smiled. "Looks like you're stuck with us—at least until tomorrow."

Fenton nodded. "All right," he said. "Let's find a hotel. But first, I want to call Hugh Nolan. There's a phone down the hall."

"Dad, wait," Frank said.

Fenton faced his eldest son.

"What happened between Nolan and Peterson that Nolan hates him so much?" Frank asked hesitantly.

"*Hate* isn't the word I'd use." Fenton shook his head ruefully. "It goes back twenty years—to that case Sam and I had, the one that eventually put Moran away."

"You've never told us anything about it," Frank said.

"For good reason," Fenton replied. "It was a particularly ugly case—one I don't like to think about too much. A fire happened in what used to be one of the worst sections of Brooklyn. Where the Jefferson Heights townhouses are now."

"That neighborhood where Moran lives?" Joe asked incredulously. "That was a bad section of town?"

"It sure was," his father replied. "But the townhouses were planned to change all that. They were supposed to revitalize the whole neighborhood. But there was one small problem—there were already apartments there, with families living in them." He sighed deeply. "It was a mess. The developers were fighting to have the apartments condemned, the families living in them were fighting to stay. All the papers followed it for months. For a while it looked as if the whole deal might fall through.

"Then one night, there was a fire. Half a block of those tenements burned to the ground. Twelve people died. And the Jefferson Heights townhouses got built after all."

"How did you get involved?"

"Sam and I were assigned to the case about two days after the fire, when evidence of arson was discovered. We found out immediately that a lot of the families had been complaining about harassment by the developers for weeks, but nothing had been done. Hugh Nolan was the officer in charge of investigating the original harassment charges.

"I went to Hugh—we'd known each other

for some time—and he assured me there was no harassment. Sam felt differently. He thought the developers had paid off Hugh to look the other way. He said as much."

"And you? What did you think?"

"Well—there were a lot of suspicious incidents, but I'm from the old school. Innocent until proven guilty. And we never found anything linking Hugh with the developers. Then later, Hugh came forward with evidence that helped us prove Josh Moran had ordered those fires, and even Sam had to admit he'd been wrong to accuse Hugh. But it was too late to salvage Hugh's career—the damage had been done."

Joe frowned. "Was that when Moran still worked for Carew?"

Fenton nodded. "That's right. The townhouses were Carew's project—from start to finish. He bankrolled the developers, and we know he had to have ordered Moran to set the fires. Of course, we could never prove any connection there. With all the legal delays and stalling tactics, it took ten years for Moran's case to come to trial. But he did end up behind bars. As for Hugh . . ." Fenton sighed. "He took early retirement and missed out on his pension. He wanted Sam to intercede on his behalf, but . . ."

Frank nodded silently.

"Anyway," Fenton said, checking his

watch, "I'd better make that call before it gets too late."

Hugh Nolan was fine and happy to hear from Fenton. When he heard they were in town, he insisted on putting them up for the night in his small Lower East Side apartment.

"It's not much," he said, smiling as he led the Hardys into the living room after giving them a brief tour. They all took seats. "But it's home."

"It's a lot better than staying at a hotel," Fenton said. "Thanks."

"You're quite welcome. Now—you never did tell me why you were in town."

Fenton leaned forward in his chair. "Hugh—have you heard about Daniel Carew?"

Nolan grunted his assent. "Sure. Someone should have plugged him ten years ago, if you ask me."

"Be that as it may," Fenton said. He took a deep breath. "There was another incident today. Someone tried to poison Sam Peterson."

"What!"

"Frank and Joe were with him when it happened. That's why I'm here—they called me."

Nolan's face had gone pale. "Sam was poisoned? Is he all right?"

Fenton nodded. "He'll be fine. We just left him." He took a deep breath. "Hugh, we think both incidents might be connected."

"Moran's will, you mean."

"Exactly. Our murderer may be someone who wants to increase his share of that money very badly."

Nolan was silent for a moment. "I won't kid you, Fenton. I could really use my share of that money. But anyone who'd do something like this . . ."

Fenton nodded. "We all—all the beneficiaries—have to be especially careful. It might not be a bad idea for you to get out of town for a while."

"I guess you're right—though I'm not sure where I'd go—"

"Well," Fenton said, "I think we ought to talk to the police about that. If you like, I'll speak to them tomorrow."

Frank saw Nolan's face tighten involuntarily. Then he relaxed.

"All right," he said. "I'll leave the details to you." He stood and stretched. "I'm going to turn in now. You three can stay up if you want—"

"No, we'll turn in, too," Fenton said. He looked pointedly at Joe and Frank. "The boys have to get an early start tomorrow—they have work to do at the library."

Frank checked the clock on the wall. It was after eleven, so he decided not to argue with his father—in spite of his desire to talk about the case some more.

They all said good night. Fenton Hardy and Joe each took a twin bed in the smaller bedroom, while Frank settled in on the living room couch.

But he wasn't ready to sleep just yet. He wanted to sort through the day's events before going to bed. That story his father had told—about the arson in which twelve people were killed, and Moran's will—he'd bet the two incidents were somehow connected.

Frank yawned. Suddenly he was having trouble staying awake.

He thought about Hugh Nolan. For someone who supposedly hated Chief Peterson, he sure looked concerned when we told him that the chief had been poisoned. . . .

Frank's eyes snapped open. I must have drifted off, he realized. The clock on the wall said 1:30.

He was thirsty. He got out of bed and walked down the hall to the bathroom to get a drink of water. Then he stepped back out into the hall.

An arm snaked around his neck.

"Don't move," a voice whispered in his ear. "Don't speak. Don't even breathe."

The man's grip tightened, the crook of his arm pressing into Frank's neck. Two or three seconds of pressure, Frank knew, and he would pass out.

Any more than that—and he'd die.

Chapter
7

FRANK'S FIRST THOUGHTS were that he'd stumbled into the person who'd been killing the beneficiaries and that he was about to become the killer's next victim.

"Who are you, and what are you doing here?" The man's viselike grip tightened slightly, prompting Frank to answer.

"My name is Frank Hardy—I'm a guest here," he choked out.

"Hardy?" Frank heard the question in the man's voice, which suddenly sounded much less threatening. "Hold on." The man pulled Frank back a few steps, his grip not slackening for an instant.

A click and the living room lights were snapped on. Frank found himself face-to-face with his attacker: a young man a few years older than himself.

"Frank Hardy," the man said. "Fenton Hardy's oldest son. I've heard a lot about you." He spoke in a clear, unaccented voice and in the light didn't look at all threatening. He had dark hair just like Frank's—a little longer, maybe—and his face seemed somehow familiar. . . .

That was it. Frank snapped his fingers.

"You must be Hugh Nolan's son," he said.

"That's right," the man said. "Ned—Ned Nolan."

He stuck his hand out, and the two of them shook. Frank's other hand went to the back of his neck, to rub some feeling back into the place where Ned had grabbed him.

Ned saw and smiled. "Sorry about that," he said. "But if you walked into your father's apartment after midnight and found somebody tiptoeing around—"

"I understand," Frank said. "You have even more reason to be suspicious today."

Ned frowned. "I don't understand."

"This afternoon, someone tried to kill Chief Peterson."

"What!" Ned's eyes grew wide with surprise.

Just then one of the doors leading into the hall opened, and Joe Hardy stepped through.

His hair was tousled, and he wore only the bottom half of a pair of pajamas.

"Hey," he whispered, glaring at Frank. "Keep it down, would you? Between Dad's snoring, and the racket out here . . ." His voice trailed off as Joe caught sight of Ned.

"This must be your brother Joe," Ned said smoothly.

"Who're you?" Joe asked.

"I'm Ned Nolan," he said. "Hugh's son." He raised his eyebrows. "The owner of your pajama bottoms. Glad to meet you."

Joe laughed slightly, then nodded. "Glad to meet you, too."

Ned turned back to Frank. "Is that why you two are here? Because Chief Peterson was attacked?"

Frank nodded. "Not just us—our father's asleep back there, too."

"Your dad invited us to stay tonight," Joe said. "He's the one who lent me your—uh, pajamas."

"Your father's here as well? Good," Ned said firmly. "The more people around, the better. Especially if one of them is Fenton Hardy." He eyed Frank and Joe questioningly. "But I don't quite understand your role."

"Well—" Frank shrugged. "Joe and I were in town, we read about Daniel Carew getting shot, and we just got involved."

"Just like that? You got involved in a murder

case?'' Ned asked. He didn't seem to believe it.

"Sometimes we try to help our father out," Frank replied. He didn't bother to mention the fact that he and Joe had also handled numerous cases on their own.

"Well, I suppose I can understand it, in this instance," Ned said. "I should probably get more interested in this case myself—seeing how deeply it affects my father. Come on," Nolan turned and headed for the kitchen, motioning Frank and Joe to follow. "Let's sit down and talk. There's a fresh bag of potato chips in the bread drawer if you're interested."

Joe smiled his thanks and opened the drawer Ned pointed to.

"So, tell me about this from the beginning."

Frank started by recounting what had happened when he, Joe, and their father had gone to the reading of Moran's will. He had gotten as far as the shouting match between Tommy Poletti and Daniel Carew when Ned interrupted him.

"I was thinking about going with my father that day, but—" Ned shook his head. "I wasn't sure I could be responsible for my actions with all those people there. After they stymied his career—" He broke off in midsentence and looked across the table. "I guess I'm not making much sense, am I?"

Frank and Joe exchanged a quick glance.

"Yes, you are—we heard about what happened to your dad from our father."

"He got a raw deal," Ned said angrily. "You know, after my mom left, he did everything for me. *Everything.* So when those people start calling him names . . ." His voice trailed off.

"For what it's worth, I'm sorry," Frank offered.

"Yeah," Joe said. Frank saw he was about halfway through the big bag of potato chips already.

"Thanks." Ned smiled. "Anyway, that was all a long time ago. So—you were at Moran's house. What do you think? Are both these killings related to that will?"

"Both these attacks—Chief Peterson didn't die," Frank said, correcting him. "And my gut feeling is—yes, they're related, somehow."

"I don't think Tommy Poletti killed Carew," Joe said. "But it does seem like an awfully big coincidence for the two incidents to come so close together—and at this particular time."

Ned was silent for a moment. "All right—if it isn't a coincidence," he asked, "then who's doing it? Which one of the other beneficiaries?"

Frank ticked off the list on his hand. "We started with Hugh Nolan, Johnny Carew, Daniel Carew, Samuel Peterson, Fenton Hardy, Thomas Poletti, and William Delaney. Daniel Carew is dead, Peterson's been attacked—"

"So—Delaney, then," Joe cut in. "It's got to be him."

"I don't know very much about any of those people," Ned said. "But my money's on Johnny Carew."

"You think he'd shoot his own son?" Frank asked dubiously.

Ned shrugged. "No, I suppose not. But from what my father's told me, he seems like the most coldhearted of the bunch. And don't forget," he said, "there could be more than one killer."

"Boy, we've been down this road before." Joe yawned and pushed his chair back from the table. "I think I'm going to hit the sack, guys. See you in the morning."

"Good night, Joe," Ned said.

"Good night." Frank leaned forward over the table. "I think the police are going to get a lot more serious about this case—and its connection to Moran's will—now that Chief Peterson's been poisoned."

"I hope so," Ned said. "Have they found any trace of the man who attacked him?"

Frank shrugged. "I don't know yet, but I doubt it. I probably got a better look at him than anyone, and I don't think I'd recognize him if he walked up to me and shook my hand."

"I suppose that's understandable," Ned

chuckled. "A white shirt isn't exactly an identifying mark."

Frank vainly tried to stifle a yawn. He was
falling asleep at the table. "I guess I'm a little
tired, too."

"It is late," Ned said, nodding. He cleared
the table and led the way back into the living
room.

"I think your father has my bed," Ned said,
staring down the hall.

"I'll flip you for the sofa," Frank offered.

"That lumpy old thing?" Ned shook his
head. "It's all yours." He picked up the sofa's
back cushions and arranged them into a makeshift mattress. "I'll make do with these."

"Good night, then." Frank said. He settled
back onto the couch—and within minutes was
fast asleep.

Frank woke to the smell of frying bacon and
the warmth of the sun in his eyes. He show-
ered, dressed, and went into the kitchen.

Hugh Nolan, Ned Nolan, and Frank's father
were sitting around the breakfast table, eating,
and reading the morning paper. Joe was there
as well, but he had pushed his chair about three
feet back from the table and was keeping his
eyes away from anything that looked like food.

"Morning, everybody."

"Morning, Frank. Help yourself to bacon
and eggs," Hugh Nolan said.

Frank nodded his thanks, even though he wasn't particularly hungry yet.

Joe groaned. "It feels like there's a lead weight in my stomach. I don't think I'll ever be hungry again."

"That's why you're not supposed to eat after midnight," Frank said.

"The papers say the police have released Tommy Poletti," Fenton Hardy said, sipping his coffee.

"They finally figured out he's not guilty," Joe said. "I guessed that all along."

"That also means the police are back to square one in their investigation," Fenton said. "Poletti was their only suspect."

"So they don't know any more about who the killer is," Ned said thoughtfully. "Or who might be next."

The doorbell rang.

Frank and his father exchanged a quick glance.

"You expecting anyone, Hugh?" Fenton asked.

Nolan shook his head.

"I'll get it, Dad," Ned said, standing.

"Careful," Fenton Hardy said, instantly serious. Frank noticed the bulge of a shoulder holster beneath his father's sport jacket.

Ned returned with two men, one tall and thin, the other short and stocky. Both were dressed in suits.

"Fenton Hardy? Hugh Nolan?"

Fenton and Hugh stood.

"I'm Detective Martin," the smaller man said, flashing a badge. "This is Detective Stevens. Could we talk to you for a moment? In private?"

Fenton and Hugh led the men to the living room.

"What's this all about?" Ned asked.

Frank shrugged. "Your guess is as good as mine."

When the four men returned a couple of minutes later, Fenton Hardy spoke first.

"These men have just come from a meeting with Chief Peterson and the mayor, boys. The word's come down from the top on this one. It's been decided that the three of us—that is, Hugh Nolan, myself, and Chief Peterson—should disappear for a while." He smiled. "I think I know the perfect place, but we'll have to stop at home first."

"Where's that, Dad?" Frank asked.

Fenton shook his head. "It's better that we keep the location secret," he said. "I'll tell your mother that a case has come up for me but that she should expect you and Joe home tonight."

"But, Dad—" Joe began.

Fenton Hardy shook his head firmly. "No buts. You two get to the library and get to work."

"Anytime you're ready," the smaller of the two detectives said. "We'll take you to the chief."

The two older men said their goodbyes—and then, just like that, they were gone.

"I don't like this at all," Frank said, staring out the living room window. On the street below, he saw the four men get into a squad car and drive off.

"Me neither," Joe said.

"What can you do about it?" Ned said. Then, assuming the subject was closed, he switched to another. "So, are you two going to the midtown library today?"

Frank met Joe's eyes, then shook his head.

"We're not leaving the city."

"But your father said—"

Now Frank stared at Ned.

"Whoever's behind the killings—if we assume for the moment that it's one person—he's already managed to infiltrate a precinct station and almost kill the chief of police."

"So?" Ned asked.

"So, what if the killer has a contact inside the police department? There's a great chance he could find our fathers, no matter where they hide." Frank shook his head. "We're not leaving until this killer is caught."

Chapter

8

"ALL RIGHT," Ned said. "What can I do to help?"

"Well," Frank said, "I think a good place to begin is with that list of beneficiaries."

"Motive and opportunity?" Joe asked. That was where they usually began when they had a list of suspects—narrow it down by checking to see who had the motive and who had the opportunity.

"They all have the same motive," Ned pointed out. "Moran's money—ten million dollars. That leaves us with opportunity."

Frank shook his head. "The police are probably doing that right now. And they have a lot more than three people to check out alibis," he said.

"Well—if we can't check opportunity, and they all have the same motive—" Joe smiled suddenly. He saw what Frank was getting at. "They might not all have exactly the same motive, right?"

"Right," his brother replied.

"What do you mean?" Ned asked.

"We're talking about ten million dollars here," Frank said. "Which is admittedly a lot of money. But to, say, Tommy Poletti, it's worth more than to Johnny Carew, who's probably got at least that much already."

"I see," Ned replied. "So what do we do now?"

"We find out how much they're worth," Joe said.

Frank nodded. "Exactly."

"How are we going to do that?"

"I've got a couple of ideas," Frank said. "I'll tell you on the way."

He stood to go.

"On the way where?" Ned asked.

"Just north of the Wall Street area," Frank said.

"Hold on," Joe said. "Let me get a little something to eat."

"I thought you were never going to be hungry again," Frank said.

"Well," Joe said, piling a few slices of bacon and a big spoonful of scrambled eggs onto his plate. "Detective work always gives me an appetite."

* * *

An hour and a half later the three boys were in the waiting room of Vance Johnson's office.

It had been Frank's idea to start digging at the lawyer's for information: impartial information on the people they were most interested in—Billy Delaney and Johnny Carew.

"Mr. Johnson will see you now," Johnson's secretary called out. She led them into the lawyer's office—a large, airy room with high ceilings and a wall of bay windows that looked out onto lower Broadway. Thick, meticulously arranged law volumes lined the floor-to-ceiling bookshelves along one wall. Another wall was dominated by oil portraits of several very distinguished-looking individuals, and the fourth wall was almost completely hidden by a line of massive oak filing cabinets and an old-fashioned water cooler.

It all seemed very proper and respectable. Yet Joe wondered how much of that respectability Johnson had was genuine. After all, he had been Joshua Moran's lawyer.

Johnson was seated behind the massive oak desk, scanning a single sheet of paper. Other than a small stack of papers piled neatly in front of him, his desk was bare. He rose as the three boys entered.

"Mr. Johnson," Frank said, stepping forward, "thank you for agreeing to see us." He nodded in Ned's direction. "This is Ned Nolan."

"Hugh's son, I assume," Johnson said crisply, shaking hands with all of them. "So, I gather this is about Mr. Moran's will."

"That's right," Joe said. "We—"

"Well then, gentlemen." Johnson laid his palms flat on the table and stared directly at them. "My time is valuable—how may I be of service to you?"

Frank seemed slightly taken aback at his formality. Joe, too, knew that was a bad sign, but Johnson's attitude was understandable. He'd probably been grilled by the police more than once during the last few days and obviously wouldn't welcome more questions—especially from three people he probably saw as little more than overly enthusiastic teenagers. Check that, Joe told himself with a glance at Ned, who was past his teens. Two teenagers.

Joe was trying to think of something witty and charming to say when he noticed a large, framed photo. In the photo Johnson was standing with another, much younger man, whom Joe recognized instantly.

"Hey," Joe blurted out. "That's Tommy Poletti."

"Why, yes. That picture was taken the day after the Rose Bowl, the year Tommy was Heisman winner." Johnson nodded. "USC lost, but Tommy was magnificent."

"Five touchdown passes, nineteen straight completions," Joe said. "I remember watching it." Truthfully, he did. It was one of the first football games he'd seen on television—and still one of the best.

"Greatest single game a quarterback has ever had—in my opinion," Johnson said. "But then, Tommy wouldn't settle for doing any less, once he got to the Rose Bowl. That's just the kind of boy he was. Is. I've been close friends with the family for years—worked for his late father for almost four decades."

Joe had a sudden hunch. "The Poletti family—that's how you came to work for Mr. Moran, isn't it? Tommy's relationship with Emily?"

"Why—yes," Johnson said. He seemed somewhat surprised. "When the two of them first started seeing each other in college, Tommy asked me to keep an eye on her family's affairs."

Joe glanced questioningly at Frank, who nodded. Joe knew that that nod meant, Go ahead—it's your show. "Mr. Johnson, we'll try not to waste your time. I'm sure the police have already asked you questions, but we're"—he indicated the three of them—"personally interested in this case in a way that they can't be. It's our fathers' lives that are at stake."

"I see," Johnson said. He crossed to a group of armchairs in the far corner of his office and sat down, indicating that the Hardys and Ned should follow suit.

"I understand your particular closeness to this case, but I'm not sure what I can do to help you."

"Well . . ."

Frank broke in. "We're trying to find out a little more background—financial background—on some of the people Mr. Moran named as beneficiaries. Especially Johnny Carew and Billy Delaney."

Johnson thought for a moment. "Well, as I was telling the police, I know very little about Mr. Carew's activities. I can only make inferences, based on conversations I had with Mr. Moran before his death."

"Every little bit helps," Ned said.

Johnson nodded. "Mr. Moran felt that Mr. Carew's various real-estate holdings were worth upward of one hundred million dollars. His own personal fortune, he estimated at somewhat less than half of that."

"So ten million dollars would still be a lot of money for him," Frank said.

Johnson nodded.

"But would he kill for it?" Joe asked.

"That's the thing about money," Ned put in. "No matter how much you have, you always want more."

"What about Delaney?" Frank asked.

Johnson snorted. "Ten million dollars would be a fortune for him."

"But I thought he'd been running Moran's"—Joe was about to say *gang*, but stopped himself in time—"businesses for him while Moran was in jail."

Johnson nodded. "Running them into the ground."

"I noticed he and Tommy didn't get along too well."

"Nor do he and Emily," Johnson said. "She's particularly uncomfortable having him live in that townhouse with her."

"They live together?"

"It was her father's request. But now that he's gone—well, I expect Delaney will be moving out shortly."

"How does she feel about all this—the killing, I mean?"

Johnson sighed deeply. "She's quite upset. She has me working to find a way to invalidate her father's will."

Joe was surprised. "Why? Won't that affect her share of the estate?"

"Perhaps," Johnson said. "That's uncertain. But she really has very little interest in that money, if you can believe it."

"I do find it a little hard to believe," Ned said quietly.

Johnson glowered at him. "Emily wants only to marry Tommy, and she would just as soon never see a penny of her father's wealth. She was never close to him."

Joe decided he'd bet money that Johnson had gotten involved with Joshua Moran only at Tommy Poletti's prompting—and quite reluctantly, at that.

"What do you think?" Frank asked. "Is there a chance of getting Moran's will set aside?"

"I hadn't thought so until recently. However, I think I may have found something. . . ." He pulled out a manila folder.

"Ah, yes," Johnson said, thumbing through the pages. "It occurred to me that if we can prove that Mr. Moran lacked testamentary capacity at the time he made out his will, we may be able to have the entire document declared void."

"Testamentary capacity—you mean, whether or not he was in his right mind?" Ned asked.

"Exactly," Johnson replied.

"Your ten-thirty is here, Mr. Johnson," his secretary said over the intercom.

"Thank you, Mrs. Hunter. I'm afraid that's all the time I can spare, boys. I hope I've been of some help."

"You have, Mr. Johnson," Joe assured him. "And thanks."

They shook hands all around, and Johnson promised to keep them up-to-date on his efforts to have Moran's will nullified.

Back down on the street, they talked about the information the lawyer had given them.

"He had a lot to say," Ned said. "Especially after you recognized that picture, Joe."

"True," the younger Hardy replied. "It seems to me that he's anxious to put this whole affair behind him."

"One thing seems certain," Ned said. "From what he told us, Delaney needs the money a lot more than Carew."

"With Josh Moran dead, he could begin to lose control of his gang," Joe said. "Add that to his financial problems—"

"And you get a prime suspect," Ned said, finishing Joe's thought. "Delaney could be our man."

"Johnson doesn't like Delaney very much, though," Frank said thoughtfully. "We have to consider the possibility he's not giving us entirely accurate information."

"That's true," Joe admitted. "And Delaney can't be the actual killer—he's a lot bigger than the man I ran into in the hospital."

"On the other hand, Delaney could have hired someone to do that," Ned suggested.

Frank nodded. "I think it's worth our paying Mr. Delaney a little visit."

To their surprise, Delaney himself answered the door at the Moran brownstone.

"Yeah?"

He obviously wasn't in a good mood. It didn't make his face, which Joe had remembered as rather homely, any more attractive. But Joe had forgotten the man was so big.

"This'll just take a second, sir," Joe said. He slid his foot inside the door so Delaney couldn't slam it on him.

"It'll take less than that, sonny," Delaney said. "You're Hardy's kid, ain't you? What're you doing, nosing around here?" He tried to shut the door and failed because Joe's foot was in the way.

"We just have a few questions—" Frank began, moving up next to Joe.

"Trouble, boss?" Another man came to the door behind Delaney. Joe recognized him as one of the mob who'd gathered around Delaney at the reading of the will.

The newcomer saw Joe, then Frank, and his eyes widened.

"It's the Hardy kids, boss," the man said. "Both of them."

"You two got a lot of nerve, showing your faces around here," Delaney continued.

Without warning, Delaney's arm shot out and grabbed Joe's coat collar. Delaney began dragging him forward, as easily as if he were a rag doll. The man was incredibly strong.

Joe realized suddenly that he might be in a lot of trouble.

"I guess we're going to have to teach you

some manners, smart guy," Delaney said. By now, he had pulled Joe so close that their noses were almost touching.

"Yeah," the other man chimed in menacingly. His eyes never left Frank as he slowly moved in on him. "Starting now. Right now."

Chapter

9

"Mr. Delaney, you don't need to do this," Frank began, sidestepping to throw his would-be assailant off balance. The man behind Delaney couldn't maneuver close enough to Frank to grab him now.

"I don't have to," Delaney growled. "But I want to." He drew his arm back as if he was going to swing at Joe.

"Let him go, Mr. Delaney," Ned said, moving into the space Frank had left.

Delaney snorted. "Who are you?"

"Ned Nolan—and I'm telling you—"

"Hugh Nolan's kid? That weasel?" Delaney barked out a laugh. "If you're anything like your old man, I could just—"

Things happened fast then. There was a flash of movement, and suddenly Delaney wasn't holding Joe anymore. He was holding his own hands and rubbing them.

"Watch what you do to my friends," Ned said. "And especially watch what you say about my father."

"Oh," Delaney said, looking up. "So you want to play rough." He stepped forward, and swung at Ned. Frank could feel the air move with the force of his blow, which was surprisingly fast for a man of his size. Ned ducked it easily and threw a punch of his own. The big man staggered on his feet, gasping for breath.

"That's it, pal." Delaney's hood moved forward with a drawn gun. "Beat it."

Frank held both his hands up and stepped in front of Ned again. "All right, things got a little out of hand, but—"

"I said beat it!" Delaney's hood slammed the door in his face, leaving the three of them standing on the stoop.

"That settles that," Frank said.

"Wow," Joe said, staring at Ned. "What did you do to Delaney?"

"Taught him some manners, I expect," Ned said, smiling. He laid an arm on Joe's shoulder. "Are you all right?"

"Yeah, I'm fine," Joe said. He paused a moment. "You didn't have to do that, Ned."

"It was my pleasure."

"No, Ned," Frank said quietly. "Joe means you shouldn't have done that."

Ned turned to face him, a surprised look on his face.

"You cost us a chance to talk to Delaney," Frank said.

"What should I have done, Frank? Let him strangle your brother?"

Joe shook his head. "He wouldn't have strangled me."

"Really? We're talking about the man who probably killed Daniel Carew—and tried to kill Chief Peterson," Ned said coldly. "Need I point out that your father—or mine—could be next?"

"We don't know that Delaney killed anyone," Frank said. "Ned, you can't let your emotions run away with you if—"

"If I'm going to be a detective, is that it?"

The two of them stood silently staring at each other.

"Yes," Frank said finally.

"Well, then maybe I shouldn't be a detective," Ned said angrily. "I'll leave the field to you two."

"Ned, wait." Joe grabbed his arm. "You don't have to—"

Ned threw Joe's grip off and stalked off without looking back.

"Let him go," Frank told his brother. "He just needs to cool off."

They stood on the bottom step of Delaney's brownstone, staring after him.

"Hey!"

Frank turned. The voice belonged to Delaney's friend, the man who'd pulled the gun on them. He was leaning out the front door of the townhouse, glaring down at them.

"Didn't I tell you guys to beat it?"

Joe turned toward him angrily, but Frank laid a hand on his shoulder before he could speak.

"We're on our way," he said, pulling Joe away. "We're not going to get anything accomplished here, that's for sure," he muttered under his breath.

"So what's next?"

Frank looked at his watch. It was almost one o'clock. "Well—there is one thing we do have to do this afternoon."

"What's that?"

"Our research at the library."

Joe groaned.

Joe actually did have a very productive afternoon at the library.

He finished his work early and decided to look into the incident that seemed to be at the heart of the case. He watched microfilms of newspaper articles from twenty years ago, when the Jefferson Heights townhouses had been built—when that terrible fire, which killed twelve people, had taken place.

It was all there, just as his father had told

them. And the more Joe read, the more suspicious that fire looked. He dug back farther, searching for more information on the deal that had been struck to tear down and "renovate" the Jefferson Heights area.

The earliest mention he found came complete with pictures of Josh Moran himself. One showed Moran at city hall, during discussions regarding the Jefferson Heights project. The photographer had caught Moran in midsentence, making a point. He was probably in his early forties then—a handsome man, with jet black hair and precise, angular features, which his daughter Emily had clearly inherited.

Joe recognized few other people in the picture, identified as city officials, including the then-mayor of New York, a few police officers—

His heart stopped.

He moved the viewer in closer, enlarging the photographed image.

There, directly behind Moran, his face partially obscured by that man's arm, was Hugh Nolan. His presence there was proof of nothing, of course, but Nolan was smiling in the picture, and Joe got the sense that he and Moran were connected in some way.

Suddenly he wasn't sure Ned's father had gotten a raw deal after all. He and Moran clearly knew each other.

He looked through a few more articles on

the project but found nothing else of interest. After returning the microfilms, he found Frank and sat down to tell him about his afternoon's work.

"So Hugh Nolan may be a suspect, too," Frank said thoughtfully. "Which leaves us with the question of how this all fits together. It's got to relate back to what happened twenty years ago."

"It seems pretty obvious to me," Joe said. "Moran took the fall for Carew, so he was mad at him. He was mad at Dad and Chief Peterson for putting him away, and he came up with a very creative way of getting back at all of them."

"But what about Tommy and Hugh?" Frank asked. "And who's doing the killings now—and why?"

Joe shrugged. "That I can't help you with."

"But that's what we've got to figure out," Frank said. "And we've got to find someplace else to do our figuring, I guess. We're probably not going to be too welcome at the Nolans' anymore."

But when they returned to the Nolans' apartment to return the keys Hugh had given them, they found a note waiting for them.

Frank and Joe,
   Sorry I got so angry with you earlier. Please feel free to stay and use the apart-

ment. I may be out late tonight, but I'll catch up with you tomorrow.

Ned

"Well," Joe said, slumping down on the couch. "That's good. At least we have a base of operations. So, what do we do tonight?"

"Well . . ." Frank sat down next to him. "We can't go back and see Delaney—"

"Or Emily, since she lives in the same place." Joe thought a moment. "Maybe we should try Johnny Carew."

Frank shook his head. "How about we talk to a friendly face this time?"

"Whom did you have in mind?"

"Tommy Poletti."

Joe nodded. "That's a good idea. But how are we going to find him? I don't expect a former Heisman trophy winner has a listed address."

"I know where he lives," Frank said. "I caught a glimpse of the police file on him when we went to see Chief Peterson that first time."

"He's got a record?" Joe asked, clearly upset. "Why? What for?"

"I couldn't see that part of the file," Frank said.

Joe shook his head. "I don't believe it."

"You can ask him about it when we get there, then," Frank said, grabbing his coat. "Come on."

"Where're we going? Where does he live?"

"Where everybody connected with this case seems to live," Frank replied. "Brooklyn."

After grabbing a bite to eat, the brothers took the subway back to Brooklyn. They got off at the first stop, and from there it was just a five-minute walk to Poletti's apartment.

Tommy lived right next to the Brooklyn Bridge, in a beautiful neighborhood of brownstones. As they turned onto his block, a figure emerged from one of the brownstones ahead of them and walked out onto the street. A tall, dark man who looked in both directions before heading directly toward them.

It was Tommy Poletti. Frank pretended not to notice him.

"Wait," Joe said. "That's him. Let's catch up and—"

"No," Frank said, grabbing hold of his brother's arm and dragging him across the street. "He obviously doesn't want to be followed."

"So?" Joe asked.

"So let's see where he's going before we announce ourselves."

"All right," Joe said reluctantly. "We'll tail him for a while."

Frank studied his brother closely. Was Joe letting his admiration for Poletti cloud his judgment? He hoped not.

Frank began tailing Poletti, keeping on the

opposite side of the street and half a block behind the man. Joe fell back a half block behind his brother. As Frank walked, he pulled a wool ski cap out of his pocket and put it on. Whenever he and Joe did a two-man tail, they used the hat, or something like it, as a signal. If Frank felt the quarry was getting suspicious of him, he'd take off the cap and fall back, letting Joe pick up the man's trail. His brother would then follow the same procedure.

But in this case, all their precautions turned out to be unnecessary. For Poletti walked straight across the Brooklyn Bridge at such a brisk pace that Frank had trouble keeping up with him. Poletti was clearly on some kind of schedule—he kept checking his watch—and didn't even look back once. Halfway across the bridge, Joe caught up with Frank.

"He's sure in a hurry," Joe said, breathing heavily.

"To go where?"

"Maybe this is how he keeps in shape," Joe suggested with a grin. "This feels like a waste of time to me, Frank."

Frank shook his head. "Let's just see how it develops before we do anything."

Joe nodded resignedly and fell back behind Frank again.

Poletti continued his rapid pace as he left the bridge and crossed into Manhattan. He strode by City Hall and continued north, past all the government buildings. Just before Chinatown, Poletti took a left and headed west, toward the Hudson River. Within a few minutes Frank was trailing the man through a maze of four- and five-story commercial buildings in an old manufacturing district.

Then Poletti stopped. In the middle of the block ahead of him a long line of limousines was parked, and a crowd of people were gathered at the entrance to a building.

Frank crossed to the other side of the street and continued walking, past Poletti and directly toward the crowd. As he passed them, he heard an insistent, thudding beat coming from inside the door. And a small sign above the door, white letters on a black background, read simply Cosmos.

Suddenly he felt very foolish. The place was a nightclub. Joe had been right after all. Poletti was simply going out, probably meeting someone here.

Another limousine pulled up in front of the club, and an older man emerged from the driver's seat. He walked around the car, opened the rear passenger door—and Billy Delaney stepped out.

The two doormen immediately parted the crowd to let Delaney's men and Delaney pass through the entrance to the club.

Was this what Poletti had been waiting for? As soon as Delaney entered the club, Tommy started walking again—this time past the entrance, toward the end of the block.

Frank shook his head. Why, if Poletti had come here to meet Delaney, wasn't he going inside?

Frank could think of only one reason.

Poletti hadn't come here to meet the man. He'd come here to kill him.

Chapter
10

FRANK HAD TO MAKE a quick decision—should he follow Poletti, or see what Delaney was up to inside the club?

As he thought about it, he decided he didn't have much choice. Poletti may have been pre-occupied, but Frank had walked directly past him. He must have been seen—and it would look too suspicious if Poletti saw him again.

Frank took off his ski cap and joined the crowd waiting to get into Cosmos. As he pushed toward the front of the mob, he saw Joe race down the corner after Poletti.

"Cover charge is twenty dollars tonight, kid." Frank looked up to find one of the doormen, a large black man with a shaved head, studying him from behind the roped-off entrance to the club. "And I'm going to need some ID—with a picture."

Frank groaned. ID—he'd forgotten all about it. In New York, you had to be twenty-one to get into the clubs. Now what was he going to do?

Improvise.

"I just came from in there," Frank began, "and I think I left my wallet inside—"

"Hey, look, kid," the bouncer said, turning his full attention to Frank. "If you don't have an ID, step out of the way." The man folded his arms across his chest and glowered threateningly at him.

"Never mind," Frank said, turning away. Now what was he going to do? He had to get inside to find out what Delaney was doing— and if necessary, warn him that Poletti was after him.

He trudged away from the club, so deep in thought that he almost missed the iron fence blocking an alleyway that ran right next to the club. He took a quick look around. The only people on the street were those at the entrance to Cosmos, and the only thing on their minds was getting into the club.

Taking a deep breath, Frank jumped up, caught the top of the fence, and carefully boosted himself up and over the spikes on top. He jumped, bending his knees to land quietly on the other side.

A door from the club was pushed out into the alley just then.

Frank dropped to the ground and lay still.

A man, wearing a white apron over a plain white T-shirt, stepped through the door carrying a large trash bag in each hand. Whistling happily, he dropped the bags in the alley next to a pile of about twenty others, wiped his hands, and went back inside. The door swung shut behind him.

Frank got up slowly and dusted himself off. This must be my lucky day, he said to himself.

He was right. The door was unlocked—and when Frank cracked it slightly, he heard whistling and the muffled thump of noise from the club.

He pulled the door open a hair farther and peered in.

The man he had seen take out the trash was at a sink off to the left, about twenty feet away. His back was to Frank, and he was scrubbing a large pot and singing along with the music coming from inside the club.

Directly opposite Frank was a set of double doors with small square windows. Through them, he could see pulsing lights.

Frank eased the door back and slid inside. He strode quickly and quietly toward those lights, taking off his jacket as he walked.

Walking into the club was like being on the

fifty-yard line during the Super Bowl halftime show.

The first thing that hit him was the music—the song playing had a thudding, droning, synthesized beat and was turned up so loud he could actually feel the thump of the bass drum in the pit of his stomach. Lights flashed on and off, making the white shirt he was wearing change colors, from orange to green to red—and back to orange again.

Inside, Cosmos was one huge round room, broken up into different levels with what looked almost like construction scaffolding. And standing on that scaffolding were some of the strangest looking and most strangely dressed people he had ever seen.

In the center of the room was an enormous, sunken dance floor. Across the room, almost directly opposite Frank, was a horseshoe-shaped bar.

In the crowd at the bar, Frank saw the man who'd pulled the gun on them at Delaney's.

As Frank watched, he took two bottles of what looked like champagne from the bartender and headed up some metal stairs toward the rear of the club.

Frank circled around the dance floor and followed the guy up the stairs. They seemed to go on forever, leading Frank away from the club. As Frank got closer to the top, the noise from below faded, and the stairs dead-ended on a large landing at a plain gray metal door.

Private, it read. No Admittance.

Frank tested the knob. It turned silently in his hand. He nudged the door open slightly and risked a quick peek behind it.

He caught a glimpse of a large, comfortable-looking room, with wood paneling, skylights, and a desk on the far wall. Seated on a large couch in the center of the room was Johnny Carew, smoking a cigar. Two men in turtle-necks and dark sport coats stood behind the couch, flanking him. Billy Delaney sat with his back to Frank on a chair in front of the couch; the two men he'd brought with him to the club sat in chairs behind him.

Frank eased the door back, leaving it ajar an inch, his ear up against it, and listened.

"And I want to assure you I had nothing to do with Daniel's death." That was Delaney speaking.

"If I thought for a moment you had killed him," Carew said, his voice clear and ringing, "you would have been dead within an hour, Billy."

"Maybe," Delaney said. "And maybe if you'd come gunning for me, you'd have been the one to end up dead."

There was an uncomfortable few seconds of silence. Even through the door, Frank could sense the two glaring at each other, each waiting for the other to back down.

Delaney cracked first.

"Look, Johnny, there's no sense in *our* fighting," Delaney said. "Especially with Emily trying to have the whole will nullified. You know that'll turn it into a free-for-all."

Carew still said nothing.

"The only way to make sure we keep control of the situation is if you let me remain in charge of Josh's concerns," Delaney continued. "I'll see you get a percentage, of course."

"A percentage?" Carew demanded loudly. Frank heard the scrape of a chair against the floor. "All right, I'll take a percentage. How about one hundred percent?"

"Johnny, you have to negotiate with me," Delaney replied.

"I don't have to do nothing," Carew said. "You've got no power, Billy. It all dried up and blew away when Josh Moran died. You don't even have Emily Moran to count on. So I'll take back the territory Josh stole from me, sure—but I won't give you anything for it."

Delaney's voice hardened. "Then maybe we should be talking about fighting, Johnny. Because I won't—"

Suddenly there was a sharp *crack!*—followed instantly by the tinkle of shattering glass.

Frank risked another peek inside.

Blood Money

Four of the men in the room had drawn guns. All of them were staring straight up at a skylight.

And on the floor, lying motionless at Johnny Carew's feet, was Billy Delaney.

Chapter

11

JOE TRAILED TOMMY POLETTI around the block to an abandoned building, his thoughts paralleling Frank's. He'd watched Delaney arrive at the club, and Poletti had obviously timed his arrival to coincide with that of Josh Moran's former lieutenant.

The big question was *why?*

Huge letters painted on the side of the building, now long since faded, announced it as the home of Schickelman Importers—New York's Largest. But Schickelman, whoever he had been, was obviously long gone, along with his importing business. Now as Joe watched Poletti lift himself up and over the sill of a window and disappear into the building, he grew even more suspicious. He hoped his suspicions would turn out to be misplaced.

Giving the man a few seconds' lead, Joe

boosted himself up and in, landing in a pitch-black space.

When his eyes adjusted to the small amount of light filtering through the filthy windows, he saw that the inside of the former warehouse had been completely gutted. Toward the back, he just made out Poletti climbing the only staircase. Joe stole across the vast floor, his feet scratching the gritty dirt against the hardwood. He climbed up after Poletti and found himself on the roof of the building itself.

He scanned the adjoining rooftops. Nothing. There was no sign of Tommy Poletti. Had the man managed to slip behind him? Joe turned to head back down into the warehouse.

Then a sudden, all-too-familiar crack echoed behind him. The crack of a gunshot.

Joe whirled. The sound had come from off to his left. And running straight toward him from that direction was Tommy Poletti.

Joe ducked behind a chimney. As Poletti ran even with him, Joe tackled the former football player.

They rolled over on the hard rooftop together. Poletti might not have played football for several years, but he was still in excellent shape—beneath the jacket he was wearing, the man was solid muscle.

He threw Joe off easily and sprang to his feet.

"What did you do?" Joe asked shakily, also

standing up. He couldn't believe it. Poletti was the killer after all. "Where's the gun?"

"Gun? What are you talking about?" Poletti was furious. "What did you tackle me for?"

"That gunshot," Joe said, his voice shaking. "Who did you kill?"

"Kill? Are you nuts?" Poletti said. He looked at Joe for the first time. "Hey—you're the Hardy kid. You were at the reading of the will, weren't you?"

"That's right," Joe said. "What are you doing here?"

"I could ask you the same thing," Poletti said.

"I'm following you," Joe said. "And I just heard a gunshot and saw you running away—"

"I don't have to tell you what I'm doing here," Poletti said defensively.

"Maybe not," Joe said, unable to keep the bitterness out of his voice. "But you'll have to tell the cops."

"Cops?" Poletti shook his head. "Oh, no, I'm not talking to any more cops."

"I'll tell them about this," Joe said fiercely. "Unless you kill me, too."

"All right," Poletti said, shaking his head. "But you're wrong about this, kid."

"Maybe I am," Joe said, but he didn't believe it. As far as he was concerned, the evidence was doing all the talking.

*　　*　　*

For what seemed like forever, Frank watched as no one in Carew's office moved.

Finally one of Delaney's men bent over his boss's body.

"He's dead," the man announced.

"The shot came from up there," Carew said, pointing up at the skylight. He turned to a couple of his men.

"Monk, Moses, you two check it out."

Both nodded and turned toward the door.

Frank started to ease the door shut, preparing to step away from it and rush back down the stairs.

"Hey—what are you doing up here?"

Frank turned. A lean, sharply dressed man with straight blond hair was standing a few feet to the side of him, glaring.

"I guess I got lost," Frank said. He smiled and shrugged.

The man wasn't having any of it. "And I guess you just decided to listen in to what Mr. Carew was saying, is that it?" He clenched his hands into fists. "We'll see what he has to say about this."

Frank shook his head slowly and pretended to look scared. "Please," Frank said. "Don't—"

When the man was just a foot away, Frank sprang into action. Backing up, Frank grabbed the stair railing with both hands. He kicked at the man approaching him, slamming both feet into his chest. The man tumbled back, stunned.

Frank turned and tore down the stairway.

"Hey! Stop that guy!"

At the next landing another man was standing, blocking the stairs going down. He made a snatch at Frank, arms wide. Frank ducked and caught the man in the side with his elbow as the man lunged past. Frank bolted down the next flight of stairs, to the next landing—the one closest to the club floor.

This landing was packed with people, talking and staring down at the dance floor below. The stairs leading down were so crowded that it would take him a full five minutes to travel that one flight, and his pursuers would be all over him by then.

As he was figuring out how to negotiate his way down, a man forced his way up through the crowd on the stairs to the landing. It was the bouncer from the front door. When he caught sight of Frank, he did a double take.

Clearly the man remembered Frank from earlier. Anger darkened his face, and he began heading straight for Frank, parting the crowd between them with no more effort than he would have expended wading through a creek.

Frank looked up and behind him. The two men he'd fought with earlier were down the stairs, closing on him.

He pushed his way to the edge of the landing and looked out over the railing and down the scaffolding to the dance floor a good twenty feet below him.

It was too far to jump, so he swung over the railing and began climbing down the scaffolding, hand over hand, toward the floor.

It was actually an easy climb—there were plenty of handholds and joints in the scaffolding where he could rest his feet. He got about halfway down before he looked up to check on his pursuers.

Carew's men were leaning over the railing, yelling. But the music was so loud, no one on the dance floor could hear them. One of them drew a gun, but the bouncer grabbed his arm, and shook his head. Then Frank couldn't see them anymore—they had disappeared from the railing.

He guessed they were going to try to beat him down the stairs to the dance floor.

Redoubling his efforts to reach bottom quickly, Frank noticed that a lot of people were now aware of him. Several had even stopped what they were doing to look up at him. As he swung to the floor, many of them started applauding.

So much for trying to be inconspicuous, Frank thought.

"Cool, man," one dancer said. "I never saw anybody climb up that high before."

"Or down," the girl with him said. "That was really neat."

Frank nodded, breathing heavily. The crowd blocked his view of the staircase, but he was certain he'd beaten Carew's men down. Now to get out of there . . .

He began threading his way through the crowded dance floor. But it was jam-packed with people, and it was impossible to move very fast. By the time he reached its edge, he knew that whatever time he'd picked up on Carew's men was lost. His only hope was that he'd lost them in the crowd.

He broke through—and suddenly, right in front of him, was the entrance to the club.

The bouncer was standing directly in front of it, looking right at him.

Frank scanned the room desperately. The double doors he'd entered from the kitchen—

One of the men he'd fought on the stairs was standing there, blocking that exit, too. Frank was trapped.

There was no way out. No way at all.

Chapter

12

FRANK DECIDED to head for the front door. It was closest to him, and if he was lucky, the bouncer wasn't on Carew's payroll. . . .

The bouncer saw him coming and grinned.

Then Frank broke into a grin of his own.

Detective Mike Lewis was standing at the door, just behind the bouncer. Joe was just behind Lewis. Frank didn't know what either of them was doing there, and at the moment he didn't care.

Frank walked straight toward the front door as Lewis reached up and tapped the smiling bouncer on the shoulder.

He turned.

"Detective Mike Lewis, NYPD," he said. "Mind if we come in?"

"This guy's really keen on getting ID, Detective Lewis," Frank said. "Better show him yours."

Lewis flashed his badge.

The bouncer growled in frustration and motioned the detective forward.

"We found the gun right behind the skylight—up on the roof," a uniformed officer said, handing a revolver to Lewis. Twenty minutes had passed, and the detective, several uniformed officers, and Frank and Joe were gathered on the street outside Cosmos. Delaney's body had already been taken away by an ambulance. Carew was inside the club, refusing to answer any questions.

"And that's where you say you traced Poletti to?" the detective asked Joe. Lewis, along with a squad car, had been assigned to watch Johnny Carew—and so he had been in perfect position to grab Joe and Tommy Poletti after the shot had been fired. They'd been expecting this "summit" between Carew and Delaney for months, Lewis explained.

"That's right," his brother nodded glumly. "Although I didn't actually see him fire it."

"Of course he didn't!" Poletti shouted. "Because I didn't have anything to do with this!"

"Maybe you'd better wait till your lawyer gets here before saying anything, Tommy," Lewis said, not without a touch of sympathy in his voice.

"I don't need any lawyer," Poletti said fiercely. "Why would I have come with the kid"—he indicated Joe—"so willingly if I shot Delaney, anyway? Huh? Answer that!"

Lewis shook his head. "That's not my job, I'm afraid." He opened the rear door of the squad car. "My job is to get you downtown now."

Poletti exhaled and climbed in the backseat—but not before shooting Joe an angry look.

"I'll let you know what happens," Lewis said.

Lewis nodded. "Good work, boys," he said.

"Yeah—" Joe stood shaking his head as the police car drove off. Right then he didn't feel as if he'd just done anything that anyone would call "good work."

"Well, I'm just not sure, that's all," Frank said. It was morning and he was sitting in the Nolans' living room, discussing the case with Ned and Joe. Delaney's killing had happened too late to make the morning papers, but the news had been all over the radio.

"How can you not be sure, Frank?" Ned asked. "They've got the murder weapon, and the killer."

"Think, though," Frank said. "Why? Why would Tommy Poletti kill to increase his share of ten million dollars when he's going to get a lot more than that once he marries Emily Moran?''

"Murderers don't reason that way," Ned said firmly. "Or maybe he's not going to marry Emily—I don't know. What I do know is that this seems to be over. We can tell our fathers to come home now."

The phone rang. Ned answered it.

"It's for either of you," he said, holding out the receiver.

"I'll take it," Frank said. He grabbed the receiver.

"This is Frank Hardy."

"Frank, this is Detective Lewis. Just thought you and your brother would want to know. We ran a ballistics test on that gun. It's the same one that killed Daniel Carew." Lewis was silent a moment. "We're charging Tommy Poletti with murder one."

"You're sure?" Frank asked.

"Sure as we can get without a confession."

Frank sighed. "All right—thanks."

He hung up the phone and turned to his brother, who'd been unusually quiet all morning. The news of Poletti's guilt had hit him pretty hard.

"They say they're going to charge Poletti," Frank told them.

"It's over, then," Joe said.

"I don't think so," Frank replied firmly. "What about this, Joe? Johnson said Emily

Moran had asked him to find a way to invalidate the will—don't you think Poletti knew about that? Why would he risk his neck killing Carew and Delaney when the whole document might be nullified?"

"It's over, Frank—face it," Joe repeated. "We're not going to find some magic clue the police overlooked this time."

"I'm not looking for any magic clue," Frank said. "I'm looking for the truth—and if you're going to sit here moping all day, I guess I'll have to look myself." He stood up and grabbed his coat.

Joe didn't move.

"I'm going to try to talk to Emily Moran," Frank said. Without another word, he stalked to the front door and threw it open. He sucked in air and gave a low whistle.

Framed in the doorway were two men. Carew's goons. He recognized one of them from the club.

"Oh," the man said, smiling. "Now this is a pleasure we didn't anticipate." He drew a gun with one hand, and with the other he roughly shoved Frank back into the apartment.

"I've been looking all over town for you—and you show up here." He pointed his gun at Frank. "I guess this is going to be my lucky day."

Chapter

13

His companion stepped in behind him and shut the door.

"So you're Ned Nolan," the man said to Frank.

"No, I'm Ned Nolan." Ned and Joe had appeared in the arch between the hall and the living room. "What's going on here?"

"Frank, who is this guy?" Joe asked.

"I'm his fairy godmother," the man said. "It don't matter who I am. What matters is this," he said, flicking his gun. He motioned Ned and Joe toward the door. "Let's go, all three of you."

Joe shrugged and stepped forward, then suddenly stopped and planted his feet. He swung his elbow to the side and knocked the goon's gun out of his hand.

In a flash his hand was inches from picking it up. He stopped half bent over when he heard the unmistakable sound of a trigger being cocked.

Joe looked up. The second gunman had a revolver to Ned's head.

"Leave the gun alone," the man said simply.

Joe had no choice. He stepped back.

"One more trick like that, kid," the first guy said, bending over to pick up his revolver, "and you'll be staying here—permanently. Now let's go."

The three of them were taken back to Cosmos—and to the office Frank had seen the previous evening. Johnny Carew was there himself, waiting.

"What's going on, Terry?" Carew asked the man who'd brought them there.

"This"—he waved his gun at Ned—"is Nolan's son. And this"—he indicated Frank—"is that punk who was in here last night. I don't know who the other one is."

"Ah, but I do," Carew said, carefully scrutinizing first Frank, then Joe. "You're Hardy's two boys, aren't you?"

"That's right," Frank said.

"Playing detective, are you? Hope to follow in your father's footsteps?" Carew asked the question with a smile, but there was underlying malice to his words.

"Why are we here?" Joe demanded.

"Feisty, eh? I like that." Carew laughed and sat down behind his desk. "All right, I'll tell you."

"It has to do with Josh Moran's will, doesn't it?" Frank asked.

"It does at that," Carew nodded. "Moran's will—and my son's death." He silently stared off into space for a moment. When he began talking again, his voice was lower, more intense.

"I had a funny thought last night, when the police were hounding me with questions about Billy Delaney." He lifted his gaze to Frank's. "I was thinking how funny it would be if one of the people the police would never think of questioning—one of the 'good guys'—had actually killed my son. Somebody who could really use Josh Moran's money—somebody like Hugh Nolan, for instance, or maybe even Fenton Hardy.

"So I sent Terry and Monk"—he nodded at the men standing guard at the door—"to find those two and bring them here for a little talk. Instead, I got you."

He nodded to Terry, who moved forward and laid a hand on Frank's shoulder and guided him, none too gently, into a chair in front of Carew's desk. Joe and Ned were also marched over and made to sit in chairs next to Frank.

"So," Carew asked, folding his hands and

leaning forward on his desk. "Where are they?"

"We don't know," Frank said.

"Come now—that won't do," Carew said, shaking his head. "Where are they?"

"He just told you," Ned said. "We really don't know. Besides, haven't you been paying attention? The police have your son's killer—and Delaney's—in custody. Tommy Poletti."

Carew waved a hand in dismissal. "That's a load of garbage."

Joe did a double take. "You don't think Poletti killed your son?"

Carew shook his head. "Tommy Poletti? A killer? Never. The police will figure that out soon enough. If they don't, they're even bigger fools than I thought."

Frank leaned back in his chair and exchanged a look with Joe.

"I don't know where my father is," Frank said. "That's the truth. But you're wrong if you think he's had anything to do with the killings."

"Your father's a man of principle—is that it? Well, we're talking about ten million dollars here, sonny," Carew said. "That much money buys a lot of principles."

"Not my father's," Frank said firmly.

"Or mine," Ned added.

At that, Carew laughed harshly. "Hugh Nolan? Not interested in money? You don't know him very well—do you, sonny?"

"What do you mean by that?" Ned asked angrily, rising from his chair. He was upset enough to attack Carew with his bare hands.

The gang lord studied Ned calmly for a second, then shook his head. "Never mind. All right, you say you don't know where your fathers are. I'll accept that—for now." Now Carew looked directly at Frank. "But the next time you want to play detective, you play with someone else, okay?"

"We don't play at being detectives, Mr. Carew," Frank said calmly. "Especially where our father's life is concerned."

"And I don't play around when it comes to whoever killed my son!" Carew slammed his fist down on the desk. "You make sure you understand that."

He glowered at Frank for a moment, then snapped his fingers. "Get them out of here."

Terry and Monk escorted them down to the street.

"Carew doesn't think Poletti did it either," Joe said, more to himself than anyone else. "Guess I'm beginning to believe the killer is still on the loose."

"I told you," Frank said. "I'm going to see Emily Moran. You two coming?"

Joe grinned. "You bet. Ned?"

Ned shook his head slowly. "No, I don't

think so." He was still clearly upset by Carew's accusation—an accusation Joe decided might be right after his discovery in the library.

But in Ned's mind they were still just doubts—and Joe didn't want to upset Ned any further without real proof.

"Well, we'll see you back at the apartment later," Frank said. "Come on, Joe—let's go play detective."

This time, their reception at Emily's was slightly more pleasant. Emily Moran, even though she looked even more tired and upset than the last time they'd seen her, was happy to talk with them.

"We appreciate your taking the time to see us, Ms. Moran—especially today," Joe said. Delaney's death had apparently enabled Emily to rid herself of the man's entourage as well. The house seemed deserted except for the three of them.

She nodded distractedly. "Yes, I talked to Vance, and he said you were trying to find the killer." She forced a grin. "Besides, there's not much else I can do right now. The police are questioning Tommy again."

"I hope you don't think this is rude," Joe began, "but—why did your father put Tommy Poletti into his will?"

"Dad didn't exactly like Tommy," Emily said. "He was in jail of course when I first met

Tommy, and he never approved of him. I think my dad wanted me to see someone who could help run his business." She stopped suddenly to look at her watch. "The police are supposed to call me when they're finished questioning him," she said, apologizing.

"They take a long time sometimes," Joe offered sympathetically.

"Don't I know it," Emily said, smiling. "You're talking to Josh Moran's daughter, after all." It was the first time Joe had seen her genuinely amused at something, and it made her look about five years younger.

Suddenly Joe wanted very much for Tommy Poletti to be proven innocent.

"I just wish there was something I could do to help him," Emily continued.

"There may be," Frank said. "Announce that you've found a way to have your father's will nullified."

Emily looked confused. "How will that help Tommy?"

Joe explained. "By flushing out the real killer."

"So you don't think Tommy's guilty?" Emily asked, her eyes glistening.

Frank and Joe both shook their heads. "No," Joe said.

"All right," she nodded firmly. "Give me a minute—I'll get my coat. Then we'll go talk to Vance to have him make the announcement."

It was just after two o'clock when they reached Johnson's office. The place was completely deserted.

"That's strange," Frank said, shaking his head. "I wonder where everybody is."

"Out to lunch?" Joe suggested.

"I don't think so," Frank said. "Look." He pointed at a half-eaten sandwich lying on the secretary's desk. Next to the sandwich, her computer was still running.

The brothers exchanged a puzzled glance.

Emily Moran crossed to Johnson's office door and rapped on it loudly.

"Nobody in there either," she said.

"I guess we come back later," Frank said. He turned to go.

"Joe! Frank!" Emily Moran screamed. "Here!"

She was standing next to a copier and pointing at the floor. Both brothers rushed to her side.

Johnson's secretary—Mrs. Hunter—was lying on the floor, still and unmoving.

Frank bent down and felt her wrist. "She's alive."

"Get her some water," Emily Moran commanded, lifting Mrs. Hunter's head onto her lap.

Frank scanned the area for a refrigerator or a water fountain. Nothing. Then he remembered the water cooler in Johnson's office. He

ran for the door, reached out to yank it open—
and pulled his hand back instantly.

The doorknob was hot.

"Look!" Joe said, pointing at the space
around the door. A thin wisp of smoke was
wafting out.

"Oh, no," Emily said, a look of horror
spreading across her face. "It's on fire!"

Chapter

14

"YOU TWO GET her out of here," Frank said to Joe and Emily, taking off his jacket. "I'll see how bad the fire is."

"Frank!" Joe yelled. "Wait—"

Whatever else his brother had to say was lost to Frank as he grabbed the doorknob with his jacket and burst into Johnson's office.

There was smoke everywhere. He'd barely opened the door before it was in his eyes, his nose, his throat. Frank coughed once, covered his mouth and nose with a handkerchief, and pushed into the room, closing the door behind him.

From the right, waves of intense heat washed over him. He staggered toward his left, where he remembered the huge bay windows were. Frank groped along the wall, searching.

His right hand touched glass, then the metal frame and the window crank. He turned the crank and opened the window. He leaned out and took a deep breath of fresh air.

Looking down at the street below, he saw Johnny Carew's goons, Terry and Monk. They were standing on the sidewalk opposite the office, looking straight up at him. In the distance, he could hear the wail of fire engines approaching.

The two men turned and quickly disappeared down the street.

"Carew," Frank whispered, his eyes still tearing from the smoke. He must have had the fire set. Frank had to tell Joe. But first things first . . .

He turned back to the office only to discover the heat and smoke were stronger than ever. The fire was spreading—partially because he'd fed it by opening the window and letting air into the room.

He and Joe would never be able to put the fire out themselves.

Taking a last, deep breath, he shut the window, and turned back toward the office door. He bumped into something heavy and solid behind him.

The water cooler.

Frank rammed it with all his strength, pushing the cooler toward the right of the room and the source of the heat.

The huge glass tank hit the floor with a loud plop. Instantly the seams ripped and Frank heard water lapping out. Suddenly the room was full of billowing smoke.

That's the best I can do, Frank told himself, and he dropped to the floor, where the smoke was less damaging. He moved on all fours toward the door.

He was so intent on focusing on the doorway that he crawled directly into a body on the floor.

"Oh, no," Frank said, rolling the man onto his back. Vance Johnson's eyes were shut, and Frank couldn't tell if he was alive or not. Frank struggled to his feet and backed out of the burning office, dragging Johnson under his arms.

Joe was rushing down the hall toward Mrs. Hunter's office, carrying two small fire extinguishers. Behind Joe, next to the entrance to the stairwell, Frank could see Emily Moran sitting with Mrs. Hunter, who was now conscious and talking.

"Forget it!" Frank yelled to his brother. "It's out of control! Just get out of here!"

Joe dropped the extinguishers and gave Frank a hand with Mr. Johnson as the first of the fire fighters were arriving.

A half hour later the blaze was under control, and both Johnson and Mrs. Hunter were conscious and being attended to by emergency personnel.

"They'll be fine," one technician assured Joe. "We just want to take them to the hospital to make sure there's no real harm done."

The EMS technicians stepped in front of Joe and lifted Johnson's stretcher.

"I'll go with them to the hospital," Emily volunteered, climbing into the ambulance.

Joe and Frank silently watched as the ambulance drove away. "We've got to find out who's doing this," Joe said angrily.

Frank shook his head. "I know who did it— well, the fire, anyway." He told Joe about Carew's two thugs.

Joe snapped his fingers. "Before he died, Delaney told Carew that Emily was trying to have the will nullified. If Carew didn't want that to happen, he might try to kill Johnson. Come on, let's find out what he's up to."

"Wait a minute, Joe," Frank said. "I don't think it would be too smart to go charging into Carew's office by ourselves."

"Who said anything about charging into his office?" Joe grinned. "I've got an idea."

"So do I," Frank said.

"That's right," Carew said, putting his feet up on the desk. "You can deal directly with my boys from now on—not Delaney's." He listened to whoever was on the other end of the line and laughed. "Don't worry. Moran's lawyer had an unexpected visit from the fire department today." Carew laughed. "I'll talk to you later. So long."

He hung up the phone and leaned back, taking a long, satisfied draw on his cigar.

From the skylight twenty feet directly above him, Frank was disconnecting the contact microphone they'd used to listen in on Moran's conversation. He turned to Joe.

"It *was* him," Frank said to his brother, who was sitting next to him, rubbing his hands together to keep warm. At Joe's suggestion, they'd sneaked back into the old Schickelman building and onto the roof over Cosmos to eavesdrop on Carew.

"And listen to this. Not only did Carew have his thugs start that fire so Johnson would never be able to challenge Moran's will in a court of law, he also thinks the fire destroyed some very special business contracts Moran had. He's going to take away Moran's territory without having to fire a shot."

"All right," Joe said. "That solves one mystery. But what about the murders and the attack on Chief Peterson?"

Joe was cut off by a crunching sound directly behind him—the sound of someone stepping on rooftop gravel.

Both boys turned.

Terry and the bouncer from Cosmos were standing there, guns raised.

"I wouldn't be too concerned about those murders right now, if I were you," Terry said. "You've got problems of your own—like how you plan on staying alive."

Chapter

15

"YOU KIDS MUST THINK I'm dumb," Carew said. "Somebody took a shot through my skylight, and I'm going to leave it unguarded after that? Give me a break."

"I guess that it was kind of stupid of us," Joe agreed. He and Frank had been marched into Carew's office, where they were now standing, side by side, in front of Carew's desk. "Maybe as stupid as you were to leave that skylight unguarded in the first place."

"Hey!" Terry said, moving toward them. "You keep a civil tongue in your head, or I'll—"

"No, no, Terry, it's all right," Carew raised a hand, and his employee backed off. "I'll chalk up that outburst to his youth."

"Of course, Frank, there is another possibility," Joe said. He raised a finger to his lips and pretended to be deep in thought. "Maybe Mr. Carew never left that skylight unguarded at all."

Frank stopped to consider this. "Why—then how could anyone have gotten up there to kill Delaney? Wouldn't he have been seen? Oh, I get it," Frank said. "You're saying Carew did have someone up there guarding that skylight—someone who was up there to shoot Billy Delaney."

"That's right," Joe agreed. He turned away from his brother now and faced Johnny Carew directly. "What about it, Mr. Carew? Is that how it happened? Is that how you killed Billy Delaney?"

The man's face went through a series of expressions, from surprise to anger to shock, and back again. Finally he just started laughing.

"You really are Fenton Hardy's sons, aren't you?" Carew said. "So what? So what if it was me who had Delaney killed. You'll never prove any of it."

"I guess not," Joe said. "But tell me, where did you get the revolver—the one the police found up on the roof?"

Carew raised his eyebrows in mock disapproval. "What? Even you don't know the answer to that one, sonny?"

"Maybe you could help us out with it," Joe suggested.

Carew looked at Joe strangely for a second and then burst out laughing all over again.

"Help you out on it?" he asked, shaking his head. "Sure. Why not? I found that revolver at the scene of my son's death. I decided to hold on to it—thought it might come in handy."

"Guess it did, huh?" Joe asked, leaning forward on Carew's desk.

"Yes, it did at that," Carew said. "You know, suddenly I'm tired of you two," he said, all traces of his good humor suddenly gone.

He waved Terry forward.

"Take care of them, will you?"

Terry grinned. "With pleasure, boss." He drew his gun and motioned the Hardys back, away from Carew's desk.

"Come on, fellas," Terry said. "We're going for a little trip."

"What are you going to do—kill us?" Frank asked.

Carew nodded. "You got it, smart boy. We're going to kill you."

"Good," Joe said. "That's what I was waiting to hear."

The old man looked at him strangely.

Then, without warning, the door to Carew's office banged open, and a half-dozen uniformed police officers charged in, their guns drawn and raised high. Detective Lewis strolled in just behind them.

"What's this?" Carew roared. "Breaking and entering! You'd better be prepared for—"

"We're prepared, Johnny," Lewis said, holding out a folded piece of paper. "Here's our warrant."

"Suspicion of murder?" Carew asked, reading off the paper. "You got no proof of any of this." He sneered. "What're you going to do—hold me downtown on some half-baked charge—"

"Not half-baked, Johnny," Lewis said. "Not this time." He held up a small box for Carew to see. "It's all down on tape."

Joe stepped forward and began pulling off the hidden microphone he'd been wearing.

Involving Lewis in their plan had been Joe's idea. And when the detective had suggested he wear a wire, thinking that the crime lord might be looser with his tongue in front of a couple of teenagers, Joe had readily agreed.

Now he stood in front of Johnny Carew, holding up the recording device for the gang lord to see.

"Surprise," he said, smiling at Carew.

The old man shook his head, his mouth moving wordlessly.

Lewis snapped the cuffs on him.

"You have the right to remain silent," the detective began, leading Carew away. "Any-

thing you say may be used against you in a
court of law. . . ."

Two hours later Frank was fixing himself a
cup of tea in the Nolans' kitchen and listening
to the news on the radio. He was waiting for
the news to break about Johnny Carew. Right
then the day's big story involved the weather.
Experts were predicting the arrival of the decade's worst blizzard sometime the next day.
Joe was sitting at the table behind him, finishing off the bag of chips he'd started the other
night.

It was early evening, and they were waiting
for Ned to come home. It looked as if he hadn't
been at the apartment all day.

"He was really upset after what Johnny Carew said this morning," Frank said. "It'd be
nice to pass on some good news to him."

Joe nodded his agreement. "You'd be upset,
too, if someone accused Dad of being a
crook."

Frank had a sudden thought. "Joe, could
Hugh Nolan have been the guy at the police
station—the one in the wig who poisoned Chief
Peterson?"

"No," Joe said decisively. "The man at the
police station had to be a lot younger, and he
didn't have Nolan's limp. And I'll bet the police have checked all the beneficiaries' move-
ments that day a thousand times. If Nolan was

anywhere near that station, they'd know about it.''

Frank shook his head. "If we could only find out who that man at the station was."

"Well, we don't have a lot to go on," Joe pointed out. "A white shirt isn't exactly an identifying mark."

Frank laughed. "You know, Ned said the same thing the other night—"

The shock of realization struck him like a physical blow. He almost dropped the mug he was holding.

"Frank?" Joe asked. "Frank, are you all right?"

His head was spinning. Frank sank down heavily into one of the kitchen chairs, next to his brother.

"Two days ago—I should have seen it two days ago," Frank said.

"What?" Joe asked.

Frank shook his head, still lost in his own world. "How could he have known?"

Joe frowned. "Frank, you're talking nonsense. What are you trying to say?"

Frank slowly turned to his brother. "That first night we stayed at the Nolans'," he began, his voice growing firmer. "That first night we met Ned."

"Go on," Joe urged.

"After you went to sleep, we stayed up a little while longer, talking—"

In his mind, Frank could hear their conversation replaying itself, word for word. . . .

"Have they found any trace of the man who attacked the chief?" Ned asked.

"I don't know yet, but I doubt it. I probably got a better look at him than anyone, and I don't think I'd recognize him if he walked up to me and shook my hand."

"I suppose that's understandable. A white shirt isn't exactly an identifying mark. . . ."

"A white shirt isn't exactly an identifying mark," Frank repeated. "Ned said the same thing you did."

"So what?" Joe asked.

"So this," Frank said. "It was the night of the attack. We'd barely discussed the incident at all, and there weren't any reports of it in the news. So how did Ned know the guy was wearing a white shirt?"

Joe let out a long, low whistle. "I see what you mean," he said.

"It was Ned, Joe," Frank said. He laid his palms flat on the table and looked at his brother. "Ned is the killer."

Chapter

16

"I DON'T KNOW, FRANK," Joe said, shaking his head. "It feels right, but—it's awfully thin. We'll need a lot more proof to make it stick."

"Okay—what about this?" Frank stood and shut off the water he'd been boiling for tea. "Who needs the money more than Hugh Nolan?" he asked. "Look at this place. Look at the way Nolan lives. And if it is Ned, he had a good reason for getting Daniel Carew—he's Johnny's son. And a better reason for getting Chief Peterson. He was the one who slandered his father's name and ruined his career."

"If it was slander," Joe pointed out. Then he had another thought. "What if Hugh and Ned are working together?"

"What if," Frank agreed, nodding grimly. "If that's the case, Dad's in a lot of trouble."

He thought a moment. "I think we need to find out a little bit more about Ned before we go to the police."

"Agreed," Joe said. "His father mentioned he'd just gotten out of the army. Let's start with that."

Frank picked up the phone—and within a few minutes he was speaking with an army lieutenant he and Joe had met on a previous case.

"I can't get you the man's complete service record," the officer said.

"What can you tell me about him?" Frank asked.

"What it says here is that Ned Nolan served in the special forces and was an expert in unarmed combat. He was honorably discharged last year."

"Thanks, lieutenant," Frank said. He hung up and told his brother the information.

"Nothing conclusive there," Joe said. "But that guy in the white shirt was certainly an expert in unarmed combat."

"All right," Frank said. "Let's go tell Lewis."

Even at that time of night they found the detective hard at work in his office. His desk was swimming in paperwork, but he welcomed them just the same.

"Good news, fellas," Lewis said. "We got

the D.A.'s office to recommend no bail for Carew and his friends.''

"That's great," Frank said. "Detective Lewis, we have something we'd like to talk about with you—" Frank began.

"Let me guess," Lewis interrupted. "You want us to bring back your father, too?"

"Too?" Frank asked.

"Yeah, Hugh Nolan's kid was in here earlier today. Wanted to know if the old man could come home yet."

"What did you tell him?" Frank asked.

"I said the case wasn't closed yet. We don't know if Carew was behind the chief's poisoning—and it doesn't seem likely that Carew would kill his own son, does it?" Lewis shrugged. "Anyway, Ned talked to his dad when the chief checked in today and found out where they are. He's going to visit them."

Frank turned pale.

Just then, Lewis's phone rang. "Excuse me a second," the detective said. He picked up the phone and started talking.

"Frank," Joe began. "If Ned knows where they are—"

Frank shook his head and quieted his brother with a glance.

Lewis finished his call and turned back to the Hardys. "So, anyway—unless you can tell me who the killer is, I'm afraid we're going to have to keep your dad out of sight."

"I understand," Frank nodded. "We just want to talk to him, though. You wouldn't happen to know where they're staying—or have any way we could get in touch with him?"

Lewis shook his head. "Not till tomorrow, when they check in again. Sorry." He looked at Frank more closely. "Say, there's nothing the matter, is there?"

Frank shook his head. "Not a thing. Thanks anyway."

"You're welcome." Lewis sat back down at his desk. "Sorry I couldn't be more help," he said, picking up another stack of papers and sifting through them.

Joe waited till they got outside before he spoke.

"Why didn't you want to tell him about Ned?"

"Think about it," Frank said. "Ned's probably killed one man already and seriously injured another. Now he's looking for his father. Why? Because he's just found out that one of the basic truths in his life, that his father got a raw deal from the police, might be a lie." Frank shook his head. "He's a time bomb, just waiting to go off. If that happens while he's with Dad and Chief Peterson—"

"But how are we going to find them?" Joe asked. "We don't even know where to start."

"You're wrong—we've actually got a pretty good idea," Frank said, pulling a train schedule out of his back pocket and checking it over carefully.

"Come on, if we hurry, we can get the last train out of Bayport."

" 'I think I know the perfect place—but we'll have to stop at home first,' " Frank said, repeating the words his father had said just before he, Hugh Nolan, and Samuel Peterson had gone into hiding.

" 'Home' has to mean Bayport, but 'the perfect place'?" Joe shook his head. "You've got me there."

They were sitting across from each other on the train, trying to figure out what their father's cryptic words had referred to.

"And why would he have to come home first?" Frank added.

"Mom would have talked to him," Joe said. "She'll know."

The boys got in late and slept in their own beds until almost seven in the morning. Their mother was up by then working, trying to fix the faucet in the kitchen sink.

"Hi, Mom," Frank began. "Have you—"

"What in the world—" Laura Hardy turned to face them, an expression of shock on her face. "Where have you two been?"

"We meant to call, but—"

"Your father told me to expect you a couple of days ago!" Laura Hardy yelled, throwing down the pliers she'd been using. "And all you can say is *you meant to call?*"

"Mom," Frank said, "we need to find Dad."

"I don't know where he is. He came home in a rush—" She stopped yelling suddenly and looked closely at her two sons. "What's the problem? Are you in some kind of trouble?"

"No, Mom, that's not it at all," Joe said quickly. "We have a message for him."

He hated lying to his mother, but he didn't want her worrying—or calling in the police.

"Two days ago your father rushed through this house like he had a tiger on his tail," she said. "All he told me was that he had some kind of urgent case that was going to take him out of town for a while—he didn't know how long."

"And he didn't say where he was going?" Frank asked.

"Not to me."

"Thanks, Mom." Frank turned to Joe. "Let's check his office."

"Wait a minute," their mother said, smiling. "What are you going to do now—just run off again without telling me where you're going?"

The brothers exchanged a quick glance.

"Mom," Frank said, "when we find out where we're headed, you'll be the first to know." With that, he and Joe disappeared into their father's office.

An hour later, though, they were no closer

to finding out where their father, Chief Peterson, and Hugh Nolan were hiding—and where Ned Nolan was heading.

"Nothing," Frank said, shutting down his father's computer. "Whatever that perfect place was, there's no record of it here. We're going to have to split up—comb the town—and find anyone who might have seen Dad leave or might have talked to him."

"Don't go far," their mother said as they were walking out the front door. "They're expecting a big storm later this afternoon— might even turn into a blizzard. I want you home before that happens."

"We'll be back before long, Mom, don't worry," Joe said.

"And if you find your father, remind him about that foreign film festival he promised to take me to. It's only running another couple of days, and I want to see it!"

"We'll do that," he assured her.

Frank's first stop was Callie Shaw's house.

"I've been all over town the past few days, Frank, and I haven't seen your dad anywhere," his longtime girlfriend said. The two of them were in the Shaws' den, standing in front of the fireplace. Callie was wearing a green sweater, jeans, and the thick gray socks Frank had given her for Christmas. She'd been curled up in front of the fireplace, reading a book, when Frank had rung the doorbell.

"In fact, I haven't seen your dad since Christmas, Frank," she continued. "Not that I've seen much of you since then, either. What's going on? You and Joe were supposed to be back from New York a couple of days ago."

"I can't talk about it now," Frank said. "But if you do see my dad, or talk to anyone who has seen him in the past few days, call my house and let me know. Thanks." He kissed her on the cheek and headed for the front door.

"Wait a minute!" Callie chased him as far as the front door, then stopped. She wasn't wearing any shoes.

"You could at least say goodbye!" she yelled.

"Goodbye!" he yelled back. "I'll call you later!"

She stood there in the front door for a minute, hands on her hips, staring after Frank as he drove off down the street.

Chief Collig hadn't seen their father.

Fenton Hardy's poker partners hadn't seen him.

Even Chet Morton, who practically lived downtown, where their father usually worked, hadn't seen him.

Joe was trudging down Bayport's main street when he felt a hand on his shoulder.

"Hey, Joe. What's the matter? You look like your best friend died." Joe turned to see Officer Con Riley—the one member of the Bayport Police Force he and Frank always got along with.

"It's not that serious," Joe said. Yet, he added silently.

"Good," Con replied. He glanced up at the sky and shook his head. "Say, you'd better get back home. That blizzard is supposed to kick in about an hour from now. And when it does, the roads around here are going to be just about impossible to drive on."

"The blizzard," Joe muttered, shaking his head. "Terrific." He'd forgotten all about it. More good news.

"It will be—for anybody who wants to get some skiing done," Con said. "You really ought to try to make it up to my cabin sometime."

Despite his black mood, Joe managed to smile. "I will—that's a promise." Con Riley had a little cabin way back in the Vermont mountains, right near a beautiful set of ski trails, that he just loved to get away to for weekends. He'd issued an open invitation to the whole Hardy family to join him up there "whenever you all aren't too busy solving crimes," as he put it.

"Say—how come you're not up there now, Con?" Joe asked.

"It's a little too crowded at the moment," Con said, a mischievous smile on his face.

Joe stopped suddenly in his tracks and stared at the man.

"Whoops," Con said. "Guess I let the cat out of the bag, huh?"

Joe grabbed the older man by the shoulders. "Con—that cabin. Is my dad up there now?"

Con must have sensed something in his voice, because he immediately turned serious. "That's right, Joe. What's the matter?"

"Nothing," Joe said. "Not anymore. Not as soon as you give me directions to your place."

"You're not going to go up there today? Not with the blizzard coming?" Con asked incredulously.

"I've got to," Joe said grimly. "That blizzard's not the only trouble heading their way."

Chapter

17

JOE CALLED FRANK, who had just returned home, and told him what he'd found out.

They were on the road within the hour.

"Based on the directions Con gave us, we ought to be there around dinnertime," Joe said. He reached into the cooler on the seat between him and Frank and pulled out a soda. Before they'd left home, they'd completely stocked the van with enough food, drink, and supplies for a very long trip, which Joe sincerely hoped this would not be.

"Sit back and relax," he told Frank. "It should be smooth sailing from here on out."

The blizzard hit about five minutes later.

It was as if someone was standing in the road in front of them shoveling snow onto their windshield. Within seconds it was coming down so hard Joe had to cut their speed in half. He was thankful for the new snow tires he'd put on the van and the extra set of wiper blades he had in the glove compartment. At their highest speed, the blades could barely keep the windshield free of snow long enough to give Joe a look at the road fifty feet ahead.

"Can you see okay?" Frank asked.

"Just barely," Joe said. "At this speed, we ought to be pretty safe." He didn't bother adding that at this speed, they'd be lucky to reach Vermont by dinnertime, much less Con Riley's cabin.

This stretch of the interstate was almost completely straight, well-lit, and not at all crowded. Had it been anything but all three of those, Joe would have had to slow down even more. As it was, at several points during the day he had to stop completely and wait for the storm to ease up a little.

"Decade's biggest blizzard," Frank said during one of those stops. "You can't say they didn't warn us."

"Weather forecasters," Joe grumbled. "They're never right—except when you don't want them to be."

They soon lost track of the passing time— the storm was so fierce, it kept playing havoc with their radio reception. They were never able to keep one station coming in clearly for very long at all. It was almost midnight when they finally crossed over into Vermont and left the interstate.

Joe pulled the van off to the side of the road and shut down the engine.

"It's all small roads and mountain driving from here on out," he told Frank. "And we can't go up one of those ridges in the middle of a blizzard, in the middle of the night."

"Agreed," Frank said, yawning. "Let's get some shut-eye." They unrolled their sleeping bags and slept on the floor in the back of the van.

In the morning Frank didn't have a single muscle that wasn't sore.

"My neck," he muttered, climbing out of his sleeping bag and stretching. "That's the last time I sleep in this van."

He opened the back door of the van and stepped outside.

It had stopped snowing. The air was clean and crisp and still; the entire world looked as if it had been outlined with a white paintbrush. A few hundred feet back from the road they had parked on, huge power lines stretched off toward a range of snow-capped mountains, just barely visible in the distance.

"That's where we're headed," Joe said quietly. He had woken silently and was standing behind Frank, leaning out the back of the van.

"All right," Frank said. "Let's get going."

Sleeping in the van had given them one advantage; they were able to get right back on the road. They hadn't gone far, though, before they ran into another problem.

Their route up into the mountains was completely blocked by a huge, overturned tree.

"It'll take us half the day to clear that away," Joe said.

"Maybe we don't have to," Frank told him. "Look." He pointed to a signpost on the side of the road that had been partially bent by the falling tree. " 'Ranger Station—Two Miles.' They ought to have a tow truck or something."

The station, a small concrete building, was a short, fairly painless half-hour hike up the mountain road.

"Hello?" Frank called out, banging on the front door. "Is anyone here?"

Joe bent down and picked up a piece of paper off the ground. He handed it to Frank.

" 'Back at eight A.M.,' " Frank read. "It's dated today."

"And it's after eight o'clock," Joe said. "Let's try the door."

It swung open at his touch. Exchanging a worried glance with his brother, Joe pushed through and inside.

The building was set up just like a police station: a front desk, with a small, open office area behind it. Two other doors led off the main room.

"Where is everybody?" Joe asked.

"They did just have a blizzard," Frank said. "They're probably out helping people." Joe opened one of the doors that led off the main room and stepped inside; Frank decided to try the other.

He found himself in a bedroom, with a bunk bed and sink in the corner.

"Nobody in here," Frank called out, swinging the door shut behind him. "You find anything—"

The question died on his lips as Ned Nolan stepped out from the other room, carrying a revolver in his right hand.

"Frank Hardy," he said, smiling and moving forward. Frank unconsciously backed up a step.

"What an unexpected pleasure."

Chapter

18

"WHERE'S JOE?" Frank asked. "What have you done with him?"

"He's all right," Ned said, nodding behind him. "I expect he'll be awake again shortly." He shook his head. "I must admit, I really didn't expect to see you ever again," he said.

"You killed Daniel Carew," Frank said. "And the coffee vendor in the police station—that was you, too."

Ned smiled. "That was me," he said and nodded. Frank's guess had been right. Ned was the mystery killer.

Ned was keeping the gun down at his side—too far down to use at close quarters, Frank noted. If he could get near enough . . .

"I didn't get Peterson the last time, thanks

141

to you," Ned continued. "But I'll get him now."

Frank took a step forward. "Why are you doing this, Ned? The money?"

"For one thing," Ned agreed. "My father deserves the inheritance more than any of those crooks, wouldn't you agree?"

"All right," Frank nodded, keeping his eyes straight ahead, willing Ned not to notice him inching ahead. "But isn't one and a half million dollars enough for him?"

"No!" Ned said angrily. "No amount of money can ever compensate for what they did to him—"

"And that's why you're trying to kill them all?" Frank asked.

"That's right," Ned said. "I think it all ties together rather nicely, actually." His voice turned cold and hard. "Don't try to stop me. I don't want to hurt you or Joe, but I will if I have to." He smiled quite suddenly, and Frank saw that his eyes were totally bloodshot.

He looked as if he'd gone insane.

"I will if I have to, Frank," Ned repeated. "Make no mistake about that."

"All right," Frank said. He took another step closer. "What if—"

Without warning, he launched himself at Ned, his arms outstretched, reaching for the gun.

Ned spun in a sudden side-kick and slammed

Frank square in the chest. Frank stumbled backward and lay sprawled out on the front desk.

Ned was standing over him, his hand raised like an ax, poised to chop down.

Frank rolled out of the way, just as Ned's punch connected with a loud crack on the desktop.

Frank drew both his arms forward and jammed his elbows into Ned's side.

Ned backhanded him viciously across the face; Frank felt his lip split and tasted blood.

Ned raised his hand again, and Frank tried to step aside, to dodge the blow. But he was moving too slow, too slow. . . .

The world went black.

Frank groaned and struggled to his feet.

His lip was swollen; he could still taste blood in the cut. That meant he hadn't been out long.

Ned was gone.

Frank rushed into the other room. There, he discovered Joe and a young woman in a Park Ranger outfit lying on the floor. Joe looked like he'd be all right, but she had a nasty-looking cut on the back of her head.

Frank found some smelling salts and brought Joe around first, and then the ranger.

"Ow," his brother said, sitting up and rubbing the back of his head. "What hit me?"

"Ned Nolan," Frank replied. He filled Joe in on what had happened.

Next to them, the park ranger was also trying to get to her feet.

"Who are you?" she asked, looking up at Frank. "What are you doing here?"

Frank introduced himself and Joe. Then he told the woman—whose name was Kathleen Little—why she'd been attacked and why they needed her help.

"We have to get to that cabin first," Frank said. "Or someone else could be killed."

"Yeah," Joe said. "We need help moving a tree that's blocking the road a couple miles back, so we can get to our van."

"Forget your van," the forest ranger said, climbing to her feet. "I'll show you how we get around up here."

She led them around to the back of the station—where two snowmobiles were sitting.

"We usually have three," she said, frowning. "It looks like your friend's taken the other one. These machines are better, though."

"Then we'll catch him," Frank said positively.

"I hope so," the ranger said. "The trail will be covered over, but you should be okay if you just follow the line where trees have been cut. Good luck—and be careful. I'll get down the mountain and send up some help."

"Thanks," Frank said. He turned to Joe,

who had already mounted one snowmobile. "You know how to drive these things?"

"Sure," Joe said. "Just like a motorcycle. Throttle on the left hand, brake on the right."

"All right," Frank said. "I'll follow you."

They gunned their motors and set them to go forward, slowly at first, then gradually picking up speed.

They rode along the silent snow-covered path through an endless sea of evergreens. The only sounds were the shush of the front skis as they cut through the snow and the low rumble of the snowmobile's tread.

"There it is," Joe said, turning around to shout at his brother. Frank couldn't hear him, but he followed the line of Joe's arm pointing at the bottom of the next ridge. Just barely visible through the forest, Frank could see a little cabin, smoke pouring out of its chimney.

If they were lucky there was still a chance Ned hadn't reached the house.

Suddenly there was a loud crack, then something clanged off Frank's snowmobile. Another crack, and something hit home on Frank's vehicle. It was as if someone had thrown rocks—

Or fired bullets.

Frank's snowmobile sputtered. He watched as a trail of gasoline streamed out of the tank. The engine coughed one last time and died.

Frank turned in his seat to see another snow-mobile roaring up the slope behind him.

Joe took in the situation and flashed back to his brother.

"It's Ned," Frank yelled, racing for Joe's snowmobile. He hopped on behind Joe, clapping him on the shoulder. "Go—he's got a gun!"

Joe kicked the snowmobile into overdrive.

Within seconds they were shooting through the woods, far faster than Joe would have liked to go. He had to forget everything but driving, concentrating on following the path where trees had been cut—or they'd crack up and end up just as dead as if Ned had shot them.

A bullet clanged off Joe's snowmobile now—then another.

"He's gaining," Frank said. "I thought this was supposed to be a faster machine."

Joe shook his head, keeping his gaze forward. "Must be the two of us, weighing the machine down."

Suddenly they burst out of the woods and into the open. For a second Joe was dazzled by the glare of sunlight on the snow. Then his eyes adjusted, and he saw a ridge stretching out ahead of them. On the left it was bordered by more forest—on the right, the ridge overlooked a sheer thousand-foot drop to the valley floor below.

And just ahead, a hundred feet ahead, the

ridge bent sharply to the left, at almost a ninety-degree angle.

At their present speed, they'd never make the turn.

"I can't hold it!" Joe yelled. "Jump!"

A second later, the snowmobile flew off the ridge and landed hard, ten feet down the steep slope. The gas tank exploded. The machine rolled over once, slowly, and then again, faster—and again, and again.

It burned all the way to the bottom.

Ned Nolan brought his snowmobile to a halt at the edge of the ridge to study the wreckage below.

A smile of satisfaction crossed his face.

From behind a large snow-covered boulder a bit farther up the mountain, Frank and Joe Hardy watched Ned view their supposed deaths.

"He bought it," Joe said.

Frank nodded. They'd just managed to get off the machine before it crashed. "There he goes," Frank said, watching the snowmobile head off toward the cabin. "Come on."

The brothers set off in a dead run. Ten minutes later Frank burst through the front door of the cabin.

His father and Samuel Peterson were sitting on a couch in front of a roaring fire, Hugh Nolan in a chair beside them.

Ned was kneeling by the fire, turning a log.

They were all staring at Frank with varying degrees of surprise on their faces.

"Frank!" Fenton Hardy rose from the couch. "What are you doing here?"

"It's a long story, Dad," Frank said. Then he raised his arm and pointed at Ned. "And he can tell you most of it."

"Once again, I'm very surprised to see you, Frank," Ned said. "Very surprised indeed."

Fenton Hardy's eyes went back and forth between the two of them.

"What's going on, boys?"

"What's going on is simple," Frank said. "You're looking at the man who killed Daniel Carew—and tried to poison Chief Peterson!"

"Hold on a minute, Frank," Samuel Peterson said, standing. "That's a serious accusation."

"But I'm afraid it's true," Ned said. Without warning, his arm snaked out, and he grabbed Fenton Hardy in a stranglehold.

"Ned!" Hugh Nolan stepped forward, shock registering on his face. "What are you doing?"

Ned pulled out his gun and pressed it to Fenton's head. "What I have to do, Dad—to make sure you get what you deserve."

"And to stop the lies—isn't that right, Ned?"

"Yes, Frank," Ned said. "To stop the lies."

"Lies?" Peterson asked. "What lies?"

"He's talking about the money Josh Moran gave Hugh Nolan to keep quiet about the fire in Jefferson Heights," Frank said.

"That never happened!" Ned shouted. He cocked the gun and pressed it against Fenton Hardy's temple. "That never happened!"

"Frank," Chief Peterson said, circling around next to him and whispering, "I sure hope you know what you're doing."

"Oh, Ned," Hugh Nolan said, shaking his head slowly. "They're not lies."

Ned's gun hand wavered slightly. "I don't understand."

"They're not lies," Hugh Nolan repeated. He faced his son. "I did take that money from Moran, and I've regretted it every day of my life. Those people who were killed . . ." He shook his head. "I still see their faces at night. I couldn't sleep for the next few years—I mean, literally. I started drinking, I—" he stopped talking and buried his face in his hands.

Frank stepped forward.

"Give me the gun, Ned," he said.

"I don't think so," Ned said, backing slowly toward the front of the cabin, dragging Fenton. He reached behind him and opened the door.

A snowball slammed into his head, knocking the gun from it.

Another caught him in the head. His grip slackened—and Fenton Hardy broke free.

Ned moved like lightning. Before the gun had even hit the ground, he was halfway into a side-kick, his foot aimed for Fenton Hardy's head.

But Fenton Hardy was even quicker. He caught Ned's foot with one hand and, before Ned could react, delivered a crushing right-hand punch to the younger Nolan's jaw.

Ned dropped as if he'd been poleaxed.

Rubbing his neck with one hand, Fenton Hardy bent down and picked up the gun with the other.

"Sorry, Hugh," he said.

"Not half as sorry as I am," Nolan answered.

Joe Hardy walked forward, carrying a snowball in each hand. "How'd I do?"

Frank clapped his brother on the back. "Tommy Poletti couldn't have thrown a more accurate snowball, Joe."

Fenton Hardy smiled. "And here I thought you wanted to be a running back."

"Who knows?" Joe asked. "Maybe I'll take up another position."

"Johnson succeeded in getting Moran's will set aside—provisionally," Peterson said, hanging up the phone. They had returned to the ranger station to see Ned delivered into police custody—and to wrap up a few loose ends. "I suspect the money will all wind up in Emily Moran's hands eventually.''

"And I suspect she'll end up giving a lot of it away,'' Frank said.

"You might be right about that,'' Peterson said. "I don't know how to thank you boys. You saved my life—twice.''

Frank smiled. "Believe it or not, it was our pleasure.''

Peterson snapped his fingers. "I know. You can all come back with me to New York—my treat. I'll get us tickets to a hockey game—''

Frank shook his head. "After that snowmobile ride, no more winter-related sports for me.''

"All right,'' Peterson said. "How about a basketball game?''

Joe grinned. "Now you're talking.''

"The boys can't go, I'm afraid,'' Fenton Hardy said. "They have work to do at home. Some papers they've been putting off writing for quite a while, I think.''

Joe's face fell.

"Though if you're dead-set on seeing a game, Sam, I wouldn't mind going.''

"Uh-uh, Dad,'' Frank said. "You can't go either.''

"Oh?'' Fenton Hardy said, raising an eyebrow. "And why is that, young man?''

"The foreign film festival, remember? You

promised Mom you'd take her. I'd hate to tell her you chose a basketball game over that.''

Their father opened his mouth to protest, then shut it.

"I think you're licked, Fenton," Chief Peterson said.

"All right," Fenton Hardy said. "But we wrap up this case, see the game, and go home. That's it.''

"Absolutely," Joe said. "We promise.''

"Then that settles that," Fenton said. He turned to go.

"Unless, of course, something else comes up," Frank whispered.

"What was that, Frank?" Fenton Hardy asked, turning. "Did you say something?''

"Nothing, Dad," Frank said. "Nothing at all.''

COLLISION COURSE

Chapter

1

"Isn't she beautiful?" Seventeen-year-old Joe Hardy said, slipping his mirrored aviator sunglasses on top of his head.

His older brother, Frank, turned to see which girl had grabbed Joe's attention. But of course he realized in the next second that Joe meant the bright yellow-and-red machine gleaming in the sun before them.

The reflected light from its sleek body glinted in their eyes, and Joe absently pulled his sunglasses down over his blue eyes as he approached the car.

The term *car* hardly described the automobile the boys were looking at—it was more like a fighter jet on wheels, with wings in the front and back, and air intakes like airplane engines attached to each side of the bullet-shaped body.

1

"It looks like it could take off and fly, doesn't it?" Joe turned to greet Scott Lavin, the speaker and owner-driver of the race car. Scott was a few inches shorter than Joe and several years older. His racing jumpsuit—and protective gear underneath it—padded out his wiry frame. His hair was light brown, cut short on the top, but long in the back. At twenty-four Scott was young for his profession, but the deep creases around his green eyes made him look older.

"It sure does." Joe grinned. They both knew the car was designed to do just the opposite: it would hug the ground at high speeds and in tight turns.

"It seems so *small* for a race car," Joe added. "Look, the top of the roll bar doesn't even reach my waist."

"Well, it has to be built low to the ground," Scott noted, "and it is a tight fit in the cockpit. The whole thing's pretty compact. But the engine can crank over six hundred horsepower, and I've gotten her over two hundred miles per hour on the straightaways."

His teeth flashed in a wide grin. "Formula One Grand Prix race cars aren't very much like those stock cars that chase each other around in a circle."

"This baby's a whole different breed." Joe ran a hand along the side of the speed machine. He thought it was just about the most beautiful thing he'd ever seen.

2

"It's been a long time coming," Scott reminded him. Three years earlier, when Joe was only fourteen, Scott had been organizing and racing in amateur road rallies in Bayport. Now he had returned to his hometown with his own Formula One racing team.

"We had some good times with that old Porsche, didn't we, Joe?" Scott went on. "You may have been too young to drive it, but you sure weren't too young to take the engine apart and put it back together again."

"Not many people would have given me the chance at that age." Joe smiled at the memory. "But you accepted me without a second thought. My favorite part was when we'd road test it on the rally course that you mapped out."

"Ah, yes!" Scott chuckled. "The old Bayport Road Rally. I remember it well."

The business people of Bayport remembered the road rallies, too. Scott's careful planning and attention to detail had created a popular local event that had brought money into the city. The city council, always looking for ways to bring in *more* money, decided to expand on Scott Lavin's idea. This year they had hired a slick racing promoter named Russell Arno to organize a Formula One Grand Prix race in Bayport.

"Well, I'm not too young to drive now," Joe said, bringing his mind back to the present. "And I sure would like a chance to give this baby a spin."

"It takes more than a driver's license to handle one of these." Scott looked with pride at the car he had built himself. "But maybe you'll get your chance."

While Joe talked cars with Scott, Frank scanned the crowed, shielding his brown eyes against the sun. "There sure are a lot of people here—mostly out-of-town reporters," he said.

"Maybe we should hire a promoter like this Arno character," Joe said, flashing his brother a smile.

Frank laughed. "Yeah, our last case, *Blood Money*, should have been good for a series of comic books. All those mobsters falling over one another, trying to grab that inheritance—and Dad caught in the middle!"

Their father, Fenton Hardy, was a private investigator and former police detective. His name wound up on a hit list when a dying gangster left a fortune to his enemies. Frank and Joe had been forced to risk their own lives to protect their father from greedy mobsters.

"You'd probably feel more at home investigating Russell Arno than making a deal with him," Scott said. "He's got some kind of deal going now with Angus McCoy. I don't like the guy, but he sure knows how to pull in the racing fans."

"Angus is the former world champion Grand Prix driver," Joe added for Frank's benefit.

"McCoy is a crowd pleaser. That's why all the reporters are here. The race is still three days

4

away, but they all turned up for McCoy's official qualifying lap around the course."

Scott shrugged. "The time trials are important because the driver with the best time gets the best starting position. But the rest of us aren't 'noteworthy'—not when the press can cover Angus McCoy's thrilling race against the clock."

"He was the best in his day," Joe said, catching the bitterness in Scott's words. "But he's past his prime now."

"He still may be the best in this crowd." Scott stared at the assorted drivers, reporters, photographers, and race officials who were gathered for McCoy's time trial. "Everybody thinks he'll have the best lap time."

Joe saw McCoy standing next to Arno, both men surrounded by reporters. Like Scott, the lines around the champion's eyes made it hard to judge his age, and his wavy red hair and fair skin made him look like a big kid. But Joe could tell by McCoy's piercing gray eyes that he was no innocent kid.

As if sensing Joe's gaze, McCoy turned his eyes toward Joe and stared. Joe could almost feel the driver's confidence. He pulled his eyes away and put a hand on Scott's shoulder. "He'll have to be pretty fast if he wants to beat your time, Scott. Your average speed was almost one seventy!"

"Ya," came a fourth voice, with a slight German accent. "He even beat me. But I expect to do better tomorrow."

Scott turned to greet the newcomer. "Reinhart! Good to see you. Joe and Frank Hardy, meet Reinhart Voss. Reinhart is the number-two driver for the McCoy racing team."

"How many cars does McCoy have?" Frank asked.

"We used to have three," Voss said. "But times have been hard, and now we have only two. Let's hope nothing happens to McCoy's car today—or else he will end up driving mine and I will have nothing."

"That's what happens when you're number two," Scott said, laughing. "I don't have that problem. Of course, I also don't have a second car either. So if something happens to my car, I'll be sitting in the grandstand with you!"

Joe looked back in the direction of McCoy and Arno. McCoy had worn his fireproof racing suit to the press conference and was now pulling on his crash helmet as he walked to his car. Completely covered in protective gear, anybody or any*thing* could have been inside that outfit, Joe observed. Even with the helmet visor up, the driver's identity was a mystery. In fact, Joe thought that the fire retardant face mask—resembling a ski mask with two large oval holes for the eyes—made the guy look like an alien from an old sci-fi movie.

"Can we meet McCoy?" Joe suddenly asked Voss.

"Ya, sure. Come. I will take you to him."

But as the group of four moved toward the center of the crowd they were intercepted by Russell Arno. "Well, if it isn't Reinhart Voss and Scott Lavin, two of my favorite drivers. Having a good time?"

"We were just going to introduce my friends, Frank and Joe Hardy, to Angus," Scott replied curtly.

"The Hardy brothers? You boys have made quite a name for yourselves in Bayport."

Frank looked at Arno curiously. The promoter looked as if he were a middle-aged banker. His hair was thinning on top, and he was a little overweight—but his tailored suit was cut beautifully and made him look thinner.

"Where did you hear that?" Frank asked.

"When Scott asked me to put your names on the guest list for the press party, I made a few inquiries," Arno explained. "I make it a point to know something about all my guests. And I would be delighted to introduce you to Mr. McCoy, but as you can see, he's getting in his car now. Perhaps some other time?"

"That's okay," Joe said. "We'll just hang around until he finishes."

Arno flashed a toothy smile. "Say, I've got an idea! We're videotaping his entire lap from my helicopter. Why don't you come along? You can see the whole race course from the air and witness the historic event from the best seats in the house!"

Joe didn't care much for Arno's tone or manner. The slick way he had breezed into town and taken all the credit for Scott's work didn't sit well with Joe. Still, this was too good an opportunity to pass up. "Sounds great," came Joe's reply.

"How about you, Scott? Arno asked, smiling at the young driver.

"No thanks," Scott said, looking Arno straight in the eyes. "I've seen McCoy drive before, and I'm quite familiar with the layout of the course. You and your pals on the city council didn't bother to give me any credit, but those are my course maps you used as the blueprint for the Bayport Grand Prix."

"And I have no great love of flying," Voss said, breaking the awkward silence that followed Scott's quiet outburst. "I like to go fast—but I prefer to do it on the ground."

Joe felt a twinge of guilt as he and Frank moved away from Scott, toward a cargo helicopter that had been modified to hold a video crew and cameras. He almost felt as if he were deserting his friend. Arno hustled them on board and introduced them to a short man with a notepad. "I'd like you to meet T. B. Martin. He's writing McCoy's biography."

The writer wore thick, wire-rim glasses and a photographer's vest crammed with notebooks, pens, and even a small tape recorder. His dark hair and beard were trimmed so short that they bristled. "Actually, I'm just a ghost writer," Martin said. "McCoy will get the credit."

"Oh, so it's supposed to be an autobiography," Frank shouted as the large turbine engine started to wind up.

"Sure, it's an *auto*-biography," Joe cut in, laughing as the lumbering machine lifted off the ground. "McCoy drives *cars* for a living, doesn't he?"

As the helicopter rose higher, Frank could see the whole city of Bayport spread out below, as well as Barmet Bay and the Atlantic Ocean beyond that.

Joe outlined the course for his brother. "It's kind of a sloppy U-shape, with a few squiggles thrown in. It starts at the Bayport Fairgrounds and then runs south through the middle of town and curves around the bay to the ocean.

"Down there," he shouted, pointing again, "it swings back behind the city to the west. Then it runs into the highway and heads up a long straight section due north. Up there, it turns east and runs to the cliffs on the coast north of town. Finally, it swings back along the bay again."

"This course reminds me of Monte Carlo," Martin shouted above the din of the engine and the rotor blades.

Joe focused out the window again and saw

McCoy's race car, a tiny ant-mobile, crawling around the turn at the south end of the course. Now it was heading back inland. Because of the helicopter's height and speed, McCoy seemed to be barely moving, but Joe knew he must be topping 190 as he headed into the long straightaway that ran to the north before the course turned uphill to the northern cliffs at the ocean's edge.

"Yeah," Joe yelled back to Martin. "The only difference is the tunnel at Monte Carlo doesn't lead out into a blind hairpin turn!" He was talking about the tunnel cut through the cliff that ended just before the road made a tight westward turn away from the ocean to follow the curve of Barmet Bay. Everyone in Bayport knew about the hazardous curve. It had been the scene of many accidents over the years—some of them fatal. "If you miss that turn, it's a long, rough ride down to the bottom."

The helicopter swung out over the ocean as McCoy disappeared into the tunnel. It seemed like an eternity before he came out the other end, although it couldn't have been more than a few seconds. The car came rocketing out of the tunnel, hugging the road surface in an impressive display of aerodynamic technology. But something was wrong.

"He's going too fast! He won't make it!" Frank shouted. Before anyone could respond, the car smashed through the guardrail on the hairpin turn.

For a second it looked as if the car could fly. But its forward momentum quickly gave way to the pull of gravity, and the car plummeted toward the cold, waiting waters of the Atlantic two hundred feet below.

The impact with the water barely seemed to slow it down. The car knifed cleanly through the surface—and sank without a trace.

Chapter

2

THE HELICOPTER QUICKLY swooped down to the spot where the race car had plunged into the ocean. Concentric waves rippled across the water, but there was no sign of McCoy or the car. The bullet-shaped vehicle had sliced straight to the bottom.

Frank Hardy looked over to see his brother fumbling at the laces on his shoes. "What are you doing?"

"I'm going in after him!" Joe unbuttoned his shirt as he lunged out of his seat. "He might still be alive, trapped down there!"

Frank leapt up and stepped in front of the sliding cargo door before Joe could reach it. He grabbed his brother by the shoulders. "Stop for a second and think, Joe. The water is at least fifty

12

feet deep here, and you know what the currents are like."

Joe struggled against his brother's arms. "We can't just leave him down there!"

Frank pushed Joe away from the door. "The impact from the two-hundred-foot fall probably killed him before the car sank. If you jump in without scuba gear, you'll just beome another casualty."

"He's right," T. B. Martin agreed grimly. "People like McCoy court death for a living. He knew the risks. Living on the edge was what he was all about. For McCoy, it was fun. But he wouldn't want someone else to risk his own life needlessly."

Frank put his hand on his brother's shoulder. "Come on, Joe. Sit down. You're not going anywhere."

Joe's shoulders slumped. He knew they were right—but he couldn't help thinking they had to do *something*.

Frank was one step ahead of him. "Tell the pilot to radio the police and put the chopper down on the road where the car went through the guardrail," Frank said to Arno.

Russell Arno was just staring out at the ocean. He seemed distracted—or maybe it was just the shock of the accident. After a moment Arno nodded and shouted into the pilot's ear.

Frank and Joe were the first ones to jump out of the copter when it touched down. They headed straight for the twisted remains of the guardrail. It looked like a licorice stick that had been casually ripped in half—except this licorice stick was made of steel, Joe reminded himself.

The guardrail wasn't the only thing damaged by the crash. Debris lay all over the place. The thin "wings" attached to the needle-nose front of the race car had been ripped off and were now lying crumpled on either side of the gash in the barrier.

Frank stooped down to examine some of the parts that didn't make the final voyage and were now scattered on the road. There were some shards of glass, a sideview mirror—and something else that caught Frank's eye. He picked it up to inspect it more closely. It appeared to be some kind of electronic device.

"This doesn't look like a normal car part," he mused, thinking out loud.

A voice from behind Frank broke his train of thought. "Nothing on these Formula One machines is 'normal.' " Frank turned to see Arno peering over his shoulder. "This is the cutting edge of automotive high tech," Arno continued. "Half the stuff under the hood is top secret—so the driver can *keep* his edge. McCoy did a lot of his own mechanical work. There's a good chance that the only person who can tell you what you're holding is down there." Arno motioned down to the deceptively calm waters.

Joe looked over at Arno, noting how composed

the promoter seemed, given the circumstances. "You don't seem too concerned about McCoy's death," he said, trying to control his temper.

Arno shrugged. "It's like Martin told you— McCoy lived on the edge. All good racing drivers do. The danger is part of the thrill. Some of these guys, like McCoy, think they're so good they can cheat death. And when you start thinking like that, death sneaks up behind you.

"But you're wrong to think I'm not concerned," Arno added, sadness creeping into his voice for the first time. "McCoy and I worked together a long time. He was a hard man to like, but I'll miss him."

Their conversation was interrupted by the arrival of a squad car carrying two of Bayport's finest. The driver got out and lumbered over to the small group, while the other officer walked toward T. B. Martin to take his statement. The uniformed man who approached Frank and Joe was large, more than a little out of shape, and sported a sizable paunch. Joe wondered how he managed to keep his pants up, before he noticed his nameplate: "Reed."

"Okay," Officer Reed huffed. "What happened here?"

Before either Frank or Joe could say anything, Arno started in. "A tragic accident," he began smoothly. "Mr. McCoy miscalculated the turn, and at one hundred fifty miles per hour it was a deadly mistake."

"Stupid race car drivers," Reed grumbled. "There's a reason for the posted speed limit, you know."

"At the posted speed limit"—Arno jerked his thumb back toward the sign that said 15 MPH—"the engine would have stalled out, and he would have had to push the car around the turn. That would *not* have produced a spectacular lap time."

The police officer looked back toward the tunnel, and then his eyes moved from the tunnel exit to the gaping hole in the guardrail. "Well, what kind of lap time do you suppose he'll get now?" He frowned. "The only thing 'spectacular' here was his crash. Maybe they'll cancel that stupid race now."

"I doubt it," Arno said curtly as he walked away.

"What do you think of this?" Frank said, holding out the electronic device he had found.

"What am I supposed to think?" the police officer retorted gruffly. "Some stupid gizmo to make a car go too fast and ruin a perfectly good guardrail. This is going to cost the county plenty, you know."

Frank and Joe gave the officer their statements, and then Reed lumbered off to join his partner, who was radioing in a report to headquarters. Frank surveyed the scene again, then turned to his brother. "I don't like this."

"Who does?" Joe responded grimly.

"Come on," Frank said, tugging at his brother's arm, "I want to ask Martin a few questions. Something just doesn't add up."

The Hardys approached the writer, who was standing by the edge of the cliff. He was staring into the blue waters below. "Excuse me, Mr. Martin," Frank said quietly, "but I was wondering if I could ask you something."

"You know," the writer began in a distracted tone, "you think you're prepared for this sort of thing. After ten years of covering the racing circuit, you think you've seen it all. Guys get killed every year. No big surprise. But somehow, you're never really ready when it happens."

He was silent for a moment, then he said, "I'm sorry. What was it you wanted to know?"

"Were the two of you close?" Frank asked.

"Close?" Martin repeated. "Nobody was close to Angus McCoy. Everything was a competition for him. He never let up, never wanted to lose the edge.

"You know, he hated having a ghost writer, wanted to do the book himself. But his publisher saw the first couple of chapters and had the ugly task of telling Angus he couldn't write worth beans. If it weren't for the contract, he would have fired the publisher."

"What happens to the book now?" Frank pressed. "Will the publisher cancel it?"

"Are you kidding?" Martin laughed. "This is the kind of ending publishers dream about! I can just see the title now: *The Fast Life and Tragic*

17

Death of Angus McCoy! And we've got the whole thing on videotape! The publisher will love it. Pictures of the famous racing driver's last moments! It'll sell millions!''

The writer laughed again, but both Frank and Joe could see the laughter was forced and bitter. Martin turned back toward the ocean and was silent for a while. Finally he said, ''Does that answer your question?''

''Actually, that wasn't the question I wanted to ask,'' Frank said apologetically. ''Something just doesn't make any sense to me. McCoy knew the layout of the course, right?''

''Sure. He'd driven it several times to get familiar with it,'' Martin said.

''And he didn't really have any serious competition in this race, right?''

''Right.''

''So why would he push so hard? And why did he drive as though he didn't know the turn was there?''

''The answer to the first question is easy.'' Martin smiled. ''Race drivers always push hard. They're not just racing against other drivers and the clock—they're competing against themselves.

''Angus was getting a little old for the game,'' Martin went on. ''There were guys who said he was all washed up, so he had something to prove. As for your second question,'' the writer continued after a brief pause, ''I don't have an answer. Angus was a much better driver than on that last turn. And it's not like this is the only course with a hairpin turn."

He shrugged. "Angus was a world champion. I don't understand it, either. This is the kind of mistake a newcomer would make."

"What about sabotage?" Frank ventured.

The question surprised both Martin and Joe. "Who would have a motive?" Joe cut in.

"Somebody who wants to win," Frank replied simply.

At that moment Russell Arno joined them at the cliff's edge. He kicked at a small rock, and Joe watched it roll and bounce down the steep incline. He barely made out the tiny splash it made when it hit the water below.

Arno turned to him and casually said, "Well, now that McCoy is out of it, it looks like your friend Scott Lavin is the new favorite."

Chapter
3

THE NEXT DAY was one of those late-summer days when the sun felt somehow cooler, even though the temperature was as hot as mid-July.

Joe Hardy was sitting on his front porch, thinking that even the shadows cast by the sun were different at this time of year. Softer. Maybe the morning seemed special because he knew summer was almost over. But Joe was sure he could recognize this kind of day even if he were set down in the middle of it, without anyone telling him what season it was.

Joe had been up for a while. The day before had been long, but he had slept well. Joe rarely had trouble sleeping. There wasn't any problem that wasn't easier to tackle after a good night's sleep, he thought.

Frank Hardy emerged from the house about

one o'clock, stretching and yawning. "You look like you could use a couple more hours of sack time," Joe remarked.

"I was up most of the night doing some work on the computer," Frank explained. The Hardys had a sophisticated computer setup, complete with a telephone modem to access other computers, and they often used it to help solve cases. If information was available over a phone link-up, Frank knew how to get at it.

"It took quite a while," Frank went on, "but I found out some interesting things. About Scott Lavin," he added.

"Oh?" Joe said, raising his eyebrows. "Let's hear it."

"Building and racing Formula One cars is very expensive," Frank began. "It takes a lot of money—and that means sponsors and investors. Scott got started with seed money from a few investors, but that money is almost gone now. He's been looking for sponsors—advertisers who will pay him to promote their products. But Scott doesn't have enough of a reputation on the Grand Prix circuit yet. He needs a big win to get that rep."

"Go on." Joe fought to keep his voice cool. Scott Lavin was his friend, and he didn't like where this conversation was leading.

"Look, Joe, I know how you feel about Scott," Frank said softly. "But right now he's the only suspect we've got. I think we should investigate."

21

"Suspect? Investigate?" Joe forgot about being cool. "What are you talking about? How do you know McCoy's death wasn't an accident? And even if it wasn't, Scott wouldn't murder anyone just to win a race. Besides, he's a top-notch driver and had a shot at winning—even with McCoy in the race."

Frank looked at his younger brother. He knew Joe was smart, but sometimes Joe's short fuse didn't allow him the logic to think things through. "You don't believe that crash was an accident any more than I do," Frank told him. "He hit that guardrail like it had a bull's-eye painted on it. Either he was struck by a sudden suicidal urge or there was something wrong with his car."

"Like what?" Joe demanded.

"I don't know. The brakes or the steering, probably. Take a look at this thing." Frank was holding the electronic device he had found at the crash site. "What does it look like to you? It looks like part of a radio-control setup to me. Flip a switch and *zap!* No more brakes."

Frank could see doubt flicker in his brother's eyes. "There's something you're forgetting," he continued. "Scott is probably bitter about this whole race. This is his course and his hometown, and Arno and McCoy just walked in and took away the spotlight. That's got to hurt.

"Maybe the money and the sponsorship wouldn't be enough, but throw in a little need for revenge. Maybe that pushed Scott over the edge.''

There was an awkward silence after Frank finished talking. ''You're all wrong about Scott,'' Joe snapped. ''You could be right about the crash. It didn't look like an accident exactly, but I think we should check out some other people first.''

''Okay,'' Frank said. ''Who?''

''Well, what about this Arno character?''

''The promoter? What's his motive?''

''He said he had a 'financial interest' in McCoy.''

''Yeah. An interest in keeping him alive to bring in the big attendance on race day. What does he gain by McCoy's death?''

''I don't know,'' Joe admitted with a sigh. ''I guess it wouldn't hurt to start by talking to Scott.''

After eating a late lunch, the Hardys drove over to Scott Lavin's garage and parked their van outside. They walked in the open door and found Scott and his head mechanic hunched over the engine of the yellow-and-red race car. Joe took one look at the machine, and some of the excitement of the previous day returned. Ever since he could remember, he had been in love with cars, and he couldn't help but share his enthusiasm with his brother.

''The wings at the front end and behind the

rear tires act just like the wings on an airplane, only in reverse," Joe said. "They create negative lift, thousands of pounds of downforce to keep the car on the road in high-speed turns.

"And see those side panels sticking out from the chassis, running the length of the car? They look like jet engines or something, but they're really upside-down airfoils. They scoop up air through intakes in the front and create an area of low pressure underneath, sucking the car to the road surface like a vacuum cleaner. It's called ground effects."

"If you're going fast enough," Scott Lavin said, not even looking up from his work, "you can generate enough downforce to ride a track upside-down. At least, that's what the designers tell me. I've never actually tried it."

Scott stood up, wiped his hands on a rag, and smiled at the Hardys. "Formula One racing entered the space age back in the late sixties when airplane designers started tinkering with Grand Prix cars. The old stainless steel carrot is still under there, somewhere, buried in state-of-the-art aerodynamics. Except it's not even stainless steel anymore. It's aluminum and high-tech fibers with names you can't pronounce.

"Just about the only old-fashioned part is the open cockpit. It seems as if it would make more sense to cover it with a smooth canopy—just as they've covered everything else."

"Except the tires, of course. The tires are

something of a technological feat themselves," Joe said.

Frank noticed that the rear tires were larger than the front ones and almost twice as wide. "Almost no tread," he observed.

"Touch one of them," Scott suggested. "It's a special rubber. It's sticky. At the end of a race the rubber looks like it's about ready to drip off the wheels. The tires last only about three hundred miles. One race and that's it."

Joe pointed to the V-8 engine. "This is a little old-fashioned, too. They've eliminated turbocharged engines."

Scott nodded. "They were generating just too much power. Formula One racing was getting too dangerous."

"As if it isn't dangerous now," Frank said, thinking of Angus McCoy's car at the bottom of the Atlantic Ocean. "It looks a lot like the cars they drive at the Indianapolis 500."

"It *is* a lot like an Indy car," Scott agreed. "There's a lot of cross-breeding between Grand Prix and Indianapolis. Rear-mounted engines, wings, and ground effects were all developed in Formula One before making the jump to Indy. Indy cars outweigh Formula One cars by about three hundred pounds—even though they carry less fuel and have smaller wings."

"Why the differences?" Frank asked.

"Different conditions," Joe said. "There are no pit stops in a two-hundred-fifty-mile Grand

Prix race, so you have to start with all the fuel you're going to need. And the wings on a Formula One car have to handle a lot of different and tight turns. Indy cars go in one direction around nice, banked oval curves.''

"All of this technology must take a lot of money," Frank commented, looking at Scott.

Scott laughed and said, "There's an old saying in racing circles: 'Speed costs money. How fast do you want to go?' " He glanced from one brother to the other. "Did you guys come down here to discuss my finances?''

"No, no," Joe replied quickly. "We just came by to see how things were going.''

"Well, they could be better," Scott said.

"Was everybody pretty shook up about the crash yesterday?" Frank ventured.

"I hate to sound callous," Scott responded, "but that's the least of my problems. I feel bad about McCoy, but the show goes on. This is a dangerous profession. At Indy, if there's a big accident on the course, they delay the race until they clear away the wreckage. In a Grand Prix race, they just stick in a guy with a flag to warn you that you're about to drive into a disaster area. McCoy's not the first world champion to die in his car—not even the first to die during time trials.

"I guess if they got really concerned about the dangers, they'd stop having races on the open road. But Grand Prix racing is just starting to catch on in the U.S. now. Cities like Dallas and Detroit realized they could make money off Formula One racing without spending any money to build a track.

"These cars may be safer than they were twenty years ago, but fatal crashes still aren't all that unusual. A lot of drivers *assume* that's how they'll go."

Scott scowled. "My problem is far more immediate and practical. One of my crew just up and quit, and we still have a lot of work to do." He paused for a second, then looked at Joe. "Hey, Joe, you said you wanted to get your hands on one of these babies. Here's your chance. It's not driving, but it's hands-on experience. How would you like to join my crew for a few days? Just until the race is over."

"Sure!" Joe blurted out, before his brother had a chance to say anything.

Frank glanced at Joe out of the corner of his eye and then shifted his attention back to Scott. "Actually, we *did* want to ask you a few questions, Scott," he began.

"No problem," Scott interrupted. "Maybe later. Right now Joe and I have a lot of work to do. Right, Joe?"

Joe hesitated for a moment, torn between his brother and something he had dreamed about—the chance to be part of a Grand Prix racing team. Maybe McCoy's crash *had* been a simple accident, he told himself. Even if it wasn't, Scott

27

couldn't be responsible for it. Suddenly, finding out who *was* responsible didn't seem so important.

"Right!" Joe heard himself say, agreeing with Scott.

Scott Lavin put his arm around Joe's shoulder, and together they walked away from Frank.

Chapter
4

AFTER CHECKING OUT the garage for an hour or so, Frank left alone. He didn't know if he should be mad at Joe or worried or both. There's no hard evidence against Scott Lavin, he reminded himself. But Joe's judgment was clouded by friendship and fast cars. If Scott's setting him up for some reason, Joe won't see it coming. In fact, Scott could have offered Joe a job just to get us off the case. Scott knows our reputation.

All these concerns ran through Frank's head as he got in the van and drove off in the direction of Phil Cohen's house. At a traffic light he opened the glove compartment and checked to make sure the electronic device was still where he'd put it before going into Scott Lavin's garage.

Frank didn't know a lot about race cars, but he was sure this thing didn't belong on one. It looked jury-rigged from something intended for another purpose. But what was its purpose now? Frank still didn't know.

If anyone could find out, it was their old friend, Phil Cohen. Anything Phil didn't know about electronics wasn't worth knowing. Frank parked the van in front of the Cohens' house, took the metal object out of the glove compartment, and walked toward the front door. A passing car caught his eye—a silver gray Lotus sport coupe. Not too many cars like that around Bayport, Frank thought.

He shrugged off a nagging feeling that he had seen the car before and rang the doorbell. No one answered. He waited a minute and then tried knocking. Still no response. Frank started to walk back toward the van, and then he realized that Phil was probably out in the garage.

Phil's passion for electronic gizmos had threatened to engulf the Cohen house. They spilled out of Phil's bedroom and into the guest room. Finally, his folks had exiled his electrical empire to the garage, which was fine with Phil. It meant he could work late at night without waking anybody up.

Frank followed the path from the house to the door on the side of the garage. He could hear Phil singing inside. "Sounds more like a goose honking," Frank muttered. "But at least it means Phil's home."

Frank knocked on the side door. No answer,

Phil just kept singing. Frank knocked again and was greeted by more loud goose noises. He tried the handle. The door was unlocked. He pushed it open and saw Phil sitting at a workbench, facing away from the door, wearing a pair of small headphones from a portable cassette player.

Something's strange about those headphones, Frank thought. But what? He looked more closely. There were no wires leading to the cassette player lying on the workbench. But Phil was obviously listening to something because his head was nodding in time to a beat Frank couldn't hear.

Frank walked over and tapped Phil on the shoulder. Phil jumped up, knocking his chair over in the process. "What—" he exclaimed. "Oh, it's you," he shouted over the music in his ears.

Phil took off the headphones and handed them to Frank. "Check this out. I'm working on a set of cordless headphones. Not exactly a radical concept, except I'm trying to come up with an infrared sender-receiver small enough for a hand-held portable cassette player."

Frank noticed that the tape player on the bench was wired up to a black box with an infrared sensor. The box was larger than the tape player. "Still needs some work," Frank observed.

"Yeah. Well, but you know me—I'll just keep hacking away until I figure it out. Then I'll patent it and retire on the royalties." Phil grinned.

"Think you could figure *this* out?" Frank

asked, handing over the piece of evidence from the fatal crash.

Phil took it, turned it over, inspected the connections of a few of the exposed wires, set it down on the workbench, and began methodically attacking it with a screwdriver. He took off the face plate and revealed several intricate circuit boards. After fiddling with it for a few minutes he said, "I'm not sure. It could be some kind of radio receiver."

Frank nodded. "That's what I thought. But to receive what kind of signal?"

Phil shrugged. "I'd have to run some tests, check out a few things. What's this all about, Frank?"

Frank told Phil everything he knew, and then something clicked in his head. "Check it out completely, Phil. Let me know what you find out."

"It could take a while."

"That's okay. I'll call you later. Right now there's something I have to do."

Frank got back in the van and started driving toward the Bayport Fairgrounds, which had been temporarily transformed into makeshift garages and pits for the race. Something Phil had said about royalties reminded him of the writer, T. B. Martin. Frank was hoping he could find him at the fairgrounds.

It wasn't a straight drive to the fairgrounds. Like much of downtown Bayport, the fairgrounds were blocked off from regular traffic for the duration of the race. Frank parked the van about half a mile away and walked the rest of the distance. He didn't get there until seven o'clock.

He found Martin in the aluminum shed that served as the portable garage for McCoy Racing. The writer was talking to Reinhart Voss, the number-two man on the McCoy team. Martin recognized Frank and waved him over. "Frank Hardy, right? I wanted to talk to you and your brother. I'm working on the final chapter of McCoy's biography. It may sound gruesome, but I want to get eyewitness descriptions from everybody who saw the crash."

"Let's make a trade," Frank replied. "Answer a few questions for me, and I'll tell you what I saw."

"Sounds good. What can I tell you now that you didn't get out of me yesterday? You guys sure ask a lot of questions. Maybe *you* should be writing a book."

"Will you make royalties off the sales of McCoy's biography?" Frank asked.

"Posthumous autobiography," Martin corrected him. "Sure. For every copy sold, I'll make a few cents. It won't make me rich, but if the book hits the best-seller charts, I won't have to worry about a paycheck for a while."

"What happens to McCoy's share of the profits now that he's dead? Do you get it all?"

The writer eyed Frank suspiciously. "If you're

asking if I'd benefit from McCoy's death, the answer is no. Dead or alive, McCoy's share goes to a company called Clarco Industries. It's in the contract."

Martin paused and then said, "What are you getting at, anyway? The crash was an accident, wasn't it? Do you know something that I don't?"

"Nothing yet," Frank responded. He noticed that it was starting to get dark out. "Listen, it's getting late. I've got to go."

"Okay—but you owe me an interview!" Martin called after him as Frank headed out the door.

Somehow the day had gotten away from Frank. The late start threw him off. He jogged back to the van. It was dusk, and he had to turn on the headlights for the drive back to Scott Lavin's garage. He knew that Scott and his crew would be finishing sometime soon, and he wanted to be there when Scott closed up the garage.

Unlike the out-of-town drivers and racing teams that had to make do with temporary arrangements on the fairgrounds, Scott still kept a private garage in Bayport. Frank had noticed a sophisticated burglar alarm system on his earlier visit, and that was what interested him now.

Frank pulled the van into a dark alley across from the garage, took out a pair of binoculars, and waited. Finally three figures emerged. One of them was the mechanic, one was Scott Lavin, and the third was Joe Hardy. Frank felt bad. He was spying on his own brother.

Frank lifted the binoculars and focused on Scott. The burglar alarm control panel was on the outside of the garage. Anyone trying to get in couldn't even open the doors for a second without setting off the alarm. Scott opened the control box, and Frank shifted the binoculars slightly to zoom in on the control panel. There was a calculator-style keypad with an LED display screen at the top. Even in the dark, Frank could see the sequence of glowing numbers that Scott quickly punched in: 3-3-1-4-6-1. The alarm was activated, and Scott closed the control box.

Frank watched the trio depart and then waited a few more minutes. He climbed between the two front seats into the back of the van and opened the tool chest. "Let's see, I'll need the flashlight—and this—" he muttered, taking out a flat case and slipping it into his back pocket. Then he opened the back door of the van, hopped lightly to the ground, and closed the door softly.

He walked across the street casually, approaching Scott's garage as if he owned the place. Frank strolled right up to the burglar alarm and flipped open the control box. He looked around to make sure no one was in sight. Then he turned back to the control panel and punched in the same sequence of numbers Scott had used earlier: 3-3-1-4-6-1. Finally he pressed the Alarm Off button. The burglar alarm was now deactivated. No problem.

Now came the tricky part. The door was

locked, of course, but Frank was prepared. He reached into his back pocket and pulled out the soft leather case that he had taken from the tool chest. Unsnapping the cover, he opened the case, revealing an assortment of thin metal strips in a variety of lengths and widths—a lock-pick set.

Breaking and entering didn't rate high on Frank's list of favorite investigative techniques. If things had gone down differently, he might have had Joe set up a diversion while he searched the place in broad daylight. But he was working alone now, and he didn't have a whole lot of time. In a few days the race would be over, and Scott Lavin would pack up and head out for the next Grand Prix race, probably in another country. Any chance of uncovering evidence would be gone.

Frank wasn't planning on taking anything. He was just going to look around—to see if he could find any radio equipment that might provide a link to the mysterious device now in Phil Cohen's workshop.

He worked the lock like an expert. The Bayport police frequently gave home security seminars, complete with demonstrations of the various burglary tools used to break into houses. Frank always made it a point to attend the classes.

The lock mechanism began to turn, and he felt the deadbolt slide back. He slowly turned the doorknob and then eased the door open. He slipped into the garage and closed the door quickly, feeling certain he had avoided detection.

The garage was pitch-black, but Frank wasn't going to turn on the lights. He didn't want to attract attention. He switched on the flashlight, and abruptly the garage came alive with shadows that wavered and jumped as Frank moved the beam around in the dark, scanning all the unfamiliar machinery. He spotted what appeared to be a pile of electrical equipment and figured that it was as good a place as any to start looking.

Then Frank heard it—a faint noise behind him, like a shoe being scuffed on the cement floor. He stiffened, realizing suddenly that he'd forgotten to lock the door behind him.

Pivoting on one foot, he whirled to face whoever it was and caught a blow to the side of his head. He tottered on his feet for a second—then Frank Hardy's world faded to black.

Chapter

5

IT WAS LATE when Joe Hardy got home. He walked in the front door and headed for the kitchen in search of something to eat. He found his aunt Gertrude making a cup of tea. "Sorry I missed dinner," Joe said as he opened the refrigerator. "Anything left to eat?"

"Well, at least you called," Gertrude said. "Here it is, already past nine, and your brother isn't home yet. He missed dinner and didn't even call. You two went out together this afternoon. What happened?"

"Nothing much." Joe grabbed a loaf of bread and some peanut butter. "We went to see Scott Lavin, and then I hung around to help out with Scott's car. Frank took off in the van. He didn't tell me where he was going. I figured he was headed back here."

"Did you two have a fight?" Gertrude asked, a hint of concern edging into her voice.

Joe took a big bite of his sandwich to buy time while he chose his words. Finally he said, "I wouldn't call it a *fight,* exactly. We just didn't agree."

"Oh?" Gertrude replied. "And what, exactly, didn't you agree about?"

Just then the telephone rang. Joe jumped up and said, "I'll get it!" And then he muttered under his breath, "Saved by the bell."

"Hardy summer home," Joe spoke into the receiver. "Some are home and some aren't."

"Hi, Joe. Is Frank there?"

Joe recognized the voice right away. "Hey, Phil. No, he's not here. And I don't know where he is. Did you see him at all today?"

"Yeah," Phil said. "He came by this afternoon. There was something he wanted me to check out. Have him call me when he gets in, okay?"

"Sure thing," Joe said. "Say, did Frank tell you where he was going when he left your house? Aunt Gertrude's getting a little worried about him," he added in a soft voice so Gertrude wouldn't overhear.

"No—he just said there was something else he had to do. I doubt if that's much help."

"Maybe more than you think," Joe said. "Thanks, Phil."

He hung up the phone and turned to his aunt. "I've got to go out again."

"What for?" Gertrude asked suspiciously.

"I think I left something at Scott's place," came the reply as Joe shot out the front door.

"Couldn't it wait until tomorrow?" Gertrude called after him. But there was no answer. Joe was gone.

Joe didn't know where Frank had gone after he'd left Phil, but he had a hunch where his brother might be now. Since Frank had taken the van, Joe had to walk. He could have asked his parents for their car, but he didn't want them asking any questions. Aunt Gertrude's were bad enough.

Besides, he wasn't sure if his hunch was right. And if it was, what was he supposed to tell his aunt? He shook his head as he imagined himself saying, "Gee, Aunt Gertrude, I think Frank's trying to break into Scott's garage, and I just thought I'd go down to see if he needs any help."

Somehow he doubted that that would make his aunt feel any better. Of course, the only "help" he intended to give Frank was to try to stop him before it was too late.

Joe wasn't sure what Frank was up to, but he knew his older brother pretty well. If Joe was right, he wanted to get there before anybody else did. He broke into a jog as he backtracked along the route he had taken just a little while earlier.

Joe was breathing heavily by the time he

reached Scott Lavin's garage. He slowed to a walk about twenty yards from the door and let himself catch his breath as he scanned the area. His eyes had adjusted to the dark, and he could make out the faint outline of the van in the alley across the street. He headed for the van and tried the door.

Locked. Joe pulled his key chain out of his pocket, fumbling in the dark for the right key. He opened the van door and poked his head inside. Frank wasn't there, but Joe did notice something in the back of the van.

The tool chest was open. Joe climbed inside and over the front seat, switching on the overhead light as he went. He already suspected what he would find in the tool chest—or, more exactly, what he *wouldn't* find. He was right—the lock-pick set was missing.

Joe climbed out of the van and doubled back across the street in the direction of Scott Lavin's garage. From the middle of the street he could now see that the door to the garage was ajar, even though all the lights were out.

A mental warning alarm went off in Joe's brain. Frank wouldn't be so careless. The slightly open door was as obvious as a flashing neon sign proclaiming, "Burglars at work!" Joe stood at the threshold and tried to get a look inside the garage, but his eyes couldn't penetrate the darkness within. He drew in a deep breath, gritted his teeth, plunged through the door—and almost tripped over his brother's body, slumped on the floor.

Frank Hardy struggled through a fog to see his brother's face staring down at him. "Joe?" he croaked. "What happened?"

Joe was sitting cross-legged on the floor, cradling Frank's head in his lap. "You almost got yourself killed from the looks of it," he said.

"Somebody knocked me out!" Frank exclaimed, struggling to sit up as the mist started to clear from his brain.

"Yeah," Joe agreed. "*You* did." He pointed to a heavy duty hoist and a racing engine lying on its side on the garage floor, under a single light that he had switched on. "You must have tripped the hoist release by accident, stumbling around in the dark like a blind cat burglar. If you'd been standing a little more to the left, that engine would have done more than just knock you out before it crashed into the floor."

"How did you know where to find me?" Frank asked as Joe helped him get up.

"It wasn't too hard," Joe snapped. "Phil couldn't tell you if there was any connection between that hunk of electronics you found and McCoy's accident, so you came back here, hoping to dig up some other evidence. But you're on the wrong track this time."

Frank rubbed his aching head—and remembered something. "There was somebody else in the garage. I heard him—just before my lights went out. He whacked me on the side of the head, and then he must have released the engine from the hoist to make it look like an accident."

"Just look at that engine," Joe said. "We'll be lucky to get it fixed before the race. You can't blame this on Scott."

He scowled and stared around the garage. "You know, Frank, there are other drivers besides Scott in this race. Maybe somebody *did* sabotage McCoy's car, but it wasn't Scott."

"Maybe I was getting too close to the truth," Frank persisted, "and Scott trashed his own engine to put me out of commission and throw me off the trail at the same time."

Joe's anger blew away his concern for his brother. "You don't give up, do you?" he shouted. "I *know* Scott Lavin, and I'm telling you he didn't do it!"

"And I might have known I'd find the two of you here," another voice interrupted. Frank and Joe whirled around to see police officer Con Riley. "If there's trouble in Bayport, the Hardy brothers can't be far away."

Riley hoisted the service revolver that he had pointed at the Hardys a moment before. "But somehow I can't see the pair of you as car thieves," he continued. "Someone reported seeing a prowler break in here, and I arrive on the scene to find Frank and Joe Hardy. I can't wait to hear the explanation."

If the Hardys had a friend on the Bayport police force, it was Con Riley. Riley would be willing to cut them a little slack, but he wouldn't let them walk away from a breaking and entering charge—at least, not without a *really* good explanation.

Before Frank could say anything, Joe started talking. "I'm working for Scott Lavin, helping him get ready for the race," he said quickly. "I came back to finish up some work."

Riley glanced at the damaged engine lying on the floor. "Scott's really going to appreciate your dedication," he observed dryly. He looked around some more and said, "I don't see any signs of forced entry, but why don't we give Scott a call and check out your story?"

"Sure." Frank abruptly changed the subject. "Say, Con, do you know if the divers have recovered Angus McCoy's body yet?"

"Not yet, and they probably never will."

"Why? What do you mean?"

"They finally did find the car, but the body wasn't there. They think the currents must have carried it out to sea."

"I don't get it." Joe frowned. "He was strapped in with a double shoulder harness, a lap belt, and leg straps. How could the body go anywhere?"

Riley shrugged. "He was a race car driver and trained to react quickly in emergencies. Maybe he popped the belt releases, hoping he could survive the crash if he didn't go down with the car. Now I think you boys had better make that call to Lavin."

But before they could find a phone, Riley was interrupted by the squawk of his two-way radio. "All units in the vicinity of the twenty-four-hundred block of Grant Street," the radio blared, "proceed to two-four-oh-two. We have a report of a three-alarm fire. Repeat: fire at two-four-oh-two Grant Street."

"That address sounds familiar," Joe said.

"Twenty-four-oh-two Grant? That's Phil Cohen's house!" Frank shouted. "Phil's house is on fire!"

Chapter
6

"COME ON, LET'S GO!" Frank Hardy shouted, sprinting for the van. "We've got to get to Phil's right away!"

Joe and Con were just a split second slower in reacting to the radio report of the fire at Phil's house. Joe followed Riley to his squad car and grabbed the officer's arm before he slipped into the driver's seat. "Look, I know this isn't exactly normal police procedure—but do me a favor."

"Now what?" Riley asked impatiently.

Just then Frank backed the van out of the alley and yelled, "Joe, you coming or not?"

Joe nodded quickly, then turned back to Riley and said, "Phil's our friend, and Frank has his reasons for wanting to get there in a hurry. So how about giving us a police escort on the streets that are blocked off for the race?"

"What?" Riley responded in disbelief.

"Could you lead the way?"

Riley stared at him for a moment. "Okay. But just this once!"

Joe smiled and said, "Anything you say, *Officer* Riley." He dashed over to the van, but instead of going around to the passenger's side, he opened the driver's door and said, "Move over, brother, I'm driving."

Frank didn't have time to protest. Joe backed up his instruction with a firm shove, then scrambled into the driver's seat. The cruiser was pulling away from the curb, lights flashing and siren blaring. Joe slammed the van into gear and took off after it.

"What's the big idea?" Frank complained. "Don't like my driving?"

"No, no," Joe said. "I think you're a great defensive driver, but this calls for a little more *aggressive* driving. Like racing."

"And you've had so much racing experience since you got your regular license this year," Frank replied sarcastically. "In fact, now that I think about it, I've been driving twice as long as you have!"

"Yeah—but Scott told me about a few racing tricks today," Joe said as he edged the car over into the left lane, braking slightly at the same time. Then he shifted his right foot back to the gas pedal and started to speed up as he followed the police car into a right-hand turn. The maneuver cut the distance between the two vehicles in half.

"Do your braking *before* the turn," Joe explained as the van continued to pursue Riley's cruiser. "Enter the turn from the far side to reduce the angle and gradually accelerate through the curve—so that you're pretty much at full throttle when you come out of the turn."

"A nice trick—as long as nobody's coming at you in the left lane."

"Okay," Joe admitted. "So it's only practical when all the cars are going the same way—or when the street's blocked off to all traffic."

Joe swung the van all the way over to the far right side of the road. Ahead of them, Riley's police car skidded through a left turn, and the van followed close behind. But instead of skidding, Joe took a low angle into the curve, drifting slightly across the yellow median before nosing back into the right lane.

As they came out of the turn, the van was just about touching the rear bumper of the squad car. "What do you think you're doing now?" Frank burst out, his right foot instinctively reaching for a brake pedal that wasn't there.

"This is Grant Street," Joe said. "Home stretch!" Then he punched the gas pedal to the floor and swerved into the left lane just as Frank thought they would rear-end Riley's car. Even though the police car was still accelerating, the van was going even faster, and it shot out in front as Joe brought it back into the right lane.

"I didn't know this van had that much power," Frank said in wonder.

"It doesn't," Joe replied as the van slowed to enter Grant Street. "It's *air* power. The car in front acts as an air-breaker—cutting down wind resistance and leaving a vacuum for the car behind it. You can accelerate faster and build up enough momentum to push ahead. They call it slipstreaming. Neat, huh?" He brought the van to a halt behind a lime green fire engine.

Frank didn't respond. His attention was riveted on a small fire blazing away next to Phil's house. The house wasn't on fire—only one half of the garage. He jumped out of the van and ran over to the nearest fire fighter. "Was anyone hurt?" he asked.

"Doesn't look like it," the man said. "The neighbors said the folks that live here are on vacation, and it's only the garage, anyway."

Frank clutched the man's arm, almost pulling him off balance and shouting, "You mean nobody went inside to check?"

Joe was right behind Frank then. "What's the story?" Joe asked.

Frank whirled around to face his brother. "Phil's folks are out of town—but Phil didn't go with them. He might still be in his workshop, and that's in the garage!"

The two brothers glanced at each other. Without saying anything they both bolted toward the side door of the garage. Con Riley, who had joined them, realized what they were doing and grabbed a hose from a surprised fire fighter. He aimed the nozzle at the boys, soaking Joe and Frank with water before they crashed into the garage.

Through the smoke they could just make out Phil's limp form on the floor. They crawled to him so they remained down low where there was less smoke. But still the heavy black air seared their throats, making them cough uncontrollably. They were half-blind, their eyes stinging and clouding over with tears. Frank grabbed Phil's left arm and Joe took his right, and together they started to drag their unconscious friend toward the side door. The front doors were already a wall of flames.

But it was too late. A burning rafter crashed down just in front of them, sealing the exit. The intense heat and smoke made it hard to breathe and impossible to talk. Frank looked around desperately, knowing that if either he or Joe passed out now, all three of them would die.

They were surrounded by flames now. But Frank spotted a window where the fire was less intense. He ripped one of the wet sleeves off his shirt and wrapped it around the lower part of his face, covering his nose and mouth. He motioned to Joe to do the same, then pointed to the window.

Joe looked at the window. It was about three feet wide and four feet off the ground. He gave his brother the okay sign, got into a linebacker's crouch, held his breath, and ran straight for the window. He took a flying leap, shielded his head with his arms, and crashed through the glass. Just before he hit the ground outside he did a tuck and roll, landing on his feet on the grass.

The fire fighters were stunned by Joe's sudden appearance, but what he did next was even more stunning. He ran back to the burning garage, ripping the cloth off his face and tearing it in half. Joe wrapped the two pieces of cloth around his hands and smashed out the glass shards that jutted up and out from the shattered opening.

Frank couldn't see what was going on outside, but he knew that his brother had made it through the window. At lease *one* of us will come out of this alive, he grimly told himself, grabbing Phil under the arms and dragging him toward the window. Coughing and gasping for breath, Frank kicked and shoved burning debris out of the way as he made a narrow path through the flames.

It seemed as if it took forever to reach the window. By the time he finally made it there, Frank was too tired to push his unconscious friend through to safety. He hoped someone on the other side would help with the job.

Joe reached in to grab Phil's body. Frank smiled weakly and let his brother take the burden off his hands. Even though he felt as if he was about to pass out, Frank couldn't leave the inferno yet.

After Joe hauled Phil through the window, he carried him over to the waiting paramedics. Then he sprinted back to help his brother. But Frank wasn't there. Desperately, Joe tried to scramble back inside the burning garage. Con Riley ran over, grabbed Joe's arm, and yanked him away.

"Back off!" Joe yelled. "Frank's still in there!"

"There's nothing you can do now!" Riley insisted. "The fire's out of control!"

Joe stared numbly. "He was right here at the window. Then he was gone." Fatigue and smoke inhalation were starting to take their toll, but Joe fought back. "I can't leave him in there! Help me or get out of my way!" He pushed Riley aside so hard that Con fell down.

Joe gripped the broken frame with both hands. He put his right foot on the sill and was about to pull himself up and in when he heard a raspy voice croak, "Got an air conditioner on you, brother? It's *hot* in here."

With a final surge of energy, Joe Hardy hauled his brother Frank out just before the roof caved in.

They both lay on the grass, exhausted, ignoring the fire fighters scurrying back and forth in a vain attempt to put out the fire. After a few minutes, Frank sat up, wiped some of the soot off his face, and said, "What happened to Phil? Is he okay?"

At that, Joe jumped up and kicked his brother in the shin. "Ow!" Frank yelled. "What was that for?"

"You don't care about Phil," Joe shouted.

"What do you mean?"

"I mean you were more concerned about that electronic gizmo than you were about Phil."

"Now, wait a min—"

"No, *you* wait," Joe shouted. "You went back to get that thing, didn't you? Phil could have been dying for all you knew, and I could have gotten myself killed."

Frank looked closely at his brother. They were both tired and upset, but Frank struggled to remain levelheaded. "That 'thing,' as you put it, is the *only* thing that could have led us to the person who just tried to kill our friend."

He should have let it go at that, but Joe's accusation had pushed the wrong button, and Frank pushed back. The words seemed to take on a life of their own, and he heard himself saying, "Of course, you seem to be more concerned about helping the guy who might have done it."

Frank was sorry as soon as the words left his mouth, but he couldn't bring himself to apologize. He saw Joe clench his right hand into a fist, and he tried to remember the last time he had gotten into a fistfight with his brother.

Frank didn't want that. He knew he could easily deflect the blow, but he just stood there and waited for it to happen. Maybe he deserved a good punch. Maybe they would both feel better afterward. He didn't know anymore—he just wanted to lie down and go to sleep.

It took Joe a few seconds to realize what he was about to do. He stared down in disbelief at his own balled fist. Was he actually going to hit his brother? No. He commanded the tensed muscles in his arm to relax. Just let it go, he told himself. Just walk away.

Before Frank could say he was sorry, Joe had turned his back and disappeared into the night.

THE HARDY BOYS CASES

Chapter

7

JOE HARDY STOMPED OFF, angry and confused. His gut instinct told him that Scott Lavin was innocent, but he couldn't just dismiss his brother's suspicions.

First the fatal crash of McCoy's race car, then the "accident" at Scott's garage, and finally the fire at Phil Cohen's house. They all had to be connected somehow.

Joe realized that the electronic device Frank recovered from the crash wreckage had to be a link. Someone who knew that Frank had found the device could have followed him, waiting for the best chance to ambush him and steal it. He or she—whoever it was—knocked Frank out at Scott's garage.

When he didn't find the device on Frank's body, he backtracked to Phil's house. Then he jumped Phil and set the fire to cover his tracks. The fire was so intense that no one could ever be sure if the device had been stolen or destroyed in the blaze.

"Whoever it was," Joe grumbled, "had a very busy day."

Suddenly he froze in his tracks and smacked his forehead with the palm of his hand. "That's it!" he muttered to himself. "It *couldn't* be Scott. He might have a motive for wanting McCoy out of the race—but how could he have known Phil had the gizmo in the first place? Scott couldn't have tailed Frank because he was in his garage with *me* all afternoon."

Joe did an abrupt about-face and started to walk back toward Phil's house, hoping Frank would still be there. He picked up the pace as he turned the problem over in his mind, trying to look at all the angles.

Suddenly he stopped again. There was a small hole in his argument that got larger and larger the more he tried to ignore it—and he knew Frank would see it right away. Joe could just imagine the very short conversation they'd have.

Joe: Scott couldn't have known Phil had the device.

Frank: He could have had an accomplice.

Joe: My gut instinct tells me Scott didn't do it.

Frank: Then ask your gut instinct for a list of other suspects.

Joe shook his head. Sometimes his brother was just *too* logical and rational. Instinct and intuition weren't enough for Frank Hardy.

Joe started walking again. He would just have to come up with a better suspect, he told himself. "Okay, gut instinct," he muttered to himself, "tell me who did it."

There was no answer. Even though Joe sometimes acted without thinking, this was different. This wasn't action, it was just a different kind of thinking—sort of thinking without thinking.

He slammed his fist into a tree and winced with pain and frustration. "Intuition," he concluded out loud, "isn't helping me out right now."

Joe had been walking for some time, not thinking about where he was going. He plunged out into an intersection without even glancing at the traffic light. The blare of a car horn and the squeal of tires snapped him out of his fog, and he leapt back to the curb.

"Watch where you're going, idiot!" someone shouted from a passing car.

Joe looked around and realized he was less than a block from Callie Shaw's house. Callie was Frank's girlfriend and mostly a pain in Joe's neck. "I can't figure that girl out," he grumbled. "Sometimes she does the weirdest—"

Joe suddenly stopped without completing his

thought—because another one had just taken its place. Girls, he thought, are supposed to know a lot about stuff like intuition. Maybe Callie can help me out. He headed for her house.

It was late, but Joe was in luck. Callie was still up, working with her video equipment.

"Get lost on the way to an all-night launderette?" Callie quipped as she invited Joe in. "You look like you could use the heavy-duty machine."

Joe looked at himself in the hall mirror. He was a mess. His blond hair had turned brown with dirt and ashes. His face and clothes were grimed with soot, and one sleeve was missing from his shirt.

"And you smell like you've been barbecuing old tires," she said, sniffing.

"Nice to see you, too, Callie," Joe replied. "Making movies of yourself again?"

"Gee, it's fun to stand here and trade insults with you, Joe, but it's kind of late and I've got work to do. Maybe we could make a date to continue this later."

Joe paused a second and then said, "Look, I'm sorry. Let's start over, okay?"

Callie took a closer look at Joe. She could see that something was troubling him. "Okay, Joe," she said. "What can I do for you?"

Joe slumped down and sat on the floor to tell Callie about the events that followed Angus McCoy's fatal crash, concluding with, "I don't

58

have any *proof*—I just have a *feeling*. Know what I mean?"

"Well, this is a switch." Callie smiled. "Are you asking for my *advice*, Joe?"

Joe shrugged. "Yeah, I guess I am."

"Guys always make jokes about 'female intuition' and complain that women aren't rational. They don't understand that it's possible to see things from a different angle. Sometimes you have to pay more attention to emotions than physical actions." Callie looked up. "Are you with me so far?"

Joe nodded. "Yeah, I think so."

Callie chuckled. "Sometimes it's better *not* to think. Some things don't have logical explanations."

"Like my coming here tonight," Joe said.

"Well, yes," Callie admitted. "Look, let me put it another way. Scott Lavin is your friend, right?"

"Right."

"Then if he's guilty, you've got lousy instincts when it comes to picking friends. But I know most of your friends, and I think you have pretty good instincts.

"So, other than Scott Lavin," she prodded, "who has the most to gain—or lose—in this race?"

Joe ran a mental checklist and then said, "Russell Arno, the race promoter, and Reinhart Voss, the other driver for McCoy Racing. With McCoy out of the way, Voss would be the number-one driver for the team, and he would have a better shot at winning."

"What about Arno?" Callie asked.

"I can't give you a reason," Joe admitted. "I don't know that much about him—or even what a promoter does. I just don't trust the guy."

"Okay," Callie said. "Now, which one does your instinct tell you is the more likely suspect?"

Joe didn't even have to think about it. The answer just popped out. "Arno," he said. "I think he's hiding something."

Callie stood up. "Then let's go check him out," she replied, grabbing her purse and heading for the door.

"Wait a minute!" Joe burst out. "Where do you think you're going? I don't need a girl tagging along."

"Okay." Callie smiled. "I'll go by myself— and I have a car. How were *you* planning to get to his office?"

Joe grinned weakly. "I don't suppose you'd consider giving me a lift?"

"There's not enough room in my car for your macho self-image," Callie chided him. "You'll have to leave it here and pick it up later."

When they got to the Bayport Fairgrounds it was late.

"What'll we do if Arno's not in his office?" Callie asked.

"We'll cross that bridge when we come to it," Joe whispered as they reached the mobile trailer that served as Arno's traveling office.

He walked up the steps and tapped lightly on the door. It was unlocked and creaked open slightly as Joe knocked. He pushed the door open all the way and stuck his head inside. The lights were on, but no one was in sight. "Hello?" he called. "Anybody here?"

Joe cautiously stepped inside. Somebody else had been through the place recently, and he doubted that it was Arno. Papers and file folders were scattered on the floor, along with several drawers that had been yanked out of the desk. Joe whistled softly. "This guy is one lousy housekeeper."

Callie brushed past Joe and started to pick things up and examine them. "We'll call Dial-A-Maid when we're through," she joked, picking up a heap of folders and leafing through them. "We don't even know what we're looking for," she said. "Tell you what, Joe—you look through the files while I watch TV."

Joe noticed a color television in the corner, with a videocassette recorder stacked on top of it. "That VCR looks unusual," he observed.

"Yeah," Callie replied as her hands skimmed over the control panel. "It's a professional model."

Joe sat down in Arno's chair. "Well, I guess that's part of what a promoter does," he said.

"He makes a lot of flashy, full-color videos of fast cars and—"

Joe stopped in midsentence, his eyes riveted to the name typed on the front of one of the file folders on the desk. "Bingo!" he called out. "This one has McCoy's name on it."

Joe opened the folder and shuffled through the papers inside. He kept up a running commentary. "Press releases, pictures of McCoy and his car, a couple of contracts, some canceled checks. It looks like Arno was paying McCoy to appear at races."

Joe turned over one of the checks and looked at the back. Then he flipped over several more. "Mmm—this is strange. McCoy endorsed all of these checks to some outfit called Clarco Industries. But I don't see anything here worth killing him for. . . ."

Joe's voice trailed off as he pulled out one of the documents. The silence drew Callie's attention, and she turned to look at Joe. He wasn't sitting anymore; his feet were planted firmly on the ground, and he was leaning over the desk, reading intently.

"What is it?" Callie asked.

Joe didn't reply. He just kept on reading.

"Come on, Joe," Callie urged. "What *is* it?"

"An insurance policy," he said at last, looking up with a triumphant smile. "A *life* insurance policy for a million bucks."

"So Arno has some life insurance. So what?"

"Arno has some life insurance," Joe repeated. "But not on his own life. This policy pays off on *McCoy's* death!"

Joe jumped up and waved the piece of paper in Callie's face. "Do you know what this means?" he asked excitedly.

Callie didn't say anything. She was staring at something over Joe's shoulder—something in the doorway, Joe realized.

"It means you're in the wrong place at the wrong time," a cold, smooth voice answered.

Chapter

8

JOE HARDY KNEW the voice that had just threatened him, and he didn't like it any more now than he had the first time he heard it. Well, Joe thought, I came here looking for Russell Arno, and now I've found him.

Joe was in a tight spot. He had his back to Arno, and Arno was blocking his only exit. Joe thought about spinning around and trying to take Arno by surprise. That might buy enough time for Callie to get away. But the man could be armed. Joe gritted his teeth and decided to go for it anyway.

I got Callie into this, Joe told himself. It's up to me to get her out.

Callie was looking right at Arno, and she spoke before Joe could act. "Oh, Mr. Arno! Thank heaven you're here!" she exclaimed, clasping her

64

hands together as if she was about to start praying. She was doing her best imitation of a little lost girl. It was almost good enough for an Academy Award, and Joe hoped it was good enough to fool Arno.

"We were just passing by," Callie continued, "when we saw your door was open. We came in to make sure everything was all right. We were afraid something might have happened to you."

Joe was impressed. Callie might just pull this one off. He felt a slight tug on the piece of paper he was still holding in his hand. He looked down and realized that Callie was trying to pry it loose and quietly stuff it in her purse.

Joe shielded her with his body, hiding Callie's actions from Arno's view. He turned to face the promoter as Callie closed her purse with the insurance policy tucked inside.

"So you were taking a little stroll around the fairgrounds at—" Arno paused to glance at his watch. "Not a very convincing story. What do you think, Mr. Hardy?"

"What are *you* doing here this late?" Joe countered.

"That's none of your business," Arno snapped. "But I have nothing to hide. I was in my room at the motel when someone tripped the silent alarm in the office."

"Wait a minute," Joe said. "How did you know the alarm went off?"

"Mobile phone," Arno said simply. "The

alarm here sends a signal to my personal phone. I take it everywhere—a clever device, don't you think?''

"Wouldn't it make more sense to hook up the alarm to notify the police?" Callie asked.

"It might," Arno admitted. "But I'm on the move a lot, traveling from city to city, following the racing circuit. I'd have to make special arrangements with the police in each city. It's easier this way."

"So why didn't you call the police?" Joe persisted.

Arno shrugged. "The motel is closer to here than the police station. I didn't want the burglar—excuse me, *burglars*—to get away before the police arrived."

Joe reached across the promoter's desk and grabbed the telephone. "Look, Mr. Arno, we're telling you the truth. The place was like this when we got here. But if you don't believe us, let's phone the police right now." He was bluffing, and he was betting Arno wouldn't call.

Who would believe that the two of them had just sort of stumbled onto the scene? Joe had already talked his way out of one tight spot that night. If Arno called his bluff—and the cops—things could get very ugly.

Arno moved around the desk and sat down in his chair. His hand rested on the telephone for a moment as he sized up Joe and Callie. Joe's gaze was steady as he returned the man's stare. Go ahead, Joe's eyes dared, make your move.

Finally Arno let go of the phone and moved his hand to his inside coat pocket. "No," he said, "I don't think that will be necessary. But the question is, now that I have you, what do I do with you?"

Now who's bluffing, Joe wondered. Does he have a gun? Joe's whole body went tense, ready to leap across the desk and crash into the promoter at the first glimpse of a concealed weapon.

"I guess you could just shoot us." Joe smiled, raising the stakes. "But that would be too messy, wouldn't it? Too many loose ends. Too many questions."

"What are you talking about?" Arno replied, pulling a pack of cigarettes out of his pocket. "I don't suppose either of you has a light? No, you wouldn't. Nobody does anymore. This is the only place I can smoke without being nagged." He gave them a foul look.

"But we weren't talking about my bad habits, were we? We were talking about murder, I believe. And you were just about to tell me why I would want to shoot you."

"You probably wouldn't," Joe said. "Shooting isn't your style. Accidents are more convenient, aren't they?"

"Ah, that's it," Arno said, laughing. "You and your girlfriend are slinking around playing junior detective. You think Angus McCoy was the victim of foul play, and I'm the closest thing you have to a suspect. You came here looking for evidence and tore the place apart when you couldn't find anything."

"I told you we didn't ransack your office," Joe snapped. "And I think I have a pretty good idea why you would like to see McCoy dead." Joe was tightly gripping the edge of the desk with both hands. He leaned over to look directly into Arno's face—and accidentally pushed one of the file folders onto the floor.

It landed with a soft plop, and Joe glanced down at the noise. Nice move, Joe, he said to himself. Brilliant timing.

The label on the file read: "McCoy, Angus."

A hand reached down and picked up the folder. "Find any worthwhile reading in here?" Arno asked, opening the file and sorting through the contents.

"We weren't looking for anything," Callie insisted. "We were just—"

"I know, I know," Arno interrupted. "You were just passing by." He took a key ring out of his coat pocket and unlocked the top desk drawer. He casually pulled out a gun and leveled it at Callie. "And I'm sure you're both quite anxious to leave. But would you mind if I search you before you go? Something seems to be missing, and I don't like it when people walk off with my property."

Joe mentally kicked himself. He had let Arno's slick routine lull him into letting down his guard.

Callie opened her purse slowly. "There's no need for that, Mr. Arno," she said, removing the crumpled insurance policy. "I think this is what you're looking for."

The promoter reached for the document with his free hand, but Callie let go of the paper just before he grasped it, and it fluttered to the floor. Arno stooped down to pick it up, and his aim wavered slightly.

Joe moved like lightning. Still clutching the edge of the desk, he heaved it up and over on top of Arno. Then he slammed all his weight into it, pinning the man down.

"Oof!" the promoter grunted as the weapon flew out of his hand and skittered across the floor.

"Grab the gun!" Joe shouted to Callie.

"Ugh," Callie replied, carefully lifting the automatic pistol. "I hate these things."

She looked at Joe. "Now what?"

"I'll hold him while you call the police," Joe said.

"Great idea," Callie said. "Where's the phone?"

"Down here," a muffled voice came from underneath the overturned desk. "I'd make the call myself if the thing were still working. I guess it wasn't designed to have large pieces of furniture dropped on it. Come to think of it," Arno groaned, "neither was I. How about letting me out from under here? I think we can clear up this whole misunderstanding.''

''Only after you hand me that insurance policy,'' Joe demanded.

Arno stuck out his hand and waved the document like a white flag of surrender. Joe snatched it away and handed it to Callie. He dragged the desk off Arno and said, ''Okay, you can get up now—but *slowly*.''

Arno grabbed on to a leg of the toppled desk and hauled himself up. ''That insurance policy doesn't prove anything,'' he said. ''It's common business practice. McCoy was my star attraction. The deals I make with cities like Bayport guarantee that McCoy will be there for the race. Without McCoy, I could lose a lot of money.''

''So why'd you pull a gun on us?'' Joe asked roughly.

''Look, kid,'' the promoter snapped. ''I'm getting tired of your questions. You say you didn't break in here. You say you were just passing by and found my office this way. I'll take your word for it—but don't press your luck.''

He glared at them. ''Now get out of here before I change my mind—and leave the policy and the gun here. It would be real unfortunate if the police found you with a stolen firearm.''

Joe took the document and the pistol from Callie. He deftly removed the clip and cleared the chamber, ejecting the bullet that had been loaded and ready to fire. "You go ahead, Callie," he said. "I'll be out in a minute."

He handed the piece of paper to Arno and tossed the unloaded weapon into the farthest corner of the office. "You be real careful where you aim that thing," Joe said as he stormed out the door. "Next time I might just make you *eat* it."

"I still don't trust him," Joe muttered to Callie as they walked away. "But I don't have any evidence!"

"You ever wonder why girls always lug around big, heavy purses wherever they go?" Callie asked.

"Huh?" Joe frowned. "What's that got to do with—"

"It's just in case they come across some evidence," Callie grinned, reaching into her handbag and pulling out a videocassette. "While you were reading files, I was reading tape labels. Check this one out."

Joe squinted in the dark trying to read the handwritten scrawl on the side of the plastic case. He stopped under a streetlight and held up the cassette to catch the light. " 'Master tape,' " he read aloud. " 'Angus McCoy Bayport Grand Prix Time Trial.' "

"Maybe this is what whoever broke into Arno's office was looking for," Joe mused. "But why didn't they take it?"

"Because they couldn't find it," Callie answered. "It wasn't on the shelves with the other tapes. It was in the VCR."

Joe just stared at Callie. "I can't believe it," he said. "Frank and I have both been so busy trying to unearth clues that we forgot Arno had the whole thing on videotape!"

Chapter

9

IT WAS ALMOST noon the next day before Joe Hardy stumbled out of bed and staggered downstairs, looking for his brother. Joe hadn't meant to oversleep, but it had been a long night.

Frank wasn't anywhere in sight. Only his aunt Gertrude was home, puttering in the garden.

"Is Frank around?" Joe asked. "There's something I want to show him."

"You just missed him," Gertrude said, looking up from her tomato plants. "Callie picked him up a while ago, and they drove over to the hospital to see that nice Cohen boy. Poor thing. Did you hear what happened to him last night?"

"Yeah, I kind of heard something about it," Joe said evasively. If his aunt ever found out that Frank and he had almost gotten killed saving Phil

Cohen from the fire, she'd have a heart attack on the spot.

"I think I'll go over to the hospital, too," Joe told his aunt. He dug in his hip pocket, fished out the keys to the van, and loped across the lawn to the driveway.

"Oh, that reminds me," Gertrude called after him. "Your brother told me to tell you to take the van and meet him at the hospital."

Joe turned and smiled at her. "Say, Aunt Gertrude, you know what I think I'll do?"

"What?"

"I think I'll take the van and meet Frank at the hospital."

"You do that," she said, nodding as she plucked a ripe tomato and dropped it into her basket.

Joe drove to the hospital by the fastest route. He wanted to make sure Phil was okay—and he was anxious to talk with his brother.

When Joe got there, he found Phil sitting up in bed, talking with Frank and Callie.

"Come on in, Joe," Phil greeted him. "Your brother tells me you saved my life. I guess I owe you one."

"I had a little help," Joe replied, looking right at Frank.

"Hey, what are brothers for?" Frank said.

"Look, Frank," Joe started, "I'm sorry—"

"No, *I'm* sorry," Frank interrupted. "We both said some things we really didn't mean, but at least you had a reason. Scott's your friend, and maybe I should have checked out all the other leads before pointing my finger at him.

"Well, I'm beginning to have my doubts, too," Joe admitted. "I haven't exactly done a tremendous job of digging up evidence that will stick to any other suspects. I thought I had something on Arno, but that guy's got an answer for everything."

"We were lucky he didn't have us arrested for assault," Callie added.

Phil coughed and said, "That reminds me. It took me a long time to go over that electronic device that seems to be so popular with the assault and arson set."

"Did you find out anything?" Frank asked.

"Hard to say for sure. The circuitry was too complex for a simple remote triggering device. So if you were thinking it was some kind of detonator for a small explosive or something, you'll have to think again."

Phil shrugged. "I could probably tell you more if I had whatever it was connected to."

"Then I guess that's what we'll have to find," Joe said. "I wanted to do a little swimming before the end of the season, anyway. How about you?" he added, nudging his brother. "Last one in is a rotten diver."

"Wait a second," Callie protested. "Before you both go leap into the bay and get sucked out to sea by the tides, how about watching a fascinating documentary over at my house?"

Joe slapped his forehead, realizing he had forgotten to tell his brother about the videocassette. That was what he wanted to talk to Frank about in the first place.

"That's okay," Frank said before Joe could open his mouth. "Callie told me all about your little adventure last night. I just can't let the two of you go *anywhere* without me, can I?"

Frank Hardy clapped his brother on the back and laughed. Then his tone shifted. "From now on," he spoke seriously, "we stick together wherever the trail leads. Agreed?"

"We both get in too much trouble alone." Joe chuckled and grasped his brother's outstretched right hand. "Agreed."

Joe and Frank decided to take a detour past the Bayport Fairgrounds, so they told Callie they'd meet her at her house.

"Why don't we check out Reinhart Voss," Joe suggested. "With McCoy gone, he'll get the whole team effort for the race. I don't think that's enough to make him kill the guy, but it's a start."

"Maybe he was tired of racing in McCoy's shadow," Frank ventured as he pulled the van into a parking space near the Bayport Motel, the closest spot they could park to the fairgrounds.

"Yeah," Joe said, opening the van door and jumping out. "And maybe he trashed Scott's engine to have an even better shot at winning the race.''

They walked to the fairgrounds. Fuel and exhaust fumes drifted through the air. The entire grounds had been transformed into a giant outdoor garage, bustling with activity.

They passed one of the sheds where a Formula One engine was being revved up. The noise was deafening. ''I guess mufflers are optional on these things!'' Frank yelled.

They found Voss with his head mechanic, making some last-minute adjustments to his car for his final time-trial run.

''Is it not a beautiful thing?'' The German driver smiled broadly, gesturing with both hands to indicate his 900-horsepower pride and joy. ''You are just in time to watch me get the pole position with the fastest qualifying time!''

Joe stooped down and ran his hand over the smooth, sleek surface of the car. It was contoured to cut through the wind like a knife. ''With McCoy gone and Scott Lavin's engine damaged,'' he began casually, ''I guess you're feeling pretty confident.''

Voss's smile quickly faded. ''I learned much from Angus,'' he said quietly. ''I will miss him— and I will also miss the chance to beat him. It is good to win, but better to win against the best.''

''Do you really think you could have beaten him?'' Frank asked.

''He was getting old,'' Voss replied bluntly.

"Maybe I would not have beaten him here. But next year I drive for Ferrari."

"You're leaving McCoy Racing?" Joe cut in.

"Yes," Voss said. "As long as I stayed with Angus I would have been number two, always getting the second-best equipment. So when Ferrari offered me their number-one slot, I jumped. This is my last race for McCoy. Maybe I can leave the team with a small victory. It should not be too hard."

Frank gave him a puzzled look. "What do you mean?"

"This is an exhibition race," Voss explained. "Most teams are here just to test out new equipment. Some of the top drivers are not even here. This is the kind of race that gives the younger drivers a chance."

"Like Scott Lavin?" Frank suggested.

"Why, yes," Voss agreed. "A win here would look very good for Scott."

The Hardys looked at each other as the German driver climbed into the cockpit of his car and put on his crash helmet. Joe knew what Frank was thinking.

The powerful engine roared to life, and Frank put his fingers in his ears. Joe leaned into the cockpit and tapped the top of the driver's helmet. Voss flipped up the visor and cocked his head in Joe's direction. Joe cupped his hands around his mouth and shouted, "But Scott's out of the race, right? His engine's no good!"

In response, Voss shrugged his shoulders in the confined space and jerked his right thumb over his shoulder, pointing behind him. Then he punched the accelerator, the tires screamed and smoked in protest, and the race car swerved out onto the roadway and took off down the course.

Joe and Frank both turned in the direction Voss had pointed and saw the familiar yellow-and-red Formula One barreling down the course, heading straight at them.

The Hardys jumped back as Scott Lavin's car screeched to a halt right next to them. Scott was laughing as he took off his helmet. He shut down the engine and squirmed out of the cockpit, handing the crash helmet to Joe as he climbed over the side of the car.

"We're back in the race, Joe!" Scott exclaimed. "When I got the police call and came down to the garage last night, I thought it was all over. But we worked all night and half the morning to fix the engine."

Joe was staring at the ground, his hands stuffed in his hip pockets, waiting for the bomb to drop. The police report would have put Frank and Joe at the scene, and Scott was bound to want some answers. Joe swallowed hard. "About last night," he began.

"If it weren't for you guys," Scott interrupted, "we never could have pulled it off."

"Huh?" Joe mumbled. Frank kicked him, signaling him to shut up.

"I don't know how you did it, but a cop named Riley said you guys reported the break-in and chased off whoever did it before he could do any real damage.

"Anyway," Scott continued, starting to climb back into the race car, "I just wanted to say thanks." He paused with one leg in the cockpit and the other on the ground. Then he looked at Joe and said, "Say, since you're already holding the helmet, why don't you put it on and drive this baby back to the shed?"

Joe's mouth dropped open. He could barely believe what he was hearing. Ever since he could remember, he had loved cars. He was the first person in line to get his driver's license. It seemed he had waited half his life for it. Now he was actually getting a chance to drive the ultimate racing machine.

But as badly as Joe wanted to get behind the wheel, he remembered his promise to his brother. They had agreed to stick together, and Joe wasn't about to let a car come between Frank and him. "Thanks, anyway, Scott," Joe said, shaking his head. "But I don't think so. We've got stuff to do."

Frank knew that it took a lot of willpower for Joe to decline Scott's offer, and he was proud of him. "Oh, go ahead," he urged his brother. "I'll meet you back at the van. I want to see if I can find that writer, T. B. Martin, and ask him a few more questions."

Joe didn't need any more encouragement. He put one hand on the roll bar and the other on the wind screen, stepped into the cockpit, and slid down into the seat. Scott reached in and grabbed the metal catch-plate attached to the "antisubmarine" straps—the straps that come up between the driver's legs. Then he helped Joe buckle in the two shoulder harnesses and both ends of the lap belt. The catch-plate connected all the straps together, like a six-pointed star, right over Joe's navel.

Joe shifted his weight around to get comfortable in the half-sitting, half-lying position and stared at the dizzying array of controls. "How come all these gauges are tilted?" he asked.

"We rotate them," Scott pointed out, "so the needles point straight up at optimum levels."

"Okay." Joe nodded, scanning the dials. "I think I've got it." But something was missing. "Hey," he said, frowning, "Where's the speedometer?"

Scott laughed. "The only speed we worry about is the other guy's. If he's going faster than you are, then you aren't going fast enough. But today let's take it nice and slow," Scott cautioned. "These monsters aren't exactly designed for idling. If you let your RPMs drop too low, she'll stall. So you'll have to kind of roll your right foot between the brake and the accelerator, braking and revving the engine at the same time. Got it?"

"Uh-huh." Joe nodded eagerly. "Here goes nothing."

Joe pushed in the clutch with his left foot, gripped the stick shift with his right hand, and shoved it into the first-gear position. With his right foot on the gas pedal, he watched the tachometer needle jump as he revved the engine. Then he eased his left foot off the clutch, and the car lurched into gear.

Frank saw his brother give him a thumbs-up as he steered the race car onto the road. Scott Lavin turned to him and said, "He's pretty good. Most guys stall out the first time they get behind the wheel."

"Joe's a fast learner," Frank replied. He started to walk away but turned back when he heard a shout rise up from the small cluster of spectators. Looking around to see what had caused the commotion, Frank saw a few people standing up, pointing down the road.

A black cloud began to billow over the race course. The trail of acrid smoke led down to a burning vehicle, and Frank could see that it was the same color as the flames that engulfed it— yellow and red.

Horror crept up on Frank as he realized slowly it was Scott's car and Joe was still in it!

Chapter

10

JOE HARDY HAD just been starting to get the feel of the race car when he heard a muffled explosion over the loud thrum of the engine behind him. His eyes darted from one side mirror to the other, and both showed him the same thing—billowing smoke and flame.

Joe didn't panic. He slammed on the brakes, reached down with his right hand, and hit the fire extinguisher release switch. Within seconds, he knew, the cockpit would be sprayed with a layer of fire-retardant chemicals, giving him time to get out safely.

But nothing happened.

He hit the switch again. Still nothing. "Great," he muttered. "No protective clothes, no fire extinguisher—and no time! I've got to get out now or I'll end up the main course at a surprise cookout!''

Joe slapped the release button on the restraint straps, threw the shoulder harness back over his head, and grabbed the lip of the cockpit to haul himself out. "Yarrghh!" he screamed in pain, wrenching his hands away from the searing hot metal.

He was trapped! He was wedged so tightly in the tiny space that he couldn't move without using his hands and arms for leverage. "No pain, no gain." He grimaced, psyching himself up to take hold of the burning metal and pull himself free.

Joe reached out with both hands—and felt a cool mist pour down on him.

Frank sprinted into the nearest shed and grabbed a fire extinguisher off the wall. Then he rushed back out and starting running toward the burning car. He caught up with Scott Lavin, who was headed in the same direction.

"He'll be all right," Scott huffed, trying to keep up with Frank's desperate pace. "There's an on-board fire extinguisher."

"I'm not taking any chances!" Frank yelled. A small knot of onlookers blocked his way. He shoved his way through the crowd, swinging the fire extinguisher to clear a path. "Out of the way!" he bellowed. "Coming through!"

Frank emptied the fire extinguisher into the

cockpit of the burning machine and tossed the canister aside. He grabbed Joe's arms, yanking him out with one tremendous heave. The two brothers tumbled away from the blaze.

The small crowd that had gathered at the scene quickly scattered as an ambulance and a fire engine rolled up. The fire fighters jumped off the truck, and within seconds the blaze was out, leaving nothing but a cloud of smoke and steam—and a smouldering heap where a high-performance race car had been a moment before.

Frank helped Joe to his feet, then looked at the burned-out hulk that had been Scott Lavin's first and only Formula One car. He glimpsed Scott standing off to one side, staring in wide-eyed disbelief, his dream disappearing in a cloud of smoke.

Joe turned his gaze to his brother. "We've got to find out who's behind this before anybody else gets killed," he said grimly.

Frank and Joe showed up at Callie Shaw's house about two hours late. "You guys always seem to think that the shortest distance between two points involves two or three stops in between," she commented after hearing the story. "Does this mean you've whittled your list of suspects down to none?"

"Well, you have to admit," Joe said, "that Scott Lavin would have to be pretty desperate to blow up his own race car."

"We need more facts," Frank replied. "Maybe the videotape of McCoy's crash will tell us something."

"I still don't see why we couldn't watch it on our own VCR at home," Joe protested as they followed Callie through the house.

"I told you," Callie said. "Mine is a *professional* video cassette like Arno's. It uses wider tape than home models. The cassette wouldn't even fit in the slot on your machine." She led the way down the basement stairs.

"My folks let me use the den down here for my video equipment," Callie said. "I've got a professional-format VCR hooked up to the wide-screen TV." She took the videocassette over to a large, black box with an imposing set of knobs and dials on the front and a maze of wires snaking out the back. She pushed the cassette through a slot in the machine. "It's show time!" she announced.

Frank pulled over some folding directors' chairs, and they all sat down to watch. "Just fast forward to the part where McCoy goes through the tunnel," Frank said.

Callie pressed a button and the action flew across the screen at a breakneck speed. Joe remembered how, looking down on the scene from the air, McCoy's car hadn't seemed to be moving very fast. Now it was comical the way it whizzed down the course and darted around the turns. "Is that some kind of digital clock?" he asked, pointing to a row of changing numbers at the bottom of the screen.

"Yes," Callie said. "Video master tapes have a time code for editing purposes. It keeps precise track of the time down to hundredths of seconds."

"Here it comes," Frank cut in, staring intently as the race car entered the dark mouth of the tunnel. "Slow it down now."

Callie pressed another button, and the tape slowed to normal speed. The digital clock slowed down, too. The Hardys watched as the car disappeared inside and the helicopter swung out over the ocean to record the scene from the exit point of the tunnel.

"Hold it right there!" Frank commanded. "Now play it in slow motion." They could see the low-slung profile of the race car as it gradually emerged from the tunnel. "It's hard to tell from this angle," Frank noted, "but it looks like he's weaving a little."

"Like he lost control *before* he hit the turn," Joe said. "And it seems like he's awfully low in the cockpit. You can barely see the top of his helmet."

"Like he was unconscious and slumped over?" Frank suggested.

The videotape kept rolling in slow motion, and they watched the race car push out the guardrail as if it were sliding through a wall of butter. "I wish we had a better camera angle," Frank muttered.

The car rolled slightly to one side as it fell toward the water. "Now you can't see him at all!" he complained.

"Great shot of the axles, though," Joe said, trying to joke.

As gruesome as it was, they replayed the scene several times, looking for anything they might have missed. "Okay, Callie," Frank finally said. "You can shut it off. This isn't going to tell us enough."

"Looks like it's time to go diving," Joe said.

"Looks that way," Frank agreed.

They left the videocassette with Callie and headed home to pick up some equipment. "The scuba gear's loaded in back," Joe said as he climbed into the van's passenger seat.

"Good," Frank replied. He was already behind the wheel, and the engine was running. "Then let's get going." He backed the van out of the driveway and headed down the street.

When they got to the end of the block, Frank turned left. "Hey, this isn't the way to the marina!" Joe protested. "Aren't we going to take the boat?"

Frank smiled. "I thought we'd take the scenic route."

Joe glanced at Frank and knew he wasn't going to get any more information out of him. So Joe bided his time reading the street signs and trying to second-guess his older brother.

After a few minutes Joe said, "Frank, I think you just made a wrong turn. This road leads to—"

"I know," Frank nodded. "You want to take a look at McCoy's car, and I want to take another look at the crash site." He turned the wheel sharply and the van swerved onto an old dirt road.

They bumped along the twin ruts for a couple miles, until they came in sight of Barmet Bay. "I'd forgotten about this old access road," Joe said as he opened the back door of the van and started to take out the scuba gear.

"Good thing I didn't," Frank said, hoisting a coil of thick rope. "With the highway blocked off for the race, we would have had a long walk."

Frank crouched down to look at something. "What is it?" Joe asked.

"It looks like someone else has been here recently," Frank replied, running his hand along the ground. "Footprints."

Joe shrugged. "Probably somebody came up for the view. Come on. Let's get moving."

The two brothers clambered down a steep incline to the paved road that skirted the cliff. They then followed the road around the hairpin turn. Joe stopped by a pair of wooden barriers with flashing emergency lights bolted to them. They were blocking the ragged gash in the guardrail where McCoy had crashed.

Frank kept walking all the way to the tunnel, scanning the roadway as he went. "Just as I thought!" he shouted. "There aren't any skid marks!" He trotted back to where Joe was standing. "Do you know what that means?"

"Yeah," Joe nodded. "Either he didn't even hit the brakes or nothing happened when he did. He just plowed over the edge without slowing down."

"And that means it definitely wasn't an accident," Frank added, moving around the saw-horses.

"You'd think someone like Arno or the police would have noticed that," Joe said.

Frank shrugged. "They had already decided it *was* an accident. They weren't really looking for anything else."

He motioned to Joe. "It looks like we can climb down most of the way without using the rope."

"Then what?" Joe asked.

"Then you put on the scuba gear and I lower you down into the water."

"Why don't I lower *you* down?" Joe suggested hopefully, slinging the bulky air tank over his shoulder. He didn't care much for the idea of rappeling down the cliff in a wet suit with that thing on his back and flippers on his feet.

"Because that's not part of my plan," Frank insisted. "If you don't like it, you can think up the plan next time."

They worked their way down to a rather large

90

ledge with a single scraggly tree that grew up against the cliff. Frank lashed the rope to the tree trunk to support Joe's weight while Joe put on the scuba gear. He double-checked the pressure in the tank, ran his hand over the air hose, and tested the regulator by breathing through it to make sure he was getting air from the tank.

"Okay, I'm ready," Joe announced when he was sure everything was in working order.

Frank tied the other end of the rope around Joe's chest, under his armpits. Then Frank took a firm stance with his legs wide apart and his knees slightly bent. Standing with his back to the tree, he wound the rope once around each of his arms and gripped the line tightly.

"I'll do most of the work," he explained. "I'll let out the rope slowly. The tree will be a backup to hold you. You just keep yourself away from the cliff wall."

Joe gave a tug on the line and then leaned backward over the edge. "Everybody into the pool!" he yelled, and pushed off with both feet.

It worked perfectly. Joe relaxed a little as he inched downward. When he was close to the water line, he gave a firm shove with both feet, pushing himself out to clear a jumble of rocks at the bottom of the cliff. But suddenly the line went slack, and he splashed into the cold Atlantic, gasping and spluttering for air.

The force of the fall had ripped the regulator from his mouth. A few swift kicks brought him back to the surface. "Nice going, ace!" he shouted up at his brother.

There was no response. From this angle, Joe couldn't see the tree, the ledge, or Frank. He ducked underwater for a moment to wriggle out of the rope.

Joe popped back up again and yanked off his face mask. He looked up again. He thought he caught a glimmer of movement, but he couldn't be sure. He was just about to shout again when he saw something hurtling over the side of the ledge.

It was Frank—his arms and legs flailing—plummeting toward the rocks!

Chapter

11

FRANK HIT the water hard, barely missing the rocks jutting out from the foot of the cliff. Stunned by the impact, he sank deeper and deeper beneath the waves into an engulfing darkness.

At last, the cold, salty wetness woke him. At first he didn't know where he was or how he got there. I was standing on the edge of the cliff, he recalled. Then I was in the air, and now I'm underwater—with my hands tied behind my back!

He thrashed around and discovered that his hands weren't really tied. He was just tangled up in the climbing rope. Frank unwound the rope and let it drift away from him. Then he kicked his way upward. His head broke the surface, and he greedily gulped in fresh air.

Frank started to tread water and looked around

to get his bearings. Suddenly someone loomed out of the water right in front of him, startling him.

"Take it easy! It's only me," Joe exclaimed, pushing the diving mask up over his forehead. "Are you okay? That looked like a vicious fall."

"Yeah," Frank said, wiping the hair out of his eyes. "If this were the Olympics, it would have been a perfect 0.0 dive."

"What happened?" Joe asked. "Did the rope break?"

"It had to have been cut back by the tree," Frank stated flatly.

"What?"

"I did a nosedive into the dirt on the ledge," Frank said. "I thought the tree must have snapped or something."

"So what changed your mind?"

"Well, there I was, starting to get back up and feeling pretty proud of myself for keeping hold of the rope—when somebody sneaked up behind me and gave me a nice, hard shove over the edge."

"Well, whoever it was is gone now," Joe remarked, squinting up the face of the cliff.

"I think we can get back up by climbing that rockfall," Frank said, pointing to a spot where the cliff had collapsed and a jumble of boulders sloped into the ocean. "I'll swim over and check it out."

He started swimming but looked back over his

shoulder. "You might as well dive down to the wreck and see if you can find anything."

"You read my mind, brother." Joe smiled, slipping the diving mask back down over his eyes and nose. He glanced at his diving watch and said, "See you in thirty." Then he slipped under the waves and was gone.

It was a short, easy swim to the rock fall. Frank was just pulling himself out of the water, thinking about how nice it would be to let his clothes dry off in the sun, when he heard the faint whine of an outboard motor. He turned to see a boat approaching from the direction of the Bayport Marina. Tracing a line from its wake, Frank could see that it was headed straight for the floating marker, bobbing up and down in the swells, that the police divers had attached to McCoy's sunken race car.

Frank lay flat on his stomach and crawled around a large boulder. Whoever it was, Frank wasn't ready to announce his own presence. He hoped his brother was alert enough to notice the oncoming motorboat—and patient enough to stay out of sight and wait for the intruder to make a move.

Joe sighted the wreckage lying upside down on the ocean floor, the wheels turning slowly in the deep currents. Like it doesn't know it's not going anywhere, Joe reflected as he closed in on the object, his legs pumping up and down, beating a steady rhythm through the water.

He enjoyed the silent solitude of the sea. It gave him a chance to let his mind wander. So he was annoyed when he heard the muffled churning of a propeller disturbing the water nearby. He stopped kicking and hovered a few feet above the bottom. Looking up, he could see the sunlight reflecting on the surface and the hull of a boat cutting a wake through the water.

The boat stopped directly above the wreck site, and Joe watched as an anchor sank rapidly, trailing air bubbles as it fell. Instinctively, Joe held his breath so that he wouldn't leave a telltale path of air bubbles. He looked around, veered away from his original course, and glided down behind an outcropping of rock.

A school of fish feeding on the surrounding plants stirred up the water, allowing Joe to breathe again without being detected. Then he waited, knowing what would come next.

Sure enough, after a few minutes, something else splashed through the surface and descended toward the overturned race car. It was a diver. It could even be somebody I know, Joe thought. But with the wet suit and diving mask, I can't see his face or even the color of his hair!

Joe let the current gently push him to the other side of the outcropping so he could get a better look at the diver. He was moving slowly along the under side of the vehicle, brushing his hands over all the mechanical parts. Like he's looking for something he dropped, Joe thought. Or something he doesn't want anybody else to find.

The diver finished his inspection of the exposed drive shaft and axles. But Joe didn't see him remove anything. Then the man—or woman—ducked under the wreck and wriggled, head first, into the cockpit. The ocean carried the sound of metal banging on metal back to Joe's ears, and the diver soon reemerged. Now Joe could clearly see that he was holding something in his left hand.

With his right hand, the mystery diver sheathed the knife he used to pry the thing loose. He floated in the water for a moment and then pushed off from the submerged race car and shot straight up toward the waiting motorboat.

Joe burst from his hiding place, swimming furiously after the diver. If he doesn't see me, Joe prayed, I can catch him by surprise and grab the evidence.

Joe could see that he was too far behind. The diver would reach the surface—and the safety of his boat—before Joe got there. But there wasn't any choice. Got to go for it, Joe urged himself.

Joe kicked as hard as he could and reached the line that attached the anchor to the vessel above. He gripped it firmly and started hauling himself up, hand over hand. Added to the powerful motion of his legs, the straining muscles in his arms helped him gain on the unknown diver.

Joe kept his eyes fixed on his objective as he

closed the distance. But he could see that the man had reached the surface and was starting to climb into his boat.

With a final burst of energy and a desperate lunge, Joe grabbed a flippered foot and dragged the diver back in the water.

It didn't go exactly as Joe had planned. The diver fell on top of him, jostling Joe's face mask loose. Salt water filled the mask, stinging his eyes and making it hard to see.

Joe's only advantage was that the guy didn't know what had hit him. Joe knew he had to take him out fast and hard.

Joe reached out and ripped off the diver's face mask. At least now we'll be even, he thought. And I can see who you are. But the other man was flailing around so much that air bubbles filled the water and made it impossible to see the man's face.

Joe hit the diver in the stomach with both feet as hard as he could. Even though the water slowed his kick, he was able to double the man over. Joe used the kicking motion to push himself away so he could get a better angle of attack, but the move put him above his opponent.

Joe knew that underwater pressure made it easier to move up rather than down. Brilliant tactics, bozo, Joe chided himself. Now the Creature from the Black Lagoon has the advantage! He can come at me faster than I can make a move on him.

As if he could read Joe's mind, the diver suddenly lunged upward, his right arm stabbing through the water. Joe caught a glint of metal. Too late, he realized it was the knife the man had used earlier.

Joe knew he couldn't move fast enough to dodge the blade. He twisted sharply to avoid the fatal blow, and grimaced, waiting for the painful bite of cold steel. But the diver's arm swung away from Joe's body to sever his air hose.

While Joe struggled to the surface for air, the mystery diver made his escape. Joe got a good look only at the motorboat as it sped away from the scene. It was not a welcome sight.

Exhausted by the time he made it back to the rocks, Joe gladly accepted a helping hand from his brother. "I saw the diver go into the water," Frank said, helping Joe take off the scuba tank. "A little later I saw him again, starting to climb back aboard his boat. Then suddenly he kind of flopped back into the water."

Frank shook his head. "You guys were making more commotion than a breaching humpback whale. You probably ruined the fishing for miles around."

Frank paused for a second when Joe shot him a look that could incinerate.

"After that," he continued after a beat, "the next thing I saw was you popping up some distance away from the boat. The other guy surfaced next to it, got in, and bugged out.''

Joe filled Frank in on the missing details. "Whatever it was we thought we'd find on that wreck," he said, "just sailed off into the sunset.''

Frank nodded. "If he wasn't holding the device when you hauled him back into the water, he must have dropped it on the deck first. I don't suppose you got a good look at it?''

Joe shook his head.

"Okay," Frank persisted. "How about the guy? What did he look like?''

"It all happened too fast," Joe said, "and we were both wearing diving gear. I didn't get a good look at him.''

Frank scowled.

"But I didn't have to," Joe added. "I got a good look at his boat, and I recognized *it*.''

"Well?" Frank prodded.

Joe Hardy sighed. "The boat belongs to Scott Lavin.''

Chapter

12

FRANK AND JOE scrambled over the rockfall and edged their way along a narrow path back to the ledge where the other half of the climbing rope was still tied to the tree.

"Just as I thought," Frank said, cradling the rope in his hands and holding out the end for Joe to see. "No frays or anything like that. The rope didn't break. It's a clean cut."

"It looks like you were right all along," Joe replied. "Somebody wants to win this race badly enough to kill for it."

"Yeah," Frank agreed. "It seems like a miracle we're still alive." He clapped Joe on the shoulder and turned his head to study the twisted route they'd have to climb to get back to the road above.

Joe followed his brother's gaze. He laughed

softly, shook his head, and said, "I'm glad this was *your* plan, not mine."

"Why's that?"

Joe unslung the scuba tank from his back and thrust it into Frank's arms. "Because it means *you* get to lug this stuff back to the van."

"Hey, hold on a sec—" Frank started to protest.

"No, no," Joe insisted. "I'm sure I heard you say that was part of your plan. The best part, I think."

The Hardys were bone tired by the time they dragged themselves back to the van. "Let's go home," Joe suggested, slouching down in the passenger seat and resting his feet on the dashboard. "I'll sleep; you drive."

"Remember what Callie said," Frank replied, shifting into gear and pulling hard on the steering wheel, spinning the van around on the dirt track. "The shortest distance between two points always involves a couple of stops along the way."

"I'm too wiped out to remember anything," Joe mumbled, closing his eyes and pretending to sleep as they bumped back down the road. "But I think I can guess where we're headed. Let me take a shot in the dark."

"Fire away!" Frank said.

"We're going to the marina to see if we can catch Scott Lavin there."

"Yes and no."

"Huh?"

"Yes, we're headed for the marina, but there's not much chance of running into Scott there. He had a big head start on us."

"Oh, right." Joe nodded. "We're going there to take a pleasure cruise."

"No," Frank said, flicking the turn signal and pulling into the entrance of the Bayport Marina. "We're here to see if anybody saw Scott take his boat out."

"Why? It didn't go out by itself."

"No—but you said you didn't get a good look at the diver. We have to make sure it was Scott and not somebody else in his boat."

They pulled into a parking space and got out of the van. Frank strode over to a small building. A sign over the door read Harbor Master.

As he reached for the doorknob, Joe caught up and put a hand on his shoulder. Pointing down the dock to one of the motorboats moored there, he said, "If someone stole Scott's boat, they were nice enough to return it."

"Hey, whose side are you on, anyway?" Frank asked. "I thought Scott was your friend."

"He *was*," Joe replied sullenly, "until he tried to kill me."

"But he *didn't* try to kill you," Frank pointed out. "He had a chance, and all he did was cut your air hose."

"So what does that prove?" Joe demanded.

"I don't know." Frank shrugged, opening the

door to the small office and waving his brother inside. "Humor me for a while."

The harbor master was a grizzled old guy with a white admiral's cap perched on his wispy hair. "Old sailors never die," Joe whispered. "They just get desk jobs."

"What can I do for you youngsters?" the man asked in a friendly tone.

"We were supposed to meet Scott Lavin here." Frank smiled. "Have you seen him today?"

"That I have," came the reply.

"Really? How long ago?" Joe cut in.

"Let's just check the log," the harbor master said, turning to a large book on the desk behind the counter. "It's all here, you know."

"Does the log say when he took his boat out and when he came back?" Frank asked.

"That it does." The old man nodded. "Wrote it down myself, don't you know. Ah, here it is. See for yourself." The self-styled admiral staggered under the weight of the huge volume as he brought it over and set it on the counter.

Joe and Frank both studied the most recent entries in the log. "Well, that does it," Joe said. "The times fit perfectly."

They thanked the harbor master and walked back to the van in silence. Joe was downcast, Frank lost in thought.

As they drove home, Joe finally said, "It looks like you were right about Scott from the start.

Boy, was I a pinhead. He *used* me. He probably even rigged that engine fire and set me up to be the toasted marshmallow.''

"Possibly," Frank said, nodding. "He could have thrown away his chances of winning the race and torched his own car to throw us off the trail."

Joe nodded. "Yeah. It sure beats a murder rap—and when he saw me at the race course, he figured it was better to risk my life than his own."

"It's *possible*," Frank repeated as he turned the van into their driveway. "But it doesn't do much for me," he said as he switched off the ignition and killed the engine.

He opened the door and hopped out of the van without saying anything else. Joe followed him around to the back of the van. "What do you mean?" he asked as his brother opened the rear door and started piling gear into Joe's arms.

Frank stopped unloading and turned to look at Joe. "Think about it."

"We know Scott was the diver who took something off the wreck. We know when he left the harbor and when he returned."

"So?" Joe retorted.

"So who was up on the ledge cutting our climbing rope?" Frank turned away and walked toward the house. Opening the front door, he called back over his shoulder, "Are you coming or not? I don't know about you, but I'm exhausted. I'm going inside."

Joe stared at the pile of gear in his arms. "Aren't you going to help me with this stuff?"

"Sure—I'm holding the door open for you." Frank smiled. "It's all part of my plan."

Joe groaned. "Next time I'm definitely coming up with my own plan." Lugging the scuba gear into the house, he said, "Scott could have had a little help. An accomplice."

Frank started to climb the stairs. "I might have bought that two days ago," he said. "But not now."

"How come?"

"Scott didn't know we were checking things out until the day after McCoy's crash."

"So?"

"Somebody's been following us, dogging our every move since I first picked up that electronic souvenir." Frank pushed open the door to his room.

"Maybe Arno told Scott that you found something," Joe suggested.

"Maybe. But I don't think so."

"Why not?"

Frank smiled again. "Call it a hunch—gut instinct."

Joe chuckled. "Okay, you've got me there. But why did Scott dive down to the wreck and rip off evidence?"

"Beats me." Frank shrugged. "When we find him, we'll ask him."

As if in answer to Frank's statement, they

heard their aunt Gertrude calling, "Boys? Are you up there? You have a visitor. It's that nice Scott Lavin."

The Hardys hurried downstairs and saw Scott standing in the doorway.

"You've got a lot of nerve coming here," Joe growled. "What do you want?"

Scott was holding something in his hands. He tossed it at Frank, who caught it reflexively. "I want you guys to help me find out what that thing is," Scott said.

Frank turned the metal object over in his hands, shrugged, and handed it to his brother. "Where did it come from?" Frank asked casually.

"I got it off McCoy's car at the bottom of the ocean," Scott admitted.

"You almost killed me for this thing!" Joe rasped, advancing on his friend.

Scott studied Joe with a look of disbelief. Then his eyes widened as the puzzled expression changed to one of shocked surprise. "You mean that was *you* down there?" he exclaimed.

He shook his head. "All I knew was that someone jumped me while I was trying to get back in my boat," he continued. "I was just trying to get away. I'm sorry, Joe. I didn't know!"

Frank quickly stepped between them and put his hand on his brother's tensed arm. "Why don't we go into the living room and talk about this some more?" he suggested calmly.

"I never trusted Arno," Scott explained, as they all sat down. "After the two 'accidents' that took me out of the race, I wanted to find out if McCoy's crash was fixed, too.

"So I took a dive down to the wreck and found that thing attached to the steering column," Scott continued, gesturing to the device in Joe's hands. "I know almost everything there is to know about Formula One design—and if that's a legit part of McCoy's steering system, I'll eat my car."

"Well, at least it's already been cooked," Joe joked halfheartedly.

"The steering system," Frank repeated. "That's it!"

Scott gave Joe a confused look. "What's he talking about?"

"Joe," Frank began, "remember what Phil said about the electronic device we found at the crash site?"

"Yeah," Joe nodded. "He said it was too complicated for a simple triggering device. It had to be part of something more complex."

"Right! Remote control steering! McCoy couldn't handle the car on the hairpin turn because someone else was steering by remote control!" Frank exclaimed, jumping up from his chair.

"But the remote operator would have to know exactly when the car got to the hairpin turn," he continued, pacing around the room as his mind unraveled the puzzle.

Joe could see where his brother's train of thought was going. "That means," he cut in, "it had to be someone who could *see* the car! And the only people who could see the car were—"

"The people in the helicopter." Frank finished the sentence with a smile. "Excluding you and me, that leaves the writer, the cameraman, the pilot, and—"

"Excuse me, boys," Gertrude interrupted, poking her head into the room. "But you have another visitor."

"Thank you, ma'am," a familiar voice came from behind her.

Russell Arno strode into the room, a coat draped over his right arm. "And now if you'll excuse us, the boys and I have some business to discuss."

Gertrude smiled. "Such a nice gentleman." She turned and walked out. "If you need anything," she called out, "I'll be in the kitchen."

"Oh, I think we have everything we need right here," Arno said coolly, pulling back the coat to reveal the automatic pistol in his hand that was aimed right at Joe.

"Don't we, boys?"

Chapter

13

ALL EYES IN the room were riveted on the gun. "I think you have something that belongs to me," Arno said.

Joe started to stand up. "I told you what I'd do if I caught you waving that thing around again!" he snarled.

Frank reached out, put his hand on Joe's shoulder, and said, "Sit down, Joe. If the man wants something so badly, let's give it to him."

Joe glanced at Frank and caught the slight wink in his brother's eye. He felt the weight of the object in his hand and turned back to the promoter. "Sure thing," he said, and smiled. "Here—catch!"

Joe hurled the device at Arno's head as Frank surged out of his seat, making a tackling dive for the man's legs. Arno managed to dodge the chunk of metal whizzing past his head, but the diversion was good enough.

Frank hurtled into him, hitting him just above the knees and knocking his legs out from under him. Arno crashed to the floor, the gun still clutched in his hand. Joe hesitated for a fraction of a second and then leaped for the arm holding the weapon. The promoter swung wildly, and a lucky blow cracked Joe on the head, the butt of the pistol slamming into his temple.

Joe fell back, dazed, pain shooting across his eyes. Everything went dark for a moment. He shook his head hard. Don't black out, he commanded himself. There's too much riding on this. He opened his eyes—and didn't like what he saw.

Arno was still on the floor, Frank's body sprawled across his legs, pinning him down. His hands were free, and in the right one he still clutched the gun. Now the barrel was pressed against the side of Frank's head.

"Move *very* slowly," Arno instructed. "Or your brother will have a very big hole in his head."

Joe staggered to his feet. "Look, you can have the thing," he said, pointing to the metal object lying on the floor. "Take it and get out. Just leave my brother alone."

Arno's gaze shifted to include Scott. "Hands on your head," he ordered the race car driver. "Bring that here," he said coldly to Joe, indicating the device. "But this time, *hand* it to me."

Joe picked it up and walked toward him. "That's close enough," Arno warned, reaching out with his free hand. "Now get your brother off me."

"I'm all right," Frank protested. "I can get up by myself."

"I'm sure you can," the promoter said. "But I want everybody's hands where I can see them—and I want them occupied."

Arno swung the gun around to include all three boys.

"Very good. Now I want you," he continued, poking Frank in the head with the gun barrel, "to clasp your hands behind your head. And I want you"—he nodded at Joe—"to pick him up. Scott, stay where you are."

Joe moved to help his brother up. "Not until I give the word!" Arno barked.

Joe froze. "Anything you say. You're the boss."

"That's better." Arno smiled. "Now, on the count of three. Ready? One—two—three."

Joe stooped down and took hold of Frank's arms near the shoulders. He grasped his brother firmly and pulled him to his feet. Joe gave Frank an apologetic look, and Frank just shrugged his shoulders. Things happen, the gesture said.

The promoter stood up, holding the gun in one hand and the device from the race car in the other hand. "Sit down, gentlemen," he ordered. "Now let's pretend I don't know what this is." He tapped the device lightly with the pistol. "And you're going to tell me all about it."

"If you don't know what it is," Frank said as he eased back into his chair, "why are you here, waving a gun in our faces?"

"I made the error of playing twenty questions with your brother," Arno began. "I won't make that mistake again. I'll hold the gun—you'll do the talking. Got it?"

A puzzled expression passed over Frank's face. "Okay. We'll play it your way," he said. "We got it off McCoy's car."

"Cute trick," Arno responded, "considering the fact that McCoy's car is at the bottom of the ocean. Try again."

"No, really," Scott Lavin interjected. "He's telling you the truth. We found that device attached to the steering column. The crash was no accident. That thing made it happen."

Joe shot Scott a look. Shut up, his eyes shouted, before you dig our graves any deeper!

Frank made a desperate attempt to gloss it over. "That's just a theory," he cut in. "What do we know? Right? A couple kids and a frustrated driver with a lump of charcoal for a car. We can't prove anything."

"No, no," Arno countered. "I think that's an excellent theory. You're probably right on track. Excellent work. I never would have thought of that. But you don't mind if I hold on to this for a few days, do you?"

"You mean you'll give it back?" Joe asked doubtfully.

"Look," Arno replied, his words dripping with impatience, "I didn't have anything to do with McCoy's death but I can't have a murder investigation delaying this race. This may sound cold-hearted to you, but time is money—and I'm only in it for the money."

"So what do you want from us?" Frank asked.

"The videotape your brother stole from my office," Arno said. "I didn't realize it was gone until this morning."

"Why didn't you just call the police?" Joe prodded.

"More questions," Arno snapped. "Just give me the tape and I'll be on my way."

"Aren't you worried that we might have watched it already?" Frank asked.

"There's really not much to see," Arno said. "Besides, it's a professional tape. Wrong format for a home VCR. Now, where is it? I'm getting impatient."

"It's not here!" Joe blurted out. "It's in a safe place."

"Oh, I see." Arno smiled thinly. "So the girl has it." He motioned to the door with the gun. "Come on. We're all going for a little ride."

Arno took his coat and draped it over his arm again, concealing the pistol in his hand. As the four of them headed for the front door they were intercepted by Aunt Gertrude. "Leaving so soon?'' she said. "I was just coming to ask if you'd like some coffee or something.''

"Why, thank you, ma'am,'' Arno said, oozing with charm. "But we really must be going now.''

"Oh?'' Gertrude responded, raising her eyebrows. "It's getting awfully late, boys. Do you really think it's a good idea to go out now?''

"Under the circumstances,'' Frank said, shifting his gaze from his aunt to the coat slung over the promoter's arm, "I think it's a very good idea.''

Joe saw what his brother was trying to do. "A *very* good idea,'' he repeated forcefully, his eyes rapidly darting between his aunt and the concealed weapon.

"We'll only be at Callie's house, anyway,'' Frank added. "You know where to find us.''

"Well, then I guess it's all right,'' Gertrude conceded. "Have a nice time—and don't stay out too late.''

"I'll see that they're home by a reasonable hour,'' Arno assured her as he hustled the Hardys and Scott Lavin out into the yard, prodding Joe with the barrel of the gun.

Frank saw two cars parked in front. One, he knew, belonged to Scott. The other, he reasoned, must be Arno's. It was a two-seater sports car.

"Oh, too bad! Your car's not big enough for all of us,'' Frank said with mock disappointment. "How about if we take the van and you follow us?''

115

"Yeah, great idea!" Joe chimed in. "We'll go real slow so you don't get lost."

"Let's all go together," Arno replied, shoving them toward the van.

"I'll drive," Frank stated flatly, heading for the left front door.

"Not so fast!" Arno retorted. Frank's hand was already on the handle. "You and Scott get in back with me," he said, nodding to Frank. "And you," he ordered, poking Joe in the back with the pistol, "drive."

They all climbed into the van, and Joe got behind the wheel. He started the engine, released the emergency brake, and rolled the van down the driveway toward the street. He knew his brother was up to something. He could tell by his tone of voice when he volunteered to drive. Frank's got some kind of plan, he told himself. I just wish I knew what it was!

Frank sat cross-legged on the floor of the van, his gaze never leaving Arno, sizing up the nervous promoter. There was no way he was going to let Arno get his hands on Callie. But it was going to be close, because he didn't want to take any chances in the van. If he tried to take Arno out while they were still moving and something went wrong, they could all be killed. Just have to wait until we get to Callie's house, he told himself, and hope Joe gets my signal.

Finally Joe pulled the van over to the curb and

shut off the engine. "Here we are," he said reluctantly as he set the emergency brake.

"You get out first," Arno instructed Joe. "Then come around and open the back door."

Joe hesitated. He glanced at his brother and saw that glimmer of a wink again. "Go ahead," Frank said. "Do what he says."

Joe started to open the door. "And don't forget the emergency brake," Frank added casually.

Joe stifled a smile as he got out of the van, quietly reaching down and releasing the brake with a smooth motion, unseen by Arno. "Right," he replied. "Almost forgot."

Frank couldn't tell for sure, but he thought Joe had gotten the message. Shifting his attention back to Arno, he waited for his brother to walk around to the back of the van. He had to make sure the promoter was the last one out.

As Joe swung the back door open, Frank said, "After you, Mr. Arno."

Arno shot him a suspicious look, and then smiled. "I'm calling the shots—if you'll pardon the expression—and I think you and Scott should get out first. That way all three of you will be in front of me, where I can see you."

Scott hopped out of the van, and Frank followed. He looked at his brother, and they shared a brief glance.

"Make sure your hands are where I can see them!" Arno barked as he started to climb out.

"Yes, sir!" Joe replied. "They're right here on the door!"

"Not your hands!" Arno snapped. "*His* han—"

While Joe distracted the promoter, Frank suddenly whirled around and lunged under Arno, shoving the bumper with both outstretched hands. The van lurched forward, and Arno pitched out headfirst.

This time, Joe didn't wait for him to hit the ground. He jumped out and drove his shoulder deep into the falling man's stomach.

"*Woof!*" Arno grunted as the wind was knocked out of him and the gun flew out of his hand. But Joe had hit him too low. Their combined momentum flipped Arno over Joe's back, and he landed right next to the weapon.

Arno snatched it up and scrambled to his feet. "Nobody move!" he screamed. "Or I start shooting!"

Frank picked himself up off the ground and advanced on the man. "You're not going to shoot anybody," he said calmly. "You've had plenty of chances, and you haven't fired a single shot. Give me the gun before somebody gets hurt."

As Frank reached out to take the weapon, Arno raised it high and swung down at him.

Frank threw his arms in the air, crossing them at the forearms to form an X over his head. He easily deflected the blow and trapped Arno's gun-wielding hand between his crossed arms. Then he twisted his body toward the promoter and grabbed hold of him at the wrist and just above the elbow. With a single, fluid motion, Frank flung Arno over his shoulder and onto the pavement.

Frank grasped Arno's wrist with both hands, making sure the gun wasn't pointed at anyone, and quickly moved in to put his foot in the promoter's armpit. "One hard tug," Frank said roughly, "and I'll dislocate your shoulder. I hear it hurts a lot."

Arno didn't say anything—but his hand went limp, and the weapon clattered harmlessly on the street.

"Now get up," Frank ordered. "You've got a lot of explaining to do."

Arno staggered to his feet. "You're right," he gasped.

Suddenly a shot rang out. Scott whirled in the direction of the sound, and Joe and Frank instinctively dove for cover.

Frank looked up and watched as Arno clutched at his chest, grimacing with pain. Then the promoter crumpled to the ground, blood seeping between his fingers and staining his shirt in a large circle.

Chapter

14

FRANK AND JOE lay flat on the ground. Out of the corner of his eye, Frank could see Scott Lavin crouching behind the van. "Stay where you are!" Frank hissed in a loud whisper. Scott probably wasn't going to move an inch until they pried him off the side of the van with a crowbar, but Frank wanted to make sure everything was under control before he made a move.

Frank turned his head toward Joe, who was lying next to him. "I'm going to see if I can drag Arno out of the line of fire." He started to squirm along the ground to where Arno lay motionless. A loud *crack* split the air, then a bullet *thunked* into the pavement, inches from Frank's head. A shard of concrete shrapnel sliced across his cheek, and he flattened and froze.

Pinned down—perfect, Frank thought. He

glanced at the promoter again. From the slowly spreading stain on his shirt, Frank could tell that the bullet had hit him in the shoulder.

"Mr. Arno!" he called out huskily. "Can you hear me?"

"Oooooh," came a low moan in reply.

Frank wasn't sure if he had really heard it or just imagined it.

Then it came again, louder this time. *Aaaooooh!*

It was a police siren—and it was getting close!

Frank heard footsteps running away, a door slamming, and a car engine starting.

Frank and Joe leapt up at the same time. "There he is!" Joe shouted, pointing down the street.

Frank caught a glimpse of the car as it squealed around the corner and out of sight. It was a Lotus sports coupe. And although it was too dark to make out the color, Frank was willing to bet it was silver gray.

The pulsing red and blue lights of a police cruiser came into view. The wail of the siren got painfully loud, and then abruptly stopped as the squad car pulled up to the curb.

"That was an awfully fast response," Joe commented, shielding his eyes from the flashing lights as the silhouette of a uniformed figure approached them.

"Not that we're complaining, mind you," Frank added. "But who called in the shooting?"

"What shooting?" came the tired voice of Con Riley. "Your aunt phoned the station and said you boys had been kidnapped by some guy with a gun hidden under his coat! Said he was going to nab Callie Shaw next."

The two brothers looked at each other and smiled. Aunt Gertrude had come through in the clutch.

"So where's this dangerous criminal?" Riley asked impatiently.

The smile faded from Frank's lips. "You'd better call an ambulance," he began, taking hold of Riley's arm and guiding him over to the injured promoter. "And you better put out an APB on a silver gray Lotus sports coupe."

The Hardys sat on Callie's front steps, under the eerie yellow glow of the porch light, and filled her in on the evening's events. They idly watched the police forensic team dig out the bullet that had kissed the pavement a hairbreadth from Frank's head. The lights were on in most of the neighbors' houses, and a throng of people in bathrobes, pajamas, and fuzzy slippers were milling around on the sidewalk.

"Most excitement they've had in years," Callie said.

"It's like some weird, late-night costume party," Joe muttered.

They could see that Scott Lavin had just finished giving his statement to one of the police officers. As the last of the police cars finally pulled away, he loped across the street to join the threesome. Callie turned to Frank and said, "So now you know Scott wasn't behind all this."

Frank nodded. "And Arno knows something, but he's not talking."

"Do you think that bullet he took was meant for us?" Joe asked.

Frank looked at his brother. "It fits the pattern. Before, they were just trying to scare us. Now they're playing for keeps."

"Now all you have to do is figure out who *they* are," Callie said.

Frank stood up. "Arno claimed there wasn't much to see on the videotape. But why would he go to so much trouble to get it back if there wasn't some crucial evidence in there somewhere?"

"Maybe we should take another look at it then," Joe suggested. "And maybe Scott can see something that we couldn't."

Frank grinned. "You read my mind, brother."

It was almost dawn when they replayed the tape for what seemed like the bazillionth time. "I'm sorry I can't help," Scott finally said. "But we already know *what* caused the crash. I can't see anything here that will tell us *who* caused it."

"And I don't see why we have to look at those stupid time codes ticking away at the bottom of the screen," Joe complained. "Isn't there any way to get rid of them?"

"They're permanently encoded on the master tape," Callie explained. "But I can set the machine so the time codes don't appear on the screen."

"That's it!" Frank shouted, jumping out of his chair. "The time codes!" He stepped quickly over to the video cassette machine. Frank had been watching Callie operate the thing for a couple of hours, and he practically had it memorized.

He hit a button on the console and the tape started to play from the beginning. "Not again!" his brother groaned.

Frank hit another button, and the scenes rushed by at a blurring rate. "What are you doing?" Callie asked.

"I'm going to cue up the scene where McCoy enters the tunnel," Frank said. "Right . . . here!" He pressed a third button, and the car froze on the screen, the cone-shaped nose just edging into the dark mouth of the tunnel. The digital clock at the bottom of the screen stopped, too. The time code was frozen at 00:09:33:18.

"Somebody write down the time," Frank ordered.

"I've got it," Callie said, taking a clipboard and a ballpoint pen from one of the shelves. "That's nine minutes, thirty-three seconds, and eighteen hundredths."

"Good," Frank said. He pressed the play button and the car started moving again. When the tape reached the point where the car started to emerge from the other end of the tunnel, he hit the freeze-frame again. Now the time code was 00:10:32:52.

"That's ten minutes, thirty-two seconds, and fifty-two hundredths," Callie read off the numbers as she wrote them down.

Scott Lavin frowned. "That's almost a full minute," he said.

"Doesn't seem very long to me," Joe responded. "It's a long tunnel."

"Not when you're going two hundred miles an hour," Frank pointed out. "How long do you think it would take, Scott?"

"Lap time is real important in racing," Scott explained. "So we keep track of time constantly. We know how long it should take us to get through each leg of the course. On my qualifying lap, I took that tunnel in about forty-four seconds. McCoy took fifteen seconds longer," he continued. "For a racing driver, that's forever."

"Long enough to stop and get out of the car?" Frank pressed.

"I guess," Scott said. "But why would he want to?"

Suddenly the answer dawned on Joe, and he was on his feet, pointing at the scene on the television. "So he wouldn't be *in* it when it went over the cliff!" he exclaimed.

"Then who was driving?" Callie wanted to know.

"McCoy," Frank answered.

"But you just said he wasn't in the car when it crashed," she countered.

"He wasn't," Joe agreed. "He was driving by remote control!"

"He faked his own death!" Frank laughed. "He's had us all running in circles!"

"Great theory, guys," Callie said, turning off the television and settling back down in her chair. "But what's his motive?"

"I heard he had some big debts," Scott offered. "Race cars are an expensive habit. McCoy's career was just beginning a downhill slide. He was losing sponsors. Maybe he did it for the insurance."

"I don't think so," Frank murmured. Something had just occurred to him, a conversation he'd had with someone. " 'This is the kind of ending publishers dream about,' " he mumbled. " 'The Fast Life and Tragic Death of Angus McCoy'."

He looked up and saw the others were staring at him. "Run that by me again," Joe said, furrowing his brow.

"It was something that writer, T. B. Martin, said," Frank explained. "Remember, Joe?"

Joe nodded. "That's right. He said McCoy's death would make a great ending for the book they were writing together. So maybe McCoy faked his own death to—"

"Turn an unsellable biography into the best-selling story of a racing legend's tragic and untimely death?" Frank finished the thought.

"But how would he collect his profits from the book sales?" Callie asked sleepily.

The sun's early rays were slanting in through the small windows set high in the basement walls, near the ceiling. Frank stifled a yawn. "Martin told me McCoy's royalties would go to a company called Clarco Industries. Maybe he can fill us in on the details."

"Does anybody know where to find him?" Scott asked.

Joe squinted through a shaft of light that had fallen across his face as the sun steadily rose in the sky outside. "Right now, he's probably having breakfast," he said. "But I know where he'll be in a couple of hours."

"Where's that?" Frank wanted to know.

"At the starting line of the Bayport Grand Prix," Joe said. "It's race day."

Chapter

15

"IT'S A BEAUTIFUL DAY for a race," Scott said softly as they walked out into the morning sun.

Joe looked at the sad expression on his friend's face. "I'm sorry about your car, Scott. If only we could have—"

"It wasn't your fault," Scott said, cutting him off. "In fact, you may have saved my life. Who knows what would have happened if I was out on the back stretch of the course doing a hundred eighty or a hundred ninety when that engine fire started."

Frank held open the van door while Scott and Callie climbed in. "Maybe it *is* our fault," Frank said.

"What do you mean?" Scott asked.

"The sabotage to your car was an afterthought. McCoy wanted us to think that somebody was trying to win the race by taking out all the front-runners. But if we hadn't pushed the investigation in the first place, he wouldn't have had to go to all the trouble."

"That's right," Joe agreed, settling in behind the wheel. "The police were more than ready to believe McCoy's crash was an accident. McCoy was afraid that sooner or later we'd stop asking the *wrong* questions and start asking the *right* ones."

Joe started the engine, checked the side mirrors, and put the van in gear. "Do you want me to drop you off someplace, Scott?" he asked.

Scott smiled weakly. "No, that's all right. I think I'll just tag along. Even if I'm not in the race, I have to see it. It's in my blood."

Traffic was much heavier than usual. Bayport was crammed with vehicles, all headed in the same direction as the Hardys' van. The pace soon slowed to an agonizing stop-and-go crawl.

Frank gazed out the window and chuckled. "People from all over pile into their cars to go two miles an hour, so they can go watch somebody else drive two *hundred* miles an hour. Unbelievable."

Finally they reached a police barricade. It was just a wood two-by-four that slanted down from a simple A-frame and rested on the pavement. On the side of the wood beam was stenciled: Police Line—Do Not Cross. It would be easy to move it out of the way—but the police officer guarding it made sure that no one did.

On the other side was the street that passed right through the middle of downtown Bayport. Scott showed his racing pass to the officer guarding the barricade, and the man picked up the end of the beam and swung it aside to let the van through.

In a few hours the street they were on would be full of screaming race cars, but for now they had it all to themselves. It was clear sailing until they got near the fairgrounds. There they ran into another kind of traffic jam—pedestrians.

Joe maneuvered the van slowly through the bustling congestion of mechanics, drivers, and race cars dotting the fairgrounds. They eventually worked their way to the shed that housed what was left of the McCoy Racing team and parked next to it. As they got out, Joe looked over at his brother. "Where's Callie?" he asked.

"She fell asleep in the back," Frank replied. "I didn't have the heart to wake her."

Reinhart Voss was in the shed, crawling around the huge rear wheels of his car, peering underneath the chassis, making his final inspection for the race. He saw Scott and got up, dusting off his knees and wiping off his hands. "I am glad you are here, Scott," he said. "There is something I would like to talk to you about."

"Before you get started," Frank interrupted.

"We're looking for the writer, T. B. Martin. Have you seen him?"

"Yes." Voss nodded. "He was here, but he forgot his tape recorder and went back to the motel to get it."

"Then that's where we're going," Frank said.

"Catch you later!" Joe called back to Scott as he hurried off after his brother.

The Hardys threaded their way back to the Bayport Motel and headed for the front desk. Frank approached the clerk behind the counter and smiled. "I'm T. B. Martin. Could I have my room key, please?"

The clerk turned to a honeycomb of cubby holes on the wall, each with a number below it. He reached for one and then turned back to Frank, empty-handed. "Your key isn't in your slot," he said with a frown. "Could I see some kind of identification?"

"Sure thing," Frank agreed cheerfully, reaching into his right back pocket. His smile faded as he tried his other back pocket. "Uh-oh. I must've left my wallet in the car. I'll be right back."

Frank and Joe turned around and headed back in the direction of the front door. When they were sure the desk clerk wasn't watching, they swerved over to the elevators.

"Eighth floor," Frank said, stepping into the elevator after his brother.

"Right," Joe replied, running his finger down

131

the bank of numbers and pressing one of the recessed buttons. A tiny light winked on to indicate the one he had touched. "The clerk reached for the slot marked eight-thirteen. That must be Martin's room."

The light inside the button marked 8 winked off as the elevator door slid open and the Hardys got off. "Wouldn't it have been easier to just call him from the lobby?" Joe asked as they walked down the hall.

"That would spoil the surprise," Frank said.

They passed Room 811 on the left and Room 812 on the right. At the next door on the left, Frank stopped and raised his hand to knock. But the door swung open before he could complete the motion.

T. B. Martin strode out, clutching a small portable tape recorder in one hand. "Well, if it isn't the Hardy brothers," he said. "I hope you guys weren't coming to see me. I'm in kind of a hurry."

He closed the door to his room and brushed past the Hardys, walking toward the elevator. Then he paused, turned around, and looked at Frank. "You know," he said, "I was just thinking about you. Well, not so much you personally, but something you asked me about the other day."

Frank raised an eyebrow. "Oh? And what might that be?"

"You were asking me about McCoy's share of

the profits on his book," Martin replied. "I told you about the contract and Clarco Industries."

"Right," Frank nodded. "I remember."

"Well, I just got a registered letter this morning from the Clarco offices. It appears the company has gone belly-up—bankrupt—and the book contract was bought by some guy named Jason Drake."

"Do you have any idea who this Drake character is?" Joe asked.

Martin shook his head. "None whatsoever. So now I've got a silent, invisible partner." He paused as a large grin spread across his face. "With any luck, he'll *stay* that way, and I can write this biography *my* way.

"Are you guys going to the race?" he asked as he turned to walk down the hall.

"Not right now," Frank responded, nudging Joe and following the writer. "But we'll ride down in the elevator with you."

"Okay," Martin said as they descended to the lobby. "But don't forget you still owe me an interview."

The Hardys watched Martin leave the hotel and head off in the direction of the fairgrounds. Then they strolled back into the lobby and found a couple of empty chairs.

"What now?" Joe asked, slouching down in a seat facing his brother. "We know the name McCoy is using—but we don't know where to find him."

Frank closed his eyes, lost in thought.

"McCoy must have gone to a lot of trouble to set up a new identity," Frank finally said after a long pause. "And we know he was still in town a couple of hours ago."

"Right," Joe agreed. "He took a couple whacks at us with a high-powered rifle and hit Arno by mistake."

"He probably has some kind of disguise," Frank continued, "but he still wouldn't want to be seen in public too much. So he'd need a place to stay."

"Well, we're sitting in the lobby of the nearest place to do that," Joe observed.

"Exactly," Frank said with a grin.

Joe sat up straight in his seat. "You mean you think he's *here?*"

"There's an easy way to find out," Frank replied.

He got up and walked over to the front desk. Joe was right behind him. "Excuse me," Frank addressed the desk clerk. "Could you tell me if you have a Jason Drake registered at the hotel?"

The man behind the counter squinted suspiciously at Frank. "Haven't I seen you before?"

"Not likely," Joe cut in. "We just flew in from Pocatello, Idaho. Ever been to Pocatello?"

"Ahhh—no," the clerk replied in a flustered tone. "I'm sorry, I must have been mistaken." He looked down at his computer console and started typing on the keyboard. "Let's see—Mr.

Drake checked out. In fact, I just sent a bellhop up to his room to help him carry down his bags."

"And what room might that be?" Frank asked, leaning across the counter and craning his neck to get a look at the computer screen.

"Now I remember you!" the clerk exclaimed. You were here a little while ago. You told me you were—"

"Got to go!" Joe interrupted, grabbing Frank's arm and hauling him away from the counter. "Don't want to miss our flight back to Idaho!"

They turned and walked quickly out the front door, leaving the desk clerk spluttering to himself.

"How do we find Drake now?" Joe asked. "Follow everybody who leaves the hotel?"

"We don't have to find him," Frank replied. "He's going to find us."

Joe glanced at his brother. "And where is he going to find us?"

"Over there," Frank said, pointing to the motel parking garage.

It wasn't hard to find the silver gray Lotus. Joe and Frank spotted it right away. They crouched behind the car next to it and waited.

"How do we know he won't have the parking attendant drive it around to the front entrance?" Joe asked.

"When you own a car like that," Frank said, "you don't let anybody else even touch it."

"The guy goes to a lot of trouble to conceal his identity," Joe whispered, "and then he drives around in a flashy sports car."

Frank shrugged. "Old habits die hard."

They heard footsteps echoing through the garage, moving in their direction. Frank put his index finger to his lips, and Joe nodded. The footsteps grew louder and then stopped nearby. There was a jingle of keys and the sound of a car door being unlocked. Frank got down on his hands and knees and peered under the car. All he could see was a pair of expensive leather boots against the open door of the silver gray sports car.

Frank signaled to Joe, and they both circled around the car from opposite sides, trapping the man between them.

Frank smiled. "Angus McCoy, I presume."

Chapter

16

THE MAN STANDING next to the sports car froze, his back to Frank. "You've made some kind of mistake," he said with a slight British accent. "My name is Drake."

"It is *now*," Frank agreed, closing the distance between them. "But a couple days ago it was—"

Suddenly the man spun around, swinging a heavy suitcase in his outstretched right hand, and cracked Frank square on the jaw. The blow knocked Frank backward, and he sprawled across the trunk of the car behind him.

"That's the last cheap shot you take at us!" Joe growled, coming at the man from the other side. He got a good look at "Drake." Joe guessed that he was about the same size as McCoy, although the cowboy hat perched on his head made him look a little taller. The wide brim of the hat made it hard to see the man's hair and eyes, but it was McCoy.

"Come on," Joe said sharply, shifting his weight on his feet and gesturing with his right hand. "Just you and me now, one on one. I can take you."

The man looked at Joe, sizing him up. Then he shrugged his shoulders and smiled. "You probably could," he agreed, and bolted for the garage entrance.

Joe ran over to his brother and helped him to his feet. "Are you okay?"

"I've been better," Frank muttered, rubbing his jaw. "But don't stop on account of me—let's get after him!"

The Hardys ran out of the garage and looked up and down the street. "There he goes!" Joe yelled, pointing off in the distance. "He's headed for the fairgrounds!"

They charged after him, running side by side. "Can't let him get too far ahead," Frank said, huffing, "or we'll lose him in the crowd."

"I don't think that's going to be a problem," Joe replied, watching the cowboy hat bobbing and weaving through the throng of racing personnel and curious spectators. He saw the hat veer off to the right and caught a glimpse of the man as he darted into one of the nearby sheds.

There was some muffled shouting and then the earsplitting roar of a Formula One engine. A race car lurched out of the shed, with a couple of very angry men in pursuit. One of them was obviously the guy who was *supposed* to be in the car, Joe noted, because he was wearing a one-piece protective driving suit.

The sleek, low-slung racing machine swerved out onto the roadway and took off down the course. "That's him!" Joe shouted. "He just stole that car!" Then he looked at his brother and said, "Well, two can play that game."

"What do you mean?" Frank asked. But Joe had already surged ahead through the crowd.

Joe ran straight for the McCoy Racing shed. He skidded to a stop out in front and peered inside. Scott Lavin and Reinhart Voss were absorbed in conversation. The mechanic was putting the last of his tools away. Joe took a deep breath and walked calmly up to the race car. He swung his right leg over the side, then his left, and sat down on something hard and uncomfortable. It was Voss's crash helmet. Joe quietly fished it out from under him and slid the rest of the way into the cockpit. Then he pulled on the helmet and strapped himself in.

Joe held his breath and reached for the starter switch. Lucky these babies don't need *keys*, Joe thought, a brief smile passing over his lips. Otherwise I'd look pretty stupid sitting here.

He flipped the switch and was rewarded with the deafening blast of the 900-horsepower engine behind him bursting into life, the painful sound reverberating off the aluminum walls of the shed.

Frank arrived just in time to see the race car squeal out of the shed and onto the road. The sight of Reinhart Voss and Scott Lavin staring in amazement only confirmed what Frank already knew.

He didn't waste any time. He hurried over to Voss and said, "There's a two-way radio in that thing, isn't there?"

Voss just gave him a glazed look.

"We can *talk* to him, can't we?" Frank prodded.

"Oh, yes. Sure," Voss said after a moment. "We have a whole control center here, with a radio to communicate with the car anytime."

"Then let me talk to him," Frank urged.

The other driver had about a thirty-second lead on Joe, but he was hampered by scattered pedestrians on the course. The race wasn't scheduled to start for another hour, and people were still milling around, sometimes darting across the roadway, looking for a better vantage point to view the race. The lead car had cleared the way for Joe, and he could see it ahead as he rocketed down a straightaway.

Joe was surprised at how bumpy the ride was. His head was buffeted from side to side, and he could feel every little flaw in the road. Then he remembered that the car was designed that way— the aerodynamic "ground effects" practically sucked the bottom of the car to the pavement for better handling.

No wonder racing drivers wear helmets, he thought as his head slammed into the back of the seat and then rocked forward again. It keeps them from getting punch drunk.

He was closing in on the other car when it dawned on him that he had no idea what he was going to do once he caught up with it. Suddenly he heard a tinny voice squawking in his ear. "Joe, are you there? Can you hear me?"

"Great," he said out loud. "Now I'm hearing voices. Maybe it's my conscience—but why does it sound like Frank?"

"Joe," the voice came again, "if you can hear me, hit the talk-back switch on the console."

Joe realized it was the cockpit radio and flipped the switch. "Hey, brother!" he shouted over the roar of the wind and the engine. "What's shaking?"

"Sounds like you are," Frank quipped over the speaker. "Listen, I've got a plan."

"I hope it's better than mine."

"All you have to do is keep him on the race course. He won't even try to get off until he's well away from the congested downtown area, and even then he'll have to stop the car, get out, and move a barricade out of the way."

"I'm with you so far," Joe replied, switching his right foot from the gas to the brake and cranking the wheel hard to the left for a tight turn. He felt the back tires start to slide, and he pulled the wheel back to the right. The race car fishtailed wildly as it came out of the turn, and Joe thought he was going to lose it.

"Whoa!" he yelled as he fought with the steering wheel.

"Joe!" Frank cried. "Are you all right?"

There was silence on the other end, and then, "Um—no problem. Everything's under control now. So you were saying?"

"All you have to do is stay close enough to prevent him from driving off the course onto some side road," Frank explained. "No heroics, okay?"

"Hey, you know me," Joe said.

"Yeah, that's what I'm afraid of," Frank replied. He handed the microphone to Scott Lavin and said, "Try to talk him through it."

"Where are you going?" Scott asked.

"I'm going to take a little drive myself," Frank said.

Frank hopped in the van, which was parked outside the shed, and started heading directly across the fairgrounds. The rough ride on the open terrain jostled Callie Shaw awake. She rubbed her eyes and said, "Where are we going?"

"McCoy stole a Formula One car and took off down the course, trying to escape. I don't have to tell you who's chasing him in Voss's car." Frank was silent for a moment, devoting his attention to a tight turn. Then he added, "I'm going to head them off."

Callie glanced at Frank. "In this thing? How will we even *catch* them, much less head them off?"

"Simple," Frank began. "The fairgrounds are in the northwest part of Bayport. The race course runs along the eastern border of the fairgrounds and then south through downtown. Then the course swings way out to the west and up the highway before turning back east to the ocean.

"We're taking a little shortcut to the north," he finished.

"But that will take us right out onto the cliff road!" Callie protested.

Frank nodded. "That's the idea."

"How are you holding up?" Scott's voice squawked in Joe's ear.

"I'm okay on the straightaways," Joe grumbled, "but he keeps moving farther ahead of me on every turn."

"What did you expect?" came the reply. "He's a pro. Just remember what I told you. Slow down before you hit the curve, and don't do a lot of down-shifting. Keep it in a high enough gear so you won't lose a lot of time shifting back up when you come out of the turn.

"Keep your hands at the ten and two o'clock positions on the wheel," Scott went on. "Cross your arms on the turns if you have to, but don't move your hands."

Joe's hands were gripping the wheel so tightly that they were turning white. "Right," he said. "I think I've got that one down pat. But I've got to close the distance somehow."

Joe saw the car ahead of him veer over to the side and slow down near a blocked-off cross street. "We'll have another driving lesson later!" he shouted. "It looks like he's making his move!"

He punched the accelerator to the floor and tore down the road, heading straight for the other race car. McCoy saw him coming, swerved back to the middle of the road and sped up again—but not fast enough. Now Joe was right on his tail, in his slipstream.

Joe eased off the accelerator slightly, letting the air currents in the wake of the lead car pull him along for the ride. "Got you now!" Joe yelled. "I'm hanging onto your tail, and I'm not letting go!"

The car in front careened from one side of the road to the other and back again, trying to shake Joe off. But Joe matched it move for move. They blasted up the long north straightaway, locked in an invisible embrace. Joe knew they must be doing close to 190, but the constant bumping and rocking, with his head just a few feet off the ground, made it feel as if they were about to break the speed of sound.

Still he felt oddly calm as the eastward uphill

turn loomed ahead. It was a right turn, and Joe was ready when the lead car moved to the left side of the road to reduce the angle of the curve and take it at the fastest speed possible.

Joe followed the maneuver easily, staying right behind him. Looking at the shadows cast by the late-morning sun, Joe couldn't tell where one car ended and the other began. The flared rear wing of one merged with the tapered nose of the other.

Then suddenly the car in front swerved back into the right lane and the driver downshifted, lurching to a reduced speed. Joe shot past him and realized, too late, that he was going way too fast to make the turn.

Joe slammed on the brakes, making another disastrous mistake. The nose dipped down and scraped the pavement. The rear end bucked up and the back tires lost their grip on the road, sliding sideways and throwing the car into a deadly spin.

Joe fought the wheel, but there was no response. The car was completely out of control.

Chapter
17

THE RACE CAR spun around violently and skidded backward onto the shoulder of the road. Any other vehicle would have flipped over, crushing the driver underneath. But the low center of gravity kept the Grand Prix racer upright.

Joe was rattled but unhurt. He pried his hands off the steering wheel. They were shaking badly. He willed himself to calm down, but he remembered to keep his foot on the gas pedal, keeping the revs high enough to prevent the engine from stalling out. He glanced at the array of gauges. Everything seemed okay. None of the needles were poking into the red zone.

All of this took a matter of seconds, although it seemed like an eternity to Joe. He was now pointing in the wrong direction, and he could see the other Formula One car in the side mirror, dwindling in the distance.

Joe eased off the clutch, the wheels kicking up gravel as the car moved off the side and back onto the pavement. Joe pulled the wheel hard to the left and made a tight U-turn, skirting the outer edge of the shoulder on the opposite side. Then he grimly pressed the accelerator to the floor, his head jerking backward as the car took off in pursuit.

Frank pulled the van out onto the cliff road about a half mile down from the hairpin turn. He glanced at his watch as he raced up the road. It had only been nine minutes since McCoy had fled the fairgrounds in the stolen car.

"What happens if they come zooming right down our throats?" Callie asked nervously.

Frank flashed a tight grin. "The van will end up with a very exotic hood ornament. But don't worry—we've still got at least a minute and a half."

Frank slowed down for the tight curve where McCoy's race car had crashed through the guardrail from the opposite direction just a few days ago. He steered the van onto the narrow shoulder at the edge of the cliff and then backed it up so that it was now blocking the road.

Frank leapt out of the van and Callie chased after him. "How do you know we have that much time?"

"Because of the time codes on the videotape," Frank reminded her. "It took McCoy ten minutes and thirty seconds to get to this end of the tunnel.

"Here, help me with this," he grunted, swinging the barricade with the flashing lights away from the gap in the guardrail, and blocking the outer shoulder of the road with it.

"But why here?" Callie pressed.

"Because this is the best place to stop him," Frank explained. "This hairpin turn is the trickiest part of the course. He'll be slowing down as he comes out of the tunnel, so he'll be able to stop safely when he sees the van blocking the road. There won't be enough room to turn around, and Joe will shut him in from the other end."

Frank looked at his watch again. He went to the back of the van and opened the rear door.

Callie rolled her eyes. "What now?"

"Still thirty seconds left," Frank said. "You get behind the van. I'm going to set out some emergency flares just to make sure he gets the idea."

He took out the flares and set one in the middle of the road, about twenty yards in front of the van. Then he ran back and knelt down next to the barricade on the shoulder, setting another flare in front of it.

Frank was about to stand up when he heard a rumbling noise behind him. He looked over his shoulder and saw a Formula One car come roaring out of the tunnel and screech to a halt near the first emergency flare.

Frank swore softly under his breath. Too late, he remembered the extra fifteen seconds it had taken McCoy to get out of his car on the day of the crash. And now he's caught me off guard, Frank realized. Right out in the open.

He couldn't make out the driver's identity—his face, from the nose down, was blocked by the lip of the cockpit. But Frank could see his steel gray eyes. They were locked on him, staring *through* him.

As Frank heard the powerful engine rev up, he knew that the man behind the wheel of the race car was going to try to smash through the wooden barrier and take the narrow outer shoulder around the van. He was willing to risk his life for his freedom—and he wouldn't hesitate to run Frank over if he was in the way.

The driver popped the clutch and the car jumped forward. Frank dove for the side of the van. He looked up to see the race car angling toward the barrier, still not going too fast. Then he heard a familiar rumbling sound. Another car was coming through the tunnel!

The second car slowed and came out of the tunnel to smash into the left rear side of the first one, twisting it sideways on the road. As the back end of the lead car swung around from the impact, the driver bashed his head on the side of the cockpit. The man inside slumped forward, and the engine sputtered and died.

The engine of the other race car revved to a high-pitched whine in triumph. Then it settled back down to a low rumble before the driver switched off the ignition. He climbed out, took off his crash helmet, and ran his hand through his blond hair.

It was Joe. He glanced inside the other car, and then he looked at his brother and smiled. "Looks like a TKO to me. Does that mean I win?"

They pulled Angus McCoy from the cockpit and laid him down gently next to the race car.

Frank reached into the car Joe had been driving and flipped the radio talk-back switch. "You better get an ambulance up here. It looks like the reports of Angus McCoy's death were greatly exaggerated."

A police cruiser escorted the ambulance to the scene. Officer Con Riley got out of the police car, followed by Scott Lavin and Reinhart Voss. "Looks like I was wrong about you boys after all," Riley scowled. "You *are* a couple of car thieves."

Joe shrugged. "I figured it was only fair to chase down McCoy in a car that belonged to him."

Voss looked over the Formula One machine. "There's no real damage," he concluded. "It's still in pretty good driving condition."

"What's all this about McCoy still being alive?" Riley demanded.

"See for yourself." Frank jerked his thumb over his shoulder.

A paramedic from the ambulance was helping a slightly shaken but unmistakable Angus McCoy to his feet. Joe winked. "Looks like the real McCoy to me."

"Well, I'll be!" Riley exclaimed, pushing his patrolman's hat back on his forehead.

"Before you take him away, we'd like to ask him a few questions," Frank said. "You don't mind, do you, Con?"

Riley frowned. "I don't even know what to charge him with. Impersonating a dead man?"

"Stick around," Joe said. "You might learn something."

McCoy seemed calm and relaxed, almost resigned. But his eyes still radiated a sense of confidence as they locked on Frank. "I should have known you were going to be trouble from the moment I saw you nosing around the crash site."

"You *saw* us?" Joe asked.

"Sure," Frank said. "He had to be hiding inside the tunnel, watching everything. He had to wait until we all left before he could make his getaway."

"Then what did he do?" Callie wanted to know. "*Walk* back to town?"

"Well, *part* of the way," Frank replied. "We

found footprints up on the ridge, but he probably had the Lotus hidden in the woods farther down the access road.

"He was going to leave town," Frank continued, "but he got nervous after he saw me pick up that piece of the remote control device. There's probably more evidence around here, too."

Frank turned to McCoy. "My guess is you loosened the bolts on the guardrail to make sure the car went over the edge. Right?"

McCoy shrugged. "You're doing just fine all by yourself. You don't need my help."

"You're right," Frank said. "I don't. McCoy started following us around. When Joe and I split up, he stuck with me since I was the one who found the device in the first place. He followed me to Phil Cohen's house and then back to Scott's garage."

"Right," Joe agreed. "Then he knocked Frank out and tried to make it look like an accident. When he realized Frank wasn't carrying the gizmo, he doubled back to Phil's place, sucker-punched Phil, grabbed the doohickey, and set the fire to cover his tracks."

McCoy frowned slightly. "I'm sorry about your friend. But you forced my hand."

"But that wasn't enough." Frank picked up the story. "McCoy wanted to wipe the slate clean. So he broke into Arno's office, looking for the videotape of the crash, but he couldn't find it. So he tried to throw us off the track again by sabotaging Scott's car, making it look like someone who wanted to win the race was behind the whole thing."

"And when *that* didn't work," Joe said, "McCoy decided to use us for target practice, but he hit Arno by mistake."

McCoy chuckled softly. "I don't hit people I'm not aiming at."

Frank and Joe exchanged a puzzled glance.

McCoy smiled thinly. "It looks like you boys don't know *everything*. Arno knew I was up to something. He found out about the Clarco Industries scam I was using to stash my money."

"The canceled checks!" Joe burst out.

McCoy nodded. "Sooner or later Arno would have figured out the whole thing."

"I think he may have caught on a lot quicker than you think," Joe said. "He took out a million-dollar life insurance policy on you!"

"It figures." McCoy sighed. "That two-bit hustler was always trying to cash in on my sweat and blood."

Frank looked at the world champion driver. "You seem to be taking all this pretty well."

McCoy shrugged. "A race car has ten thousand parts. Even if it's 99.9% perfect, there are still ten things that can go wrong. But there's no sense getting mad at the car. My plan wasn't perfect. You won. I lost. No hard feelings."

Con Riley slapped a pair of handcuffs on McCoy and led him away. Joe turned to Scott Lavin and said, "I'm sorry about the way things worked out. This should have been your big day, but now you don't even have a car."

"Oh, but I do!" Scott smiled. He patted Reinhart Voss on the back. "Reinhart made me an offer I couldn't refuse."

"It is nothing, really," the German driver said. "I told Scott he could drive my car. As I said before, this race is not that important for me. But for Scott it could mean much. So I said to myself, why not? And with Angus gone, who is there to say no?

"What could be more simple?" Voss went on. "Until you came along and took off in my race car like some crazy person! Lucky for you, the car is all right, and Scott will have his chance after all."

"You mean, after all this, there's still going to be a race?" Callie asked in disbelief.

Joe grinned from ear to ear and clapped Frank on the shoulder. "A Grand Prix race is like the Hardy brothers—*nothing* stops us!"

FINAL CUT

Chapter

1

"FRANK. HEY, FRANK! What are you doing? Catching flies?" Joe Hardy whispered.

Joe Hardy had been trying to catch the eye of his older brother, Frank, but caught him in the middle of a huge yawn instead. Both boys were terminally bored by speeches and ceremonies, and right then they were suffering through both. They were standing wedged at the front of a crowd listening to Town Supervisor Gilchrist speak from a raised platform. His amplified voice rang out: "My friends, this is an exciting day for Bayport!"

Joe sighed quietly and slid his silver aviator sunglasses over his blue eyes. Maybe, he figured, he could hide his impatient scowl behind them. When Joe folded his muscular arms across his chest, anyone could see why he was a star football player.

1

Frank's steady girlfriend, beautiful blond Callie Shaw, stood between the brothers and poked Joe with an elbow. "Better play it cool," she warned, gesturing toward the Hardys' aunt Gertrude, who stood next to Frank. She was drinking in every word and staring round-eyed up at the platform of the new WBPT-TV studios.

"I know a new TV studio here in Bayport is a big deal," muttered Joe, keeping his voice low. "But they could be celebrating just as well if I were at the mall. I know we promised to come with Aunt Gertrude, but enough already."

Frank Hardy, a year older and an inch taller than his brother, leaned across Callie and whispered, "Just think of it as survival training. Make a game of it and you won't be so bored."

"Not even that'll work today. There ought to be a law against speeches that last more than ten minutes! They should have a guy with a stopwatch standing on the platform, and when a politician goes over the mark, just drag him off and—"

"Frank! Joe!" Their aunt Gertrude flashed them one of her reproachful glares. "Can't you two keep quiet? Mr. Gilchrist is introducing some famous movie and TV people, and I can't hear with you carrying on!"

"Sorry, Aunt Gertrude," said Frank, raking

back his straight brown hair. "But Mr. Gilchrist does have a way of going on—"

"And on and on," added Joe. "What's more, there's a whole platoon up there ready to take his place. That guy Graham looks like he's got a nice, long, dull speech to lay on us."

"Now, Joe," Gertrude said, wagging a finger at him. "J. F. Graham has done a lot for Bayport."

J. F. Graham was a tall, distinguished-looking, gray-haired man whose face was in the local newspapers at least once a week, usually over a caption that read, "Well-known Financier." For the past twenty years his money had funded shopping centers, housing complexes, and office buildings all over the city. No one had been more important to Bayport's growth than J. F. Graham, who owned or had a controlling interest in a web of interrelated companies.

He stood beside the town supervisor. Behind them were most of the VIPs in town as well as the top dignitaries from the new studio.

Callie nudged Frank. "Is that Jim Addison up there? The actor who always plays really nasty types on TV?"

"I thought I recognized him," Frank replied, nodding.

"Do you remember him in that TV movie, *Murderous Mechanic?*" Callie asked, shuddering slightly.

3

"He's probably playing the heavy in that movie they just started shooting, *Thieves' Bargain*."

"It's not just a *movie,* Frank!" Gertrude's eyes gleamed with excitement. "It's a *pilot* for a TV series, and they might shoot the whole series right here in town. Maybe even on our street!"

"Sounds like Mr. Gilchrist is winding down, getting ready to finish," Frank noted hopefully.

"Fat chance," Joe replied, shaking his head. "He's just getting his second wind."

Sure enough, the town supervisor glanced down at his notes, and continued as if he had just begun. "At this time I want you to meet the man who will be in charge of the day-to-day operations here at Bayport Studios, an experienced Hollywood veteran and a good friend, I might add—Mr. Mel Clifford!"

A short, deeply tanned man in an off-white suit and open-necked sport shirt stepped forward. He waved, and his sunglasses reflected the glare from the hot sun.

Gilchrist went on at length about Clifford's life and excellent qualities. "And now," he said, "I wish to thank the person who deserves the greatest credit for transforming the old WBPT studios into modern ones—a leading citizen of our fair community and a man whom

I am proud to call a close friend—Mr. J. F. Graham!''

Graham smiled to acknowledge the crowd's applause as the supervisor continued.

"At the conclusion of my remarks, Mr. Graham will say a few words. . . ."

"A few words," Joe whispered, staring over Callie's head at his brother in horror. "My brain's about full right now. Words are going to start leaking out if we don't get out of here—now."

Frank shrugged helplessly. "I'm with you, but Aunt Gertrude looks like she's going to see this thing through to the bitter end. I don't see how we—"

He broke off abruptly when he noticed that Callie had closed her eyes and was swaying back and forth, a hand on her forehead. She looked ill.

"Callie? Are you okay?"

She shook her head weakly. "I don't know . . . I feel kind of sick—if I could just sit down . . ."

Frank said, "Aunt Gertrude, excuse me, but Callie's sick. Would you mind if I took her someplace to sit down and rest?"

"Oh, of course not, dear!" Gertrude gave Callie a concerned look. "You *do* look pale, Callie." She thought for a moment. "Frank, Joe, you two help her find a comfortable place to rest for a while. Don't worry about me, I'll be fine.''

"We'll see you at home," said Joe.

"I'm sorry, Aunt Gertrude," Callie said faintly.

"Don't be silly, dear, you just take care of yourself. Go on, now."

Frank, Joe, and Callie started toward the main gate of the studio, making their way through the crowd. Adding to the congestion were carpenters, electricians, costumers, and painters who were trying to work. The studio was so large that many of the workers had to ride bicycles to get from one place to another.

"Maybe it's the flu," Joe suggested. "There's been a lot of these real weird bugs going around lately."

"No, I don't think so," said Callie, giving Joe a Cheshire cat smile. She was suddenly looking very healthy. "Actually, I think I'm on the road to a complete recovery. I'd probably feel as good as new—"

"With a slice of pizza from the mall!" Frank stared at his girlfriend with respect. "You were faking it!"

Callie looked smug. "Well, we were all desperate to get out of there, and here we are. You can tell your aunt that I just needed to sit down. I'm fine now."

Joe grinned. "Unbelievable! You ought to be an actress. You really looked sick back there."

"I don't think acting is my thing," Callie replied. "Except in emergencies, of course. Did someone say something about pizza?"

Frank laughed. "Okay, okay. You've definitely earned it."

"Pretty impressive setup," said Frank as they walked on. "It's like a little city."

The studio was spread out over a hundred acres. There was a maze of streets and narrow alleys between buildings. The biggest structures were soundstages, where the actual shows were shot. The enormous doors of one stood open so they could glance inside.

"Awesome," said Callie. "You could fit our whole house and yard into just a corner of this thing."

Smaller buildings were identified by signs: Sound Recording Studio, Carpentry Shop, Wardrobe Department.

"There's the gate." Joe pointed to the right. They started past an alley between two sound stages. Suddenly they heard a loud crash, the sound of metal smashing against metal.

"What was that?" Callie yelled.

"It came from down this alley," Joe noted. "Let's check it out." They dashed to the mouth of the alley.

The harsh roar of a powerful engine being revved up filled their ears, and then a pickup truck shot toward them. Callie became rooted

7

to the gound. The truck was going to hit her head-on!

Frank spun and dove for her. The force of his charge carried them back several feet. They hit the ground just as the truck whizzed by. It took a sharp turn and raced for the gate. People scrambled and parted to clear a path for it like the wake on both sides of a ship.

A few angry pedestrians yelled after the disappearing truck as Frank asked Callie, "You okay?"

She laughed weakly. "Now I *really* need a place to sit down."

Joe helped her up and saw how scared she'd been by the near miss.

"That truck had no plates," said Joe.

"Is there anything down there?" asked Frank.

The three peered into the narrow passageway. It looked empty except for a big metal scrap bin piled high with trash at the far end. The truck must have struck the bin initially. They walked down to get a better look.

The bin was full of scraps of wood, paint cans, a broken ladder, and other junk. It looked like an ordinary scrap heap. Except—except for something sticking out that caught Joe's eye.

"Frank," said Joe, "does that look like a foot to you?"

"*Two* feet, actually," said Frank.

"Must be a dummy," Joe decided.

"Probably," replied Frank, "but we better make sure."

The brothers climbed into the Dumpster and began to remove pieces of junk. They worked quickly as more of the dummy came into view. Frank lifted a piece of wood, then suddenly dropped it to jump back.

"What's the matter?" cracked Joe. "Too heavy for you? Let me." He reached down and pulled off the board.

Sitting on the side of the Dumpster, Callie gasped.

"Uh-oh," said Frank.

"That's no dummy," Joe said simply.

Callie said nothing; she only bit her lip and looked away.

The legs were human, and they were attached to a body. The body was dead.

Chapter

2

FRANK AND JOE AND CALLIE had called the police at once. They had given them what little information they had and had been asked to wait.

Since then they had been standing off to one side, apparently forgotten while half the Bayport police department swarmed around the alley. Chief of Police Collig himself was directing the work. Technicians drew sketches, took pictures, measured, and dusted for fingerprints.

Frank finally spotted a friendly face among the ranks of the Bayport P.D.

"Hey, Con! Con Riley!"

Con Riley smiled and walked over to greet the boys and Callie. He was a big, easygoing man, one of the few local police willing to admit that Frank and Joe had helped to solve

10

some tricky cases in the past. To him they were friends, not nuisances.

"Hello there! Trust you to be the ones to trip over a body."

"Yeah, but now no one'll tell us what's going on." Joe frowned and nodded at the busy crime scene.

"What's happening, Con?" Frank asked. "Who was the guy?"

Riley thought for a bit before replying.

"Well—okay. The victim is a writer named Bennett Fairburn. Matter of fact, he wrote the script for 'Thieves' Bargain,' the TV series pilot they're shooting. He was shot by a single thirty-eight-caliber bullet less than two hours before you found the body—about an hour before the speeches began."

"Any leads? Clues?" asked Frank.

Riley smiled, raising his hands. "Whoa, slow down. We just got here an hour ago. Although, as it happens, we *do* have a possible suspect. Some of the television people tell us that Fairburn had some pretty hot arguments with an actor, a Jim Addison. They almost came to blows two days ago."

"Jim Addison!" Callie exclaimed. "He certainly *looks* nasty enough to kill somebody."

"Right, they call him the man you love to hate, I think," Con replied.

"So, what does he say?" Frank asked.

"We haven't reached him yet," said Riley,

"but we will. I wouldn't be surprised to see the whole thing cleared up in time for supper."

"That'd be nice and neat," said Joe.

Frank started to speak, then stopped, looking thoughtful. Then he turned to his brother. "I guess we might as well take off if you don't need us."

"Hang on a second," said Con, and he went over to talk to Chief Collig. After a brief conference, Riley returned.

"The chief says you can go, and that he's grateful for your assistance."

"Sure," said Joe.

"So long, guys," Con said. "Sorry, but I don't think this is one of those whodunits you like so much. Maybe next time."

After dropping Callie off, Frank and Joe headed for home. Frank didn't say a word.

Finally Joe couldn't stand it another second. "Okay, what's on your mind? Spit it out."

"I don't know exactly, but there's something weird about dumping a murder victim where you know there's going to be a big crowd, especially one with lots of media people—TV, newspapers, the works. I can see that the Bayport P.D. wants this thing to have an easy answer, but it just doesn't fit together right."

"Maybe not," agreed Joe, "but it's none of our business anymore."

As they pulled into their driveway, they spotted their dad's car and one they didn't know—a slick, sporty little foreign job, built for speed and handling.

"Dad's home," Frank observed, "and it looks like he's brought company."

Their father, Fenton Hardy, had been a detective with the New York City police department for some years before becoming a private investigator. He now had an international reputation as a detective.

"Whoever the company is, I like the choice of wheels," Joe said with an admiring look at the visitor's car.

"You wouldn't want it," replied Frank. "I bet it's a real gas guzzler."

Joe turned and gave the low-slung performance car one last envious stare.

"I could live with that," he said.

They went in to the sound of their father's voice calling out, "Frank? Joe? Is that you?"

"It's us, Dad," Frank answered. "We would've been here earlier but we found—"

"Yes, I know what you found," Fenton cut him off. "Chief Collig called. Come on into my office. There's someone I'd like you to meet."

The brothers stopped in surprise just inside the door. Seated on a couch, across from Fenton, was Jim Addison! He was a big, barrel-chested man in his late forties, with a face that could frighten children. Now he only looked worried. Beside him sat a woman wearing an elegant silk dress, lots of makeup, and an angry expression. She was talking.

"And I think that it's simply *outrageous* that the police can even *think* of Jim as a murderer! Why, he wouldn't hurt—" She broke off, noticing the newcomers in the room. "Oh. Hello, boys."

Fenton stood up. "Andrea, Jim, I'd like you to meet my sons. The brown-haired one who looks as if he's seen a ghost is Frank. The blond with his mouth hanging open is Joe. Boys, this is—"

"Jim Addison!" they said in chorus.

Addison gave a faint smile. "I hope that means that you're fans," he said.

Fenton gestured to the woman, who was giving the two brothers a dazzling smile. "And this is Andrea Stuart, Mr. Addison's personal manager."

"Delighted, I'm sure," she purred. "My, you two are good-looking! You could break a lot of teenage hearts. Have you ever thought of careers in Hollywood?"

"Uh, no, not really," Frank said. "Nice to meet you, Ms. Stuart."

"Please!" She held up a hand tipped with long, scarlet fingernails. "Call me Andrea."

Fenton spoke. "Frank and Joe assist me in a lot of my work. Do you mind if I fill them in?"

"Go ahead," said Addison.

"We've been talking about my investigating

the murder of Bennett Fairburn. At the moment the Bayport police seem to have only Mr. Addison—"

Addison interrupted. "It's *Jim*."

Fenton went on. "The police think that Jim is their number one suspect."

"Which is ridiculous!" Andrea Stuart burst out. "It's just because everyone thinks that an actor who plays bad guys has to be a bad guy in real life!"

"Actually, there's a little more to their suspicions than that," Frank said. "Con Riley said that the police know of some rather loud arguments between Fairburn and Mr.—er, Jim, here."

"Oh, really?" asked his father. "That true, Jim?"

"Oh, it was nothing," said Andrea. "Just two men blowing off a little steam."

"Jim?" Fenton asked again.

"Well," said the actor, looking uncomfortable, "before I got involved with this pilot, I'd been looking for a chance to play a good guy for a change. I was getting tired of always being the heavy."

"There's a lot more work out there if he can play nice characters sometimes, too," added Andrea Stuart. "It would give his income a nice little boost."

"We agreed to sign onto this deal only because we were told that I'd play a good guy

15

this time," Addison continued. "Also, I was told that if the pilot did make it as a series, I'd be a regular on the show. There was nothing written down about it, but—"

"We just figured we could trust them," finished the manager.

"Then we got the script, and there I was, playing a villain again! A criminal genius, the mastermind of a gang of crooks! And what's more, I was *out* of the regular cast of the series! When I complained, they said they'd work it so I escaped at the end of the pilot, and they could bring me back now and then, but—"

"But *that* means a lot less money," Andrea Stuart chipped in. "Not as many shows, and not as much money per show."

"Well, they had us," said the actor bitterly. "We had signed, and they hadn't done anything illegal. We could have sued them, but it would have cost a ton of money and kept me tied up in court all the time. So we were stuck. And when I found out that the idea to change the script came from Fairburn—well, I guess I got a little angry with him. We did have a few shouting matches—but *murder!* I wouldn't—"

"Oh, *wouldn't* you though?" Gertrude stood in the office doorway, glaring at Addison. "I saw you kill that sweet young girl in *Death at the Drive-in!* And the way you treated your own cousin in *Hot Lead and Cold Blood* was awful!"

"But—but those were just roles, just parts in movies, Miss—Mrs.—"

"This is my sister, Gertrude," said Fenton. "She, uh, sees a *lot* of movies and TV."

"Fenton, I'd be *very* careful if I were you," said Gertrude. "No one can *act* that mean without it rubbing off a little. I don't know—"

"Thanks for the advice, Gertrude," said Fenton, gently moving her out of the office. When she had gone, he turned to Addison and shrugged an apology.

"You see why I'm tired of playing bad guys?" Addison demanded. "This kind of thing always happens! People boo me when I walk into a restaurant, kids run away from me in the street, little old ladies kick me in the shins—"

"And being suspected of murder could cost us a fortune," Andrea added.

Fenton thought a few moments and said, "I think I'm willing to take your case, but first I need you to do something for me."

"Anything. Name it," Jim Addison said eagerly.

"I'd like Frank and Joe to be put to work on the project somehow. To nose around a little."

Jim Addison looked over to his manager, who gave another of her bright smiles.

"I don't think it'll be a problem. They can probably be production assistants—gofers."

Frank said, "As in 'go fer' this and 'go fer' that, right?"

"Right, sweetie," said Andrea. "You'd be little more than errand boys, doing a bit of everything—fetching and carrying, paging actors, whatever.

"Mel Clifford wants to hire as many local people as he can, so if we tell him that a couple of young local students want a job, he should be happy to agree. Especially if we get J. F. Graham to put in a good word for you."

"Would Mr. Graham do that?" asked Joe.

"J.F. will be glad to do me a little favor," Andrea assured him. "He's a pussycat."

Frank and Joe gave each other a quick grin. It was hard to imagine the dignified Graham as a "pussycat," and they doubted that Graham would care much for the label.

"So, Mr. Hardy—Fenton—will you?" Jim Addison leaned forward anxiously.

"You see to getting jobs for Frank and Joe," replied Mr. Hardy, "and I'll take the case. I'll start by getting some background on Fairburn. Frank and Joe, you sniff around and pick up any gossip about him that you can find. Any known enemies, that kind of thing."

"You got it, Dad," Frank assured him.

Jim Addison and Andrea Stuart got up to leave.

"I feel much better knowing that you're on the case," Jim Addison said, shaking Fenton's hand. "And I'll tell you one other thing," he added, looking grim. "Fairburn's friends could fit in a phone booth. You ask around, and you'll see. There are a lot of people who are glad to see him dead, and there are bound to be some who were willing to help him get that way."

Chapter

3

AT SEVEN O'CLOCK the next morning Frank and Joe were standing just inside the door of a dimly lit sound stage. They had gotten up before six A.M. and didn't feel completely awake yet.

The soundstage was enormous, like an airplane hangar. It was empty except for the far corner, where a small area was lit from powerful overhead lights. Forty feet above the boys was a network of narrow catwalks where people walked back and forth, adjusting and setting lights. Dozens of other people were milling around below, but it wasn't clear what they were doing.

"So what now?" Joe wondered.

"Look for someone in charge," Frank replied.

"It's seven A.M., and all these people look

like they've been here for hours," Joe muttered, only half awake. "Don't they believe in sleep in this business?"

Before Frank could answer, a voice called out from somewhere in the vast, dim space. "Hey! You two! Are you Frank and Jim Harley?"

A bearded, balding man in jeans and a shabby sweater came jogging toward them. Static and voices were being emitted from a walkie-talkie on his belt.

"My name's Joe, not Jim, and that's *Hardy*, not Harley, but otherwise you got it right," Joe said grouchily.

"Hardy. Yeah, right," said the man, making a note on a clipboard. "Right. Okay. I'm Hector Ellerby, the first A.D.—"

"A.D.?" questioned Frank.

"As in assistant director. I'm the guy you work for. I tell you what to do, and where and when to do it. You have any questions, ask me. You got any problems, come to me. Understood?"

"Well, actually, I *do* have a couple of questions," Frank began, but Hector waved him off.

"Not now, I don't have the time. I've got to get over to the office. Trish'll show you around. Trish? *Trish? Trish!* Come on, dear, hustle!"

A soft voice came out of the gloom. "Sorry, Hector, I was just getting—"

"Yeah, right. Look, I have to run. Fred and Jim Hardy, the new P.A.s, are out here waiting. Show them the ropes, will you? Gotta go, bye!"

"That's *Frank* and *Joe,*" called Joe, but Hector was already out the door.

"Don't let Hector get to you," said the voice from behind them. "He's all right. A.D.s are always racing around. It's part of the job."

The Hardys turned and came face-to-face with a young woman who, even in the dim light, was obviously very pretty. Her black hair was cut in a short style that perfectly framed her large brown eyes. She wore jeans and a shiny black satin jacket, which said Bayport Studios in electric blue.

"Frank and Joe, right?" She shook their hands. "I'm Trish Cochran. I'm going to direct movies someday. Right now I'm what they call a directing trainee."

"Nice to meet you, Trish," said Frank.

"I'll say," Joe agreed eagerly.

"What's a trainee, exactly?" asked Frank.

"I'm learning all about how movies and TV shows get made. Meanwhile, everybody gets to order me around. Everybody but you, that is. You guys are the only people around here that I outrank. Well, let me show you around. Come on."

Trish led them over to the brightly lit area. There, the Hardys saw that furniture had been laid out, surrounded on three sides by "walls"—large canvas flats anchored by hinged legs and weighted down with sandbags. Through a "window" in one wall Frank and Joe could see a painted backdrop of a city street.

Workers positioned chairs, changed and focused the lens of a huge camera mounted on a wheeled dolly, and maneuvered microphones on the ends of long poles. Others placed props on the desk. Apparently the set was an office of some kind. Two men stood motionless while someone put pieces of tape on the floor at their feet. A crew member measured the distance from the camera lens to the nose of one of the men, who, Trish whispered, were stand-ins.

"What are they standing in?" asked Joe.

"They're standing in for some actors," she explained. "See, they're close enough in size and looks to the actors they work for, so that they can replace them and stand in while the crew focuses the camera and sets up lights and sound. That way the actors don't get tired out just standing around."

Trish walked the brothers over to where a man sat in a canvas director's chair with the name *Ivan* stenciled on the back.

Trish said, "Ivan, meet our new P.A.s Frank and Joe Hardy. Guys, this is Ivan Kandinsky, the director."

Ivan Kandinsky wore a black jumpsuit.

Around his neck hung a viewer, which he would occasionally peer through.

"Frank, Joe. Delighted. Hardy—hmm. Have you, by chance, a relative named Andrew?"

"Uh, no, not that I—" Frank started to say.

"No, no, didn't think so."

A woman ran up with a gun in each hand just then. "Which one should he carry, Ivan?"

"Let's use the forty-five automatic, my dear." Kandinsky turned to Joe, who was staring at him. "Forty-fives have more *presence,* don't you think?"

Joe nodded and Frank tried not to laugh.

They walked over to the camera. There they met Jerry Morrall, the director of photography, a white-haired man with a bushy mustache.

"Welcome to our happy family," said Morrall.

"Nice to be here," replied Joe.

"Sometimes it is," Morrall answered.

"Bizarre," Joe whispered to his brother.

"Over here, guys," called Trish. She stood next to a young man whose hair was almost to his shoulders. He wore wire-rimmed glasses and headphones. In front of him was a rack with a complicated-looking tape recorder and a lot of electronic gear. Frank was fascinated.

"Frank, Joe, this is Teddy Silva, the sound man. Everybody calls him Headcase because he always has those headphones on."

"How you doing?" asked Headcase.

"Say, what kind of a tape recorder is that?" Frank wanted to know. "Looks pretty special."

"It's a Nagra. You find them mostly in studios. Cost about eight thousand dollars."

"Eight *thousand*—" Frank was stunned.

"More or less. Are you into electronics?"

"Definitely," Frank replied.

"Well, hey, let me show you. Trish, think you could hustle me up a cup of coffee?"

"Sure thing. Be right back, guys."

"Mind if I come along with you?" Joe asked, hopefully. He was always more interested in a pretty girl than a tape recorder.

"Sure, come on. You'll need to know where the coffee is anyway. You'll be fetching your share of it. Oh, hi, Vic." A man had wandered up just then. Joe remembered him as one of the stand-ins. He kept walking, looking very sour.

"Oops, Vic's in a bad mood," said Trish.

"He's *always* in a bad mood," noted Headcase.

"That's Vic Ritchey, Jim Addison's stand-in," Trish explained.

"What's his problem?" Joe asked.

Trish explained. "He wants to act, but all he ever does is stand under the hot lights like a statue. Then, when it's time to do the interesting stuff, he's gone. He always doubles for Jim, but he hates it."

"Sounds boring," Frank remarked.

"It's a living," replied Headcase.

"Come on, Joe, let's get the coffee," said Trish. "We have work to do."

They walked over to a food table, on which were a big coffee urn, trays full of doughnuts, rolls, tea bags, sugar, and plastic foam cups. "They go through hundreds of gallons of coffee a day," Trish commented as she got a cup. "And all the sodas and the tea and tons of doughnuts."

"Well, they must burn up lots of energy." Joe handed her a napkin.

"It is hard work, but I love it. I'd almost do it for free." Trish smiled, and Joe stepped back from the urn to give her room to pass. In stepping back, Joe bumped into something very large and solid.

A low voice growled, "Look where you're going, kid! You made me spill my coffee."

Joe turned around and found a squat, powerful man glaring at him. He was wearing a T-shirt, now coffee-stained, over a massive set of muscles. He stared up at Joe from under bushy brows.

Trish quickly said, "Joe Hardy, this is Sam Freed, one of our crew. Joe is a new pro—"

"This stuff is to drink, not to bathe in," rumbled Freed. "You got that straight?"

Joe felt his face getting red. "Sorry," he said. "I didn't mean to—"

"You want to get out of my way so I can get another cup, kid? I'm asking you real nice."

"Come on, Joe," said Trish. "Let's go."

"Yeah, that's a good idea," Freed said with an ugly smile. "Be careful and don't trip over yourself or get stepped on or anything."

Joe was stung by the man's attitude.

"Hey, I said I was sorry. If that's not good enough for you, that's your problem."

Freed stepped closer to Joe until they were only inches apart. "Listen, punk," he said softly. "You better run along, right now, or you're gonna wake up with a bunch of footprints all over your face."

"Try it," Joe answered as he tensed his body for possible action. "You may not find it so easy."

Freed reached out a big hand and grabbed a handful of Joe's shirt.

Chapter

4

ALMOST WITHOUT THINKING, Joe lashed out and broke Freed's hold on his shirt. He braced for the fight that he knew was coming.

A voice called out, "Hey, Freed! You going to take all day? Get back here!"

The big man stepped back and looked at Joe. "See you around—punk," he said softly.

Joe took a deep breath and relaxed. "That'll really make my day," he replied.

As the man walked away, Joe noticed Trish watching him with frightened eyes.

"Sorry," Joe said. "It won't happen again."

It wasn't till midafternoon that Joe had a chance to tell Frank about his run-in with Freed. They'd been on the move all morning—delivering messages, calling actors from their dressing rooms, and bringing food and drink to crew members who were too busy to leave the set. Now they were passing out coffee.

"Freed?" asked Frank. "That guy with muscles? I brought him a soda a while ago, and all he said was 'Thanks, kid.' He was nice enough."

"Well, take it from me," said Joe, "he was ready to punch me out right there."

"Well, you'd just made him spill hot coffee all over himself. Don't make too much of it."

Joe wasn't convinced. "I guess we'll see. You get any interesting information yet?"

Frank shrugged. "No time to make small talk with anyone. I've been kept running."

Joe said, "I enjoy investigations, but being a waiter is a drag."

"Come on, the camera crew wants coffee, too," a voice said from close by.

Jerry Morrall had just worked out a camera angle and chosen the lens for the next scene. Now he was sitting in his chair, watching his assistants make the necessary adjustments. Frank handed him a cup of coffee.

"Thanks, Frank. So, how do you like show business so far?" asked the director of photography.

"Oh, it's okay. Interesting people."

Morrall chuckled. "Interesting, huh? I like your choice of words. Yes, they're interesting, all right."

Before Frank could ask Morrall what he

meant, Joe came up and asked, "Who's the big guy sitting against the wall over there? He hasn't moved all day." Joe pointed to a large, round man who sat with his chair tilted against the wall, wearing a cowboy hat down over his eyes.

"Oh, that's Alvin," said Morrall. "He's the unit's driver. But his *real* specialty is sitting. You'll never find a better sitter than Alvin. He can sit there for hours on end."

"Does he ever do any driving?" Joe asked.

"Sure, now and then," said Morrall. "But not while we're shooting here."

"Did you know that guy who got killed, the writer?" asked Frank.

"Fairburn? Sure, I knew him." Morrall looked at Frank suspiciously. "Why?"

"Oh, no special reason," Frank said quickly. "Just curious. Somebody must have had it in for him, I guess," he added, trying to lead the conversation.

Morrall leaned back with his coffee. Frank could almost see him struggle with his love of gossip and his fear of talking too much. Soon, though, the urge to gossip won out.

"Well, guys, just between us, there were a *few* people here who weren't sad to see the last of Bennett Fairburn. Take Mel Clifford."

"The one who runs the studio?" Joe said.

"Uh-huh." Morrall nodded, leaned forward again, and lowered his voice. "He used to be a hotshot Hollywood movie producer once upon a time. Then he got himself into a mess. Seems he wrote a few checks and signed somebody else's name. The guy who blew the whistle on him was Fairburn. That was the end of Mel in the movies, and he figured it was Fairburn's fault that he works in TV now. So when they ran into each other here, well—"

"Jerry!" called one of his assistants. "We're ready to shoot."

"Okay," Morrall said, rising from his chair. "Hector, anytime now."

"Let's lose the stand-ins," Ellerby ordered. "Bring in the A team! Ready, Mr. Kandinsky!"

The stand-ins left, and the actors came in. The set was the office of the private eye and hero, played by tall, handsome Preston Lawrence. Monica Malone, a beautiful brunette actress, played his girlfriend. Lawrence was made up to have a bruised and swollen eye, and a bloody bandage was pasted on his forehead.

"His bandage needs blood," said Kandinsky.

"Makeup!" shouted Ellerby. "More blood on Mr. Lawrence's bandage!"

A man ran in and carefully applied some fake blood from a bottle with a Q-tip.

"Okay, now let's rehearse it once. Something the matter, Monica?'' said the director. Monica Malone was pouting angrily.

"Ivan, I *told* you and *told* you, if the camera's *here* and I'm *there* on camera right, you get my *bad* side. Why can't I be by the desk, and Preston over there where I've been standing?''

Now Preston Lawrence looked mad. "Oh, come on, Monica! If we switch places, then no one can see my black eye and bandage! I got beat up in the last scene, remember?''

Watching this exchange, Frank poked Joe with an elbow and winked. Joe stifled a laugh.

"Now, now, let's be pals," urged Kandinsky, jumping between his actors. "Monica darling, we *have* to do it this way, dear, or it won't match up with the other shots, you understand? But then we'll turn the camera *around* and shoot your *close-ups* with your *good* profile—not that you don't look gorgeous from *both* sides, dear—and it'll be *fine*. Trust me on this, okay?''

"Well—oh, all right," the actress said, giving Lawrence one last dirty look.

"Fantastic!" exclaimed Kandinsky, walking back to his chair and wiping his face with a handkerchief.

"Give me a break!" Joe whispered to Frank.

Frank nodded. "I wish Callie could see this."

With the crisis solved, the master, or the full scene, was quickly shot. Then the crew got ready for the close-ups, which meant turning the camera around, changing some lights, and moving furniture. The actors, who had seemed to be very much in love only seconds before, walked away from each other without a word. The "B team"—the stand-ins—took over.

Just then Mel Clifford came bustling onto the set and called out, "Jerry! Over here!" With Clifford was a tall, very thin man in a dark suit. Morrall joined them and the three moved away to talk in private. Frank and Joe, watching curiously, noticed that Morrall looked worried. The tall, skinny man left then, almost running.

Headcase called over to the Hardys, "Guys, come over here a sec, will you?"

They went over to the sound man's equipment. "Just stand there and sort of block me from everyone," he said. "Great, stay right there." Frank and Joe were in front of Headcase, and out of the corner of his eye Joe saw him take out a long microphone set in a plastic reflector, like a small dish antenna, and aim it at the secret powwow.

"Headcase, what *is* that thing? What are you doing?" asked Joe.

"*Don't* look at me," Headcase whispered back. "This is a shotgun mike with a parabolic reflector. It'll pick up a whisper fifty feet away if it's aimed right— Ah, got it!"

Frank was amazed. "You mean you're listening in on—"

33

"Shhh! Not now, Frank, I'm concentrating. Well, look who's here!" Headcase said.

The thin man had returned, bringing J. F. Graham with him.

After a few minutes of careful listening, Headcase announced to Frank and Joe, "We have a problem here. The film from yesterday's shooting went to a local lab for processing, and they've ruined it. That's a day's work blown—bad news on our schedule. They've decided to air-express all the film from now on to a lab in Los Angeles—at least until they know what went wrong here. Okay, guys, you can relax."

Frank stared at the long-haired sound man. "Do you listen in on private conversations often?"

Headcase looked offended. "Hey, what's the big deal? I mean, I'm not blackmailing people or anything! I just like to keep track of what's going on."

"What if you get caught?" asked Joe.

Headcase grinned. "So far I haven't been."

"But if you did?" persisted Joe.

Headcase shrugged. "With my skills, I'd have no trouble finding another line of work."

"What other kind of work?" Frank wondered.

"Oh, I'm pretty good at putting together all kinds of electronic goodies," said Headcase.

Joe shook his head. "Well, it's your business, I guess."

"Frank! Joe! Can we see you, please?"

Jerry Morrall was signaling them to join him, Mel Cifford, J. F. Graham, and the thin man.

"These are our new production assistants, gentlemen," Morrall said. "Frank and Joe Hardy. Boys, this is Mel Clifford, who runs Bayport Studios, and this is Mr. J. F. Graham, who recommended that you be given jobs here."

Graham smiled. "You're both interested in television production?"

"Yes, sir," Frank replied.

"Getting more interested every minute," said Joe.

"Splendid!" Graham said. He nodded to the thin man, who nodded back and left quietly. "I think these two young men are just the ones to help us with our problem."

"Us? How can we help?" Frank asked.

Jerry Morrall answered. "All the film we shoot today has to be rushed to the airport to be flown air-express to L.A. You guys know your way around here, right?"

Graham cleared his throat and said, 'I'd better be running along. Nice to meet you, boys." Then he was gone.

The brothers looked over at Alvin, still leaning back in his chair. "What about him?" Joe wanted to know. "Isn't this his kind of job?"

"Alvin?" Morrall said. "Oh, no, we have to keep him here in case one of the actors needs to be driven back to the hotel. Well, can you handle this? We'll send Trish along to look after the film itself."

Joe's face brightened. "It'll be a snap. Right, Frank?"

"Like he says," Frank agreed, "no problem."

Shooting ended a few hours later, and the Hardys met Trish at the stage door, carrying a big stack of film cans.

"Can I give you a hand with that?" Joe said. He took the cans from her, getting a grateful smile from the girl.

"How far is it to the airport?" asked Trish, jogging to keep up with the boys.

Frank shrugged. "Maybe twenty-five miles."

"That plane leaves in forty-five minutes," said Trish. "Can we make it?"

"No sweat," Frank assured her, opening the side door to their van, a black beauty with a powerful customized engine. Soon they were on a hilly road, which wrapped itself ribbonlike around some tight curves as it rose and fell.

"Is this the fastest way to the airport? Why not the highway?" Trish asked from the backseat as Frank whipped the van into a hairpin turn.

"This time of day, we'd get stuck in rush-hour traffic," answered Joe from the seat next to her. "This way, it'll be clear sailing all—Whoa! Sorry." As the van cornered, he slid against Trish, his seat belt stretching its full length. A second later he slid in the *other* direction, against the door. The film cans clattered beside him, sliding from side to side.

"There's no need to floor it, not on *this* road. Take it easy," Joe said, bracing himself in his seat.

Frank stared at the road, then at the speedometer, knuckles white as he gripped the wheel.

"This joyride isn't *my* idea! Grab something—we've lost our brakes!"

The van skidded through a left turn, and there, headed straight up the hill at them and filling more than its half of the road, was a huge flatbed truck!

Chapter
5

THE TRUCK LOOKED ENORMOUS, lumbering toward them like a modern-day dinosaur. Its air horn hooting angrily was almost drowned out by a scream from Trish behind. Frank struggled to stay cool as he wrestled with the wheel, the clutch, and the gearshift to edge as far as he could to the side of the road. A dense growth of trees left little maneuvering room there though.

The van was on the dirt shoulder, and tree branches whipped at the windows as it sped by. A heavy branch smashed the right sideview mirror just as the flatbed was on top of them, filling the windshield with its chrome grille.

The Hardys and Trish braced for the crash, but it never came. Horn still blaring, the truck screamed past, an inch separating it from the van. But Frank had no time to relax; he slammed the shift down into second gear and heard the engine howl in protest. It worked. The van slowed a little, just enough to keep them from flying off the road on the next out-side curve. Suddenly the downgrade ended, the road began to climb, and the van slowed even more.

"Everyone all right back there?" shouted Frank, throat dry and heart pounding.

"We're okay, I think," his brother yelled. "How about stopping this thing?"

"I think I see a place up ahead—brace your-selves!"

To the right of the road was an old turnoff, long abandoned. It ended in a few feet in a thick tangle of undergrowth. Frank dropped into first gear and slowly let out the clutch. The engine screamed as he aimed for the bushes. There was a last screech of tires, a bone-jarring thump, and they stopped with branches scratching at their doors. There was complete silence for a few seconds.

"Trish? Joe? How you doing?" Frank finally asked, rubbing a tender spot where his ribs had hit the steering wheel.

"All in one piece, I think," said Joe shakily. "Trish?"

"I—I— Wait till my heart slows down a little! Frank, if you were trying to impress me with your driving skills, you could have found an easier way!"

Frank took a deep breath and got out to join Joe in checking out the damage. After a quick inspection, Joe shook his head. "This van isn't going anywhere for a while, except behind a tow truck. The left front end is crumpled in against the wheel and the right side looks like it's been through a war."

He surveyed the area. There was no sign of anyone—no houses, no lights twinkling in the early twilight.

Headlights shone around a curve and caught them in the glare, blinding them for a second. They hardly saw the car that pulled up to a stop.

"What happened? Do you need help?" asked the driver, leaning out his window to take in the crumpled van and its dazed passengers.

"We had an accident—lost our brakes," Frank replied. "But we're okay. If you could just give us a lift to a phone so we can call a tow, we'd appreciate it."

"Sure," the man said. "There's a little diner not too far away. Hop in."

"I'll go," said Joe. "I'll call a garage in town."

"Call Hector Ellerby, too," added Trish. "He has to know we missed that plane."

"And call a taxi," Frank said.

Joe turned back to Frank halfway to

the car. "You think this has anything to do with—"

Frank cut his brother off. "Later, Joe. When we're alone. Right?"

Frank looked at Trish, who was wearing a puzzled expression, obviously trying to figure out what Joe had been going to say. She kept quiet and didn't ask any questions, though.

Sometime later the battered van had been hauled away, and Frank, Joe, and Trish were dropped off in front of the Hardy house. "Come on in for a minute, Trish," suggested Frank, "and then we'll get you back to the hotel—or wherever you want to go."

"Joe said Ellerby wanted me to drop this film at the studio," she replied. "They have to figure out how to get it to L.A. tonight."

"We'll take you in just a minute," said Joe, and the three entered to find Fenton Hardy waiting.

"Dad, this is Trish Cochran, she works on the film. She was with us when we had a—"

"Little accident," Frank finished. "Trish, this is our father, Fenton Hardy."

"Nice to meet you, Trish," said Fenton. "Is everyone all right?"

"We're fine, Mr. Hardy," Trish answered.

"That's good. Trish, will you excuse us for a minute?" Fenton led his sons into the kitchen.

"What happened?" he asked.

"There was no fluid in the van's brake cylinder," replied Frank.

"Was it an accident?" Fenton said.

Frank thought, then shrugged. "There's no evidence one way or the other."

Fenton nodded and then turned to Joe. "Does Trish know about the case?"

"We haven't said a word to her," Joe said, assuring his father. "But she couldn't be involved."

"Why not?" Frank asked. "Come on, Joe! I mean, sure she's pretty, but—"

Joe's face turned red. "That's not what I mean! All right, say someone wanted us out of the way and messed with our brakes. She was right there with us. If we'd been taken out, she'd have been killed, too!"

"As it stands, we can't be absolutely certain that she's an innocent bystander, so we have to keep her out of this for now," Fenton said. "Now, what else have you got?"

Frank and Joe quickly filled their father in on what they'd learned, especially from Jerry Morrall. Joe told them about his run-in with Sam Freed.

"What does this Freed do?" asked Fenton.

"He's a gaffer," replied Joe. "He moves scenery, furniture—heavy stuff like that."

Frank said, "He didn't seem all that bad to me. He did get steamed at Joe, but don't forget, he'd just spilled hot coffee on himself."

42

"Just steer clear of him—if possible," advised his father.

"I'm willing if *he* is," Joe replied.

"I've been checking Fairburn's past," said Fenton. "He worked as a police-beat reporter for years in Boston. I've phoned a detective I know there, and he's sending me a rundown on the man, plus copies of his big stories. Oh, I'll arrange for a rental car for as long as your van is in the shop, and tonight you can use my car to take Trish where she needs to go."

"I have a date with Callie," Frank said.

"I guess that leaves me," said Joe, trying not to sound too eager.

The three Hardys rejoined Trish, who was curled up on the couch leafing through a magazine.

"Sorry we took so long," said Frank.

"That's okay," she said. "I needed a little time to get myself together anyway."

"I can give you a lift to the studio now," said Joe, grinning at her.

In the car Joe tried to make small talk with Trish, but it seemed she had no interest in anything but television and movies.

After they handed the film to Ellerby, he got rid of them instantly.

"Thanks, kid, gotta get this film on a charter plane we have standing by. Then I gotta see about extras for tomorrow."

When they pulled up at the corner near the

front of the hotel, Joe said to Trish, "If you feel like something to eat, we could—"

Trish smiled but shook her head. "Can't tonight. I'll just grab something. The editor's going to let me watch while he does some cutting. Isn't that great?"

"Yeah, wonderful," Joe replied. He hopped out of the car and walked her to the hotel and said good night.

Joe strolled unhappily back to his father's car and wondered if there was anything other than television that interested Trish. He had his hand on the car door when he felt a steely grip on his shoulder.

"Nice to run into you again. What do you say we finish our little talk?" a gravelly voice said in his ear.

Before Joe could move, another hand shot out and grabbed his arm, twisting it painfully behind his back. Joe tried to wrestle free, but he felt a stab of pain in his shoulder as his arm was wrenched even harder.

"Keep fighting, kid, and I'll break it off."

Then the goon shoved Joe ahead of him into a dark alley just around the corner.

Chapter

6

THE ALLEY WAS a deep U shape, bordered on three sides by the rear walls of the hotel. Joe felt himself being shoved forward and didn't stop until he was smashed up against a brick wall. He tried to clear his head, but things were happening too fast. He heard faint traffic noise, too far away. His arm ached, and his face burned where it had been scraped against the bricks.

He turned slowly to face his attacker. Freed! Joe knew one thing—he didn't want to fight him right then. He needed to try to get on the man's good side if he was going to be able to stay at the studio and gather information. "I'd forget about that girl if I was you, punk," Freed growled. "Matter of fact, I'd forget about the TV business altogether. I think you ought to take an early retirement—real early.

45

Like, just don't show up tomorrow morning. It ain't your line of work, you know?"

Joe resisted the impulse to rub his shoulder or check the blood that he could feel warm on his face. He tried to think. Was Freed bullying him just for the fun of it? Or was he delivering a message?

Joe moved a step away from the wall. "What's the problem anyway?" he demanded. "What's it to you whether I work there or not? I don't get it."

Freed folded his arms across his massive chest. He looked hard and mean in the dim light. Shadows cut deep hollows in his face. "Listen, junior, I don't have to give you explanations. I don't like your face, and I don't want you around no more. How's that for a reason?"

Joe grinned at the man. "You sure know how to hurt a guy's feelings. And here I was, hoping we could be buddies and all."

Freed took a deep breath. "Okay, little man, I guess you don't listen too good. Maybe when I mess up that pretty face of yours, you'll get the message and wise up."

Joe measured Freed with his eyes. The gaffer was shorter than Joe, but he was solid—about Joe's weight. Joe just hoped he was quicker.

Freed took a few shuffling steps toward Joe,

who circled warily, keeping his distance. He wanted Freed to make the first move.

"This'll be *fun*," Freed purred, and swung up a roundhouse right that started from the hip. Joe dodged, and Freed connected with nothing but air, which threw him off balance.

Joe countered with a straight left that caught Freed square on the nose, drawing a geyser of blood. Joe stepped back, trying to keep some distance between them.

Freed blinked, lowered his head, and bulled forward, windmilling his thick arms in a hail of hooking punches aimed at Joe's ribs. Joe backpedaled and landed another left—this time on Freed's ear.

One of Freed's wild punches caught Joe just then in the side. It was only a glancing blow, but it hurt enough to make Joe realize that if the man ever connected with Joe with full force, it would be all over.

They swapped a few more punches, and suddenly Freed changed tactics. He lunged straight at Joe, ducking a left that Joe threw, and grabbed Joe around the waist. He locked his hands together and began to squeeze. Joe tried to work free, but Freed was too strong.

Trapped in the bear hug, Joe couldn't breathe. He had to break loose fast. Freed grunted, and lifted Joe off the ground while maintaining the crushing pressure.

Desperately Joe grabbed a double fistful of

Freed's hair and yanked hard. The gaffer let out a bellow, and his hold eased off long enough for Joe to squirm free.

Gasping, Joe danced back a couple of steps, and Freed charged after him. He threw a wild roundhouse right, and Joe dropped his head. The punch flew over his shoulder and smashed against the wall. Freed roared in anger and pain.

When the stocky gaffer rushed forward again, Joe slipped to the side, and Freed flew straight into the wall. For an instant Freed was stunned, unable to keep his guard up. Joe landed first a short left hook to the midsection, and then a right uppercut to Freed's jaw. The gaffer's knees turned to rubber, and he sank slowly to the ground.

As the man was struggling to get up, Joe bolted and ran for the car. He wanted to consult with Frank. He also wanted to put some mileage between himself and this gorilla.

But as he opened the car door, he heard Freed's voice from the alley. "Where do you think you're going, punk? We're not done yet!"

Quickly Joe started the car and put it in gear. As he drove by the mouth of the alley, Freed lunged forward and almost grabbed hold of the door. Joe sped away, watching the powerful form grow small in his rearview mirror. Good thing he didn't grab that door, he thought to himself, or he'd probably have torn it off.

Later that evening, when Frank came home from his date, he eyed the scrapes on his brother's face and whistled.

"Did you and Trish have a little disagreement?" Frank asked, not cracking a smile.

Joe shook his head. "Trish had a heavy date to watch film being edited. That girl has a one-track mind, so I dropped her at the hotel. Then, as I was leaving, Sam Freed grabbed me. He's the one I had the disagreement with."

Frank looked thoughtful. "It looks like you're still in one piece. How did *he* look?"

Joe said, "I was lucky. I slowed him down long enough to get away. It would take a lot to stop him. Funny thing, though"—Joe rubbed his arm and winced—"I can't figure out if Freed was just going after me on his own, or if maybe he was told to scare me off."

Frank replied, "I don't know. Maybe he's still sore about the coffee. Maybe he's interested in Trish himself and doesn't want you hanging around her. Seems like he just took a serious dislike to you."

Joe felt his ribs to see if he had suffered any injury. "I don't know why. I'm such a nice, friendly guy." Joe frowned. "Seriously, though, the coffee business was just an accident. It wasn't enough to start a war over."

"You planning on telling anyone about what happened tonight?" Frank asked.

"No way," exclaimed Joe. "Let it ride. We don't want the police all over the studio, making everybody uptight. No one'd ever talk to us."

"Right you are," agreed Frank. "Maybe tomorrow, we—"

The doorbell rang, cutting him off, and almost instantly it rang again.

"Pretty late for callers," Joe said.

"Maybe it's your buddy Freed." Frank winked at his brother.

As the Hardys went to the front door, the doorbell rang a third time, a long, insistent ring. Frank opened the door, and Andrea Stuart swept in and began to pace back and forth like a tiger in a cage.

"They'll never get away with it!" she said angrily. "We'll sue that department for every last cent!"

"Won't you come in," Frank asked dryly.

"Where's your father?" demanded the manager. "I have to see him. Now."

"Why? What's so important?" Joe asked.

She glared at him.

"I'll get him right away," Frank assured her. "Meanwhile, please sit down."

She ignored Frank and continued pacing.

Frank and Fenton appeared a moment later.

"What is it, Andrea?" asked the detective.

"Your brilliant local police just arrested Jim. He's down at headquarters now. I'll have that chief's badge for this! I'll have the best lawyers in the country here in the morning, and we'll sue the city for . . . defamation of character and false arrest and—"

"All right, Andrea, settle down," Fenton said quietly. "Let's have the facts. They arrested Jim? For murder?"

"Of course for murder! Those stupid, bumbling—"

"Something new must have come up," said Joe. "They wouldn't just arrest him for no reason."

Andrea wheeled around and nailed Joe with a long, hard look. But Fenton spoke first.

"There's no point in standing around here. Let's go downtown and find out exactly what is going on. Frank? Joe? Coming?"

"Right with you," replied Frank.

They reached the main police building shortly before midnight and asked to see whoever was in charge of the Fairburn murder. A minute later Chief Collig strode into the room.

"Good evening, Mr. Hardy."

"Chief, I didn't expect to see you down here at this hour."

"When we break a major case, it always gets my personal attention. You're here about developments in the Fairburn matter?" He barely nodded to Frank and Joe. They knew that he considered their interest in past police investigations to be unnecessary and sometimes obstructive.

"Mr. Addison has hired me to look into it," answered Fenton, "and I've been going on the assumption that he is innocent. The fact that he hired me gives some weight to my presumption."

"Yes, I could see that it might appear that way," said Collig. "But it looks like you backed the wrong horse this time, Mr. Hardy. He'll be formally charged in the morning."

"This is—of all the thick-headed—how dare you even think such a thing?" Andrea Stuart sputtered.

Chief Collig looked at her coldly. "And *you* are—"

"This is Andrea Stuart, Jim Addison's personal manager," Frank said.

"How do you do?" said Collig. "We make arrests only if we're very sure of ourselves."

"On what grounds, Chief?" asked Fenton. "I assume you've got hard evidence."

Collig nodded, trying not to show his pleasure in having solved the case so quickly. "Earlier this evening we turned up an eyewitness who saw a very nasty argument between Mr. Fairburn and Mr. Addison—"

Andrea Stuart erupted again. "Why, that's

ridiculous! Who is this—this—eyewitness any-way?"

But Chief Collig shook his head. "We don't reveal the names of witnesses, ma'am."

"Some jealous stagehand, I'm sure," she said, pacing again. "Of course Jim and Fair-burn argued. But that's no reason to charge Jim with murder. You're just trying to get publicity using Jim because he's a star."

Collig's face turned pale. "I've got a solid case here. I don't care about publicity, and you'd better watch yourself."

Frank tried to catch her eye. "Andrea, you're not helping your—"

But she wasn't listening. "Our lawyers will be here in the morning," she said, glaring at Chief Collig. "And you'll be lucky to still wear a badge once we've finished with you and your two-bit department."

Collig's lips were pressed together in a thin line. "It's a very good idea to have a lawyer here," he said to Andrea. "Make it a good *criminal* lawyer. Because our witness—not a stagehand, by the way, but a respected citizen of Bayport—heard Addison and Fairburn ar-guing only *two hours* before the body was found."

"But—"

"He was only twenty yards away, and rec-ognized them both," Collig went on. "What's more, he heard Addison say that Fairburn had a bullet coming to him, and that he'd be pleased to deliver it personally. We got the right man, Ms. Stuart. As far as I'm concerned, this case is airtight. Jim Addison murdered Bennett Fairburn.''

Chapter

7

IF THE WITNESS STOOD UP, the case against Addison looked pretty solid. Fenton Hardy had a short private conversation with the chief and came out of his office shaking his head.

"I tried to get Collig to release Jim to me," he said. "I argued that Jim wouldn't run because it would amount to an admission of guilt and because he's too well-known to stay hidden for long. Collig wouldn't buy it."

Andrea Stuart's jaw was clenched. "I'm calling J. F. Graham right now to *demand* that he use his influence to get Jim out of there."

"Even Graham might not be able to do much," Frank said.

"We'll see about that!" she snapped. "Where's a phone?"

"There's a pay phone through that doorway," Joe replied, "but—" He stopped. She was gone.

She returned wearing a satisfied grin. "J. F. is on his way here right now," she said.

"In that case, we'd better go," said Frank.

"Go?" she asked. "Why?"

"He shouldn't see us here," replied Joe. "As far as he knows, we're just a couple of kids with an interest in TV production."

The Hardys were back home and Frank and Joe ready for bed when the doorbell rang. Frank opened the door and admitted a tired, pale Jim Addison, along with Andrea Stuart, J. F. Graham, and the tall, thin man who always seemed to stick close to Graham.

"Jim, are you all right?" asked Fenton.

"I guess so," the actor answered. "But being locked up gets to you. J.F., here, told the chief he'd vouch for my sticking around."

Graham stepped forward. "Mr. Hardy, I want to tell you how pleased I am that you're working for Jim. Oh, this is my private secretary, Norris. Norris, this is Fenton Hardy, the detective, and his sons, Frank and Joe, who are helping their father out on the case."

Norris nodded to them. Though they were angry at realizing that their security had been broken, Frank and Joe kept their silence.

"Well, Mr. Graham—" Fenton began when his sister, Gertrude, appeared in the hallway.

"I heard the doorbell and the talking. Is there anything wrong? Oh, Mr. Addison! What's happened? You look just awful!"

Addison replied, "I'm fine, Gertrude, really. Just tired, that's all."

Gertrude blushed and said, "I'm sorry about the other day. I get carried away sometimes. But I know just the thing to fix you up—a nice steaming cup of cocoa. Let me just—"

"No, really, you needn't go to any—"

"Now, it's no trouble at all," insisted Gertrude, heading for the kitchen.

Andrea Stuart said, "Mr. Hardy, have you learned anything important about Fairburn's past? You said you would check on it."

Fenton replied, "I don't think we need to keep Mr. Graham and Norris any longer."

"Oh, come on, Mr. Hardy," Andrea urged. "We can trust Mr. Graham. He *is* on our side."

But Graham spoke up. "Ms. Stuart, I think it's best for me to leave. Mr. Hardy is quite right to keep things private. If there's anything more I can do, just ask."

The financier and his secretary departed, and the others went to Fenton's office.

"I think you were very rude to Mr. Graham," said Andrea Stuart. "After all he's done for us—"

"How come Graham knows all about us working for you?" asked Joe.

Andrea gave him a cold stare. "I *beg* your

pardon. Are you trying to tell me my business?"

Frank said, "It's *our* business when our cover is blown. You weren't supposed to talk about us to anybody without clearing it first."

The manager turned to Fenton. "Mr. Hardy, really. Are my dealings subject to approval by your *children?* This is ridiculous."

"Children!" Joe was furious.

Fenton gave Andrea a cold look. "Frank and Joe are absolutely right to be worried, Mrs. Stuart. The more people who know about our job, the harder it becomes, and the more dangerous as well."

"Dangerous? Oh, please!" Andrea sneered. "Let's skip the cheap melodrama. How could I persuade Mr. Graham to get your boys hired, or to get Jim out of that cell, without telling him what's going on here?"

"Melodrama, huh?" Joe said. "Well, we had a little joy ride today on a mountain road with no brakes. That wasn't melodrama, that was real life." He related the story of the van ride.

Addison was shocked. "But you're okay? You weren't hurt?"

"We were lucky," replied Joe, "and Frank is a really great driver, or you'd have needed two new gofers tomorrow."

Andrea Stuart, however, waved it off. "You don't mean to suggest that J. F. Graham goes around fiddling with brakes, do you? He isn't a hoodlum, he's a respectable businessman. It must have been an accident."

"Andrea." Fenton leaned forward and fixed her with a steely look. "Let's get this clear. You are not to talk to him or to anyone else about this case. Do we understand each other?"

"Oh, all right, if you insist. Now, what have you learned about Fairburn?"

Fairburn's past as a crime reporter suggested nothing to either Jim or Andrea.

"What about this eyewitness?" asked Frank. "Got any ideas about that?"

Addison shook his head.

Fenton said, "Jim, when I saw Chief Collig, he showed me the transcript of the eyewitness's story. I can't reveal his name, but I know the man and he's an honest citizen, with no stake in this business. He says he heard you tell Fairburn that he'd earned a bullet and now he was going to get it. We have a problem here. Can you explain it at all?"

Jim slammed his hand on the arm of his chair. "Explain it! No, it's completely crazy! I was in my hotel room, alone, until just before that opening ceremony, studying my script. I never *saw* Fairburn that day! Of course, I have no way to prove it. If you don't believe me . . ."

"You know—maybe something could be—arranged," Andrea said.

"Arranged? Meaning what?" Joe asked.

Gertrude bustled in, carrying a tray. "Here's some nice cocoa for everyone, and some home-baked cookies. Now, Mr. Addison—"

"Just Jim, please, Gertrude," said the actor.

"*Jim*, then. A cup of cocoa will make you feel much better. I'll just leave you all to your business." Gertrude quickly left the office.

"What did you mean, something could be arranged?" Frank said.

Andrea shrugged. "If we found witnesses who would swear that at the time of the murder Jim was, oh, let's say, having breakfast with them miles away, why, they'd *have* to clear him."

Joe frowned. "But Jim was alone, in his room at the time."

Andrea waved it off. "*You* know that, sweet-ie, and *I* know it, but we can still get wit-nesses—for a price."

Abruptly Fenton stood up. "That's foolish talk, Andrea. And I have to tell you that if you ever try such a thing, not only would we drop the case, but we would have to go to the police and tell them about this conversation."

Now Andrea got up and glared at Fenton. "If you cared more about helping your clients and less about little legal formalities—"

"Andrea!" Jim Addison's voice rang out. "That's enough! It's late, and we're all tired. Let's go and let the Hardys do their job. *Now*."

60

Andrea blinked and looked confused for a moment. "Yes, of course. You're right, Jim. I apologize if I— I'm sorry."

The visitors got up to go, and Jim Addison noticed the untouched cocoa.

"Thank Gertrude for her hospitality," he said to Frank with a grin. "Good night."

Fenton Hardy showed them to the door and rejoined his sons in his office.

Frank shook his head. "That Andrea Stuart is something else."

"Can you believe her trying to get us to go along with phony witnesses?" exclaimed Joe. "She could be real trouble."

Frank sat up straight. "Maybe she's mixed up with this murder herself! With her attitude toward the law—maybe she set Jim up—"

"How could she have set up the argument that witness overheard?" Joe asked. "Maybe the lady *is* bent, I don't know. But right now I'm more worried about who else she told about why we're really at the studio. Even if she's honest, she's dangerous."

"I think we should turn in and worry about it in the morning," replied Frank, yawning. "We're going to be short of sleep as it is, and tomorrow, we've got to—"

Crash!

The sound of smashing glass shattered the nighttime silence.

"That came from the living room!" Frank shouted, charging out the office door.

An engine was gunned, and someone took off at high speed.

Frank reached the living room first, and stopped short just before his father and brother joined him. Daggerlike shards of glass from the living room window lay scattered all over the carpet. In the middle of the room lay a brick, a piece of paper wrapped around it. Joe picked his way carefully through the mess to get at the brick. He carried it back to where all three of them could read the message scrawled in block letters on the paper.

"Mind your own business. Next time we'll use a bomb."

Chapter

8

THE NEXT MORNING Frank and Joe were back at work on the sound stage. Sam Freed was there, too, but he hadn't reacted at all when he saw Joe. No one had any comments about the scrapes on Joe's face either.

The Hardys had decided not to let anyone, including the police, know about the brick and the bomb threat. "If we don't keep quiet about it," Frank had said, "we won't be able to do our job because the police will be following us around to protect us."

"It sounds like a bluff anyway," Joe said. "If someone goes after us with a bomb, it's like saying that the case against Jim isn't open-and-shut after all."

While a shot was being prepared, Frank and Joe were learning about wireless microphones from Headcase.

"See, you can hide the mike on a costume, like behind a button," Headcase explained, holding up the tiny gadget, "and then the actor puts this transmitter in his pocket. I pick the sound up on this receiver. It's great, say, when the actors are in a car, and you can't use a boom mike or run wires."

"Frank, Joe!" Trish came over. "Mr. Addison needs you in his dressing room."

Jim Addison's dressing room, unlike the boxy little trailers that the minor actors had, was large and comfortably furnished. It was set some distance from the stage, isolated from the noise and bustle, with only a few equipment trucks around it.

The Hardys found J. F. Graham and Norris in the trailer there along with Addison and Andrea Stuart. Drawn curtains over the windows and the air conditioning made the room dim and cool. A stereo played softly in the background.

"Come in, boys," said Graham, smiling. "I have some information for you. I had Norris check to see if anyone working on 'Thieves Bargain' might have a criminal record. He's made an interesting discovery. Tell them, Norris."

The secretary, who wore either the same or an identical black suit, opened a folder. Then he read aloud in a thin, reedy voice: "Freed, Sam. Arrested five times on assault charges, convicted twice. Served eight months in prison after the second conviction. Released three times for lack of proof.''

"Why, the man is a gangster! Why not just have him fired?" Andrea Stuart blurted out.

"Not without definite evidence that he's committed a crime," Graham said. "The union wouldn't stand for it, and a man is innocent until proven guilty. We don't have any evidence against him, do we?"

Frank and Joe exchanged glances but said nothing.

"Then," Graham went on, "let's simply keep an eye on this fellow. He might be—"

There was a knock on the door, and Mel Clifford burst in. "Hello, J.F., I wasn't told you were going to be here today. What's this meeting all about? Or shouldn't I know?"

"Take it easy, Mel," said Addison.

"If I'm not wanted . . ." Mel said sulkily.

"Oh, that's all right, honey." Andrea Stuart hooked her arm through his. "We just want to see that Jim isn't tangled up with this horrible murder more than necessary, that's all."

Mel nodded, and then looked suspiciously at Frank and Joe. "And what about these kids?"

"They've been helping—" Andrea started to explain, but Addison cut in sharply.

"Andrea! Stop!"

Mel's eyes jumped from person to person in the room. "Oh, so there *are* some secrets, are there? What's happening? You hatching a plan to give the cops some suspect besides Jim? I mean, he's still the prime suspect, right? And with reason, right?"

"If the cops wanted another suspect," said the actor, glaring at Clifford, "they wouldn't have to look very far. Would they, Mel? You figure that Fairburn ruined your Hollywood movie career, right? Can *you* account for your whereabouts on the morning of the murder?"

"Me! Why, you big, overrated ham! We all saw you practically strangle Fairburn when—"

The two men stood up, Addison towering over Clifford. He said, "Remember, Mel, *you* have the criminal record, not me! *You're* the forger!"

Mel Clifford's face went from tan to bright red. "That's it! One more word, and I'll—"

J. F. Graham stepped between the two. "Cut it out, both of you! We have enough problems on our hands without this kind of nonsense. Mel, come with me, and cool down. Excuse us, please."

Graham and Norris left, taking the furious Mel Clifford wth them.

Once they had left, Joe spun around to face Andrea Stuart. "You just won't learn, will you? You were going to tell Clifford about us a minute ago! Why don't you buy an ad in the local papers? Then you wouldn't have to spend all your time telling everyone in person."

"I've known Mel for years!" she exclaimed. "He's a pussycat! He couldn't be involved—"

"That's not the point," Frank said. "My dad told you not to tell anyone why we're here. You might tip off the murderer that—"

A knock on the door stopped Frank. Trish poked her head in.

"Mr. Addison, you're needed on the set."

Addison took a deep breath. "Thanks. Andrea, come with me."

"Jim, is it all right if we use the phone in here?" asked Joe.

"Feel free," the actor answered. He and his manager left, along with Trish.

"Who are you going to call?" Frank asked.

"I want to tell Dad about Andrea Stuart and her big mouth before she really messes us up."

"Good idea," Frank replied.

As Joe picked up the phone there was another knock at the door. Frank opened it, and there was Trish again.

"Guys, how come you're not on the set? They're going to be looking for you."

"We have to call the garage," Frank said quickly. "About the van. It won't take long."

Joe put the phone down. "Couldn't get through," he explained to Frank. "Trish, if you have a minute, we'd like to ask you about something. Come on in, it won't take long."

"Well, okay, but this better be quick." As she stepped into the trailer she examined the scrapes on Joe's face. "What happened to you?"

"I had a little accident last night," said Joe quickly. "Tripped and fell in the driveway."

"Yeah, Joe's always tripping over his feet or something"—Frank smiled—"but we put up with him anyway."

Trish didn't look convinced.

"Frank and I have been wondering about this guy who got killed," said Joe.

"Fairburn?" asked Trish.

"Right," said Frank. "We heard Jerry Morrall talking about how Fairburn and Mel Clifford didn't get along, and then Mel and Jim Addison almost had a fight going in here—"

Trish grinned. "Jerry Morrall told you that, huh? *He* should talk!"

"What do you mean?" asked Frank.

Trish obviously enjoyed a little gossip, too. She leaned forward and lowered her voice. "Everyone on this project knows that Jerry and Fairburn hated each other's guts for years."

"How come?" asked Joe.

"They went to court once over who had the rights to a story they both wanted to film, and Fairburn won. He always teased Jerry about it to get him steamed up."

"That's one bit of information that Jerry

would never have told us about himself,"
Frank said.

"This Fairburn sounds like a real sweet
guy," Frank observed.

Trish shrugged. "I didn't really know him,
but everyone says he was a creep. He had a
nasty sense of humor and always knew how to
get at people, knew just how to needle them
and drive them crazy."

Joe looked at Frank thoughtfully. "Sounds
like people would've stood in line for a chance
to murder him."

Trish gave the brothers a suspicious look.
"Why are you so interested in Fairburn any-
way? I thought you were here to learn about
TV production?"

"Oh, yeah, we are," Frank assured her.
"But a murder is pretty exciting stuff, you
know. We just figured you'd know some of the
inside dope, since you've been working here,
around all these people, that's all."

Trish stood up. "Well, we should really be
back to work. This isn't the time to be—"

A nearby truck started up with a roar and
drowned out her voice. Trish went to the door
and turned the knob.

The door wouldn't budge.

She pushed harder, but it remained firmly
shut. She turned to look at the Hardys.

"What's going on with—" She stopped talking suddenly as she began to cough. Harsh

fumes were beginning to fill the trailer, and Frank and Joe were coughing now, too.

Joe pulled back the curtains covering the windows, but instead of a view there was an expanse of wood that completely sealed off the view—and any chance of ventilation.

"Someone's boarded over the windows!" Frank snapped, his voice breaking into coughing spasms. The fumes grew heavier.

Frank went to the door and pushed it, but nothing happened. He kicked at it beside the knob, but it didn't budge. The heavy gas was quickly flooding the room.

Joe gasped. "We're suffocating!"

The trailer had been turned into a comfortably furnished gas chamber!

Chapter
9

"HELP! SOMEBODY, HELP US!" screamed Trish, and then she lapsed into a fit of helpless coughing.

"No one'll hear," gasped Joe.

Frank saw Trish panting for breath. "Lie down flat, the air's better near the floor," he said hoarsely.

Joe grabbed a chair and smashed at the window. The glass shattered, but the boards remained in place. "No good," he wheezed.

Frank saw that Trish, lying on the floor, was barely conscious. His lungs ached as he labored for enough oxygen to keep him conscious. "Not much time," he said faintly. "Try the phone!"

Joe staggered over and picked up the receiver, then dropped it. "Line's dead. Must've been cut."

Desperate, Frank looked around. Suddenly he looked up and saw, in the roof of the trailer, a small plastic skylight. It was too high for him to reach without help.

He dragged a small coffee table directly under the skylight and picked up a heavy brass Emmy statuette from a shelf. Jumping on the table, Frank hammered as hard as he could with his oxygen-starved muscles. With his second blow he cracked it and with the next he smashed his way through.

"Joe! Get Trish up here and I'll pull her out!" Frank hoisted himself up and onto the roof. Reaching back, he took hold of Trish's semiconscious body and dragged her up beside him. Joe quickly followed, and all three sat there silently, inhaling lungfuls of fresh air.

After a few minutes the three dropped lightly to the ground. They examined the windows, which had been covered by half-inch-thick plywood. The wood had been held in place by the heavy-duty silvery adhesive tape used on TV and film sets by gaffers and referred to as "gaffer tape."

"No wonder you couldn't knock that wood loose from inside," Trish said to Joe. "That tape is made to hold heavy stuff in place."

Joe looked at the trailer door. A wooden wedge had been stuck between the door and the frame. The harder they shoved and kicked, the firmer the wedge had gotten lodged in place.

Frank had led the way around the trailer. Now he called to the others, "Come here and check this out."

A length of hose had been run from the exhaust of one of the huge tractor rigs that the studio used for hauling equipment into a vent in the wall of the trailer. Both ends of the hose had been held in place with the same silvery tape that had secured the plywood.

"Someone sure worked fast to get this set up," Joe said. "Or maybe it was more than one person."

"It would almost have to have been more than one," Frank responded. "It was done fast and silently."

"All right, you two!" Trish stood facing the brothers, and her eyes were angry as well as frightened. "I want to know what's going on here! Last night when we lost our brakes, you told me it was an accident. I suppose this was an accident, too!"

Joe focused over her head. "We aren't supposed to—"

"Hey, don't tell me that!" Trish yelled. "I could've died last night, and I could've died just now! You owe me the truth!"

Joe's eyes darted to Frank, who shrugged a reply. Then they focused on Trish once again.

"You're right," he said to her. "We couldn't

73

be sure before, but after this—I'm going to tell her," he said to Frank. "If Dad asks why, it was my idea."

"Go ahead." Frank nodded. "I agree."

Quickly Joe outlined to Trish why they had come to work on "Thieves' Bargain." As she listened, Trish's anger gave way to fascination.

"So whoever killed Fairburn may be trying to get to you before you can find out the truth," she said. "Is that it?"

"It's a good bet," answered Frank. "Who knew we were in that trailer just now?"

Joe counted them off. "Graham, Norris, Addison, Stuart, and Mel Clifford. Anybody else?"

"No," answered Frank, "unless—Trish, when you were looking for us to tell us to go see Addison in his trailer, did you ask around much before you spotted us? Who did you talk to?"

The girl thought back, and then nodded. "I checked several places before I saw you— Oh, I see, you're right. I stopped by the camera crew, I talked to people in props, wardrobe . . . And every time I left word that you should be told to come to Jim's dressing room."

"So, just about anybody on the set *could* have known that we'd be there," Joe concluded.

"Maybe someone on the set might have seen someone coming from here," suggested Frank.

The three went toward the door of the sound stage.

As they approached the door, Joe said, "There's Jim now! Maybe he saw someone. Hey, Mr. Addison! Jim!"

The figure turned and looked at them curiously as they got nearer. It wasn't Addison but his stand-in, Vic Ritchey, taking a breather. Red lights flashed around the door, indicating that shooting was going on inside, and that no one could enter or exit until the lights went off. Sitting near Ritchey was Alvin, with his hat pulled down over his eyes, in his usual director's chair leaning against the wall.

"Uh, hi, Mr. Ritchey," said Joe. "Is Mr. Addison working in there?"

The stand-in nodded glumly. "Yeah, he's in there getting his face on film while I cool my heels out here. Business as usual."

"Mr. Ritchey, did you notice anyone coming from the direction of Jim's trailer in the last ten minutes or so?" asked Frank.

"No, not since Addison did," replied Ritchey. "Of course, I was inside until they sent for him."

"How about you, Alvin?" asked Joe.

There was no response.

"Alvin?" repeated Joe

There was a slight movement from the body in the chair.

"Hello?" came a sleepy voice from under the cowboy hat.

"Did you happen to see anyone coming or going from Mr. Addison's dressing room?" asked Trish.

Alvin slowly lifted a hand to the brim of his hat and raised it so that he could see who was talking to him.

"Sure did," he said, lowering the hat brim again.

"Who?" asked Joe excitedly.

There was a long pause.

"Who what?" asked Alvin.

Frank took over. "Alvin, who did you see around Mr. Addison's trailer? It's kind of important."

The hat brim was nudged up again, and Alvin looked calmly at Frank before replying.

"Lots of folks. There are always lots of people running every which way around here. Don't know what they're in such a hurry about, racing around like they do. I never pay them much mind myself." Down came the hat brim.

"Great," observed Joe sarcastically.

The flashing red lights went off, and the stage door opened. The first one to appear was Hector Ellerby.

"Oh, good. Here you are," he said, leafing through a stack of papers on his clipboard. "Tomorrow is a big day, guys. We're shooting this humongous gun battle at the end of the picture, okay? We'll be on location downtown, and you're going to help with traffic control. Here's a map of where we'll be. Be there by seven A.M. sharp. Got that? Hey, how come you two are hanging around outside anyway? We've been working *inside*."

"Actually—" Joe began, but Hector stopped him with a hand gesture.

"Sorry, guys, I'd love to stand and chat for a while, but I have to check out the locations for tomorrow and make sure we've got the cars arranged and rigged, and I've got to make a sketch of the location for Mr. Kandinsky. See you."

And off he jogged.

The door opened again and out came Addison and Stuart. Frank caught the actor's arm.

"Something's come up. Can we see you over by your trailer?"

As they walked Addison back to his dressing room, Frank and Joe and Trish explained about their near miss with death. Addison looked grave, and even Stuart, for once, didn't make fun of what had happened.

"Who do you think could have done it?" Jim asked when the brothers had finished their story.

"We don't know yet," Joe answered. "But one thing is for sure. *Somebody* around here definitely knows why we're working on this project and wants to make certain we're stopped." He cast a quick glance at Stuart, and she looked away.

They rounded a corner and started up toward the trailer. Frank said, "I can't figure how they got that plywood over the windows. They didn't have enough time . . ."

"*I* had those windows boarded up by the crew," said Addison. "I take naps in there and I wanted to block out the sunlight and the noise."

As they came up to the dressing room door, Addison said, "I don't like it. I don't want anyone getting hurt for my sake. It's getting too dangerous for— *Hey!*"

A stocky figure had popped out from around the corner of the trailer and blundered straight into Addison. His arms were loaded with gaffer's tape and lengths of hose. It was Sam Freed.

Freed threw the hose and tape in Addison's face and took off surprisingly fast, with Frank, Joe, and Trish on his heels. Freed did have a ten-yard lead, which Frank quickly whittled down to two. But before Frank could bring him down, Freed sidestepped a stagehand pedaling a studio bicycle and threw the man and bike down in the boys' path. By the time they had disentangled themselves, Freed was racing toward the crowded main street of the lot.

"He'll probably head for the front gate. We

can't lose him in the city," Frank said as he and Joe sprinted in pursuit, Trish close behind.

They reached the main street and looked around. Joe tapped Frank's shoulder. "There he is!" Following Joe's finger, Frank saw the gaffer turn a corner and run down a narrow alley between two large buildings.

"What's down there?" asked Joe as they dashed that way.

"We'll see in a second," Frank replied as they dodged the traffic to reach the alley. It dead-ended and was empty.

Each of the buildings bordering the alley had a door, and the brothers tried both. They were locked. Trish caught up to them just then.

"Freed's vanished," Joe told her. "He ducked in here, but now he's gone."

Trish said, "The building on the left is the scene shop, where they build the sets. I'll bet Freed has a key to that door."

"Come on!" snapped Frank, and he and Joe raced around to the front of the buiding. The enormous sliding doors in front were fully open. Frank poked Joe in the arm.

"He's over there!" he shouted.

A group of carpenters and painters had just left the building, and Freed was walking with them. He appeared to be trying to blend in so that he could make his way to the main gate. But he whirled around at Frank's shout and spotted the Hardys.

He broke into a run, scattering people like bowling pins, and ducked around the corner of a huge soundstage. Frank and Joe followed him just in time to see a side door of the stage close. Trish came panting up beside them.

"He went in there," said Frank. They opened the door and peered inside.

It seemed empty and very dim. Only a few bare bulbs set high up near the ceiling gave any light. The enormous space was silent, eerie. Quietly they steppped all the way in, easing the door closed behind them. They stood motionless, listening hard, but heard nothing.

"He's got to be in here somewhere," Frank said, "but we'll never find him in the dark."

"There's a switch box over by the front doors." Trish's voice echoed three times in the empty space. "I can light up the whole place." She started toward the switch box, which was on another wall.

As Joe stood rooted to his spot, waiting for more light, he heard a creaking and then a metallic clink from somewhere high above him. Looking up, he watched spellbound as a huge object started falling through the gloom. Trish was right under it!

Chapter
10

JOE DOVE FORWARD and tackled Trish just as something large and heavy hit the concrete floor with an explosion of glass and metal that sent thousands of tiny shards whirling.

"Cover your faces." Joe spoke into his arm, and his voice was muffled.

A powerful floodlight lay a few feet from them. It would have crushed anyone standing under it.

Now they heard mocking laughter overhead.

"He's up on the catwalks!" yelled Joe, brushing off the bits of glass that clung to his arms.

Frank called back, "I'm going up after him!"

Joe turned to Trish. "How do you feel?"

She took a shaky breath, but her eyes were steady when she looked at him. "If you hadn't shoved me, I'd be . . . I would have . . ."

She couldn't bring herself to finish.

"For what it's worth," said Joe, "I think Freed probably thought it was Frank or me under him."

Trish shook her head. "I have to stop hanging around with you guys. But I'm okay, I think. Let me get those lights on."

A moment later the entire building was brightly lit. Joe saw Frank halfway up a metal ladder bolted to the wall. Directly above him at the top of the ladder stood Freed. He had a long wrench ready to throw.

"Frank! Above you!" shouted Joe.

As Freed flung the heavy tool, Frank swung out and away from the ladder, pivoting on one hand. The wrench dropped past him and clattered to the floor.

The catwalks were made of wooden planks, about four feet across, set on steel frames. They were arranged in a grid covering the whole floorspace of the soundstage, so that lights could be hung and focused on any spot below.

As Frank reached the top of the ladder, Joe was scrambling up to join him. Meanwhile, Freed ran along a catwalk, away from the Hardys.

"We have him cornered!" Joe said.

"Wrong!" snapped Frank, pointing across to the opposite corner, where another ladder was bolted to the wall. "Let's box him in. I'll cut across, and you chase him down."

The brothers raced in different directions. Joe's speed made him a dangerous receiver of deep passes during football season. Now he closed on Freed, who was alarmed to see Joe on his heels. Realizing he wouldn't be able to reach the ladder before Joe caught him, he turned onto one of the catwalks that led out over the middle of the floor.

But the Hardys were faster and in better shape. Frank quickly shifted to cut the gaffer off, and Joe raced after him in pursuit. Seconds later Freed found himself standing, his back against the catwalk's guardrail, with Frank on one side and Joe on the other.

Freed turned toward Joe and feigned a move in that direction, freezing Joe momentarily. Then he whipped around and ran full speed at Frank, ramming him hard with a shoulder. Frank was knocked against the rail, out of breath, and Freed tried to get by toward the ladder, but Frank dove and just caught Freed by the ankle, sending the thug sprawling on the planks.

Both were quickly on their feet, facing each other. Frank lashed out with a right cross. He hit Freed high on the cheekbone, backing him up a step. But Freed closed with him. He placed a foot behind Frank's ankle and tripped him up. Frank landed hard on the catwalk.

Instantly Freed was on Frank, shoving at him and rolling him. He was going to push him off the planks and down to the concrete forty feet below! Frank felt himself sliding toward the edge with nothing to grab on to.

But Joe came in behind Freed and got in a kick behind the knee. Freed's leg buckled and he lost his balance. Frank scrambled away.

Just as Joe was about to lunge forward, Freed pulled out a long and deadly-looking switchblade knife. Both brothers had to retreat just out of Freed's reach. He turned from Frank to Joe, stabbing out with the gleaming blade. Suddenly Joe darted forward, making the thug lunge. Joe then dove low for Freed's legs while at the same instant Frank hit him chest-high from the other side.

The knife went pinwheeling into the air, and Freed hit the deck with Frank on top of him. Cursing under his breath, Freed bucked Frank off and lunged at Joe, who had regained his feet.

"Not this time, Sam," Joe said, stepping out of reach and driving his knee up and into Freed's jaw. The thug collapsed and lay still.

Panting, the brothers grinned at each other. "The coach would be proud of us," said Frank.

"I *knew* all those scrimmages would come in handy someday," Joe replied. Then he yelled down, "Trish! Find a phone and call the police."

That evening after dinner Frank and Joe sat with their father in his office. They leafed through photocopies of Fairburn's old newspaper stories.

Before settling down to this chore, the three had exchanged their information. The brothers had told Fenton about their day, ending with the Bayport police hauling off Sam Freed.

"The fact that someone wants us out of the way seems to put Jim Addison in the clear," Frank observed. "That's what we told Chief Collig."

"But he said that there was nothing to tie Freed to Fairburn's murder," Joe added. "So he was treating it as a separate incident."

"Well," said Frank thoughtfully, "he may have a point. I mean, we've turned up a lot of people who hated Fairburn, but there's no history that we can find between him and Freed."

"What did you hear about Fairburn's past from your buddy in Boston?" asked Joe.

Fenton pulled a piece of paper out of an envelope. "You can read this over later if you like, but here's the gist of it: Fairburn had a reputation back then as a heavy gambler who was always in debt, always borrowing from the other reporters. He was too friendly with some of the criminals that he wrote about, in the opinion of the other police-beat writers."

"Not exactly a model citizen," said Joe.

The three Hardys continued to look through the file of stories. Suddenly Joe stopped and said, "Take a look at these." He gave his brother a handful of clippings.

Frank checked them over. "They're about a gang that pulled off a string of big heists twenty-five years ago," he said to Fenton. "Apparently when they broke up the gang, they never caught the brains of the outfit. The stories identified him only as 'Gallagher.' "

Frank tossed the copies on the desk. "These stories read just like the plot of 'Thieves' Bargain,' " he said. *"Exactly* like it. There's no way it can be a coincidence."

Joe added, "And this Gallagher is just like Jim Addison's character. The mastermind."

Fenton picked up the stories. "Well, I suppose it figures that an ex-crime reporter would turn to his own old material for a TV script," he said.

"Yeah," said Frank, "but Jim said that when he was first told about the TV pilot, it was completely different from this. Then, when Jim got the script, he saw that Fairburn had changed it. Why?"

Joe shrugged. "Maybe he just thought it was a better story than the other one."

Frank shook his head. "You don't rewrite a

script completely just before shooting. It wasn't just a little bit here and there, it was a total rewrite, and that—"

The phone rang and Fenton answered.

"Hello? . . . Oh, hello, Con . . . Yes. *What?* . . . When? . . . I'm going to put you on the speakerphone so you can tell Frank and Joe yourself. Just a moment."

Fenton put down the receiver and punched a button. "It's Con Riley. Okay, Con, go ahead."

The policeman's voice sounded strained. "Hi, Frank, Joe. I've got some bad news for you."

"What's up, Con?" asked Frank.

"Sam Freed was being taken for mug shots and fingerprints, and I don't know how it happened, but he somehow managed to overpower his guards and get away. We haven't been able to find him."

"When was this?" asked Joe.

"A half hour ago," Con replied. "We've got an all-points bulletin out on him, and we're combing the city. I figured you ought to know."

Frank's lips were pressed into a thin line. "Well, thanks for the word, Con," he said. "You'll be sure to keep us posted, right?"

"You can count on it," said the tinny voice over the speaker. "And, Frank? Joe? Stay on your toes. This guy is one mean customer. He really has it in for you two. He put two cops in the hospital, and the last thing they heard him say was that he was going to kill those two Hardy brothers!''

Chapter

11

AFTER CON RILEY'S CALL, Frank and Joe waited for their father's reaction. He said, "I guess I don't have to tell you two to watch yourselves until this guy is found."

"We'll be careful," Frank assured him. "But we still have a job to do."

"Right," agreed Joe. "Anyway, tomorrow we'll be working in a huge crowd all day. Freed isn't going to pop up there. I mean, he may be a hood, but he isn't crazy."

The next day the crew and cast were set up in downtown Bayport, on a block that had been cleared of traffic for the day. Freed was nowhere around.

"Nobody seems to miss him much," said Joe.

"A nice, friendly guy like that?" cracked Frank. "I can't imagine why."

The scene being shot was a gun battle between the gang and the police. At the end of the battle the gang would be captured, except for the character played by Jim Addison, who'd escape.

Frank and Joe had walkie-talkies. They were stationed on a sidewalk just off camera. They had to keep any passersby or curious onlookers from wandering into a shot. Hector Ellerby had actually spent a whole minute with them giving them instructions.

"Remember, guys, this kind of scene, with a lot of extras and guns and stunts and cars and fightings, costs a bundle of money. And if we have to reshoot any of it because some civilian gets in front of the camera, then it'll cost *two* bundles. "So watch the walkers and gawkers, and don't fall asleep, okay? I'm counting on you guys."

"We'll stay awake," Frank replied.

"You can trust us," said Joe.

There had been no further word from the Bayport police about Sam Freed. He was still at large. But neither of the Hardys was especially worried about his showing up on location.

"Maybe he's left town," Joe suggested hopefully but not really believing it.

Before any actual shooting, there were several rehearsals. Police cars raced up, cops spilled out, and heavy gunfire erupted between cops and robbers.

Everything had to be organized to the last detail among a hundred performers, three cameras in various locations, and all the other crews.

During breaks between rehearsals, Frank and Joe met the special-effects wizard, Max. He was a leathery older man in a baseball cap and sat at a big electronic console, where he could set off the small charges that looked like bullets striking targets by remote control.

The Hardys listened as Headcase explained how the actors were supposed to be "shot." They had very light explosive charges taped to their bodies, which were protected by thin protective shields. In some cases, in close-ups, there would also be plastic bags of stage blood designed to burst when the actor was "hit." Other charges had been fastened to walls, to look like bullets smashing into the walls when they were set off by the man at the console.

The special-effects wizard would control all this. But everything had to be carefully planned and gone over again and again, to reduce the possibility of expensive retakes. Ideally scenes like this were shot only once.

Frank and Joe found it all as interesting as did the "civilians," what the crew called everyone not involved in their line of work.

They watched everything from just out of camera range, on the nearby sidewalks.

"Where's Jim Addison?" Joe asked Jerry Morrall at one point.

"Oh, he's not here yet. On a long shot like this, where you can't really see his face, Vic Ritchey can do just as well. Better, maybe."

"How come?" Joe wondered.

Morrall gave one of his ironic smiles. "Well, Ritchey is younger and a little more athletic than Addison, so Addison generally lets Vic do the running around whenever he can. Ritchey really can look amazingly like Jim. Also, it's pretty dull and time-consuming, so Jim would just as soon sit it out." Morrall winked at Joe. "You know what they say, rank has its privileges. First we shoot the whole scene from a distance. What we call the 'master.' And then we start working on reverse angles, point-of-view shots, and close-ups—*then* Jim'll go to work."

After still more rehearsal, Addison *did* appear, hopping out of a limo and vanishing into his dressing room trailer. During a break the brothers went to see him and told the actor about Fairburn's old newspaper stories.

"What do you make of it, Jim?" Frank asked. "Does it give you any ideas?"

Addison shook his head—it meant nothing to him. He was too concerned about the scene he had to do to think about anything else.

"Could one of you stick around and go over my lines with me? I'd sure appreciate it."

Just at that moment the Hardys' walkie-talkies crackled, and Trish's voice sounded.

"Frank, Joe, we're about to shoot. Better get to your stations."

"Roger, we copy," said Joe into his mouthpiece. "Sorry, Jim, but we have to hold back the crowds of your admiring fans."

"*My* fans, huh?" Addison grinned. "Not very likely. But I'll bet you that there's a whole regiment of Preston Lawrence fans there. That's what you get when you play he-men and heroes."

On location Ivan Kandinsky gave his star last-minute instructions. Lawrence listened intently, nodding every few seconds. Then he got into a car and drove off out of camera range.

Kandinsky gave the thumbs-up signal to Hector Ellerby, who had picked up a bullhorn.

"Can I have your attention, everyone? We're about to shoot a very tricky scene, so I want you all to be alert. You people watching over there, please help us out. We're happy to let you watch, but you have to keep *absolutely silent* while we're doing this and stay where you are. If we have to retake this master shot, it'll be hours before we can get it all ready to go again. Thank you for your cooperation." He put down the bullhorn and picked up his walkie-talkie.

"Cameras ready? Sound? Special effects?" One by one, he checked in with each department and got an okay. Then he picked up the bullhorn.

"Drivers, start the cars! Wait for my signal to move! Lights!"

A battery of floodlights turned what was a bright day even brighter.

"Camera!"

Three cameras began to roll.

"Slate the scene!"

Three assistant camera people ran in front of their cameras carrying slates with the scene number chalked on them and hinged sticks, called clappers, on top. Each assistant held his slate in front of the lens, read off the scene number, clapped the clappers, then ran out of camera range.

"And—*action!* Go ahead, drivers!" yelled Ellerby.

Half a dozen squad cars came screaming around the corner into the shot, sirens wailing and red lights flashing, and squealed to a stop. Twenty-five actors and extras in police uniforms piled out of the cars and spread out behind them. A window in the building they were facing was shattered, and a gunshot was fired from inside. Then a burst of gunfire crackled as the "cops" and the actors playing the gang, holed up in a building nearby, blazed away at one another with blanks. One bad guy yelped, clutched his chest, and fell halfway out a window.

Preston Lawrence gave orders and gestured with his hands. Some of the actor/police started charging the building. There was a louder burst of gunfire. Another villain was hit, screamed, and fell all the way out of a window, landing on a thin pad below that was carefully placed just out of camera range. One of the policemen grabbed his shoulder, and fake blood dripped from between his fingers.

Frank and Joe watched the crowd from their stations with one eye but followed the scene with fascination. Joe thought that it went like some kind of super-complex football play, brilliantly run. Frank thought of a really involved chess game.

Since it was obvious that the spectators weren't trying to get too close to the action, the brothers gave more and more of their attention to the action before the cameras.

Joe was so caught up in what he was seeing, he hardly noticed when one shot sounded different from the others. It was sharper, a little louder. Then a chip of the stone from a wall near his head flew off with a whining noise.

Joe looked around but saw nothing unusual. He picked up his walkie-talkie and whispered into it, "Frank. Frank. Do you read me?"

Frank was a few yards away, and whispered

into his own transmitter, "I read you, Joe, what's—"

Suddenly another loud shot hit home above his head. Before he could duck, a bit of stonework flew, scratching Frank's cheek. He put a hand to his face, and it came away with a smear of blood on it.

He said urgently to his brother, "Joe, take cover right now. Someone's using the noise of the fake gunfire to snipe at us, and he isn't using blanks!"

Chapter

12

WHILE HUNDREDS OF ONLOOKERS gasped at the fake gunfire and staged fighting, Frank and Joe were caught up in a real fight for their lives.

Joe dove for cover behind a parked car as a bullet smashed the wall right where his head had been a second before. The crowd gasped and pointed but didn't know what was happening only a few feet away. It was just as well, thought Frank, who had knelt behind the shelter of another car. Otherwise the situation could all too easily turn into a general panic.

Joe put his walkie-talkie close to his mouth. "Can you figure out where the sniper's shooting from?" he whispered.

Frank had been scanning the area. "He has to be up on one of the roofs across the street, whoever it is."

Now Joe, also looking from one roof to the

next, saw a flash of movement from the one directly across from their sidewalk position. The barrel of a gun suddenly appeared, and somebody's arms and head. But at that distance and angle it was impossible to tell who it was.

"Frank," Joe said softly into his mouthpiece, "did you see the gun?"

"Affirmative," replied Frank. "He seemed to pop up to take another shot, and then realized that we had gone to ground. He knew he didn't have a clear line of fire."

"Let's take him as soon as the scene is done," Joe said, and Frank agreed.

The scene ended, and Kandinsky yelled, "Cut! And print!" as the crowd began to applaud.

The Hardys leapt from their cover and sprinted across the street. Reaching the door of the building where they'd seen the sniper, they ducked inside. The roof was four stories up, and they took the stairs two at a time. At the top of the last flight of steps was the door to the roof. It was standing slightly ajar.

They paused and, with great care, slowly pushed the metal door open. They leapt back as a burst of automatic fire greeted them.

"Looks like we found the right place," said Frank as they crouched behind the door. "Did you see the shooter?" Joe asked.

"Yeah," replied Frank. "It's Sam Freed."

"Looks like he *is* crazy after all," said Joe. "How do we handle this?"

"How about if one of us distracts him while the other one jumps him?" suggested Frank.

"Great idea!" Joe snapped. "Let's see, he's got an Uzi or something and we have zip. How do we distract him, with funny stories?"

"The building alongside this one is a story higher," Frank said. "You stay here. Give me exactly one minute and then slam that door open with a lot of noise. I'll come at him from behind, off that taller roof."

Joe replied, "You have to run down four flights of steps here, and then *up* five flights next door. Let's make it ninety seconds. You're not as young as you used to be."

"And you're not as funny as you think you are," responded Frank. "Okay, ninety seconds. Check your watch, starting—now!"

Frank started down the stairs, and Joe remained in a crouch by the door, keeping his eyes focused on his watch's second hand.

As Frank reached the street, he heard Trish call out to him but didn't answer as he ran into the neighboring building.

He pounded up the five flights and rushed onto the adjoining roof. He moved quietly to the edge and looked over. Freed was squatting with his back to Frank behind a large metal ventilator hood, cradling an Uzi.

As the ninety seconds ended, Joe kicked the

metal door open. It swung around and crashed into the wall. He yelled, "Here we come, Freed! Ready or not!" Then he jumped back out of the line of fire. Freed swung his Uzi and fired a burst. The bullets kicked up tar and gravel from the surface of the roof, while others smacked into the stairwell wall, barely missing Joe.

As Joe moved, Frank swung over the edge and dropped the single story down to the other building. Freed was focused on the open doorway. Abruptly he sensed someone was behind him, but before he could turn and fire, Frank hit him with a shoulder in the small of the back. The thug was knocked forward, sprawling to the ground.

"Joe!" shouted Frank. "Move it!"

Joe broke from his cover and charged Freed, whose Uzi lay just beyond his outstretched arm. Freed gave the younger Hardy a murderous look and launched himself forward. He grabbed the gun, pointed it at Joe, and squeezed the trigger.

There was a dry click. Either the clip was empty or the gun had jammed.

Frank reached down to grab him from behind, but with surprising quickness Freed whirled around. He reversed the gun and lashed out at Frank with the grip. Frank ducked, but the blow caught him on the shoulder with numbing force, and Freed kicked clear.

Joe was on him instantly. But he hit Freed high, and the tough gunman dropped lower and arched his powerful back, bucking Joe up and over him. Joe hit the roof and vaulted, disappearing from sight.

The Hardys picked themselves up and took off after Freed. The roof Freed had dropped to was one story lower. They were landing on it as Freed raced for the door to the building's stairs.

Before the Hardys could reach the door, Freed had darted through it and slammed it behind him. Joe tried it, but it wouldn't budge.

"He's jammed it or locked it!" Joe shouted, banging the metal in frustration.

They could hear footsteps pounding as Freed ran for the street below.

"Joe! The fire escape!" yelled Frank, pointing to the top of the ladder that faced the street. The brothers started down the slippery metal rungs two at a time, watching the street below for Freed to appear.

Frank was in front, and just as he reached the second story Freed came barreling out through the ground floor door. He took off at full speed, right for the spot where the crew was busy setting up the next shot. Frank catapulted over the side and dropped to the sidewalk, Joe right behind him.

Frank pointed, and the two brothers dashed after Freed, who was tearing straight through the astonished production crew. He elbowed one man out of his way and sent a script girl head-on into a pile of canvas chairs as he forced his escape route through the technicians.

Frank and Joe were faced with a mob of sightseers and film people milling around and making it impossible to run full speed. Helpless and frustrated, they tried to keep Freed in view as they struggled through the crowd. By the time they had escaped the worst of the confusion, Freed was nowhere to be seen. The man had succeeded in vanishing again.

"Which way could he have gone?" Joe demanded urgently. Frank only shrugged, realizing that every second the thug was getting farther away.

"We *had* him and we let him get away!" Joe exclaimed with a look of disgust on his face. "What a great pair of detectives we are!"

"Take it easy," said Frank, putting a hand on his brother's shoulder. "He can't be too far away. Maybe somebody saw him."

"Hey, fellas," came a voice from under a cowboy hat. Alvin was in his usual position, sitting in his chair, tilted back against a nearby trailer.

"Alvin!" exclaimed Frank. "You didn't happen to see—"

Alvin pointed with his thumb, indicating a right turn at the next corner. "A man oughtn't to race around like that. It's not healthy, and you can knock folks over when you aren't careful." Alvin carefully adjusted the tilt of his hat. "You know, I'm beginning to take a strong dislike to Sam Freed."

"Thanks, Alvin, we owe you one," said Joe as the brothers resumed their pursuit.

They rounded the corner and entered a side street, but Freed was nowhere to be seen.

"Let's split up and check these doorways and alleys," said Joe.

The two ran to opposite sides of the street and slowly checked each possible hiding place for Freed. Then, halfway down the block, Frank saw an old pickup truck sitting at the far end of the narrow alley with its motor running. There was someone in the driver's seat, but it was too far away to tell who.

He turned and called, "Joe! Come here for—" But before he could finish, Sam Freed sprang out of an entryway and clubbed Frank savagely across the back of the neck with both fists. Dazed and hurt, Frank dropped to his knees as Freed ran for the pickup.

Joe ran across the street and reached the mouth of the alley just as Freed leapt into the pickup. It sped off, reaching the end of the alley, and disappeared.

Joe knelt beside his brother. "Frank? You all right?"

"I think so," Frank answered, shaking his head to clear it. "Freed blindsided me and he took off in that truck. We lost him again."

Joe carefully helped Frank to his feet. "Did you see who was driving the truck?"

"No, it was too far away." Frank slapped the wall and scowled. "This is turning into a totally rotten day. We can't do anything right!"

"Hey, look at it this way. Freed tried to kill us and we're still alive. It's not over till it's over, right?" Joe snapped his fingers. "You know, that truck could've been the one that dumped Fairburn's body. It didn't have plates."

"We'd better call Dad and report in," said Frank, rubbing the back of his neck.

"What about the police?" asked Joe.

"We'll see what Dad says," Frank replied.

At a pay phone they called Fenton and told him what had happened.

After making sure that his sons were all right, Fenton asked Frank, "Could you tell if the driver was a man or a woman?"

"No, Dad," Frank said. It was pretty far away, and the angle was wrong. "Why, you think it might have been Andrea Stuart?"

"I wouldn't rule her out. Was she on the location today?"

"No. Neither was Mel Clifford. But Jim Addison was around."

"Are you sure? All day?" asked Fenton.

"Well . . ." Frank thought for a second. "Actually, he got here kind of late, and then he spent a lot of time in his dressing room."

There was a brief silence from Fenton, and then he said, "I don't think we can rule anybody out. All we know for sure is that there's more than one person in on this murder, and that this guy Freed is harder to pin down than we figured."

"Don't rub it in," groaned Frank.

As Frank and Joe walked back to the filming location, Hector Ellerby came up to them.

"Where have you two been? We need you guys. We still have a lot to get done today. Have you seen Freed, by the way?"

Frank said, "Well—"

Ellerby looked at his watch and interrupted. "You can tell me all about it later. Right now we're trying to shoot some close-ups, and we could use you to keep the civilians from pestering Preston Lawrence for autographs."

Ellerby trotted away. Frank grinned at Joe.

"Just as well that he can't wait around for an answer. It saves us the trouble of cooking one up."

As they resumed work, Trish came by and gave Joe a look of concern.

"Are you okay? I saw you and Frank running after Sam Freed a while ago."

Joe grinned at her. "We're fine, but I appreciate your asking. The TV business is turning out to be more exciting than I expected. But don't worry, Frank and I can look out for ourselves."

Her look remained worried. "Well, okay, if you say so. But you just be careful. Oh, by the way, one of my favorite old movies is playing in town tonight. *Casablanca*, with Humphrey Bogart. Do you want to go?"

Joe's eyes lit up. "Sure, that sounds great! I could pick you up at—"

"I tell you what," she interrupted as Frank walked up to them, "maybe Frank and his girlfriend would like to come along. Frank, what do you think? Want to see a classic movie tonight?"

Frank looked at Joe, and then back at Trish. "Uh—sure, I guess so, it sounds like fun. I'll call Callie when we finish shooting today."

"Fantastic!" Trish exclaimed, and ran off happily.

Frank gave his brother a grin. "Sounds like you're making progress. Hang in there."

Joe shrugged. "Maybe, but I think that if she had a choice between seeing me or a movie, I'd finish a distant second."

Frank clapped Joe on the shoulder. "Well, that's show biz."

Later that afternoon, as the sun dropped low in the sky, Jerry Morrall squinted at the shot he was setting up.

"Ivan," he called out to the director. "We're losing the light. I think we'll have to wrap after this one."

"Okay, Jerry," the director answered. "We got all the important stuff we needed. If we still want a few little covering bits, we can get them with a second unit, without actors, next week."

The shot was completed, and Hector Ellerby picked up his bullhorn. "That's a wrap, people. Good work today. Let's pack it up."

Technicians began putting lighting instruments away, carefully winding coils of cable and packing up reflectors.

Frank came up to Joe and said, "I just called Callie, and she and I will meet you tonight at the theater. You ready to take off?"

"I'm going to hang around while Trish finishes up here," replied Joe. "Headcase said that he'd give us a ride back to the hotel. We're going to get something to eat before the movie."

"All right," Frank said. "Don't let her talk about movies and TV. Maybe she'll notice she's having a date."

"I'll give it my best shot," Joe assured him. Frank left, driving the rental car they'd picked up.

Joe helped Trish as she passed out the next day's schedule to everyone on the crew. Then he ran a couple of errands for Hector Ellerby. By the time they had finished, it was almost dark.

Headcase called out to them, "You guys ready to go?"

At the same moment another voice called out, "Trish! Phone call for you, in the office."

She called back to Headcase, "I'll just take this call, and then we can all leave."

The company had rented a storefront to serve as a temporary office for the day. It was just around the corner from where they had been shooting. Joe walked Trish over there and waited while she picked up the phone.

"Hello?" she said. And again, *"Hello?* Anybody there?" She gave Joe a puzzled look.

"Whoever it was must've hung up."

"Well, let's go. Headcase is waiting," Joe said, opening the office door.

They walked in silence toward the corner. Joe heard a car door slam in the darkness. He ignored it, trying to figure how to get Trish to open up a little. Footsteps approached behind them. Headcase got tired of waiting, Joe thought, and turned to say hello.

But he didn't get all the way around. Something hard and heavy came down on the back of his head with crushing force. Joe felt a flash of pain. Then the ground rose up to meet him, and everything went black.

Chapter

13

"Joe! Hey, Joe!" Can you hear me, man?"

The voice was familiar, but so far away.

Joe slowly opened his eyes, and was aware of a nasty pain in the back of his head and a blurry face staring down at him. Gradually it came into focus. Headcase was kneeling over him with his customary headphones in place and a worried look behind his wire-rimmed glasses. Joe wondered what was going on. He couldn't quite remember.

Then Joe noticed that he was lying on his back in the street. He raised himself on one elbow and winced as his head started to throb. Things began to come back to him. He looked around at the dark street and tried to focus his thoughts.

There was nobody else in sight. There was

no sign of Trish. *Trish!* He had been with Trish, and then someone had bashed him.

"What—" Joe started to say, then stopped. "Headcase, have you seen Trish? How long have I been out like this?"

With enormous effort Joe tried to get up. Headcase gently put a hand on his shoulder.

"Don't move yet," warned Headcase. "You could have, you know, a concussion or something. Someone really gave you a shot, huh? I haven't seen Trish. You both walked over to the office maybe ten minutes ago. When you didn't come back, I went to look for you, and found you out cold. She wasn't around."

Joe closed his eyes and took a deep breath.

"Can you help me up?" he asked Headcase. When the soundman still hesitated, he added, "It's all right, really. Whoever knocked me out just wanted me to go to sleep for a few minutes, not do permanent damage."

With Headcase's help, Joe stood and held on to his arm a minute until the dizziness passed.

"Listen," he said, "we have to check to see if anyone saw Trish leave and if she was with anyone."

As they started back around the corner, Joe stopped and gave the soundman a serious look.

"Be careful not to give the impression that there's anything seriously wrong. We're just curious, okay?"

Only a few technicians still remained on location, and they hadn't seen her. Joe spotted Alvin, still in his chair.

"Alvin!" He approached the big driver. "Listen, did you see Trish around in the last few minutes?"

Alvin looked up from his chair. "Trish? Yeah, I saw her drive off in someone's pickup just a little bit ago. Don't know whose truck."

A pickup truck! Joe suddenly was hit by a terrible thought. Could it be the same pickup truck? Could Trish have set him up? Could she be a part of the murder?

Joe leaned closer to Alvin. "Did you happen to see who was with her?"

Alvin scratched his head and thought. "Nope, sorry. I figured it must have been a couple of guys from the crew, you know, giving her a ride back to the hotel." He looked at Joe more intently. "Something wrong?"

"No, it's no big deal," Joe said quickly. "I was just looking for her, that's all." Alvin looked up at Headcase, but the soundman simply returned the look without giving anything away. But as they walked away from Alvin, Joe sensed the driver staring after them.

Headcase took off his headset. Joe had never seen him without it. He looked very different.

"Listen," said Headcase quietly. "You don't have to tell me anything if you don't want to. I figure you and your brother are into something pretty heavy."

Joe shot him a suspicious frown. "You haven't been—you know, listening in when Frank and I . . ."

Headcase shook his head and assured Joe. "No, no, I haven't been listening in on you or anything like that. But it doesn't take a genius to figure that something screwy is going on around here, all this bad action between you and Sam Freed, and now you get knocked out cold, and Trish disappears. All I want to say is, if I can do anything, just let me know."

Joe smiled gratefully and said, "Thanks, Headcase. I appreciate it. We might just take you up on it." He went back to the office and used the phone to call home. His father answered almost at once, almost before the phone had had a chance to ring.

"Hi, Dad, I—"

"Joe," his father cut in, sounding worried, "where are you?"

"At the location. I've been—"

"Are you all right?"

"Yeah, but—"

"You better hurry home. I have something to show you," Fenton said urgently.

At Joe's request, Headcase dropped him off at the Hardy house, and he walked in to find not only Fenton, but Frank and Callie, too, waiting for him with grim faces.

"Where's Trish?" asked Frank.

Joe filled them in on the attack he had suffered, and on Trish's disappearance.

"I asked everyone who was still around, but nobody had seen where she went, or who took her."

Fenton pointed to a piece of paper lying on a table. "Read that, but be careful not to touch it. There probably aren't any fingerprints, but you never know."

Joe bent over the piece of paper, on which a message had been pasted in cut-out newspaper letters: "We have Trish. Wait for our call. Tell no one or she's history."

Joe banged a fist on the desk. "When did you get this?" he asked his father.

"Fifteen mintues ago. We got a phone call, and an obviously disguised voice told us to look in our mailbox. There it was."

Callie spoke up. "What do they want with Trish?"

Frank put an arm around her shoulders. "Probably, they *don't* want her specifically, except as a way of putting pressure on us. But there's no point in guessing. We just have to wait for their call—whoever 'they' are."

"Do you figure that anybody on the crew knows what's wrong?" Frank asked Joe.

"Well, they know that Sam Freed is a goon of some kind," replied Joe, "but I haven't heard anybody putting things together yet. Except for Headcase. He knows that something's up, but he doesn't know what, exactly. He also said that if there was anything he could do to help to call him."

The next half hour dragged by slowly. They all sat, staring at the phones in Fenton's office as if that would make the call come sooner.

When it did ring, Callie jumped a little. Fenton picked it up instantly and switched on the speakerphone so that everyone could hear both sides of the conversation.

"Is this Mr. Hardy?" The voice sounded high, squeaky, and metallic. Someone was making sure that he or she wouldn't be recognized.

"Yes, this is Fenton Hardy."

"The girl is fine. Play ball with us, and she stays that way. We don't want anyone hurt."

"What *do* you want?" Fenton asked.

"Get Jim Addison over to your place, now. Tell him to come alone. You have one hour. When we call again, he better be there. And there better be no cops."

There was a click and then dead silence.

"Addison!" Joe exclaimed. "What's going on here?"

Fenton punched out the number of the hotel where the actor was staying. "For the moment they have the upper hand, so let's just do what they say."

The detective got the actor on the line.

"Jim? Fenton Hardy here."

"Yes, Fenton, what's up?"

"Something important has come up. I can't talk about it on the phone. We need you over here right away, and alone."

Jim Addison didn't hesitate. "I'm on my way."

When the doorbell rang a short time later, Frank answered it to find Jim Addison—and Andrea Stuart.

"What's *she* doing here?" Joe was furious. "Hasn't she caused enough trouble?"

Ms. Stuart held up a hand. "Wait, please. I've learned my lesson, Joe," she said. "I won't make any more waves from here on in, I promise. But Jim is not only my client, he's a dear friend. I want to stand by him."

Fenton said, "Andrea, wait in the living room for a few minutes."

Andrea started to protest but remained behind when the others went back to Fenton's office. After she was gone, Addison said, "What's going on here? Don't tell me you suspect *Andrea?* That's ridiculous!"

"She's caused a lot of trouble for us with her mouth," said Joe, "and she sounded willing to bend the law. We can't be sure of her."

"I can't believe—" Jim started to say.

Fenton cut him off. "Jim, you have to let us do our job. Joe's right. She's still under suspicion." He quickly outlined the situation to Addison.

"How long till they call back?" the actor asked.

"About half an hour," Joe said.

While they waited for the phone call, the Hardys ran over their list of possible suspects for Jim's benefit. The people who could have wanted Fairburn dead included Mel Clifford and Jerry Morrall. Andrea was also on the list because of her attitude. "And that's just what we know now," Fenton said. "Fairburn made a lot of enemies. There may be—"

The phone rang and Fenton grabbed it.

"Yes?"

"Hardy? Is Addison there?"

Addison spoke up. "I'm here, whoever you are. What do you want?"

The voice chuckled. "You'll know soon enough. Now, listen real close because I'm not going to stay on this line long enough to be traced, you understand."

"Go ahead," said Fenton.

"We want to make a trade. Addison for Trish. We figure that the TV company needs Addison to get this show finished, and they'll pay plenty to get him back in one piece, and you want to get the girl. Now here's what—"

"Forget it," cut in Fenton sharply. "We can't be a party to—"

"Then say goodbye to that cutie you're so worried about," the voice said roughly.

Chapter

14

"I'LL DO IT, FENTON. I owe it to all of you," Jim said quickly so the voice wouldn't cut off.

"Now, that's real smart. Like I said, if everyone plays it straight, no one gets hurt. We just want to make a little money, is all. Put Joe on the phone." Fenton handed the receiver to his son.

"Here's the deal," the caller continued. "Addison and you will drive out to Black Creek Road—you know it?"

"I know it," said Joe, his emotions on a tight rein.

"Smart kid. You leave the highway and go two miles up Black Creek Road. There you'll find a dirt turnoff that goes up into the hills. Take it exactly half a mile, park in the clearing there, and just wait. You got that?"

"Got it," Joe answered. "What then?"

"Just wait. And nobody else shows up, especially no cops. Or you won't see the girl again. We'll be watching when you arrive. If you're not alone, you won't see us, or her. Ever. You have forty-five minutes."

The line went dead with a click.

Joe relayed the plan to the group. Fenton Hardy shook his head. "It's too dangerous, Jim. You're going in blind."

Addison smiled. "It's funny. All these years of playing villains, I've been wanting to play a hero, without getting my shot. Now I have a chance to do it in real life, and I'm *going* to do it. Get Andrea in here."

When the manager came into the office, Addison told her what was happening and why.

Stuart laid a hand on his arm. "Jim, that's crazy. You'll be—"

The actor stopped her. "One reason I'm doing this is that I feel a responsibility for what's happened. I want you to stay with Fenton until I get back, is that clear?"

Andrea nodded and sank unhappily into a chair.

Addison looked squarely at Fenton. "I want to go. That is, if you're willing to let Joe come with me."

Joe spoke up. "I don't see what choice we have. Like you said, Dad, they have the upper hand; they're calling the shots for now. And if what they want is money, then they probably won't let anyone get hurt.''

Fenton frowned. Then he nodded reluctantly. "All right, Joe, we'll wait to hear that Trish is safe. But if we don't hear anything in an hour and a half, we'll notify the police.''

Jim Addison jumped up, eager to be on the way. He grinned at his manager.

"Cheer up, Andrea, I'll be fine. Look, it's just like TV. The good guys always win in the end.''

Frank spoke quietly to Callie, "Yeah, except that on TV everyone follows a script. *This* script is being written as we go along, and I wish I could be sure that we're going to have a happy ending.''

They borrowed Andrea Stuart's sporty little car. Joe drove, and Jim Addison sat in the other bucket seat. They headed out to the hills behind Bayport.

Addison was stiff and tense. Joe told the actor, "Look, I've been through this kind of thing. These guys don't play by rules. Stay loose and be ready for anything, but no heroics. They don't shoot blanks.''

By the time they reached Black Creek Road, there was no traffic. It was a two-lane strip of asphalt winding through scrubby woodland.

As instructed, they drove two miles along the dark, silent street until they got to the turnoff. This took them onto a narrow lane of graded earth, just wide enough for the car to avoid the trees that hemmed them in on either side. The lane climbed steeply.

Joe watched the numbers click off on the mileage indicator as he drove slowly and carefully over the rutted, bumpy surface.

"That's a half mile," he said. There the lane widened into a clear space in the middle of the dense forest. There was no sign of another human being. They sat listening for any hint of movement. By the moonlight Joe could see Jim's face, pale and frightened.

A voice came from out of the trees right behind the car.

"Addison? That you?"

"I'm here, and so is Joe Hardy," the actor replied steadily. "Now what?"

"Get out of the car slowly, both of you. Turn around and put your hands up on the roof."

They obeyed the orders.

A pair of hands frisked Addison and tied his arms roughly behind him. He was blindfolded. Joe tried looking around, but the voice said, "Look straight ahead of you, kid. No peeking, now."

Then Joe was searched and tied. As the ropes were being tightly knotted he asked, "Where's Trish? You said—"

He was grabbed by the shoulder and turned around. Sam Freed gave him a gloating smile and growled, "I guess we kind of told you a fib, kid. Sorry about that. But I've been looking forward to seeing you again.''

A large fist drove into Joe's stomach. He sank to his knees, trying to get his wind back.

Above him he heard Freed's voice again. ''Women are nothing but trouble, punk. See what happens to you when you fall for a dame?''

Joe was hauled to his feet, and a blindfold was wrapped over his eyes. He and Addison were marched through the clearing. Joe felt a gun barrel poking into his back. He realized that there was at least one other person with Freed. Who could it be? Certainly not Andrea Stuart. ''Let's get out of here,'' Freed growled.

Joe heard the tailgate of a truck being let down, and then he and Addison were roughly thrown into the truck bed. Both cab doors opened and closed. The truck lurched into motion and started back down the hill.

At the Hardy home, Frank, Callie, Fenton, and Andrea Stuart waited for Joe's call. A full ninety minutes passed without a ring.

Finally Frank couldn't take it any longer and said, ''They've been gone too long.''

Fenton said, ''Something's wrong. I'm afraid they've changed the rules of the game on us.''

''Is Jim—are they in danger, do you think?'' asked Andrea.

''All we know for sure is that the crooks

haven't kept their part of the bargain," Frank pointed out. "We don't know why—yet."

"No choice now but to go to the police and tell them everything," Fenton said gloomily. "Chief Collig won't like it that we've been holding out on him. But we have no alternative."

"Do we have to involve the police?" asked Andrea Stuart. "Couldn't that be dangerous?"

"The situation's already dangerous," Frank said. "They probably have Jim and Joe as well as Trish." He stopped for a minute, thinking, and turned to his father.

"Dad, listen. There's no point in all of us going to the police. Why don't you and Andrea go, and meanwhile I'll scout their meeting place. Maybe Joe left some clue as to what happened out there."

"I'll come with you," said Callie.

Frank frowned at her. "I don't know if that's such a hot idea. Maybe you should wait here just in case we do get a phone call."

"We'll go together," said Callie firmly. "It'll be better if two of us search the area."

Frank sighed, but he also knew that Callie could handle herself well in a crisis. "Okay, we'll go."

"Watch yourselves," warned Fenton, "and if you find anything, let us know right away, at police headquarters. Don't go off on your own."

"Okay, Dad," Frank assured him.

After Fenton and Andrea Stuart left, Frank and Callie were almost out the door, when Frank suddenly stopped.

"Frank?" asked Callie. "What is it?"

He didn't answer.

"Frank?" repeated Callie, louder.

"Huh?" Frank looked at Callie with a smile on his face. "Oh, sorry about that, I was just— Listen, we're going to have to wait a few minutes before we go. I've got to make a call."

"A call?" Callie was puzzled, then suspicious. "But we don't have any time."

"No, no, trust me. We're just going to look around, like we told Dad, but I want to arrange a little backup, just in case someone has plans for us, too. It won't take long. Call it insurance."

Frank was on the phone for five minutes, and then, before heading out to Black Creek Road, he stopped off at Bayport Studios.

"Wait here," Frank told Callie, "I'll just be a minute."

"What are you—" Callie started to ask, but Frank had already dashed into a building. He emerged a few minutes later and got back in the car.

As they drove off, Callie gave Frank a long look. "I don't suppose you'd be willing to tell me what that was all about?"

Frank replied, "It's better that you don't

know. Honest. Can you just take my word on that for now?''

Callie shrugged. "I guess I'll have to."

He drove along the same route that Joe and Addison had taken earlier. Climbing through the wooded hills, they neared the clearing and saw Andrea's sports car.

"They're all right!" Callie said happily. "They must still be waiting."

Frank had to drive directly behind the other car before they saw it was empty.

"It's what I was afraid of," Frank said quietly. "They've got Jim and Joe now, too. Let's take a look around for starters."

They got out of the car. It was very quiet. Frank carried a powerful flashlight and shined the beam at the sports car. A rustling noise nearby made them both freeze.

They stood motionless and heard nothing further. Frank relaxed. "Must have been an animal that we spooked," he said, and aimed the flashlight at the car again.

Just then a voice came out of the darkness, chuckling. "Just like we figured. Grab one brother as bait, and the other is bound to come sniffing around after him."

Frank flashed the light toward the voice.

A gunshot roared and Frank heard a bullet whistle through the leaves just over his head.

"Turn that thing off, kid," the voice ordered.

"All you're doing is making yourself an easy target."

Frank flicked off the light. There was enough moonlight to recognize Sam Freed as he stepped out from behind a tree, holding a .45 automatic trained on Frank and Callie.

"And you brought another dame along, huh? Well, the more the merrier."

"Where are they?" asked Frank, feeling Callie's hand clutching his tightly.

"Relax. We'll take you to them," Freed said. "We'll use your car. Let's go."

Frank gauged the distance between himself and the thug, trying to decide if he could jump him, but Freed read his thoughts.

"Bad idea, kid," he said. "Take a look to your right. Just by the trees over there."

Frank and Callie looked where Freed was pointing. They saw another figure, too deep in shadow to be recognizable. But the revolver he was holding glinted in the moonlight.

"You try any dumb hero stunts and your girlfriend gets it before you move a step. So be nice. Don't be a wise guy like your brother."

Frank said, "Why don't you let her go? She's got nothing to do with this, and she won't talk to the police, not while you have me."

"Nothing doing, kid," Freed snapped. "She comes with us. That way, I figure you'll behave yourself and do what you're told. Now, move." Freed's eyes narrowed, and he said coldly, "This is the last time I'll ask you nice."

"Okay, okay," answered Frank quickly. To Callie he said, "We'd better just go along with what they want, for now."

Callie gave Frank a nod, and a nervous smile. Freed turned toward his shadowy helper. "Help me tie them up," he called.

Seeing Freed's attention turned away for a second, Frank sprang forward, reaching for the thug's gun. But Freed stepped back and chopped at the back of Frank's neck with his gun butt. Frank fell flat on the ground, dazed.

Freed snarled and aimed at Frank's head.

"No!" screamed Callie. *"Don't!"*

Chapter

15

FOR A LONG MOMENT Freed's automatic hovered an inch above Frank's head. Then Freed relaxed. "You take some dumb chances," he said. "The only reason you aren't dead right now is I want to be able to snuff you and your brother at the same time."

Frank and Callie were tied and blindfolded and dumped in the back of Frank's rental car. Freed got in front. Before they pulled out, Frank heard another engine start up. I'll bet gangster number two is driving a pickup with no plates, Frank thought.

After ten minutes the car stopped and Frank and Callie were hauled out and marched across some pavement. Then they were pushed farther, into a building this time. Finally their blindfolds were removed.

Frank looked around. They were in a large,

high-ceilinged, old brick building. Probably an abandoned factory, he thought. The rumbling sound they had heard was made by a heavy metal door rolling back as they entered. He could just make out heavy steel moorings to which machines had been attached. Dirty windows high in the walls allowed a little moonlight inside, and a few dangling, unshaded bulbs shed weak light.

A section of the vast room directly across from the huge door was better lit than the rest, and Freed took Frank and Callie there. As they walked, Frank noted that the windows were too high to offer any chance of escape. He couldn't spot any other doors in the gloom.

As they neared the opposite wall, Frank saw that a couple of portable electric lamps had been lit there. Huge rings set into the walls to anchor machinery had been fitted with chains, leg irons, and handcuffs. Three such setups were already occupied, by Addison, Trish, and Joe.

"Is everyone okay?" whispered Frank.

All three nodded.

"Hey! Get over here and make yourself useful!" barked Freed at his accomplice, who had been hanging back in the darkness. "Get these two chained up!"

The dim figure who had been with Freed now stepped into the brighter light.

It was Vic Ritchey, the stand-in.

Under Freed's guard, he quickly shackled Frank's and Callie's legs. But he ignored the handcuffs, leaving their arms tied with rope. He stepped back to survey the scene with a satisfied smile. Then he stepped forward to where Jim Addison sat on the ground. Bending down, Ritchey delivered a stinging slap to the actor's face.

It was clear to Joe and Frank that Addison was shaken, but the actor kept quiet. Next to Joe, Trish gasped. Callie stared at Ritchey, horrified by his maniacal glare.

Ritchey was fixed on Jim Addison. He began to speak softly.

"Eighteen years now, I've been your stand-in. Never getting a chance to act. Never allowed to have *my* own career, *my* own shot. Never getting the big money. All thanks to you. Eighteen years, and I've hated you every minute."

Frank looked from Addison's shocked face to Ritchey's. His eyes were burning with a crazy light. Carefully, quietly, he began to move his hands behind him, trying to loosen the ropes.

"Vic," Jim said at last, "I saw to it that you had a job wherever and whenever I did. I didn't hold you down, Vic. You'd never have been able to make a success as an actor, you—"

Ritchey cut Addison off with another slap. A

thin trickle of blood ran down from the corner of Jim's mouth. He said nothing more.

Frank suddenly said, "*Now* I understand!"

"Understand what, Frank?" asked Trish.

"Joe, don't you get it?" Frank went on. "Don't you see how the eyewitness swore that he had seen Jim threatening Fairburn?"

"Of course!" Joe said. He looked disgusted. "How come we didn't catch on sooner? I mean, even *we* mistook Ritchey for Addison from twenty yards away. That's why he was Jim's stand-in."

"Right," Frank agreed. "Same build, similar features . . ."

Ritchey's laugh echoed in the room.

"That's right, smart boys. It was *me* that guy saw with Fairburn. I made sure that someone was near enough to see when I picked a quarrel with Fairburn. I saw to it that he got a real good look at us before Freed took Fairburn away to finish him off."

"You ought to watch your mouth," growled Freed. "You'll run it too much someday."

But Ritchey didn't seem to hear, or care. He stooped down. Now his face was only inches away from Addison's.

"I'm getting a lot of money for this, big shot," he sneered. "But you know what? I would have done it all just for the chance to have you where I can tell you what I really think of you, where I can give you what you deserve."

Ritchey stuck his gun in Addison's face, and for an instant Joe was certain he would shoot the actor right then. But Freed yanked Ritchey away. "That's enough for now," he ordered. "You keep popping off and you won't live to spend that money you're talking about."

Ritchey shrank back from Freed's flat, cold stare, looking pale and nervous.

Frank's wrists felt raw and scraped, but he also felt that his knots had loosened just a fraction.

Joe turned to Freed and said, "That answers *some* questions about this racket, but there's still the big one: who's paying Ritchey? Who's paying you? Who's running this show?"

"You'll find out soon enough, punk," Freed said with an ugly grin. "Too bad you won't be around to tell anybody else."

"I believe that I'm the one you're looking for," said a voice disembodied by the surrounding darkness. Footsteps echoed, coming closer. Frank strained to make out the figure just walking into the light.

"Well, what do you know!" Joe exclaimed.

"I don't understand," Callie said.

Frank looked at her and said, "Callie, meet Mr. J. F. Graham."

Chapter
16

FOR FRANK AND JOE, the last piece of the puzzle had now fallen into place. They also knew that their time was short. Frank decided they might gain more time by getting Graham involved in a conversation. He continued to flex his wrists and work the knots loose as he talked.

"Tell me, Mr. Graham, did you live in Boston once upon a time?" asked Frank.

"And did you go by the name of Gallagher?" asked Joe, picking up the thread of his brother's idea.

Graham smiled at the Hardys. "Clever boys. I figured that you'd get to the bottom of things sooner or later—unless we stopped somehow.

"Yes, I'm the Gallagher that Fairburn wrote about. We did quite well, that old gang of mine—until we were busted."

"And Fairburn knew you?" asked Joe.

Graham nodded. "We were partners. He was greedy, always in debt. He'd get info as a reporter that I could use in planning heists. Fairburn got a cut."

"But you got caught," prompted Frank.

"Not me," Graham went on. "I gave the police the slip. I came to Bayport twenty-five years ago with the money I'd put aside. I took the name Graham and set myself up as a businessman, strictly legit. I even became a community leader.

"Then I got involved with this studio business." Graham scowled. "And I met the writer of Bayport Studio's first project, 'Thieves' Bargain.' "

"And he recognized you," said Joe.

"Yes, and I recognized him." Graham shook his head. "Fairburn was still greedy. He saw a chance for some blackmail. He showed me the new script he'd written. It was the story of the old Gallagher gang, thinly disguised, with the names changed of course.

"He said that unless he was paid well, he would see to it that the press knew who I was. I knew he'd never leave me alone. He had to be eliminated," Graham finished simply.

"How did you work it for Freed to get hired on the movie?" asked Frank.

"Nothing to it. I called an old underworld friend and asked him to find me some muscle with a union card for TV work. He gave me Freed's name. I brought him here, and he got hired because there weren't many experienced gaffers around. The rest was easy. Freed told me about Vic Ritchey's hatred for Addison. It looked like Addison would be the perfect fall guy—and easy to set up.

"When Andrea Stuart asked me to help get you jobs at the studio, she told me that you'd be helping your father investigate the murder. I knew Fairburn's past would be checked, and that you had to be stopped," Graham went on. "Norris sabotaged your van. I hoped that if you were hurt, your father would drop the case."

"*Norris* did that?" asked Frank in surprise. "He doesn't look like the type."

Graham laughed. "He did all our driving. He may look like a bank clerk, but he's quite good. He was my wheel man in the old days.

"However, we didn't stop you. Even that little message through your living room window didn't scare you off. I figured the time had come to take my getaway fund and run.

"But Freed and Ritchey got out of control." Graham frowned at Freed, who glared back. "You see, I don't kill except when it's necessary. I'm a businessman. But Freed and Ritchey—well, they wanted blood. Freed got Norris to help in an attempt to gas you in that trailer. Then he tried to shoot you, using Norris to drive the truck.''

Graham shook his head. "That was stupid. What was worse, they failed both times. But we *still* could have cut and run, even then.''

"Why didn't you?" asked Frank.

"Because Freed wanted to see you two dead, and Ritchey wanted Addison. So they kidnapped this young lady," Graham said, pointing to Trish, "to get you three in their hands. I was totally against it, but Freed threatened to finger me to the cops if I didn't cooperate. So you see, *I'm* not to blame for your present situation. As a matter of fact, Freed would probably shoot *me* for telling you all this, except that then he wouldn't get the rest of the money I owe him.''

"So what happens now?" asked Joe.

"Well, I'll hold off your father and the cops by using you as hostages until I can get out of here. There are countries where I can live happily, with no questions asked, as long as my money holds out. Norris is getting my emergency fund right now. He has also called the police to let them know that we have you all here and that any police interference would be *very* bad for your health, but that you will eventually all be released unharmed.''

Graham shook his head slowly. "That is what I would *like* to do, believe me. But Mr.

Freed and Mr. Ritchey have other ideas. So, you see, it's really out of my hands."

Freed stepped past Graham, gun in hand. "Enough talk, Graham. Ritchey, you ready?"

Ritchey stepped over to Freed's side, now holding his own forty-five automatic. Both men cocked their guns.

Joe looked up at Freed. The thug was grinning, and the mouth of his automatic looked huge. This is when the cavalry should show up, he thought. But there wasn't a bugle to be heard. He looked over at his brother, and waited for the sound of the gunshot, the last sound he would ever hear.

Chapter

17

FRANK HARDY LAUGHED.

Freed glared at Frank. "You got some weird sense of humor, punk. What's so funny anyway?"

"You are, Freed," replied Frank. "You figure you're on top of the situation, right? But the truth is, Graham is playing the two of you for chumps, and you don't even know it. That's pretty funny, wouldn't you say?"

Frank laughed again. He tried to ignore the pain in his wrists. A few more minutes and he might be able to work his right hand free.

"Cut it out," snapped Freed, whose face was flushed with anger, "or your girlfriend here takes the first bullet—now."

Quickly Frank quieted down.

"Now, what are you talking about? Talk straight, and talk fast."

"I thought you knew the ropes," Frank said, shaking his head. "Graham is too smart for you, Sam. He hired you because he wanted someone he could give to the law. All this time he's been setting you up to take the rap. You'll end up with every cop in the country looking for you, and Graham will end up with a bagful of money, setting up a nice new life in another country. Wake up, Freed! You're being had!"

"Just a second—" Graham started angrily, but Freed waved him silent.

"Go ahead, kid. I want to hear all of this," the thug said, looking coldly at Graham.

Joe quickly realized that Frank was trying to turn the gang against one another. It looked like the best bet to stay alive awhile longer.

"That's right, Freed," said Joe. "Frank and I know about your record—two assault convictions, eight-month stretch after the second one. Some other arrests, but you were released because there wasn't enough proof. How do you think we found out about that?"

"How did you?" growled Freed.

"Graham told us," explained Joe. "He wanted to make sure that the cops would have someone to go after. A guy with a record like yours is perfect—you'll take the rap for everything."

Frank watched Graham, fidgeting, out of the corner of his eye. If the businessman had been holding a gun, he figured, he and Joe might be dead right now. But Graham was scared of Freed's temper and would try to talk his way out of trouble.

"Graham says that personally he'd just as soon have us live," Frank said. "That's a lot of smoke, Freed! With us gone, *you're* the only one tied to any crimes."

"Right!" said Joe. "Graham wants us dead more than you do, but you and Ritchey do his dirty work, and he walks away with clean hands."

"That's ridiculous!" said Graham sharply. "You don't believe that nonsense, do you, Freed? The boys are just trying to save their skins."

"I don't care if it's true or not," Ritchey muttered. "I just want to put a bullet into Addison, and I'll take my chances afterward."

"Wait a minute," Freed said. He turned to face Graham. "How *did* these punks know about my record? Did you tell 'em?"

"Of course not," Graham replied. "They're lying, I told you. They're stalling, can't you see? Look, Freed, get on with it. We can't hang around this place forever."

Frank and Joe saw that Freed's attention and anger were fixed on Graham. They had to keep it that way and play for time.

The heavy steel door rumbled back far enough for Norris to come in.

"Everything's set. I've picked up the money and notified the police."

"So, you looked up my record, huh?" Freed asked with a murderous look at Graham. "You wanted to put me on the spot, did you?"

Norris paled and backed away. Graham said, "Come on, Freed, use your head! Of course I checked your record, that's why I hired you! I needed a man who was tough."

Freed stayed suspicious. "I don't know, Graham. If you're setting me up for a fall . . ."

Graham backed off a step, holding up his hands and making a show of bafflement. "Freed, haven't I taken care of you up till now? Come on, do the job, and let's get out of here."

"Yeah, let's get it over with," growled Vic Ritchey.

But Freed came forward and grabbed Graham by a fistful of collar. He dragged him forward until their faces almost touched.

"What good does killing these punks do for *me?*" he demanded gruffly. "I can see where getting rid of them helps *you* out, but there's other witnesses out there who know what *I've* done. Why should I whack these people out for you?"

"Very well, Freed," Graham replied, carefully removing Freed's hand from his collar and smoothing his clothes out. "I'll pay you an additional twenty-five thousand dollars, you and Ritchey both. That ought to be—"

"Make *him* do it," shouted Frank, cutting in on Graham.

Freed stared at Frank and thought a moment. "What do you mean, kid? What's your point?"

Frank gestured with his head toward Graham. "Make him do some of the shooting. That way he'll have blood on *his* hands and you'll have something on Graham. It's only fair, right?"

Freed stared down at Frank, and then eyed Graham. Abruptly he walked over to Vic Ritchey.

"Gimme your gun," he ordered.

"But I—" Ritchey sputtered, and then stopped as Freed stared at him stonily.

"It's not fair," he whined, *"I* was—"

Freed said nothing. He held out his left hand and fixed Ritchey with a flat, unblinking stare. The stand-in handed over his gun and slouched away.

Freed walked back to Graham and held out the second automatic.

"Take it," he said.

Graham looked down at the gun and then back at Freed. Then he said, "Now, see here—"

"Take it, I said. The punk is right. It's time you did something aside from giving orders."

Freed thrust out his left hand, holding Ritchey's automatic. When Graham still wouldn't pick up the gun, the tough aimed his own weapon at the mastermind's forehead.

"I ain't fooling around here. You take that gun, Graham."

Graham took it. It was clear to Frank that Graham wasn't used to guns and didn't like them. The financier looked around and saw Norris.

"Norris," he ordered, "take this and—"

"No dice," Freed said. "Not Norris, friend. *You're* going to pull the trigger, and I'm going to watch you do it. I'm going to watch you shoot this punk here." He pointed to Frank. "Seeing as how it was his idea and all."

To the Hardys' eyes, Graham no longer looked like the dignified businessman. His face was pale and sweaty. He stared at Freed's gun and nodded, slowly running his tongue around his lips.

He walked up to Frank and reached out a shaking hand until his weapon was only inches away from Frank's head. Frank still couldn't free his hands. He willed himself not to flinch, to look straight at Graham, who wouldn't meet his eyes. The gun shook, and then steadied.

From the darkness a voice was heard. It said, "I wouldn't do that if I were you."

Chapter

18

GRAHAM LET OUT A CRY of surprise. Freed whirled around. "Who is that?" he barked. "What's going on here?"

Joe let out a breath of relief. He didn't know what was happening, but at least Freed had been distracted. He turned to give Trish a look of reassurance. "Hang in there," he said softly.

From another part of the old building another voice came out of the gloom. "Give it up. You don't have a chance."

"Who are you?" shouted Ritchey. He stared into the unlit expanse of the factory and then jumped in panic as a voice was heard from directly opposite the last one.

"We have you surrounded," it said. "Drop the guns and put your hands up."

Freed aimed at the sound of the last voice

143

and fired. The bullets whined as they ricocheted off the bricks of the wall.

"This is your last chance, Freed. Drop your guns right now." Shouts were coming at them from all around. "Don't be stupid," said one. "It's all over," said another.

"Mr. Graham, what's happening?" called Norris, his voice pitched high with fear.

"Shut up, Norris!" snapped Graham, scanning the room, his gun in front of him.

With one final, all-out effort, Frank yanked his right hand free of the ropes. He leaned over and whispered to Joe, "I've got my hands free."

"Freed's got the key to all this iron," Joe whispered back. Let's see if we can get him within reach." Frank nodded, keeping his hands behind him.

One of the voices spoke again. "This is your last warning," it announced. "You don't have a—"

Freed fired again, aiming toward the voice, and it was suddenly cut off. There was a shower of sparks.

"What's going on here?" snarled Freed savagely. He picked up one of the electric lamps and pointed it toward where he had just shot.

A small portable speaker stood on the floor. Next to it were the remains of an amplifier which had just taken a bullet in the transistors. Crouched alongside the amplifier with a microphone in his hands was Headcase. He wore his headphones and was carrying the shotgun mike that he used to pick up whispered conversations.

"Who *are* you?" shouted Graham.

"He's the soundman on 'Thieves' Bargain,' " Freed snarled. "They call him Headcase, and he *is* a headcase, too, walking in here like that. All right, you little freak, how *did* you get in here?"

"I sneaked in after Norris," the soundman replied. "You guys were all too busy to notice."

"How did he find us?" Joe asked his brother quietly.

"Tell you later," Frank whispered back. "For now, let's just try for that key."

Freed turned to Graham. "We're not surrounded at all. This long-haired nut sneaked around in the dark putting speakers all around and talked over them with a mike, trying to panic us." He looked at Headcase, and brought his gun up. "You stuck your nose in the wrong place for the last time, wise guy," he growled, aiming.

But at that moment another voice was heard from outside, over a loudspeaker.

"Attention inside the building. This is Lieutenant Weller of the Bayport police. We have this building surrounded. I repeat, this building is surrounded."

"Cops!" squawked Vic Ritchey. "The cops are here! Freed, what are we going to do? There's cops out there!"

"Shut up!" Freed bellowed, whirling to give the stand-in a look that instantly quieted him. "Just keep your mouth shut, or I'll shut it for you—permanently."

"Frank!" whispered Joe. "The key's on a ring sticking out of Freed's hip pocket! If we can get him closer, maybe you can fish them out."

Freed turned his attention back to Headcase—but Headcase wasn't there anymore. He had taken advantage of Freed's distraction to slip away into the darkness of the building.

Meanwhile, Lieutenant Weller's voice continued. "Attention, you inside the building. You will throw your weapons outside the door and come out after them with your hands up. You will not be harmed. You have thirty seconds."

Frank noticed that Norris was growing increasingly fearful, his eyes darting wildly around the room. He whispered to Joe, "Watch the secretary. He's beginning to crack. Maybe he'll give us the distraction we need."

Joe nodded back.

Norris scuttled over to Graham and said, "It's all over! We're caught! Let's give it up before we all get shot!"

Graham was scanning the building for possible escape routes. He gave his secretary an angry glare.

"Shut up, Norris! This is no time for panic. We're not caught yet, and we're going to get out of this. Just calm down and do as I say."

But Norris wasn't about to calm down. He backed away from his employer, his eyes wide and glassy.

"No! I haven't hurt anyone!" His voice was thin and ragged. "I just drove a truck, that's all! I'm not putting my neck on the line for you, Graham! I'm giving up, and the rest of you can do whatever you like."

Freed walked up to Norris, slapped him hard across the face, and stuck the barrel of his gun under the secretary's chin.

"Nobody is walking out of here, you follow me? Nobody is making any deals with the cops! I'll shoot you right here and now, friend, you hear me? You better believe it, 'cause I got nothing to lose. So stay put and keep your trap shut."

Freed walked away, leaving Norris frozen with fear, rubbing his face where Freed had hit him.

Ritchey, who had been standing off to the side, now confronted Graham.

"Give me my gun," he demanded.

Graham shook his head. "I'm hanging on to this for now," he said.

Ritchey moved forward and shouted, "No! I

want—'' Graham fired a single shot over Ritchey's head, making the stand-in cower back.

A gunshot cracked outside, breaking the momentary silence. It was followed by a fusilade of shots, dozens of them. In a far corner of the factory, glass shattered as windows broke.

"What are you shooting at?" Freed yelled at Graham. "You see what you started?"

Graham stayed where he was, but Frank and Joe knew that he was just waiting for the right time to make a run for it. Norris crouched down, clapping his hands over his ears.

Only Freed held his ground, gun raised, coiled and tense, like a wild animal that knows it is being stalked. Intent on the threat from outside, he had backed closer to the prisoners chained to the wall.

Joe looked at Frank with a question in his eyes. Frank gave a slight shake of his head. He wasn't close enough to try to take Freed, or to go for the key.

"*Hold your fire! Cease fire!*" came the angry voice of Lieutenant Weller. The shooting died out. "Attention, you inside. Come out now, with your hands up. This is your last warning."

"*No! Don't shoot!*" screamed Norris. He threw himself at Freed from behind with hysterical energy. Fear had given the mousy secretary a desperate strength.

As Freed bucked and lurched in his attempt to dislodge the man, the key ring in his pocket dropped to the floor. Keeping an eye on the struggling Freed, Frank reached out, but the keys were a foot beyond his grasp.

"Joe!" Frank whispered urgently. "Can you get them?"

Carefully Joe maneuvered his chained legs around until he got a foot on the key ring. He kicked out with both legs, and the keys sailed toward Frank, who caught them on the fly.

Quickly he freed his own legs, then slid over to get Joe loose. "I'll take Graham," said Joe. "You tackle Freed."

The brothers moved together. Frank hit Freed with a shoulder below the knees, knocking him down along with Norris, and jolting the gun loose from Freed's grasp. The thug landed on Norris and rolled free, reaching for his automatic. But Frank grabbed one of the heavy leg irons and brought it down hard on Freed's wrist. Freed howled with pain, and Frank scooped up the .45.

Meanwhile Joe came up behind Graham, who was peering out into the building, looking for the cops. Grabbing the mastermind by the shoulder, he spun him around and hit him with a hard right in the midsection. Graham doubled over, dropping his gun.

As Joe bent down to pick it up, Vic Ritchey suddenly darted forward, screaming, "Gimme that gun!" and leapt on Joe's back, knocking him forward. Joe arched his back and, grabbing

Ritchey's arm, flipped him over his shoulder. Wasting no time, he yanked the stand-in toward him by the collar, and knocked him cold with a left hook to the jaw. Then he looked back for the gun.

It was nowhere to be seen. Neither was Graham.

Frank saw that Ritchey and Norris were both out of it. He trained the gun on Freed and said, "It's all over, Sam. Clasp your hands behind your head."

Sullenly Freed did as he was told.

Now Graham appeared from the shadows. In his hand was the automatic, and the gun was pointed at Callie.

"Drop it, Frank," Graham called, "or your girlfriend gets it."

Frank hesitated for a moment.

"You heard me, Hardy!" Graham shouted. "Do it, right now, or—unh!"

From behind him Headcase sprang out and grabbed Graham's gun arm, jerking it up. The gun went off, unloading into the ceiling. Joe raced forward to help the soundman pull the gun away from Graham.

While Frank covered the gang, Joe quickly freed Addison, Callie, and Trish. All were shaken, but basically unhurt.

"Guess you can tell the cops to come in now," said Trish.

"Oh, right!" exclaimed Frank. "I almost

forgot about that.'' He raised his voice. ''Everything is cool! Come on in.''

The heavy steel door rumbled open.

In walked Alvin, the driver. There was no one else with him. He carried a bullhorn in one hand and a metal device in the other.

Freed stared in disgust at the driver.

''I *knew* it! The punks suckered us! Serves me right for getting mixed up with a bunch of wimps and losers like this!''

Trish was still confused. ''Where—what happened to the police?'' she demanded.

''There *were* no police, Trish,'' Frank said. ''Just Alvin and Headcase and a little electronic simulation.''

''What?'' Trish asked, startled. ''I don't follow—how did—?''

''Alvin, show the girl,'' Headcase suggested. The driver stepped forward, carrying a portable electronic panel like the unit that the special-effects man had used to detonate simulated shots by remote control earlier that day.

''You mean there was nobody else out there just now?'' demanded Jim Addison. ''Just Alvin and some electronic gadgets?''

Alvin nodded with a bashful smile. ''Headcase and I followed you guys with all his equipment. Once Frank and his girl were dragged in here, we set the blanks into the walls, all around the building. Then I set 'em off.''

Joe scowled at Frank. ''This must all have

been *your* idea! It figures. Leave it to you to come up with something as scatterbrained as this."

"Hey, it worked, didn't it?" Frank said. "Anyway, Headcase had a lot to do with the planning, too."

"But how did Headcase and Alvin know where this place was?" Joe asked. "How come they weren't spotted?"

"Let me show you," Headcase said, running over to where his amplifier and microphone still lay. "It's this gimmick I put together a while back. It's a tracker, see, with about a one-mile range." He brought back a metal object like a cigar box with an antenna and a couple of lights and dials. "It receives signals from a transmitter—show them, Frank!"

Frank unbuttoned the top few buttons of his shirt. There, taped to his chest, was a small flat gadget. A wire antenna ran out of it, the top of which was taped just below Frank's collar.

"See, we just followed Frank and Callie from about a quarter mile behind. When Norris came in here, I got inside before the door rolled shut and set up my speakers. I listened in on you all with that shotgun mike, and when it looked like shooting was going to start, I spoke up. And I wore a wireless mike," Headcase finished up, showing the little device clipped to his shirt. "That way Alvin could hear what was going on from outside!"

152

Callie said, "So *that's* what you stopped off at the studio for!"

Frank shrugged and smiled. "Well, I had an idea that we could use some backup. I figured that we might not be able to send for the police quickly enough if things suddenly turned violent. So Headcase and I sort of worked this thing out. It was his idea to bring in Alvin. He doesn't talk much, but in a tight spot he does come through."

"One more thing," said Trish. "How did you break the windows in this place if you only used blanks? That's a pretty neat trick."

Alvin grinned bashfully. "What it was, was rocks. I threw some rocks, and that's what broke the windows."

"And now," said Frank, "I think we'd better call the police for real and hand this bunch over."

"Chief Collig isn't going to be too pleased with us," Joe stated darkly.

"But since we're giving him all the rotten eggs in one neat basket," Frank answered, "I don't think there's much he can do."

Trish shook her head. "You could never sell this story for TV," she said. "No one would ever buy it!"

Shortly afterward, the *real* police were called, and a whole detachment of Bayport's finest came to haul away Graham and his men, with Chief Collig in the lead. As predicted, the chief wasn't very happy with the Hardys, but he was in no position to quarrel with success.

There had been a tearful reunion between Jim Addison and Andrea Stuart. As they drove off in her sports car, Joe heard her telling the actor how she was going to make Jim's real-life heroics pay off big at the box office.

Headcase and Alvin drove Trish back to the hotel. But before they left, she came up to Joe and smiled shyly at him.

"We still have a date for the movies," she reminded him. "I'm going to hold you to it."

"Whenever you say," replied Joe. "Provided that I can take you for something to eat first."

"It's a deal," she said happily.

Later that evening the Hardys and Callie sat in their living room drinking some of their aunt Gertrude's cocoa.

"That Jim Addison," said Gertrude, smiling brightly. "What a *sweet* man he is! The *idea* that anyone could think he was a murderer— honestly!"

"Oh, that reminds me, boys," said Fenton. "I have a message for you. From Hector Ellerby."

"A note of congratulations for a job well done?" asked Joe with a smile.

"Well, not exactly," replied his father. "Here's the note."

He handed Joe a slip of paper. Joe read the contents out loud.

" 'To Frank and Joe,' " he read. " 'Your work call tomorrow is six A.M. Please be on time. We've lost a few days, and we still have a show to finish!' "